D1386074

REPUBLIC:
BOOK TWO

THE
SWORD
OF
REVENGE

REPUBLIC:
BOOK TWO

THE
SWORD
OF
REVENGE

JACK LUDLOW

Allison & Busby Limited
13 Charlotte Mews
London W1T 4EJ
www.allisonandbusby.com

Hardcover published in Great Britain in 2008.
This paperback edition published in 2008.

A CIP catalogue record for this book is available from
the British Library.

10 9 8 7 6 5 4 3 2

ISBN 978-0-7490-7917-8

Typeset in 10.5/14 pt Sabon by
Terry Shannon

Printed and bound in the UK by
CPI Bookmarque, Croydon, CR0 4TD

JACK LUDLOW is the pen-name of writer David Donachie, who was born in Edinburgh in 1944. He has had a variety of jobs, including selling everything from business machines to soap. He has always had an abiding interest in the naval history of the eighteenth and nineteenth centuries, which he drew upon for the many novels he has set in that period. The author of a number of bestselling books, he now lives in Deal with his wife, fellow A&B author Sarah Grazebrook.

www.jackludlow.com

Available from
ALLISON & BUSBY

In the Republic series

In the Conquest series

Written as
DAVID DONACHIE

In the John Pearce series

To Edward Ephraim,
who has overcome many difficulties in
a fascinating life, not least having
me as a neighbour.

PROLOGUE

The dedication of a tomb to a great man was a magnificent occasion, doubly so when the person whose life was being recalled was someone seen as honest, upright and a friend to the common people. Few doubted that the individual being honoured this day had been such a man; if he had demonstrable defects they were those of the ordinary mortal: however upright a man tried to be in his life, he could never quite stand unbowed against the malice or jesting nature of the Gods.

Born into one of the leading families of Rome, Aulus Cornelius had been a great general, the man who led the legions against, and humbled the heirs of, Alexander the Great. His victories in Greece had earned him the suffix Macedonicus and wealth beyond the dreams of avarice, but it was not just his fighting qualities that singled him out. He was remembered as an administrator who had employed, both in Rome and in the provinces, a light touch in the magistracies he had occupied, including the two occasions on which he had held the office of Consul, never bearing down on the poor and dispossessed in favour of the rich, the well-born or the powerful.

There were many ex-soldiers resident in the city who could recollect serving under him and recall his ease of manner, his natural nobility, as well as his concern for their welfare. Not that Aulus Cornelius was soft; any legions he commanded were a byword for their tight discipline and good order. But most telling, he was loved by his comrades because he had that commodity esteemed by all fighting men: he was successful. To crown a glittering career Aulus Cornelius Macedonicus had left behind him an inspiring tale to make the whole population of the city of Rome feel proud. He had died a hero's death in the province of Illyricum, leading a mere seventy men who perished with him, to hold back, in a narrow defile, a much more numerous enemy, so that the legions to their rear could prepare for battle, a contest in which they were victorious.

'Is that what they are saying?' asked Titus Cornelius, the dead man's youngest son, who had arrived from Spain the day before. 'That he and his soldiers died to give the 10th legion time to prepare. That it was a deliberate sacrifice?'

'It is what is being put about by the man who betrayed him, as well as his friends.'

Claudia Cornelia, widow of Aulus and stepmother to Titus, spoke softly, not being sure who was within earshot. Quintus, her other stepson, was preparing for the ceremonies, seemingly unconcerned that such falsehoods regarding his father's death were being openly peddled around the city.

'And does this lie go unchallenged?'

Claudia smiled ruefully. 'The supporters of Vegetius Flaminus have paid people to go to the baths, streets, markets and taverns to spread this tale. And it is clever, Titus, for it does not diminish your father. If anything it makes him more of a paragon and that goes for the soldiers with him. They are seen as dying like Leonidas and his Spartans, knowingly giving up their lives for the greater good. What could be more puissant to a Roman soldier than to be likened to the heroes of Thermopyle?'

'Then it's time to counter it.'

Titus had been told the truth in the despatch which fetched him back from his military duties; how Vegetius Flaminus, the corrupt and corpulent governor of Illyricum, had, through his rapacity, caused an uprising amongst the locals and through his ineptitude had allowed them to combine with Dacian tribesmen from beyond the borders of the province to create a full-blown revolt. Aulus Cornelius had headed a senatorial commission to investigate Vegetius and his gubernatorial record. On seeing the depth of his fellow-senator's depredations – rapacious taxation, open bribery and fiscal chicanery – as well as the way his army, more accustomed to labouring than soldiering, had ceased to be effective, he had superseded him.

The legion in Illyricum, the 10th, Aulus had brought back to fighting capacity by good training and personal example, till a rebellion that had festered for years seemed to peter out. No sooner had Illyricum been made peaceful, than yet another revolt started to the south, in the neighbouring Roman province of Epirus, one which the 10th Legion, the nearest large military force, was obliged to suppress. At the head of an advanced guard and seeking to contain what he thought was a local uprising, Aulus Cornelius had discovered the truth of what he faced, an enemy army large enough to give full battle. He sent back for reinforcements but Vegetius Flaminus had declined to throw them forward, leaving Aulus isolated with his reconnaissance cohort at a narrow gorge called the Pass of Thralaxas, forced to fight and take casualties before he was truly ready.

Had he and his men been supported, as they

should have been, their situation would not have been grave, but by his actions the titular governor had condemned to death those who could not flee. Even when it was clear that no help was coming Aulus could have left the danger with a clear conscience – it was no part of a Roman general's duties to be cut off from his command – but, typically, he would not abandon the men he had led into this death-trap to save his own skin.

'The rest of the commission…'

Claudia interrupted Titus. 'Lily-livered apologists for Vegetius Flaminus, or nonentities who would dearly love to bask in the reflected glory of his forthcoming triumph. Your father was the only upright man on the commission he led. The rest are wolves like Vegetius, or sheep too frightened to bleat the truth.'

As they talked the steady hum of the crowd, gathering in the pre-dawn darkness outside the house, had grown, with the odd shout from an impatient mourner penetrating the walls. Some of those gathered would have been drinking and have joined the spectators in the hope that the new head of the Cornelii family would chuck some coinage at their feet: it was the way of the funeral rites of the wealthy, which were as much a celebration of a life lived as a grieving over loss. A slave appeared to inform them that Quintus was ready to begin, with prayers to *Manes*, the God of deceased loved ones, at the family altar. Titus and Claudia pulled cowls over their heads, then made their way to the small chapel off the atrium, home to the Cornelii *Lares*, the repository of the family Genius.

The overseer nearly got Aquila. In place before dawn, Nicos had changed his tactics, staying still and waiting for the poacher to appear in the deepest part of the wood, rather than trying to track him as he hunted, snaring the small game and spearing the larger, stealing what was not rightfully his from the fenced-off land belonging to Cassius Barbinus. He and the men he led made sure they were downwind of their quarry, so that when the boy stopped well short of the first of his traps, he was not sure why. It was the lack of noise in a place that should not be silent: such a thing signified a threat. Remaining still, he saw no birds fly nor land in the trees and a search of the morning sky showed no hawks or kestrels, not even a high-flying eagle. If no birds sang in the woods, nor were staying still for fear of a flying hunter, that meant there was something else present, something large enough to command a hush.

Slowly and silently he backed away, watching with care where he placed his sandalled feet on a forest floor thick with leaves, twigs and broken-off branches. If it was a large predator that had made the forest still he had no desire to confront it; if it was human the chances of that being friendly were small. Aquila knew just how angry the Barbinus overseer was at his poaching, because Nicos had told everyone in the district that he knew what was going on and just what he intended to do with a whip when he caught the culprit.

The awareness he had of this wooded world had not deserted Aquila following the events of four seasons past; it could hardly be otherwise with Minca his constant companion. The huge dog was lying still, hardly breathing while Aquila checked his traps, but he stood as his master backed towards him, pointed ears pricked as he sensed danger, soundlessly on Aquila's heels as the boy passed him. Soon they were out in an open field, playing as a boy and dog should, engaged in a tug of war over a thick stick, as the sun rose over the mountains to the east to light the fields of pasture and the quietly grazing cattle.

Aquila pretended not to see the men lurking at the edge of the wood, a party that, once they moved, had made a sound that would not have disgraced a herd of those same cattle. The sight of Minca would keep them there; huge and frightening to a stranger, the animal was to a friend as gentle as the lambs he used to tend. He was also, now, Aquila's dog; Gadoric, the Celtic slave-shepherd who had raised him from a puppy, had been taken south to a place called Sicily, where he was apparently likely to die a slow and wasting death toiling in the fields, poorly fed and labouring under a killer sun.

When the boy thought of Gadoric, one-eyed, tall and fair, and in truth a warrior not a pastoral custodian, his one-time tutor and friend, tears pricked the corners of his eyes; he had been one of the few people in the world that Aquila had loved. Another was the girl Sosia, young and beautiful, like Gadoric a slave owned by Cassius Barbinus. Finally there was Fulmina, the woman who had raised him, the woman he thought of as his mother. All three had gone from his life in one horrendous day; Gadoric to Sicily, Sosia to Rome and Fulmina to Hades.

Before dying Fulmina had told him the truth of his birth; that the people he had called Mama and Papa were not his real parents, that he had been found deep in the forest, well away from any habitation, left there on the morning after the Feast of Lupercalia, exposed by someone who had not wanted him to live. Now all he was left with was a hankering for the only person to whom he could say he was close, the man he had called Papa, Clodius Terentius, serving for years in the Illyricum legion, and surely long past the time at which he was due home.

The finding of him in that forest glade had, Fulmina insisted, been a marvel. First, Clodius being in the woods, waking from a bout of heavy drinking, then the weak sun of a *Febricus* morning that lit that one patch in which he lay. Whoever had laid him on the ground had left him in the swaddling clothes in which he had been wrapped after his birth, thick enough to blunt the night-time cold. When these thoughts of loss and longing became intolerable, Aquila would visit the gurgling riverside spot where he had been found and wonder at the nature of the people who had abandoned him. He would see in his mind's eye ghostly figures on horseback – Clodius had seen hoof prints – figures whose faces were indistinct death-masks, or horrible, hooded apparitions that spoke of Hades and desecration. He would look up to the distant mountains over which the sun rose each day, one with a strange cap shaped like a votive cup, home to the soaring eagles after whom he had been named.

At other times he would go to where the hut in which he had been raised once stood. Standing before that spot he would touch the leather amulet that had been Fulmina's last gift to him, something she had kept hidden all his life. Well-tanned leather and shining with beeswax, it bore on it a raised device of an eagle in flight, wings outstretched. He never took it off his arm, because Fulmina had told him that what it contained, stitched inside, was the harbinger of his destiny. She had also made him swear not to unpick that stitching until he was old enough to fear no man, a vow he had made before the turf altar of their tiny abode, an oath which he would never break.

There was guilt too when he stood and remembered, given how little time he had spent here in the last year of Fulmina's life; in Gadoric he had found someone who had been like the soldier father he so missed. Every waking hour, as well as many a nocturnal one, had been spent in his company. Pretending to be witless and older than his years, Gadoric walked with a stoop, his face hidden by a wide straw hat, as he tended the Cassius Barbinus flock of sheep. He had certainly fooled Aquila the day they met; an intended shock to an old shepherd had turned full circle into surprise for the boy, that made doubly so by the dog he had neither seen nor anticipated. Minca would have taken out his throat if the one-eyed shepherd had not intervened.

Intrigued by the boy's strange colouring, Gadoric had taken Aquila into his confidence, revealing the truth – that he desired only one thing, a chance to return to his own homeland. He had also taken to a boy who was keen to learn and had the time to do so, until, as a trio, which included Minca, they became inseparable. The Celt had taught Aquila to use a spear he had stolen, how to fire a flint-tipped arrow and how to use a wooden sword, to stab, parry, cut and stun with the pommel. He had taught

Aquila some of his barbarous tongue, in exchange for an improvement from the boy's rustic Latin, which the Celt would need if he were to escape. By the light of a tallow wad he had told him long Celtic sagas, which the lad struggled to fully understand, yet knowing that they were tales of the kind of courage and fortitude of which he dreamt.

He was taught that birds' eggs in nests were to be left to hatch, the chickens would provide such food; care should be taken not to kill a cub, be it bear, wolf, fox, stoat or ferret, for these animals lived in concert with the trees, the sky and the rivers which were part of Gadoric's religion. He was encouraged to eat only fully grown fish and when hunting bird or beast to take only what was necessary so that the land would continue to flourish and produce until eternity.

With the sun lighting the nearby Via Appia, Aquila left the forest behind, heading for the place where he now lived, the half-built house of Piscius Dabo. He would not call Dabo's place home, for it could never be that. It was a roof under which he could lay his head till the day his adopted father Clodius came home. Then together they could rebuild the hut, which had formed the funeral pyre of Fulmina, and life could go back to some semblance of what it had once been.

CHAPTER ONE

———◆———

Those gathered for the dedication of the tomb were the relatives and closest friends of the deceased, men of station. Naturally this included Aulus's childhood companion, Lucius Falerius Nerva, one of the two reigning censors and at present the most powerful senator in Rome. While most stood around, heads bowed, he looked about him with an air that bordered on the impious, as if examining each attendee to measure the depth and honesty of their respect, by his actions implying to Titus Cornelius, even if he did not intend it, that he was, himself, lacking in that attribute.

A thin man, with narrow features and thinning hair, the ex-consul was feared as much as he was respected. He had been Aulus's friend since the time both learnt to talk and on the rare occasions when Titus's father had mentioned the man it had always been with admiration for his abilities as an administrator, with reservations regarding his use of the power he wielded in the Senate. As the hazel eyes swung onto the widow, the Falerii face took on an expression of mild disdain. Claudia Cornelia, unable to see out of the side of her cowl, did not observe the look, but Titus did. Lucius had never quite accepted the second marriage of Aulus Cornelius, seeing it as a piece of gross foolishness that a man nearing forty, and as famous and wealthy as Macedonicus, should wed a slip of a girl who, at the nuptials, was a mere sixteen.

Titus had been twelve at the time of the marriage, but you could not move in a Roman street without seeing the lubricious graffiti, or hearing the ribald comments of the lower classes regarding the match; the views of his father's peers were passed on as jokes to Titus by his gleeful contemporaries as they practised martial arts in the Campus Martius. Observing Lucius now, Titus saw a dry stick of a man who looked and acted as though sensual passion was something alien to his nature – hard to believe he had fathered a son of his own. Yet he had not been alone; Quintus had been dead set against the betrothal, and had let his younger brother know just how much he resented the replacement of his late mother by a girl younger than he, who he saw as a nonentity looking to bask in his father's fame and fortune.

Lucius eventually looked from Claudia to Titus,

the expression turning to a thin smile, tempered with a hint of curiosity, as if the older man was saying, 'I know who you are, but what are you like?' The stare was returned in a direct way that had the censor dropping his head into a reverential pose, this as Quintus began the prayers to *Jupiter* and *Juno*, the premier God and Goddess of the Roman pantheon. Titus, with a silent plea to *Honos,* God of chivalry, honour and military justice, looked up at the death-masks of his ancestors, lit from below by flickering oil lamps, with his father's the most prominent in a line that stretched back hundreds of years. He felt a surge of pride, for in his world the family was everything – the means by which a man achieved immortality – and he prayed next to the Goddess of the Future, *Antevorte*, that one day his own deeds would elevate the Cornelii name and that when his descendants said prayers at this very altar before the mask of his own likeness, they would do so in the same spirit that he did so now.

The first ceremony was over quickly and the party, led by Quintus, moved out into the atrium. Gathered there were those who had come to pay their respects, but who were not of the Cornelii blood, or close enough for inclusion in the private family prayers. Cholon Pyliades stood off to one side in the line of the family slaves. He had been close to Aulus, even closer than Claudia, having served him as a body slave in Greece, Spain, here in Rome and in Illyricum. The Greek had been sent away from the debacle at Thralaxas by his master, given a codicil to the Cornelii will that would be read out that evening, a duty that had saved his life. Given how bound he had been to the man whose death they were commemorating, it was disappointing that Quintus had not seen fit to allow Cholon to attend the private ceremony at the family altar. That would have been fitting for such a loyal servant, but knowing his brother as he did, Titus suspected that such a thing, an act of pure nobility that would have been second nature to their father, would never occur to him.

Senators, magistrates and soldiers of legate, tribunate and centurion rank were assembled, all with their heads covered and all quick to bow to Quintus. There were members of the class of *Equites* present too, as well as representatives of the allied Italian provinces. Aulus Cornelius had never actually championed the cause of the knights and the allies as they sought a share of Roman power, yet he had been inclined to listen to their grievances without dismissing them out of hand. Other men were there for less respectful reasons; as the richest man in Rome, Aulus had lent money to support many a speculative venture. Those in his debt would now be wondering if his son and heir would call in such high interest loans.

As a younger son Titus received the odd sympathetic look, following on from those given to his stepmother. His brother was now head of the Cornelii household, and as such he was accorded the respect due to a man of huge wealth, great lineage and one who would in time surely rise to be a power in the land.

The funeral party emerged into the street to the odd shout, but mostly to a reverential murmur from those who lined the streets, and that continued as they descended from the Palatine Hill, their route taking them along the Sacred Way to the Porta Querquetulana. Outside that gate in the Servian Walls a sarcophagus had been erected which marked, in sculpted marble bas-relief and written text, the deeds of the great Macedonicus – only fitting as that was the gate that a triumphant general would use, having been given permission to lead his victorious legions into the city. Behind Quintus two priests from the Temple of *Apollo* carried a second death-mask and a small casket on a cushion.

The mask was the same as that above the altar, a very good likeness taken from one of the many statues that had been sculpted of the hero. The casket should have contained Aulus's ashes, but they had been trampled into the dust at Thralaxas, as the victorious legions led by Vegetius Flaminus had chased the remnants of the rebel forces south through that same defile after the defeat of their main army. Instead it held earth from that place, brought back by Cholon, which would be placed in the sarcophagus, for somewhere in that would be a particle of the crushed bones of Aulus Cornelius Macedonicus, mixed in with the ash from the wooden palisade which he had set on fire just before he died, as well as traces of the men he had led.

Beside that sarcophagus lay a smaller, square memorial, topped by a pointed column, which listed the names of the legionaries who had died with him. Commissioned and paid for by Claudia, it was, she knew, something of which her late husband would have approved; he was a man who was fond of pointing out that however competent he was as a commander, he was only as good as the men he led into battle. Titus and Cholon stopped by that to read the names of the men listed, each of whose families would find, when the will was read, that the general who had led them to their deaths had not forgotten their dependants.

The mourners gathered by the sarcophagus, a rectangle topped by a heavy flat stone, with a panel on each side denoting some facet of Aulus's life, set on the roadside between the city walls and the Via Tusculana, so that every traveller passing in and out of Rome could marvel at his deeds. His service as a consul and magistrate was shown on one of the smaller panels, the extent of his wealth, represented by abundant corn and toiling slaves, on the opposite. The two larger panels were reserved for his martial deeds, with that facing the Via Tusculana given over to his greatest accomplishment, the defeat of Perseus, the Macedonian king. It showed that monarch being led in chains behind the chariot of the victorious Aulus, as well as the huge amount of spoils that had come with the triumph, the last part of the panel with Perseus on his knees, Aulus behind him pulling hard on the rope with which he strangled his royal captive.

Lucius Falerius Nerva stood slightly aloof at the beginning, again watching not the ceremony but those attending: Cholon, the Greek body slave, with his smooth skin, carefully tended hair and effeminate looks; Quintus, all *gravitas* and pomposity, a coming man that Lucius knew he would now have to cultivate; Titus, so physically and morally like his father, which might prove a blessing or a problem; that he would have to wait and see. Then there was the Lady Claudia, now a widow in her late twenties, still strikingly beautiful. If Aulus had been a fool to wed her, Lucius suspected he would not be the last, for the added years and her position had given her presence as well as looks. He smiled, though not at Claudia but at the knowledge he had about her and her late husband.

Years before, as boys, he and Aulus Cornelius had sworn a blood oath which bound each to attend upon the other in time of need and to aid each other in pursuit of their careers, but Aulus had failed to support Lucius at a time when he should have been present, that being the birth of Lucius's son Marcellus, on the night of the Feast of Lupercalia. Worse, with the whole edifice of empire in peril, an impious act, the bloody removal of a Plebeian Tribune, had been required to protect that *imperium*. Lucius looked to Aulus, of all people, for backing; his childhood friend had not met his obligations and neither had he offered an explanation for that failure, thus creating a suspicion that far from being a partisan of the faction that Lucius led, the *Optimates,* he had joined the ranks of his enemies, the *Populares.* Bad as that was, it was not as troubling at that which followed; Aulus, in front of the whole Senate, having defended Lucius against an accusation of murder, had gone on to declare himself independent of all factions. He had deserted Lucius and the Patrician cause at the very time when his support was vital to success.

Angry and hurt, Lucius had allowed a spy to be placed in the Cornelii house – indeed the slave was still in place – the aim to ensure that Aulus was a passive not an active enemy. Thoas, a tall and handsome Numidian, had been conjoined with Claudia's handmaiden, which put him very close to the centre of the household and even closer to the lady herself, and it transpired that it was she who was the key to the mystery of Aulus's failure to attend and say prayers at the birth of his son. It had taken several years to unearth, but eventually the truth emerged, now all written up in a scroll that Lucius kept locked in his strongbox, and if it vindicated Aulus from any hint of conspiracy, it did nothing to raise him in the estimation of the man he had failed.

On campaign in Spain, Claudia had been captured by the Celt-Iberian rebels. When found, two campaigning seasons later, she had been with child and plainly Aulus was not the father. No doubt she had been the plaything of her captors, to be used and abused at will, and though not a sensual man the thought produced, as it had in the past, a certain pulse of blood to the loins as he imagined her repeatedly taken against her will, perhaps by multiple participants. She must have been quite a prize, only seventeen and striking, so he assumed that whoever had fathered her bastard would have been from the higher reaches of the tribal society, a chieftain perhaps.

It made no odds; Aulus, who should have killed her on sight, had refused to set her aside, had, on the same night as Marcellus was born, oversaw a secret birth in a deserted villa in the Alban Hills, before taking the child and exposing him in a place where death was certain. Lucius had to repress a thought that would have made him laugh out loud if he had pursued it. He was conjuring up another carved panel for the sarcophagus, one which showed the great Macedonicus adorned with a pair of cuckold's horns.

Titus had moved to the other side of the tomb as the priests began their prayers, prior to the sacrifice of a goat, to look at the panel that represented that Iberian campaign as well as his father's heroic death in Illyricum. Lucius Falerius joined him there to examine those same images, curious and slightly troubled to note on the neck of the man Aulus had fought in Iberia a device, which on close inspection looked like an eagle in flight. Standing beside Titus he could not resist alluding to both it and the wearer.

'Brennos, chieftain of the Duncani.'

'You've seen the device?'

'No. Only heard about it from a hundred different throats. No one mentions the man without a reference to his talisman.'

Lucius nodded, as if something obscure had been made plain. 'Your father ranted to me about this Brennos after their first encounter, and by the Gods he hated him. He said the man was the greatest threat to Rome since Hannibal.'

'I judge by your tone you did not agree with him?'

'I thought him obsessed.'

'Then I too must be that.'

'I have read all the despatches from Spain these last three years, Titus. They are alarmist to say the least and I know you had a hand in the compilation of many of them. I showed them to Aulus before he left for Illyricum and he backed up everything you said.'

'My father did not exaggerate, and neither did I. Brennos is a serious threat to Rome.'

Lucius's gesture was one of uncertainty; he did not want to openly disagree with the younger man on such a day and in such a setting. 'I am apprehensive enough to ensure that I know what the fellow is up to. He is spied on constantly, as you well know.'

Titus was tempted to insist that the Senate should do more, but it was not his place to talk in such a manner to the leading man in Rome. Brennos was probably a menace greater than Lucius would grasp; the censor had not fought the man, both Titus and his father, at different times, had. A Druid from the northern islands, the man preached a message that, if implemented, would indeed make him more dangerous than Hannibal, and his name alone was a warning. Another Brennos, at the head of a great Celtic confederation, had ravaged Greece and burnt half the city of Rome hundreds of years before. His namesake was intent on uniting that same confederation, his aim not to partly burn the city but to destroy the whole empire. The carving on the sarcophagus showed him defeated, yet Brennos was far from that. Yes, he had lost a campaign, had been beaten by Aulus, but that had seemed to do no more than inspire him to continue. If anything, he was more powerful now than he had been years before.

'I came across Brennos in my last action, just before I was informed of my father's death.'

'Really,' Lucius responded absentmindedly, his eyes still fixed on the carving and quite specifically on that eagle device on his neck.

'He led a raiding party into the area of my command. A fool of a centurion, who should have known better, with a full cohort, chased them deep into the hills, ignoring strict instructions to avoid such a thing. He got them trapped in a defile from which there was no escape. The right hand of every soldier was cut off and they were sent back to us.'

'And the centurion?'

'Was hacked to pieces by Brennos, before my eyes.'

'This device around his neck, what do you know of that?'

What was it about Lucius's voice? Titus could not quite place the tone, but it lacked the assurance with which the censor had previously expressed himself. 'It is some kind of talisman. I have been told that it came from the Temple of *Apollo* at Delphi, taken by his namesake when he sacked Greece, and that he wears it because of a prophecy.'

There was a definite tremor in Lucius's voice as he repeated the word. 'Prophecy?'

'It is said that one day, a man wearing that will stand in the Temple of *Jupiter Maximus* and that man will have conquered the city of Rome.'

All that Titus noted was the quiver in the voice; with Lucius looking so intently at the sarcophagus, he could not see the man's face. If he had he would have been made more curious, because it was a countenance drained of blood, and behind that was a mind in turmoil and a heart beating too fast for comfort. As children Lucius and Aulus had made an illicit visit to a Sybil, wrong because it was something barred to mere boys. Right at this moment Lucius was recalling the events of that night – the fearful stench of the dank cave, the bones of dead creatures at their feet, made more gruesome by the indifferent torchlight, the dark wrinkled face of the old crone of a seer who had not been fooled by their purloined manly garments. She had known them for what they were, yet she had spoken a prophecy to encompass their joint futures, the words of which were burnt into Lucius's brain...

One will tame a mighty foe, the other strike to save Rome's fame.

Neither will achieve their aim.

Look aloft if you dare, though what you fear cannot fly.

Both will see it before you die.

The Sybil, without any hint of ink or stylus, had executed on a piece of papyrus the blood-red drawing of an eagle in flight, before throwing it to Lucius. As she intoned those words, and without any sign of physical contact, the drawing had burst into flames in his hand. Try as he might to laugh it off, that prophecy still affected Lucius; he had even questioned those who came back from Illyricum to see if there were any eagle signs connected to Aulus's death, yet here was one before his very eyes. The censor put a hand out, touching the cold stone of the sarcophagus to steady himself. He felt Titus's arm on his and heard, through a rushing of blood to his head, the words the young man said.

'Are you all right, Eminence?'

Lucius loosely waved his other hand; what could a carved stone eagle do to him? He could not die now, his work was unfinished. The prophecy was false; he had convinced himself of that in the past and he must hold on to his scepticism now. Seers were unreliable, prophecies couched as riddles were too obscure to claim to be absolute truth.

'I am, I am, Titus. Just overcome by the tragedy

of the occasion. Your father and I were friends all of our lives, from childhood through to being grown men with sons of our own. Is it any wonder I am affected by grief?'

Titus had to keep a straight face then, to hide his doubts. Lucius Falerius had not been given the soubriquet Nerva for nothing; he was a man of emotional steel, not the type to faint at the graveside. Lucius, keeping his face hidden, was reminding himself that this Brennos had not killed Aulus, he had been defeated by him. The prophecy was mere flummery, made up by the Sybil to justify her fee. Slowly, as he rationalised these thoughts, his heartbeat slowed and the blood returned to his face. Yet he felt he had to say something, to divert the young man standing beside him.

'Perhaps, Titus Cornelius, you and your father had a clearer idea of the menace of this Brennos than we have in Rome. I shall take heed of that.'

Claudia Cornelia too had examined those sculpted panels, many more times than Lucius, for she had had a hand in the drawings from which they had been made. It was she who had reminded Quintus of the eagle charm that Brennos wore, which he too had heard of but never seen. The look on the face of Aulus's eldest son when she had suggested its inclusion had been deeply curious, though it was an inquisitiveness that remained unrequited; Claudia would tell no one the truth. In remembering Aulus she had felt again that tenderness she had always had for a man who could truly be termed good. The thoughts of how she had failed him as a wife lay heavy, but at least, she knew, he had died in ignorance of the truth, had died thinking that the child she had conceived in Spain had been the result of a violation.

Now she was watching Titus and Lucius from the other side of the sarcophagus, wondering at the conversation that had made the older man look ill. If he had dropped dead on the spot she would have had to fake sympathy; though she did not hate the man, she did not like him. To her mind he had abused his friendship with Aulus, and her husband, being the man he was, had stuck to a loyalty that had not been reciprocated. She and Lucius had clashed in the past as she sought to barb him with the truth; that he was a devious liar and an unreliable comrade.

The need to attend to the rituals made all present concentrate. Sacrifices were made, the blood of the animals cascading forth to taint the earth at the feet of the priests. Most had their heads bowed, but not Cholon. The Greek was weeping and he wanted everyone to know how much he had loved and missed his master. The man beside him, the newly retired centurion, Didius Flaccus, who had also been saved from death at Thralaxas when Aulus also ordered him away, was actually embarrassed.

'Contain yourself, man!' he hissed.

'I cannot.'

'It is for women to weep, not men.'

Cholon, through red and swollen eyes, looked sideways at Didius Flaccus. The tanned and scarred complexion under short-cut iron-grey hair were features which marked his occupation. Flaccus had been in the legions for twenty years and he and Cholon had seen, from a distance, the early morning smoke from the fire that had consumed the bodies of Aulus and his remaining legionaries. Cholon recalled that the man had been stony-faced then, and that for soldiers in his own century.

'Men may weep and wail if they choose. Perhaps you mean it is not for soldiers.'

'I'm not a soldier any more, mate,' Flaccus spat, 'and I am as like to be a pauper if something don't turn up soon. I had hoped old Macedonicus would sort that one out and load me with booty, but he didn't, did he?'

That offended the Greek deeply: to be able to attend such a distressing occasion and stay dry-eyed was one thing; to be so callous as to consider one's own concerns was quite another.

'I heard,' Flaccus added, indicating the other, smaller memorial, 'that the general left some money for his men.'

'Only those who perished.'

'What good is that going to do the dead?'

Cholon edged away, not wanting to listen to such

words, but Flaccus barely noticed. He was staring at the sculpted images of the Macedonian triumph; Aulus on his chariot wearing a crown of laurel leaves, behind him chained slaves bearing jars filled with gold, wondering if one day, as it had been vouchsafed to him by every teller of fortunes he had ever consulted, such wealth would come to him. He had been so close to cornucopia in Illyricum, but it had been snatched from his grasp and the remembrance of that deepened his irritability.

His mood was not enhanced on the return to the Cornelii house, as, walking well behind Quintus, Flaccus was too far away to get at any of the coins the man was chucking to the crowd. Not that there was any gold in there; it would be copper at best, though there was one consolation he had on re-entering the house. He was treated to a decent meal of the kind he dare not splash out on himself. Taking care to ensure that no one was looking, Flaccus pilfered as much food as he could and drank as much wine as the servants were prepared to pour into his cup, so that by the time he left he had in his mouth the taste which made him want to continue.

The stuff he drank in his local tavern was nowhere near the quality of what he had imbibed in the Cornelii house, but what it lacked in flavour it made up for in potency, so that Flaccus was intoxicated enough to do something he normally restrained himself from; he began to recount his experiences of fighting and leading a century in the Roman army. His fellow-drinkers listened to his stories with respect but when he became really drunk, banging his fist on the table as he tried to persuade them that he had been within an inch of untold wealth, indeed a wagon full of gold, that lifelong comfort had slipped through his fingers due to the stupidity of a legionary called Clodius Terentius, attention wavered. By the time he began to recount the enigmatic prophecy he had heard so often, that indicated he would be rich anyway, he was talking to himself.

'A golden aura, that's what the man said, which means great wealth. And men cheering like I've won a great victory. It will come to pass one day, you mark my words, and when it does I shall find better company to share a drink with than you arsewipes, that's for certain.'

It was just as well he was mumbling to himself; anyone close enough to his drunken ramblings would have heard him confess to the murder of an elderly Illyrian soothsayer, in between the curses with which he damned the man for expiring without telling him the truth about his future in plain language.

In the tablinum of the Cornelii house, where Aulus had at one time conducted all his business, an increasingly angry Quintus was reading the will. Cholon heard the words that set him free and even though he had known it was coming, he was again overcome with emotion. It was not the manumission which angered Quintus, it was money; a sizeable sum had been bequeathed to the Greek so that he would be, in freedom, more than comfortable. A fortune already gifted to the Lady Claudia could not be reclaimed and Titus, too, was left a sum enough to avoid the need to beg for corporeal sustenance from his brother. But to top it all came the bequest to the dependants of those who had died at Thralaxas, laid out in a codicil that Cholon had brought back from Illyricum. Quintus first questioned its veracity and, once persuaded that the terms must be met, complained that he would be ruined. It was nonsense of course, as Claudia observed.

'My dear Quintus, you are just not the richest man in Rome any more. I dare say your father had faith in you to gain that accolade on your own merits.'

The long day ended with each of the Cornelii going to their own suites, to harbour their own thoughts. Quintus had with him a list of his father's numerous debtors and was looking through it to see whom he could force into early repayment. Titus had visited the family altar on his way and paid private obeisance to his father's memory, aware that he had been in awe of the man when he was alive and was even more so now that he was dead. Cholon went to the slave quarters for the last time to cry himself to sleep. Tomorrow he must look for a place to live; he could not abide the idea of residing under a roof of which Quintus Cornelius was the master.

Claudia, attended by her maid Callista, prepared for bed, sure that she would not sleep. She would lie looking at the ceiling and wonder, for the thousandth time, about the small russet-haired boy, her love-child by the Celtic chieftain Brennos, that Aulus and Cholon had taken from her just after his birth and exposed. Where was a mystery; she only knew that he had left on horseback and not returned till dawn the next day. Lying in darkness she would envisage gloomy woods and hungry predators, feeding on the small, still living, screaming carcass, waking dreams that were nightmares and her mind would always turn to the charm she had put around the baby's foot in the hope that someone would find him and, realising he had at least one rich and concerned parent, raise him to manhood.

Solid gold, shaped like an eagle in flight, with the wings picked out in subtle engraving, it had once hung around the neck of the only man she had ever truly loved; the boy's father, Brennos.

CHAPTER TWO

———◆———

Piscius Dabo did not like Aquila and he did not like having to provide a roof over his head, especially since he was forced daily to admit that the boy, whom he had attempted to tame, had fought him to a standstill. No blows had been exchanged: the fisticuffs had occurred between his own children, especially his eldest son Annius, though for very much the same reason: Aquila's refusal to toil in the fields. Annius, who had already put on his manly gown, was a good two years older than Aquila, but there was no difference in their height and build, nor in their willingness to fight each other. So it was a fair match, until Dabo's other children intervened, ganging up on Aquila and overpowering him by numbers.

Rufurius, Dabo's second boy, originally as willing to thump Aquila as the rest, had recently shown a marked reluctance to take part, only joining in when personally threatened, and that, allied to Aquila's increasing growth, meant beatings were rapidly becoming a thing of the past. The object of all this anger was not unwilling to work, provided the task suited him and his prowess with trap and snare. That and his ability to tickle fish meant that he contributed more to the pot than he would ever manage labouring in a field. Stolen food of course, and the Barbinus overseer would skin him alive if he found the culprit, but Dabo was not doing the thieving himself, nor averse to free food on his table, so he turned a blind eye to the source.

Aquila, when not hunting, would work happily around the villa, feeding the hens and pigs, or chopping wood for the fire, another source of friction since proximity meant that he could eat when he liked, while helping himself to the water from the well, this while the others toiled in the blazing heat with no more food or water than they could carry. And these days, given their father's prosperity, they had to work quite a distance from the house.

The dog was a real problem; Dabo's own mutts were terrified of it, hiding their tails and whining submissively if it came close. Aquila had reacted angrily the first time Dabo had suggested chaining Minca up, making it plain that both he and the animal would be off up the road at the first opportunity. The boy's blank refusal to be used as an extra farm labourer could only be altered by a sound buffet round the ears, but it would be a brave man who would do that with the dog loose. The huge black and brown animal, who would sit immobile as Dabo's children fought Aquila, bared his teeth if the older man even came close. Nor could Dabo just kill the damn thing; if he did, he knew that it would be Aquila he would have to chain up. The boy had a spear hidden somewhere and Dabo had already learnt, on the day that Fulmina died and he had sought him out in the woods, that Aquila knew how to use it. It had thudded into a tree right by Dabo's head, and he knew, from the look in the boy's eye, that he had missed deliberately.

His own children could not understand; their father constantly moaned to them about Aquila, but was curiously reluctant to do or say anything to the culprit himself. They could not know that every time the boy angered him, he conjured up a vision of Aquila running away to the nearest town, telling the tale of his life on this farm and the man who owned it, which might lead to a tax-gatherer calling at his door. That stayed the hand and whip that he so liberally used on his own offspring. As far as the Roman state was concerned, Piscius Dabo was serving with the legions in Illyricum; the fact that the person who was doing the soldiering was none other than Clodius Terentius, Aquila's adoptive father, was the cause of the aforesaid worry.

They had swapped places because Clodius was on his uppers, a landless, wage-paid day labourer, which exempted him from service. Dabo was doing well, which snared him, because in the Roman State only those with property could be trusted to defend it. A man who had lost his land – Clodius had lost his own holding because of his stint in the legions – did not qualify for the *Dilectus*. Dabo had only held on to his own farm because his father had looked after it while he was a serving soldier. So pauper Clodius, recipient of the corn dole, had been exempt from the call-up; farmer Piscius Dabo, who could feed himself and his family, was not. Never mind his sons were too young to look after the place while he was away; never mind that the fields would go to rack because he was not there to tend them. Rome had been made great by fighting farmers; it would stay great the same way. Getting Clodius drunk, and having him review a life that was far from perfect, then recalling with a rosy tint the time they had soldiered together, Dabo had persuaded him to sign up under his name.

Serving legionaries were exempt from the land tax, so for all the time Clodius served in Dabo's place he had paid not a bronze *ass* to the local legate and because of that he had enjoyed an extra degree of prosperity. One of his neighbours, who had gone off to fight in the same legion as Clodius, had left a wife and two children to look after his holding. The eldest boy, the mainstay of the farm, had died of a flux, so the place was going to ruin. All it needed was one more thing to go wrong and the wife would be forced off the land before her husband could get home and put the place to rights. So 'good neighbour' Dabo had stepped in and bought her out at a knock-down price of her harvest brought in for free, added to half of his own. He was now the owner of three farms; with one more Dabo would definitely have enough land to realise his dream and change over from crop growing to rearing cattle. He would start small, he already had a goodly number of pigs, but there was actual money to be made in ranching and sheep rearing, real copper and silver coin, instead of the near-total barter system that he was engaged in now.

A tax-gatherer seeking ten years' dues now would ruin him, for he was over-extended, busy turning his humble home into something approaching a proper villa that would go with the status to which he aspired; the future rancher had committed the small amount of actual money he had to paying for that. Hard to imagine now, in amongst all the filth and rubble and the dust blown into every chamber in the old part of the house, but it was Dabo's dream to live and die like a true gent, a knight with an income of a hundred thousand

sesterces. Ranching would bring him that – not all
at once, but in time, as with real money he could
change over from seed to pasture, then buy up a
whole load more properties from neighbours
struggling to make ends meet.

That Clodius's service had lasted ten years had
surprised Dabo as much as it had, no doubt,
infuriated his old companion. News had filtered
through that, after some great and bloody battles,
the campaign in Illyricum was over. The 10th
Legion would return to Italy to be disbanded and so
would Clodius, so Dabo only had to wait a few
more months and he would be freed from the
burden of his contract. No point in antagonising
anyone at this stage, so much to the annoyance of
his hard-pressed offspring, and at some cost to his
own blood pressure, he let Aquila do pretty much
as he pleased.

'Look at the bugger,' he said to himself, as he
spied the boy chatting to the two robbing sods who
were putting on the timbers that would support his
new roof. Aquila was standing, golden hair blowing
in the breeze, a long pole in a bucket of tar, which
he was stirring over a fire to keep it fluid enough to
coat the wood. 'What I wouldn't do to be able to
take a stave to the lazy sod's back. He'll toil for
strangers but not lift a finger for the man who feeds
him.'

Aquila enjoyed helping the two builders who had

at one time, like Clodius, been small farmers, for both had been soldiers, and were happy to talk about it. As legionaries they had built for the Roman army in many a far-flung province; now they built for customers like Dabo but were happy to answer questions about their service from a youth just as eager to work for no pay.

'Sighting a camp ain't easy,' said Balbus, removing his leather cap and wiping the sweat from the brow of a large head. 'You want high ground to start with. Mind, it can't just be set on any old hill, though half the generals in the Roman army don't seem to be aware of that.'

'Generals!' His small, stringy partner, Mellio, spat as he said that, his sunburnt face screwed up with hate. He did not like superiors of any description and he was vocal about his reasons. 'They either kill you, maim you, or beggar you.'

Aquila fanned the charcoal under the kiln to keep it at maximum heat. Minca, with more sense on such a hot day, had found a cool patch of damp earth on the shady side of the well. He lay there, tongue lolling out, watching Aquila toil at the fire.

'That hill would be a good place,' the boy said, pointing at a gentle rise that dominated the ground between the Via Appia and the foothills of the mountains. His other hand was held up to shield his face from the intense heat.

'Granted,' Balbus replied, 'but what about

water? It has to have its own water supply if it's going to be for more than one night, and it should be flowing enough to wash away the legion's shit. That's the most important thing. It's better to build on flat ground with water than to take a hill that's bone dry. Then it needs clear lines of assault that you can protect against and you don't want the natural line of attack to be comin' from the east, 'cause in the first light of a clear day, your enemy can advance on you unseen.'

Mellio cut in, to point to a clump of trees that would require to be cleared. 'An' then you use 'em to build a palisade that'll keep the sods out even if they do attack.'

'Were you ever attacked?'

'More'n once boy.' Skinny Mellio puffed out his chest. 'I've lopped the head off men trying to get over our walls, and that was the ones that hadn't been speared before they got that far. I couldn't tell you the number of times me and Balbus here had nothing but our shields, our sword arms, and a mate on our left hand between us and perdition.'

'I'd like to hear it.'

'Work first, lad,' said Balbus, 'then we can do the story-tellin'.'

Aquila was like any boy his age; he had dreams of glory, often imagining himself at the head of a great army, charging down upon a fierce, barbaric enemy, and by sheer personal bravery, routing

them. It had nothing to do with the predictions
Fulmina had made that promised that very thing;
they were usually relegated to the back of his mind
and only recalled when he happened to touch the
leather amulet on his right arm. Now, caked in dust
from head to foot, the vision was different. He saw
himself standing on a hilltop, with a plan on the
table before him, directing legionaries to build the
most impregnable fortress the world had ever seen.
Men like Balbus and Mellio would gasp with
amazement at his technical prowess, and wonder at
the number of his innovations. And they would
raise their swords to salute a hero.

Claudia had felt a genuine sense of grief at the news
of Aulus's death, and had cried copiously, earning
jaundiced looks from both Quintus and Cholon,
both of whom were aware of the cold way in which
she had treated him while he was alive. She would
not have demeaned herself by trying to explain and
knew, in the future, if anyone talked of nobility, her
thoughts would turn to him. But there was relief for
him too, and the burden of loving her he carried;
Aulus had died in battle, so his spirit, at least,
would be at rest.

   Listening one more time to a description of the
events as described to the family was distressing.
Cholon was subjected to a rigorous interrogation,
because he had been there to personally observe the

actions of Vegetius Flaminus and if anything was to
be done about the man, proceedings should be
instituted before the triumphant general, waiting
outside the city with his legion, entered Rome. Titus
had a rather austere military directness, which
precluded him from seeing the effect his questions
were having on the tender-hearted Greek.

'Please, Titus,' said Claudia, for she had seen the
chest heave, heard the quickly drawn breath as
Cholon tried to hold back his tears. 'Can you not
see the distress you're causing?'

The sound Quintus made was eloquent enough;
the mere idea that a slave, even one now free, could
have feelings worth consideration, was alien to him.
Titus, made aware, walked over to put an arm
round Cholon, wondering why the Greek threw his
stepmother such a venomous look. After all, she
had intervened to protect him.

'Brother,' Quintus barked, making no attempt to
hide his impatience. 'We are due to attend upon
Lucius Falerius. It would not do to be late.'

'I am told he often keeps people waiting,
Quintus,' said Claudia, with a mischievous twinkle
in her eye. 'Your father remarked on it more than
once.'

'Entirely due to the work he does on behalf of the
Republic, Lady.'

'True, albeit he had a very singular vision of the
way things should be.'

Quintus gave her a look that was meant to convey that she, as a woman, could hardly understand such things. He called to Titus to follow him and Cholon, not wishing to be alone with Claudia, left on their heels.

'The death of your father is a blow to the whole Republic. We shall wait a long time to see his like.'

Quintus Cornelius bowed in acknowledgement to Lucius Falerius Nerva, but added nothing to the older man's commiserations. His host might be as thin as a sapling, yet his lively hazel eyes belied any thought that he might be weak and the grip he had given Aulus's two sons upon their entry to his house had not lacked physical strength. 'He laboured on behalf of Rome, without thought for his personal well-being.'

Titus, standing to one side, had the impression that Lucius was talking about himself, not his late father, as he wondered why he and his brother had been summoned here. Surely the senator, who claimed such close friendship to Aulus, would not have diminished himself if he had called upon them!

The older man turned to include Titus in his next statement. 'You will both miss his guiding hand, will you not?' The brothers murmured in assent, as Lucius, nodding sagely, laid a thin hand on Quintus's shoulder. 'Which is why I asked you here.

Since your father is gone, I wish to offer, in his place, my humble support. The path to prominence is strewn with pitfalls for the unwary. I betray no trust when I say that Aulus himself depended on my advice.'

Lucius half-turned, his eyes fixed on Quintus in a way that excluded Titus, this as the tone of the old man's voice changed, taking on a harder edge than previously. 'After all, it was I who secured his last two appointments to Spain and Illyricum, just as I supported him in earlier times, giving up my rights as senior consul when we served together so that he could take command in Macedonia.'

Titus experienced the first faint stirrings of resentment and he fought to remain still so that his feelings would remain hidden. Old enough to see his father as more than just a hero, he was aware, as any son must be, that he had had faults; but he had stood as a paragon compared to this man, who, if rumour was to be believed, had stooped to murder to gain his political ends. Now, by the tone of his voice, Lucius seemed to be implying that Aulus Cornelius would have remained a nobody without his help.

It was almost a surprise to Titus that he spoke; the words seemed to come out of his mouth unbidden. 'I'm sure my father was properly grateful for the help he received from his many friends. They must take pleasure from the knowledge that they extended their trust to one of the most able men in Rome.'

The old man turned his penetrating gaze on the younger Cornelii. Titus had his father's height and build, as well as his features: the thick, black hair of the younger Aulus, a straight and prominent nose and the kind of brow that denoted both brains and natural *dignitas*.

'Properly grateful,' said Lucius, rolling the words around his mouth, as though tasting them. Then he turned his attention back to Quintus, moving closer and placing a hand on his shoulder. 'I have already said that I admired your father. I shall not labour the point, since that would only debase the sentiment. Above all things, Aulus was a practical man.'

Even the stony-faced Quintus flicked an eyebrow at the way Lucius had used the word 'practical', but he said nothing to interrupt; the importance of the man clutching his shoulder precluded comment.

'The Forum Romanum was not his natural home. I'm not sure he always, for instance, grasped the importance of patrician loyalty. Sometimes it was hard to see him as what he professed to be, a member of the *Optimates*.'

Lucius noticed the shocked look on Quintus's face and he turned sharply, as if aware that it would be the younger of the pair who would speak, and held his hand up as an instruction to remain silent.

It was breeding rather than respect that made Titus hold his tongue.

'I express myself in a lame fashion. I have rarely met a more upright man than Aulus Cornelius, incapable of subterfuge.' He paused for a moment, then produced a thin smile. 'Which is a handicap in politics. When I spoke of loyalty, I did not mean it in the personal sense. I meant adherence to a higher goal, namely the safety of the Republic. Aulus served Rome on the battlefield and I do not doubt that his sons will do their city the same service, but he was also needed in Rome. There are as many enemies in the city as there are on the frontiers. I asked you to call on me today so that I may be sure that you understand the nature of your inheritance.'

He was talking exclusively to Quintus now, again excluding Titus, but that was in order; the words he used could only apply to the new head of the Cornelii household. All the family responsibilities fell on Quintus's shoulders, including firing the first shafts in the campaign to bring Vegetius Flaminus to justice.

'But more important than that, I wish to stand in his place. You are heir to a great fortune and an even more illustrious name. You will both assume, in time, your place in the Senate. After that, with guidance, you could rise to become consul. I intend that you shall succeed and I hope that you will stand by me in the defence of everything that is sacred, and learn the art of politics at my side.'

Quintus bowed again and finally spoke. 'I am yours to command, sir.'

Lucius ignored Titus's frown, and patted his elder brother on the shoulder. 'You gladden my heart by saying so, young man.'

Titus nodded to the various people they passed, who wished to greet the brothers, while also, they being in mourning dress, silently condoling with them. Quintus seemed not to notice, striding down the street with his mind on distant prospects. It was no secret he hankered after high office, that he longed to serve as a consul. Quintus's whole life had been bent to that one supreme goal. His brother decided he should be brought back to earth, reminded of just how shabbily they had been treated.

'He should have called on us, and paid his respects to our stepmother.'

'Do be quiet, Titus.'

'You don't agree?'

Quintus stopped and faced his brother. 'What if I do? Am I about to tell the most powerful man in Rome that he lacks manners?'

'I think father would have found a tactful way of telling him!'

'There's a world of difference. They were of an age and had been friends for years.'

'All the more reason for Lucius Falerius to call.'

Quintus frowned. 'You're just like father, you know, blind to reality. Lucius Falerius doesn't call on anyone.'

'So you are about to join his circle of arse-lickers,' Titus snapped.

'Don't you dare address me like that again, brother. I would remind you that I am now head of the family and as such I have duties, one of which is to seek advancement.'

Titus was aware that he had gone too far; his brother's elevation entitled Quintus to a degree of deference, yet he could not bring himself to actually apologise, though he did force himself to speak with a more measured tone.

'I know that, Quintus, yet I would advise you to take care...' Titus saw the angry glare in his brother's eye, and spoke quickly to deflect it. 'I have as much interest as you in the well-being of the family. I would beg you ask yourself one question. If Lucius Falerius values father's memory and our future so much, why is it beneath his dignity to call? Or is it that he does not truly consider either of those things to be worth the trouble?'

'If a man like that offers me his good offices, then I would not refuse. Neither would our father.'

Titus spoke softly to take the sting out of his words, taking a gentle grip on Quintus's arm.

'Father was the man's equal, not his client. Do not lash yourself to Lucius Falerius any more tightly than he did.'

Quintus responded by pulling his arm free and striding off.

CHAPTER THREE

Marcellus Falerius felt his right arm go numb, but he was quick enough to transfer the stave to his other hand, dropping his head to avoid the follow-up blow. His opponent had stepped forward to deliver this, his leading leg bent to support the forward movement. Marcellus swung his stave up in an arc, stopping it just as it made contact with the leather pouch on the exposed groin, then he jabbed gently. Gaius Trebonius dropped his weapon and clutched at his genitals, more alarmed than hurt, speaking breathlessly. 'It was an accident, Marcellus.'

'No it wasn't.'

'Honestly!'

Marcellus jabbed at him again. 'Don't lie, Gaius. Never lie. You're a Roman, remember.'

'He'll be a Vestal Virgin if you keep jabbing him there,' said Publius Calvinus.

His twin brother, Gnaeus Calvinus, spoke too. 'Marcellus is right.'

'Go on Gnaeus,' sneered Trebonius. 'Lick his boots.'

Instead Gnaeus started to vigorously rub Marcellus's right arm. 'Did it hurt?'

'No,' he lied, since it stung badly; Gaius Trebonius had given it all he had, in total contravention of the rules of the game, though Marcellus blamed himself for leaving the arm exposed.

'Why do you always cheat, Trebonius?' asked Gnaeus.

'It runs in the family,' called Publius, who had picked up the fallen stave.

'Publius!' snapped Marcellus. 'Gaius is in mourning for his grandfather, who I would remind you, died as a Roman should.'

The boy named swelled with pride then; the tale of his grandfather's death at the hands of the Illyrian rebels was nearly as inspiring as that of Aulus Cornelius. He had faced the men who murdered him as a Roman proconsul should, exuding pride and indifference, with nothing in his hand except the axe and fasces that denote the power of the Roman *imperium*.

Publius pulled a face. 'Officially, maybe, but I bet he's really thinking how much closer he is to the family coffers.'

'It makes no difference. I should have thought it was obvious that remarks about his family were unwelcome at any time, but especially now. I pray to the Gods that you never insult me that way.'

Marcellus turned and stalked across the open field, his boots sending up small puffs of dust. Gnaeus ran after him and Publius sighed. 'There he goes, Trebonius. The most upright prick in all Rome.'

Gaius Trebonius laughed. 'Speaking of pricks, do you think his boots are the only thing your brother licks?'

Publius swung the stave up and hit Trebonius hard in the groin. As he doubled over he brought it down on his neck. 'The trouble with Marcellus is that he's too soft. He turns the other cheek. If you'd struck me the way you hit him, I'd have taken your head off and I don't mean the one on your shoulders. I'd make you scream like that horrible sister of yours.'

'Pax!' bleated Trebonius.

Publius lifted the stick and whacked him across the buttocks. 'Come on, otherwise Timeon, our great and glorious teacher, will fetch you a dozen of those.'

The noise of the returning children briefly distracted Lucius and made him wonder whether such boisterous behaviour should be allowed. He had noticed that Timeon, the tutor he had engaged to teach Marcellus and his neighbour's children, had been less strict of late, ever since the time his son had seen fit to give the Greek a buffet around the ears. The boy had received a sound beating for that transgression but that was only half the solution; it could not be allowed to interfere with the pedagogue's strict methods, which in the past had seen him employ a vine sapling with vigorous regularity. Timeon had cost a fortune to buy and if he was growing soft, not disciplining sufficiently the boys in his care – all of whose parents paid Lucius a good fee to share his services – he would have to be sold and replaced. There was only one way to bring up and teach a Roman, and that was with rigour, but he decided to let what he could hear be; it would not aid Timeon's authority to have him intervene.

Perhaps it was the paper before him that softened his natural disapproval of their youthful playfulness. After many years and careful disposal, he had in his hand the document which transferred ownership of two *Latifunda* farms in Sicily, the last piece of his land not within a day's journey from Rome. Never again would he be required to think about examining the accounts and organising distant planting and irrigation schemes. Not that he had been to Sicily; his grandfather had acquired these two plots in a distribution of captured Carthaginian land after the Second Punic War.

Huge and difficult to manage, they had, if anything, been a drain on his finances rather than an asset, returning such a low yield that some subterfuge had been required to extract a good price from the purchaser, Cassius Barbinus.

Challenged, Lucius would not have wanted to admit the real reason he had got a higher payment for his property than was truly justified. Cassius Barbinus had had his reasons to bid the price up; he wanted to ensure that the censor did not remove him from the senatorial list and there were grounds, he being a sybaritic fellow, a wealthy man who openly engaged in trade, one to whom the sumptuary laws governing conspicuous consumption were observed more in the breach than the letter. On top of that, the fellow was looking for advancement, even though he had never held any office on the *cursus honorum,* so generosity to a powerful man like Lucius Falerius Nerva might prove profitable.

It had been an unpleasant business; indeed it was a sign of the times in which he lived that Lucius could even consider transacting business with such a man. He had visited Barbinus at his cattle ranch near the small town of Aprilium in the company of his son, this to avoid being seen to have any kind of dealings with such a fellow, which in Rome would set tongues wagging. The luxury of the man's villa was alone enough to displease Lucius, but the open way that Barbinus had tried to bribe him with gifts had set his teeth on edge, first with some tame leopards, then with the present of a young slave girl. Having turned down the first proffered gift he had been obliged to accept the second, manners demanded it, but he had seen to it that the girl never entered his house. She had been sent to a farm between Rome and the port of Ostia.

His steward entered silently and, without distracting him, laid the latest batch of reports, fresh in from the Republic's scattered provinces, on his desk. Lucius threw aside his bill of sale and turned eagerly to read them. Illyricum was now at peace, the governorship having gone to another Flaminus, in part a recognition of his success in turning Vegetius, who had once been a political enemy, into a client, albeit a reluctant one. Locked away in his nearby strongbox he had the private correspondence that Aulus Cornelius, as head of the investigative commission, had sent back to him, reports that were enough to see Vegetius stripped of more than just his Senate seat; indeed they were so damning they could see him impeached, condemned as a thief and thrown naked off the Tarpien Rock.

He remembered the man's face as he had read them at his legionary camp outside Rome, flabby like his body, with too much wine and food, so that in his soldier's armour he looked like a buffoon instead of a general. Lucius also made it plain that he knew the truth about the way Vegetius had left Aulus Cornelius and his men to die, made it clear that his goodwill was the only thing that stood between the ex-governor and impeachment. Vegetius Flaminus had understood with an alacrity that showed his true, shameless character; as long as he toed the Falerii line and supported the *Optimates* in the house, those letters would stay locked away. Stray from that and they would be laid before the people.

That sanction not only locked in Vegetius Flaminus, it also included the faction of which he was a leading member, a group of senators who made mischief by flirting with the opposition, people that had to be continually bought off to keep that mischief from turning into real trouble. With them neutralised, Lucius Falerius now had the kind of power in the house which ensured that any vote that came before the chamber was almost certain to go the way he wanted. Over ten years it had taken to fully repair the damage done to his cause by the defection from his side of Aulus Cornelius, the pity being that he had to acquiesce in the granting of a triumph for a man he considered a slug, a man who could, on the most elementary examination, be denied that reward. There would, no doubt, be those who wanted Vegetius arraigned; they could bleat, but they had no evidence, only he had that.

For all the satisfaction he had had at the moment

he had shown Vegetius Flaminus the secret correspondence of Aulus, he had felt a pang of guilt, plus an ache for the friendship he and Aulus had once enjoyed. From boyhood they had been inseparable, an unlikely couple to many; Aulus so gifted physically, he of a lesser build, with a sharp tongue in place of a keen sword blade. Yes, he had soldiered, and though it had been far from a disgrace, it had not brought to him what it gifted to Aulus, an arena for what Lucius wished were his natural talents. Those had lain elsewhere; not in battle and command, but in supply and support. The legions to which he was attached were better equipped and better fed than any others either before or since, and because of that he could lay some claim to be, even if another was the actual commander, the partial author of their success.

Prior to the murder of the plebeian tribune, Tiberius Livonius, he had had in Aulus a man with whom he could share his innermost thoughts and concerns and it hurt him even now to admit that he missed that greatly. Marcellus would one day become his confidant, but as yet he was too young. Powerful as he was, Lucius knew he was not immune from struggle. Quintus Cornelius, if not handled properly, could easily become a focus for dissent. He must be brought to see where his true interest lay, not in pursuit of Vegetius Flaminus but in loyalty to his fellow-patricians. It was good to observe that Aulus's eldest son showed some sign that he understood, proving he had a better appreciation of his duties and prospects than his late father.

Honest Aulus Cornelius, who had sat in this very room and made him swear he was innocent of murder. Could he have admitted that he had hired the thugs who stabbed and mutilated Tiberius Livonius, a tribune whose person was supposed to be inviolate? No, he could not, any more than he could admit to a living soul that the son he so cherished was not his own, but the fruit of a liaison between his late wife and his own body slave, a man called Ragas, who, physically strong and a fine boxer, had protected Lucius in the streets of a city where violence was commonplace. That was his secret and his alone; his thugs had taken care of that slave on the same night as they had taken care of Livonius. It was an unforeseen bonus that his wife, a woman he had come to despise for her simpering infidelity, in giving birth to Marcellus, had also expired on the night of his birth.

Three very necessary deaths on one night, the Feast of Lupercalia. That killing of the plebeian tribune had been essential to stop the tide of reforms the man proposed, extending citizenship to Rome's Italian allies, changing the voting structure in the *Comitia* in a way that would dent senatorial rule, all this to diminish the power of the

Optimates. Even worse was the idea of allowing the *Equites* the right to sit in judgement in the courts. The class of knights would use that power for only one purpose: against the patricians whose families had led Rome to the greatness she now enjoyed. Empires, Lucius knew, were fragile. There had been many before and they had fallen, to his mind for only one reason: the power of the state had been diluted, so that political infighting replaced firm central rule.

With a start, Lucius realised he had allowed his mind to wander, to think on things that were past and unalterable. Now mattered, not yesterday or the day before, so he turned to the other scrolls that made up the despatches. The road-building senator, Licinius Domitius, was engaged in the last sections of the road that would run all the way from Rome to Iberia, thus helping to keep that province under control. He was experiencing some difficulty in bridging, at a point near the delta, the great river that ran south from the Alps to the Greek city of Massila; more time, slaves and money would be required. There was a hint of trouble on the border with Numidia where the sons of a client king were competing for the succession and causing trouble, but the Ionian coast was quiet and prosperous, as was the whole of Greece. There was the usual nuisance of the Alpine tribes north of the River Po in Gallia Cisalpina, but the biggest problem was, and remained, Spain, and in particular the chieftain called Brennos.

It was telling how often, in these last ten years, that name had come up in the affairs of both the state and his own life, first when he had read Aulus's early despatches from Spain, in which the man had come close, having caught the legions strung out on the march, to winning a major battle. The modesty with which his old friend had explained how he had mastered a desperate situation was still vivid in his mind – he had not, for instance, made any mention of the capture of Claudia. Despite Aulus's warnings, following on from that campaign, Lucius had seen him as a defeated foe, albeit not a dead one, going so far as to describe the man as a flea. But he was beginning to realise that this chieftain had grown to become first a gnat with a painful sting, before a metamorphosis in his power had turned him into a fully grown and dangerous spider.

It was startling just how much Rome knew about Brennos; not where he came from precisely or why, but what he had achieved since he first appeared on the Roman border. He had, against all the odds and previous experience, united the tribes that lived cheek by jowl with Rome and so very nearly turned them into a successful army. Beaten by Aulus the man had retired into the west, first to the lands of Lusitani, which bordered the great outer sea, and, once obliged to move on from there, to other tribal areas, all the time using his status as a Druid. That gained him hospitality and trust at every hearth, a trust which he abused by seeking to seduce the younger warriors from allegiance to their tribal elders.

Finally he came upon the Duncani, a tribe in decline, and there he stayed, becoming a companion to the elderly chieftain, Vertogani, a man much given to three major faults: drinking, boasting and limitless procreation. Once a great warrior, the man was old and enfeebled by his passions. He had also bred too many sons who hankered to succeed him, each of whom had been given part of the tribal lands as their own fiefdoms. These sons had not only disputed amongst themselves but sought alliances with neighbouring chieftains, foolish because such neighbours sought only one thing: Duncani territory. Many a descendant, cheated by those who had professed to be their friends, had to be allowed back into the family fold, forgiven for their stupidity.

It only emerged later that the weaknesses which this created, especially the rivalry to succeed Vertogani, were the factors that attracted Brennos, that and the location of the tribes' hill-fort. Numantia was a place of natural defence high on a bluff overlooking the confluence of two rivers. In order to gain control of that Brennos had cast off his Druid vows of celibacy, married Vertogani's favourite daughter, then proceeded to murder as many of the man's sons as were foolish enough to stay within reach. The wiser offspring, seeing that their father was in thrall to this interloper and wishing to stay alive, left before Vertogani died, to become a source of much of the information Rome had acquired.

First Brennos had taken back land that had been lost, before reducing the neighbouring tribes to clients rather than rivals. As his authority spread he became the dominant force in the interior, and at the same time the fortress of Numantia grew more and more formidable. Brennos, now the undisputed Duncani chieftain, had added ring after ring of outworks to his defences. Not that he, according to the reports, trusted to the landscape. Great trenches had been dug in front of the bluff walls to double the scaling height, the ramparts were faced with wood to make a frame filled with loose stones and great earth bastions stood behind these, so that Numantia was impervious to attack by fire.

The central area, sacred home to the original tribe, had been kept free to act as a place of worship and assembly. The small wooden temple, dedicated to the Earth God, *Dagda*, held the treasures of the tribe, much increased, it seemed, through the new chieftain's efforts. The Greeks who traded with Brennos told of gold and silver objects set with precious stones, fetched out at all the festivals of the Celtic faith and placed around the altar. This, a circular stone, stood above the spring that gushed out of the earth, providing a source of water that could not be plugged from outside. Brennos anticipated a siege, since he paid as much attention to husbandry as he did to his defences. As recent nomads, the Celts were inclined to rear livestock to the exclusion of all other staples; he had them plough the earth to plant wheat, driving the men to work as well as the women. Great storehouses had been scooped out of the formidable rock, to hold the grain that would be necessary to withstand an attack.

His wife, Cara, was certainly fertile, giving birth annually, and for all that he had seen off the sons and heirs to the leadership of the tribe, his wife had a string of cousins and nephews, so that his personal household had grown to include the male members of that extended family, who acted as his bodyguards. Lucius stopped reading for a moment, his mind playing on an idea. Brennos was certainly dangerous; he encouraged other tribes to revolt, backed them with men, then broke off his support for the insurrection as soon as the Romans gathered in strength to oppose it. That left his clients exposed. Even the Lusitani, hitherto cautious of troubling Rome, had taken to carrying out pirate raids on both sides of the Pillars of Hercules with their small galleys. Given their strength and location, that was something to which Rome found it difficult to respond.

Perhaps the way to deal with Brennos was to emulate his own rise to prominence; to encourage another male member of the tribe to supplant him, either by subterfuge or force. Lucius expected little from other chieftains. Those tribes closest to him who were not actually under his heel treated him with respect, even if they failed to acknowledge his leadership. The same men who gave Rome information about the Duncani provided them with intelligence about their neighbours. If anything, the reports coming out of these encampments were even more specific. Brennos was given to predicting that one day they would succumb to him, not through fear but through respect.

Masugori, one tribal chieftain who had made and kept his peace with Rome, was quite open about his neighbour's aims. The Duncani chieftain claimed that all he needed was a Roman army, with a general foolish enough and greedy enough to venture far beyond the limits of Latin power. Once they had been lured into the forbidding interior fastness of high plateaus and deep valleys, Brennos could inflict on them certain destruction. Let the fame and wealth of Numantia spread across the Iberian Peninsula; let it be known that there was another power as great as the Roman Republic.

He laid aside the scroll with a grim smile; everything that Brennos did to create a war fell flat. It must seem, to him, like lethargy, but it was quite the opposite. It was sound tactical sense for an empire which had time on its side. Yes, Rome would fight the tribes closest to them, in response to the raids he initiated, and reduce them till their only hope of survival was to sue for peace, but they would not come inland to attack him or any of the other hill-forts, like Pallentia, which they would be bound to consider a threat to their communications. The thought he had had earlier was fully formed now; in the absence of an enemy to fight, let the people of Numantia, with a little encouragement from Rome, indulge in intrigue, directed at the only source of power, Brennos himself!

That was the way to deal with him.

CHAPTER FOUR

———◆———

Didius Flaccus hated to be kept waiting, even if a lifetime as a soldier had inured him to such a thing. He had no choice; as a retired centurion you were only as good as the weight of your purse and he was way short of the funds he needed to set up in the style to which he aspired. He had enough money, accumulated from plunder and the depredations he had visited on his legionary underlings, like charging them for leave, to take a small apartment at the top of a tenement, but it would be rough wine and poor food he had to eat if he wanted his money to last. He could not bear the thought of that, or even worse, going back to the provincial farm from which he had set out all those years ago to be a soldier. He could return to the province of Illyricum and set up in some kind of trade, but that did not appeal either, especially since questions might be asked about the sudden demise of that old soothsayer, with him the last caller.

Silently he damned the man, for his dying words had brought Flaccus no peace. He still had a prophecy couched as a riddle, one he had extracted from more than one seer. He badly wanted to believe them all, but after the near-fulfilment of the prophecy south of Thralaxas, he was prey to even more doubt than he had entertained previously. What he could do with some money! He had his eye fixed on a ground or first-floor dwelling, with enough income to live properly and dress well, a situation that might lend itself to the acquisition of a young Roman wife. Perhaps the person he had come to see could help; after all they had once soldiered together and been companions, albeit the man had been his titular superior. So he sat in the ante-room of the house of Cassius Barbinus, waiting for the owner to summon him.

All around he could see the evidence of great wealth; the space alone, in such a crowded city as Rome, was evidence of that, let alone the statuary and furniture. The floor of the atrium, right through to the colonnade that surrounded the garden, was laid with an intricate pattern of mosaics that must have set Barbinus back a fortune. Even the goblet in his hand, presented to him by a young, sleek and handsome slave, was the kind of article he had longed to pinch as a serving soldier. The whole place smacked of Hellenism, of Greek luxury and excess;

the old centurion, who had known nothing but the army for twenty years, loved it, and gave up a silent wish to the God *Porus,* that the kind of plenty he was experiencing would one day be his.

The carefully manicured slave reappeared, requesting that he follow, and Flaccus stood up, goblet in hand, till the slave favoured him with a look of such condescension that, for all his years and seniority, he blushed, put the goblet down on the table, and followed to the door of the tablinum. Cassius Barbinus did not stand to receive him, nor did he look up, concentrating on the list of figures on his desk. Flaccus was content to look at the top of the senator's bald head, which, since he never went out without a hat, was as white as his remaining hair. A 'new man' they called Cassius Barbinus; reasonably well-born into the upper reaches of the plebeian class in a Roman colony off the Via Appia, he had done his duty as a soldier but then set aside any desire to climb the *cursus honorum*, doing what very few men of his background had dared to undertake previously. He had openly gone into trade, working in his own name instead of through middlemen and not just farming and ranching; even the most elevated patrician noble saw that as a state duty.

Cassius Barbinus had bought ships and traded with the east; taken up tax farming on behalf of the Republic; bought mining concessions and vineyards that were operated for profit rather than personal consumption and he had got his seat in the Senate, despite the rules against members openly indulging in such activities. When his more rigid peers sneered at him for this, he was apt to throw a huge and expensive dinner, in defiance of the sumptuary laws, watching amused as his fellow-senators angled for invitations to eat delicacies they could not themselves afford.

'So, Flaccus,' he said, looking up. The face above the fat body was smooth and round, the man overweight, well fed and sleek. 'You're a lot greyer in the hair, but you haven't changed much.'

'Neither have you, sir.'

Barbinus stood up, rubbing his hands over his protruding belly. 'Nonsense, man. I must be twice the weight I was when I was a soldier.'

He walked round from behind his desk and stood beside the retired centurion. Then he ran his hand over Flaccus's flat stomach, a hand that lingered just a little longer than necessary. 'What I wouldn't give for a belly like yours.'

'You don't give! It's what you do without that gives you a flat belly.'

Barbinus laughed and patted him on the shoulder. 'Well said, Flaccus. I do eat too much and business has kept me from exercising as frequently as I should. Still we're not here to discuss your figure or mine, are we?'

Flaccus's eyes lost their hard look, to be replaced by one of supplication. 'Have you thought on my request?'

'I have that, but I'm not sure that I can oblige.' Flaccus looked slightly crestfallen. Then, as if he remembered who he was with, his face took on the same blank look he had always reserved for conversations with senior officers. 'After all, you're no clerk, are you?' It was not a question requiring an answer, so Flaccus did not provide one. 'Nor are you sailor enough to captain one of my ships.'

'I thought I might act as your agent, somewhere. Ephesus or the like.'

'And rob me blind, no doubt.' Flaccus was about to protest when Barbinus cut him short. 'I would have thought if anyone would retire rich from the legions it would be you. You were such an avaricious bastard.'

'I wasn't lucky,' said Flaccus bitterly.

The other man snorted. 'Luck. What's luck got to do with it? I daresay you've had enough money, you just haven't managed to hang on to it. What was it? Too many visits to the brothel? Gambling?'

'Don't matter, but being a centurion must fit a man for something.'

'It equips a man for many things, Didius Flaccus, but not occupations that pay any more than wages and that's not what you're after, is it?' Flaccus shook his head sharply as Barbinus walked back behind the desk. He sat there for a moment in silence, before looking up again, a gleam in his eye. 'I have one job which needs doing that might fit the bill, a job that a hard-nosed old centurion might do better than most.'

Barbinus picked up a piece of paper in his fat fingers and swore gently under his breath. When he looked at Flaccus again he saw that the man was practically at attention, his face bearing the look of a soldier seeking to avoid censure. 'I'm not swearing at you, Flaccus. I've just bought the rights to some land in Sicily, a great deal of land in fact and I had to pay a lot of money for it, a good deal more than it's worth.'

'That don't sound like you.'

'Anything for a quiet life, Flaccus. One of our more elevated senators, a present censor, no less, hinted that my commercial activities, not to mention the way I spend my money, could be construed as unbecoming for a man in my position.'

'Meaning?'

Barbinus looked thoughtful for a moment, but declined to explain why, if he could be expelled for indulging in trade or overspending, he was still a senator. Flaccus would know as well as anyone, having been in the army, the difference between the rules as they were written and how they were applied.

'Censure on the floor of the Senate. Perhaps even

removal from the senatorial roll, since the present consuls are in office only because the man threatening me has put them there.'

'I don't see...'

'I bought two *Latifunda* off him, Flaccus, that is the most noble Lucius Falerius Nerva. Now there's a man who wouldn't soil his hands in trade, but he's not beyond eliciting a bribe, as long as it can be dressed up as a normal transaction.'

'Is the land worthless, then?'

'No. I sent someone to look it over. It's good wheat-growing soil, even if it has been allowed to go to the dogs. Old Lucius is too immersed in politics to supervise the place properly, so it's more like a retirement home for slaves than a proper farm. The trouble is that it's hard to make money out of wheat, since the price is controlled. It's profitable, but not profitable enough the way it is now. Lucius Falerius will use my money to buy some land closer to Rome, where he can do some ranching.'

'Can't you ranch on this Sicilian land?'

Barbinus shook his head. 'It's too hot for large-scale pasturage. No, the only thing to do is to increase the yield, which is where a tough old centurion might come in handy.'

Flaccus pulled himself up to attention again, as Barbinus, leaning on the table, fixed him with an intense look. 'You know what I'd dearly like to do to that upright patrician bastard. He's sold me this land for twice what it's truly worth, but what if I could increase the yield so much that I'd be making a profit on the sale?'

'You want to stick it to him!'

'That's right, Flaccus. I want to see the fixed smile on that stiff-necked bastard's face when I tell him that I, Cassius Barbinus, have made a profit out of bribing him. He doesn't look as though he eats much now, but when I'm finished, I want him to be truly sick at the sight of a loaf of bread. I want to stand up in the Forum and ask why we have to import so much wheat from Africa when I can get such a yield from my property, not forgetting to add, by the way, that the honourable Lucius Falerius had so cultivated the land, before I bought it, as to make my task a simple one. Do you see the beauty of it, old friend? That Falerii prick won't be able to say or do anything.'

'How do I come in?'

Barbinus fixed him with a sour look. 'Meaning what's in it for me?'

'That too,' replied Flaccus, returning the stare.

Barbinus stood and, hands on hips, stretched his back. 'You want money, I want revenge. The land is there, the seed and the sun are there, as well as the slaves. Now I know it doesn't turn in the crop yield my other farms manage, so I will give you the figure for the yield so far and provide funds for any improvements you need to make. Money for things like irrigation and I'll even provide more slaves if you can justify them. You have both places for three years and any increase in the profits you can keep for yourself. After that, the whole income from the properties reverts to me.'

'What do they turn in now?'

'A million sesterces a year, Flaccus, most of which goes straight back into the soil or some slave's belly. I know you want to have enough to be a knight. Double the yield on that land in Sicily and you'll be able to join me in the Senate.'

'I derive as little pleasure from my presence here as you do,' said Cholon.

'I need more time,' replied Quintus.

'If anything could count as your father's dying wish, it was that these behests should be paid.'

'You sound like a lawyer, Cholon,' Quintus said sourly. 'Being a free man obviously suits you.'

'There was no attempt at impertinence there, Quintus Cornelius.'

'How the world changes, Cholon. You now address me as Quintus Cornelius instead of master.'

Cholon frowned. The proper forms of address between Roman citizens were a little unfamiliar. 'Is that not correct?'

Quintus looked at the Greek. Gone was the simple gown he had worn as a slave, to be replaced by a blue unadorned toga. His problem was not that his father had freed Cholon but that he had left instructions for the care of the families of those soldiers who had died with him at Thralaxas, written instructions too. Not that it mattered; Quintus knew that Cholon would never lie about such a thing. He could refuse to pay them immediately but a man who wished to advance in the public domain could hardly relish the thought of such an accusation attached to his name.

'You have called me by my name, that is all, Cholon. I cannot forget that a few weeks ago you would not have dared.'

'I can't recall being cowed by the prospect. Perhaps it is more likely that you wouldn't have been pleased.'

'Oh yes, Cholon. My father would never have bothered if you'd called him by name. One wonders that a man can expend so much energy being humble.'

Cholon bridled; he would not have the memory of Aulus Cornelius Macedonicus sullied by anyone, even his eldest son. 'In his case it was effortless, the natural extension of his remarkable personality.'

Quintus was stung. He stood, something he had been determined not to do in the presence of this ex-slave. 'Well, that remarkable personality has been so prolific with his bequests that I'm having to call in outstanding loans, sell land and slaves to pay them. Since I have no desire to part with my inheritance at a lower price than it should command, I must move slowly. So you will forgive me if these people are forced to wait.'

'I have seen to as many cases as I can from the money your father left me.'

'What?'

Cholon smiled, speaking with perfect assurance, aware that Quintus was attempting to talk down to him. 'I know that you will reimburse me in time.'

That was the point at which Quintus lost his temper, his dark eyebrows gathering together as he sought to stare down the insolence he perceived. 'Don't be so sure, Greek!'

'But I am sure. You are not equal to your father by a long league but you're enough his son to pay the family debts.'

'Get out,' Quintus hissed. 'Leave a tally of the sums you've paid with my steward. When I have enough to reimburse you, I shall send you word.'

Cholon gave a small bow and left. Claudia emerged from her quarters as he crossed the atrium and, since she stood before him, he could hardly do as he wished and ignore her. So he stopped, bowed slightly and waited for her to speak. They looked at each other for several seconds before she obliged, with a wry smile.

'I'm aware that you don't like me, Cholon, just as I'm aware of the reasons.'

The Greek, of all people, had seen the way Claudia's coldness, after the birth of her bastard, a child he had himself placed on the cold ground to die, had affected his late master. He had also seen their relationship as it was before her capture: happy and tactile. Claudia had turned to stone from the moment she and her husband had been reunited, and Aulus, who blamed himself for her ordeal as well as her fall from grace, had suffered when to Cholon's way of thinking he should not.

'Then there seems little more to say, Lady.'

Claudia paused, hoping that he would say more, but Cholon stood silent. 'I heard raised voices.'

'Only one voice was raised.'

She smiled again. 'Quintus has a temper.'

'Indeed!'

'Would you mind telling me the cause of the argument?'

His face was like a death-mask. 'It was not an argument, Lady.'

'You seem to have acquired the stiff Roman neck very quickly,' Claudia snapped. 'It is a pity that in adopting our codes you didn't take on board our manners as well.'

The reply was calm, his demeanour imperturbable. 'No doubt I shall, in time, if I'm careful with my tutors.'

Claudia clasped her hands together, her face taking on an anxious look. 'This will not do, will it, Cholon?'

'Do for what, Lady?'

'Do you see me as an enemy?' she asked. 'There was a time, wasn't there? I hurt Aulus and you hated me for it.'

'Emotions may pass on with those who die. They tend to remain in the living.'

'I know Quintus is short of money. I wonder if you know why?'

'It would be impolite to enquire.'

'His father, many years ago, transferred a large portion of his wealth to me.' Cholon tried, but he could not keep the surprise off his face. 'Unfortunately for Quintus, it seems to be the most easily tradable part of the estate. You are aware that an eldest son normally inherits everything. Aulus felt that Quintus might be unjust to me…'

'I wonder why he felt that?' said Cholon, coldly.

Claudia's eyes dropped and she clasped her arms together and shivered slightly. Quintus had found her the day her 'captivity' had ended; it was his men who had killed Brennos's personal bodyguards to free her. He had also seen her condition and the thought that it might become public terrified him. She could remember the thoughts she had had when Quintus went to fetch his father, Claudia refusing to move from the spot where he had found her. Sitting in the wagon, she had contemplated killing herself, but the first stirring of the child in her womb had stayed that thought. Like Aulus, Cholon only knew half the truth and, tempted as she was to open up now that she was widowed, she knew she still had to keep secret the truth.

'You and I are now the only people who know what happened. I am aware of the regard you had for my husband. I doubt if I could ever convince you how much I esteemed him...'

The interruption was brutal. 'I doubt he sought your esteem.'

She reached out and grasped his arm. 'Unbend, Cholon. I cannot explain to you, neither will I demean myself to attempt it, but if we were enemies once, we can be friends now. The memory of that man is as dear to me as it is to you.'

Cholon's voice had a crack in it, half a sob. 'I cannot believe that!'

Claudia tightened her grip as she saw his head drop. 'Who will you talk to? With whom can you share your past with some degree of understanding, or will you be forever telling strangers of the greatness of the man you loved, knowing that they don't believe you, thinking that you are merely taking on airs in a famous man's shadow. You can talk to me. I know what he was worth.'

The anger returned again. 'Do you?'

'Ten times me, if not a hundred. I hurt him more than anyone alive, yet I asked him to put me aside.' Cholon looked into her eyes, seeking the truth. 'Aulus refused. In a way he inflicted the suffering on himself. He was a victim of his own nobility.'

'He loved you, Lady.'

Claudia quickly wiped a tear from the corner of her eye. 'I have money to pay his bequests, and to reimburse you.'

'You were listening?'

Claudia shook her head. 'I do not need to listen at doors. One of the soldier's wives came with her children to express her thanks. I know Quintus didn't pay her. I'm like you, Cholon. I would not want Aulus to suffer from posthumous disgrace and, sometimes, I would like someone to talk to that I know I can trust.'

Cholon bowed his head, half in acknowledgement, half to hide his distress. Thoas the Numidian slave flitted from behind a nearby pillar. Cholon, more alert than Claudia, turned and saw him. The man's colouring and height identified him, making the Greek wonder if Quintus had set Thoas to spy on his stepmother. He could quite believe it, which only served to widen the gulf between what he thought of the father and the lack of regard he had for the son. It was because he decided to say nothing that Cholon missed the point; his suspicion of Claudia outweighed every other consideration. If he had spoken, he would have found that Thoas, along with her handmaiden Callista, had been bought from Quintus as soon as the will was read.

CHAPTER FIVE

———◆———

The road was dusty, the air hot and arid, so Didius Flaccus ordered his men to dismount and walk the horses, a command greeted with blank and silent stares. It worried him that they did not grumble; he was used to the company of legionaries, and they did little else. These men were not soldiers, though a few of them must have been so at one time. They had recently been guards and instructors at a gladiator school, which had gone under due to the owner's debts; tough, scarred men and ruthless, who would spear an opponent on the nod from anyone who would pay their wages. He had offered them more than that to act as his personal bodyguard because what he had to do would be hard and dangerous. The Sicilian slaves he was about to take over would work or die, probably both, and no one man, alone, could feel secure in such a situation.

'How far've we come?' demanded Toger. 'I need a wet.'

Flaccus stopped and half-turned to answer; unlike the others, this individual actively troubled him. He was squat, lantern-jawed, with huge shoulders and a square head covered in tight curls. His eyes, small and pig-like, never ceased to move, as though he was forever on guard against some unseen attack, an impression strengthened by the worry lines that furrowed his tiny forehead. He would smile occasionally, but there was no friendliness in it. Toger's physical presence was alarming and he had a wild and unpredictable temper. The other men did not like him, though they laughed heartily enough at his feeble jokes, and never questioned any of his suggestions. They were afraid of him and it was quite possible, Flaccus thought, that the best way to ensure their undying loyalty would be to kill him.

'We're near a place called Aprilium,' he replied, looking around the cultivated fields that lined the road and stretched to the grazing land for sheep and cattle on the nearby foothills. The substantial and well-tended villas they had passed were ample evidence of the wealth such land produced, just as they were proof that the owners would not be common farmers. Barbinus himself had a property round these parts – one he had just avoided – there was no way he could take this bunch of thugs into such a place, but thinking on that reminded him of another fact. His mind went back to the pass at Thralaxas and the men he had left to die there. 'A few of my cohort came from round here, poor bastards.'

Toger snorted derisively. 'Poor bastards is right, if they have to work the soil.'

'They're even worse off than that. They were trampled into it, that is if there was anything left of them after they had been hacked to pieces.'

'Are you thinkin' of payin' any social calls?' asked Dedon, another of his ruffians.

Flaccus did not reply. Clodius Terentius had come from land that lay close to the Barbinus properties, which caused the centurion to remember two other things: Clodius had been a surrogate legionary for someone better off than he, called Piscius Dabo. The second thing was that Clodius had died owing him money. They would have to stop for the night soon, find a bunkhouse in one of the flea-ridden post-houses that lined the route. How much better and cheaper it would be to impose themselves on a free billet. Right now, Flaccus was paying for everything, their wages as well as their bed and board; a personal bodyguard had not been part of his deal with Barbinus. This lot would not consent to sleeping in a field and if they did stay at a post-house, Flaccus knew that he would probably wake in the morning to find a couple of women and several flagons of drink added to his bill.

He turned to Dedon and gave him a grim smile. 'I'm thinkin' of paying a call, though I doubt I'll be welcome.'

Toger grinned, his tiny yellowed teeth making a sharp contrast with the thick red lips. 'Who cares about that?'

They turned off the busy road slightly further south and started to ask for directions. Perhaps if Dabo had been less crabbed he might have had on his side the natural hostility of country folk for strangers, let alone a band of men such as these. That would have guaranteed a dumb response to questions about the location of his farm, but his grasping nature, as well as his parsimony, had become a local byword, so even people who had had no dealings with him, and therefore no real cause to dislike him, were happy to direct Flaccus to the right place.

The builders, Mellio and Balbus, were near to finishing for the day and, still working on the roof, they were the first to see the small band of armed men approach. What they observed made them hurry to put away their tools and for once their attitude to Aquila was as dusty as the boy himself. An air of impending trouble seemed to emanate from the horsemen as they rode into the compound, hauling their mounts to in front of the main section of the house. Minca stood, his tail stretched out behind him, the ruff along his back proud, a sure sign of danger. The workmen left from the back of the building, taking care to keep out of sight. Dabo, who had come out to greet these visitors, hurried back into the house having looked them over, sending a slave to fetch everyone in from the fields.

'Greetings,' he said when he re-emerged, squinting up at Flaccus, astride his horse with the sinking sun behind him.

'I'm looking for a fellow called Piscius Dabo.'

The idea of lying crossed Dabo's mind but he dismissed it, sure that this man knew he was at the right farm. Besides Aquila had jumped down from the uncompleted roof and wandered over to stand beside him. The dog loped across the compound and took station by the boy's leg, his presence causing some of the horses to shy away till Aquila took him by the ear, said something quietly in that heathen tongue he had learnt from the Celtic shepherd who had owned the animal, and Minca sat down.

'That's me,' Dabo replied with an air of confidence he certainly did not feel. 'And who might I be addressin'?'

'Says it all really. Here he is, Piscius Dabo of the 10th, a legionary *Hastari*, who has just spent years fighting in Illyricum, and he don't recognise his own centurion.'

'Is this some kind of joke?'

'It's no joke to Clodius Terentius,' replied Flaccus coldly.

The name froze Dabo's blood but it acted very differently on Aquila, who rushed forward and grabbed at the greave on Flaccus's leg. 'You know him?'

Flaccus looked down at the dust-covered boy, his hair standing on end, full of red stone mixed with sweat. Then Dabo spoke, his voice hard and commanding. 'Get back in the house, Aquila.'

Minca, suddenly on his feet, growled at Dabo's tone. Flaccus looked at him, then back at the boy. 'Aquila? Is this Clodius's youngster?'

'In the house,' shouted Dabo again, ignoring the threatening sound of the dog beside him.

Aquila was long used to ignoring Dabo but something unusual in the voice had him halfway to complying. He turned to go, but Flaccus's words, matter of fact and free from emotion, stopped him.

'Lad ought to know that his Papa's dead, Dabo, don't you think?' Aquila spun round and grabbed the leg again, his red-rimmed eyes looking up pleadingly at the grey-haired centurion. Flaccus continued in the same flat tone. 'Killed at a place called Thralaxas, along with the rest of my men. Heroes all of them, you might say.' He must have seen the pain but the voice hardened and he pointed his finger at Dabo. 'Died a soldier's death, lad. Trouble was, it was this man's death, not his own.'

Dabo's children, in from the fields, had gathered in a group by the well. Aquila gripped the leather greave on Flaccus's leg tightly and his head fell forward to touch the horse's sweating flank. When he lifted it again, and gave Flaccus a final look with those bright blue eyes, full of the hope that he was lying, the centurion could see the streaks of the tears that were cutting a path through the thick dust on the boy's face. He was not a soft man; years of soldiering had removed what little kindness he possessed, yet he spoke gently now, reaching down to touch Aquila's hair.

'Sorry, lad. There's no easy way to say a loved one's gone.'

Aquila pushed himself violently away from both horse and rider, causing Flaccus's mount to rear slightly at the strength of the shove. The boy ran between the other horses, heading for the group by the well. Minca followed, with each rider taking a firm grip on their reins as their mounts sought to avoid the black menace that was suddenly in their midst, barking wildly as it raced after the boy. The group by the well stood rock-like and bemused as Aquila pushed his way through, though they parted more readily for the dog, then turned to gaze as the pair ran off into the fields, heading for the woods on the other side.

'You didn't come here just to tell me that Clodius is dead,' said Dabo.

Flaccus, who had also spun in the saddle to watch Aquila's flight, turned back to face the owner of the farm, treating him to a humourless smile. 'No, I didn't.'

'So what do you want?'

'Such an unfriendly way of talking,' said Flaccus, his head weaving so that he could include the band of ruffians in his thoughts. 'What a way to greet an old comrade. Decent type would have invited me in for a drink by now and told my mates to water and feed their horses.' He fixed Dabo with an icy stare. 'You are a decent type, ain't you?'

Dabo looked at Flaccus long and hard, weighing up the odds. This grizzled centurion could make trouble for him even if the war was over, the legions disbanded and Clodius dead. What he had done was wrong and he could be punished if it was reported to a praetor, never mind the land tax-gatherer. Dabo then examined the band of men Flaccus had brought with him. Each one wore a different type of armour, tailored to the skill they had at their particular form of fighting, but the helmets and breastplates had one thing in common: judging by the dents and scratches, they had taken a pounding. Unshaven, scarred and filthy from their time on the road, it did not take much of an imagination to realise the obvious: this fellow would not need to go to a magistrate to upset things; he had enough trouble, right here with him, to ruin Dabo's life for good.

'There's drink a'plenty in the trough. If you water your horses, I'll see to some feed.'

'And my men?'

Dabo looked at them again and shuddered slightly. He would not be able to fob this lot off with polenta or bread and cheese. 'I've been meaning to roast a pig for weeks. Tonight will do as good as any.'

Flaccus grinned and raised his voice. 'Hear that, lads. Roast suckling pig for supper and I bet old Dabo here has an underground store full of good strong wine.'

Dabo nodded, advancing towards Flaccus as he made to dismount. He spoke urgently but softly, interposing his body so that the others could not hear. 'I might have been shy of goin' last time, but I was a soldier once, an' a damn good one. I can still use sword and spear, so if anybody on this farm loses so much as a hair on their head, your men might ride out of here, but you'll not.'

Flaccus leant down and pushed his face close to Dabo's. 'Don't you talk to me like that, you turd. If I give the word this lot'll tear you limb from limb. You push out the boat, you hear, or I'll leave your pretty little farm looking like the ruins of Carthage.'

Dabo tried to stare Flaccus down but there was no question of who was tougher. As his eyes dropped the centurion finished speaking. 'I'll do you one favour, Dabo. I'll let you send your womenfolk away for the night. I wouldn't want them around when my lot are full of drink.'

Flaccus could hear his men snoring in the barn and he was a good fifty paces away in an unfinished part of the house. They had eaten well – the dying embers in the courtyard pit still gave off a slight odour of the pork fat that had dripped into the ash – and drunk better, full to the brim with that grain concoction so loved by the late Clodius Terentius, the same stuff that had got him drunk enough on the night he agreed to depute for Dabo. He lay with his eyes closed, turning over in his mind what to do about Dabo, Sicily, Toger, Barbinus and his dreams of untold wealth, each thought chasing the other. It was not a sound that made him open his eyes, just a feeling that he was not alone. The boy stood, the dog beside him, framed by the moonlight from the unfinished window. He had a tall spear, too big for him, upright in his hand, so Flaccus began to reach for his sword.

'You'll be dead before you get it knee high.' The voice was cracked and deep, not the voice of an adult yet, very much the sound of a boy turning into a man. 'Minca here will take out your throat.'

'Don't be so sure, lad, he's nothing compared to the wolves I've seen off.'

'I want to know how he died,' Aquila demanded.

Flaccus did not like being talked to like that, unused to it as he was, so he growled his reply. 'How the hell should I know, I wasn't there.'

The tip of the spear came down, but the voice didn't change. 'I don't mean that.'

Flaccus was tense, wondering, unlikely as it seemed, if the boy might kill him. The dog was much more dangerous, of course, but he often found that a dog got confused if you attacked, instead of waiting for the animal to have a go at you. He considered doing that now, weighing the odds, then he realised the drink he had consumed was making him aggressive. There was no need for this. What was the point of assuming the worst? The boy just wanted to know how his Papa had died. Flaccus could tell him what he knew and if the situation still seemed dangerous after that, then he would be forced to do something about it. But first he had to get the boy to relax.

'Tell me about your Papa, boy. I only knew him as a soldier.'

So Aquila did tell him what he remembered, not much, being only three at the time; a kind soul ground down by his labours, yet who always had time for a swim or a game. And he also told him, without adding too much more, that Clodius was not his real father.

Having told the tale several times, not least to
Lucius Falerius Nerva and Titus Cornelius, Flaccus
had honed it to perfection, but to this boy, he had
to say more, to explain why a senatorial
commission had been sent to Illyricum in the first
place, though he did not include the fact that he had
gained from the depredations of the governor they
had come to investigate. Vegetius Flaminus always
made sure some of his illicit gains came the way of
his inferior officers. Nor was he going to admit that
Clodius was forever after him for leave, requests
which Flaccus turned down because the legionary
had no money to pay his centurion for the privilege.

'He was a good soldier, though, as tough as old
boots,' Flaccus said, not sure if he was telling the
truth. He had never seen Clodius in a proper fight,
only marching his daily twenty miles or working
like a slave, digging ditches or raising fences so that
Vegetius Flaminus could charge for his labour. That
was a man he was happy to damn.

'Bein' a proconsul is a sure way to make a mint,
lad, but this Vegetius I was talking about was
another case altogether. He would steal your eyes
then come back for the holes and having a province
that was not at peace suited him just fine 'cause he
could justify more taxes for defence. Mind, he
pocketed that then charged the farmers and mine
owners for soldiers to protect them.'

He had charged them for fieldworks and

irrigation schemes as well, ending up with a legion that was better trained for labouring than fighting, but Flaccus decided to leave that out too.

'When the commission arrived it was led by a real soldier's soldier, Aulus Cornelius Macedonicus, and he was a man who hated corruption. Easy for him mind, he was the richest man in Rome after he conquered Macedonia.'

'Where's Macedonia?'

'Do you know where Greece is, lad?'

'No.'

'Then there ain't much point in trying to tell you where Macedonia is, and that don't matter anyway. This Aulus made Vegetius shake in his boots, stopped all the little swindles the governor was up to, got the legions out after the rebels and had the whole place at peace in three months.'

'I really only care how Clodius died.'

'I'm comin' to that, boy, but it don't make sense if'n you don't know what led up to what happened.'

Flaccus related how, after the news came of a revolt to the south, Aulus had sent him off in command of a cohort to reconnoitre the ground. For the ex-centurion this was a painful segment to recall; not only had they watched Roman soldiers and another proconsul called Publius Trebonius being hacked to death by rebels, that was the night he and Clodius had come close to getting their hands on Publius's treasury, in a wagon well away from the place where the killing was taking place. Close, but not close enough. They had emptied the strongbox and buried the gold but when they returned the next day, with Aulus Cornelius leading in person, the sacks they had taken and buried, a mint of money, had disappeared. All they found was a heap of hacked-about Roman bodies.

'Yet Aulus was not content. Said it weren't right so south and south we went, running if you don't mind, with the general out in front, though we stopped when we saw what we were going to have to fight. Turned out we was facing an army, not a band of rebels, thousands of the sods, Illyrians and Dacians from over the border, all heading north, so Aulus Cornelius decided to fall back and hold the pass at Thralaxas. Then he sent me back to bring up more soldiers. Trouble was that slimy bastard Vegetius Flaminus wasn't havin' any of it and with Aulus Cornelius out ahead with the advanced guard there was no one to give him orders.'

That was an uncomfortable memory for Flaccus, the recollection of his standing before Vegetius, filthy, tired and hungry, while the governor quaffed wine and ate grapes, certain in the knowledge that there was nothing he could say or do to effect any change in the man's intentions.

'The men that Aulus had couldn't hold the place, not enough of 'em, and Vegetius knew that, so he was as good as condemning them to death. So, when no reinforcements appeared, they fought a delaying action then got off as many as could still run. Clodius weren't one of them, nor was the great Macedonicus and death was the price they paid. Hard to know whether the general was a fool or not, lad.'

Flaccus was sitting up now, while a glum Aquila was slumped by the window, with his back to the damp wall, the spear and Minca by his feet. 'He relied on another man to do his duty. Vegetius didn't, and they all died for it.'

'Will this Vegetius be punished?'

Flaccus laughed softly. 'Punished. He's been voted a triumph from what I've heard, lad, with the thanks of the Senate. Shouldn't have been, mind. He didn't kill enough Dacians to warrant the award, so the bastard slaughtered a few thousand of the Illyrian locals and called them Dacians to make up the numbers. Made himself a lot of money into the bargain. Those he didn't kill he sold into slavery.'

'Perhaps I should kill this Vegetius.'

'I'd wait till you're a bit older. For now, till your fields and breed youngsters of your own.'

'I don't till fields!' said Aquila sharply.

'What the hell d'you do then?'

'I do what I like. It was no part of the bargain that I should work in Dabo's fields.'

'That won't last, then. Your Papa's dead.'

Aquila's hand rubbed the leather amulet on his right arm, a constant reminder of the circumstances of his birth. 'I told you, he's not my real father.'

'Makes no difference to me, lad. Now I'm tired, so why don't you take your dog off to bed and let me get some sleep.'

'What age can I join the legions?'

Flaccus yawned and stretched, before lying back down on his cot. 'You've got a few years yet. Time to get yourself enough property to qualify. Maybe they'll call on Dabo again.'

'I'm not staying here.'

Flaccus yawned. 'Then go away.'

'I heard one of your men say you're going to Sicily.'

'That's right.'

'Will you take me with you?'

'Not on your life. Now piss off.'

'I'm not responsible for money Clodius Terentius lost gamblin',' Dabo insisted.

Flaccus gave him a wolfish grin. 'The person I played dice with was listed in the century roll as Piscius Dabo.'

'So what?'

'So that's the fellow who lost and owes me money.'

Dabo stood up and banged his fist on the table,

then walked towards the window where he could see Flaccus's men saddling their horses in the early morning light. 'I've had enough of this. You come barging in here like bandits, helping yourselves to my food, my oats, my water and my wine, without even so much as a copper ass offered in payment. Then you have the damn cheek to ask me to pay that numskull Clodius's debts.'

'Someone has to pay 'em and since you have the right handle I reckon it's you.'

'Well I'm damned if I know how I'm to do it.'

'Perhaps if we re-light the fire and strap you to the same spit we roasted that pig on last night you'll think of a way.'

Dabo saw Aquila emerge from the byre. He stood watching Flaccus's men, the dog by his side. 'You got as much chance of getting coin out of me as you have out of Clodius.'

Flaccus had stood up, unseen by Dabo, and walked up behind him. He grabbed the farmer's shoulders and spun him round, pinning him against the wall by the throat. 'Is that right?'

'I've got no coin,' croaked Dabo. 'Even if I wanted to pay you, I can't.'

Flaccus banged Dabo's head painfully against the wall. 'You shit. You send another man to do your duty then sit here getting fat while the vultures feed off his gizzard. What did you shell out for that, a few vegetables and some corn, with the odd suggestion that a wife with a husband so far away might like another to warm her bed?'

Dabo was looking at him wide-eyed, mostly due to pain, but partly wondering how he knew about the suggestions he had made to Fulmina. 'The boy told me all about you, Dabo. I don't think you deserve to live.'

'The boy. Take the boy,' Dabo gasped.

'What do I want with a lad like him?'

'He's good at hunting. Put him near a forest and you'll never be without meat in your pot.'

'I'll have as much meat as I like, shit!'

'Then put him to work in the fields. He's mine now, as good as my own son. I'll flog you him in debt bondage. Then you can do with him what you like. Sell him to a Greek brothel for all I care. With that hair he'll fetch a mint.'

Flaccus rammed Dabo's head against the wall again and the farmer's eyes and mouth opened wide with the pain. 'Killing you would be a pleasure, but I don't think you're worth the trouble it would cause me. You'd best thank the Gods I asked a lot of people how to get here. If I'd not provided so many witnesses to who I was after, I'd string you up to the nearest tree.'

The ex-centurion's knee drove hard into Dabo's groin just as he let him go and the farmer slid down the wall, doubled over in pain, to be kicked as he rolled over onto his side and finally he was spat on.

After a final curse Flaccus walked out into the cool sunlit morning, where his ruffians, having saddled the horses, stood waiting for him, with Aquila watching them in silence. The ex-centurion mounted up, hauled round the animal's head and walked it over.

'Does the turd that owns this place have a horse?' Aquila nodded. 'Then saddle it up, boy. You've got no future here. Your guardian just offered to sell you to me. I won't buy you, even to sell on. Clodius wasn't the best soldier in the world, but he did his duty and so shall I. I'm heading south on the Via Appia. You can come with me if you can catch us.'

Flaccus hauled round his horse's head and cantered out of the courtyard. Aquila wasn't looking; he was in the byre saddling Dabo's ploughing mare.

Drisia, an old soothsayer hated by Clodius, stood by the roadway. She had been a confidant of Fulmina and many's the time she had cast her bones or spat some concoction onto the dry earth floor of the hut to read the signs that she insisted only she could interpret. Flaccus and his men came by and she had a more frightening effect on the horses than Minca. They all shied and had to be forced past her and when Flaccus caught a whiff of her stink, he understood why. She opened her mouth and let out an unholy cackle, then threw a handful of fresh corn over him. He looked back to see her still laughing, rattling one hand around in a bag at her waist, the other pointed straight at him. Flaccus brushed the corn husks off his saddle and kicked his horse hard to get it moving.

The boy, now with a spear strapped to his back, rode by Drisia a few moments later, hurrying to catch up with the men ahead. The old crone hissed at him with a toothless wheeze, and uttered that one word she used, after the death of Fulmina, whenever he had been unfortunate enough to cross her path.

'Rome!'

CHAPTER SIX

———•———

Marcellus rose before cockcrow, knowing the entire household was in for a busy day. He had barely finished dressing when the summons came, so he hurried to the study, not in the least surprised to find his father already surrounded by scribes and up to his elbows in work. He waited patiently while the business was concluded and once the men who attended on him had gone, he was invited to sit opposite, preparatory to another of their talks on the state of Rome and the nature of politics.

'It has been my wish that you should be privy to my thinking, Marcellus.'

The boy composed his face in an attitude of seeming attentiveness that he had learnt early in life. From the moment when Lucius had considered him capable of reasoning, he had included his son in some aspects of his ideas, and as time had passed that had become more complex. He was now treated as a trusted ear, perhaps the only person in Rome with whom his father was truly open. Lucius insisted that if Marcellus was to come upon his inheritance and the power he now wielded, then he must know both how it had been acquired as well as the methods by which it was exercised.

These sessions had once been something to look forward to, a time when such talks had been used as a means of teaching Marcellus Roman history, occasionally talking about the ancient books of prophecies sold to Tarquinus Superbus by the Sybil at Cumae, incomplete, because the Sybil had offered them to the Roman king for a fortune in gold. When he declined to pay she burnt half the books and offered him the remainder at the same price. Another refusal led to another burning and finally Tarquinus paid the price demanded for a quarter of what he could have had in the beginning. Lucius had seen them, and even copied some out, so father and son had spent many a happy hour trying to make sense of the riddles the remaining books contained, as well as speculating on what was missing. That all seemed distant now; Lucius had long given up both on that and his history lectures in favour of dissertations on the day-to-day state of Roman politics, while his son had long since given up saying thank you for what he considered a burden.

'I have told you before this of how I wasted my youth.' Lucius leant forward, a thin smile on his face. 'Not entirely wasted, since I served as a soldier in four campaigns. I know that my good fortune stems from my appointment as *praefectus fabrum*. I withstood the jibes of my fellows, brave idiots, who could not comprehend that a good quartermaster is as vital to an army as a good commanding general. Any fool can wave a sword, but it takes more than a muscular arm to feed a legion on the march.'

Marcellus stifled a yawn; he had heard all this before, what his father called his awakening. In the hope of a slight change of tale he posed a question. 'Did Aulus Cornelius rib you?'

Lucius blinked at the interruption, his mind trapped in those far off days, forty years before, when, not much older than his son, he had dreamt of a different kind of glory, the sort of accolade that Vegetius Flaminus was to be granted this very day. The name Aulus Cornelius coloured that memory, tinting his thoughts with envy coupled with regret for the loss of the simplicity of their early friendship. He could not decide whether to be pleased or irritated by the way Marcellus so openly admired the man with whom he had entered upon a military career.

'No, Marcellus, he did not. Quite the reverse. Alone among those I served with, he encouraged me to accept the post. We were close in those days, and I for one would have had it stay that way. But it was not to be.'

Marcellus opened his mouth to speak, to ask how such an honourable man could cease to be a close friend and how such a villain as Vegetius Flaminus, who had plainly left the same man to die, could be voted a triumph, but his father removed the opportunity.

'You will oblige me by not interrupting me again!'

'My apologies, father, but I wish you'd talk more of your days in the army.'

If Lucius noticed the implied hint that he talk less of politics, it didn't show. 'You will experience your own time as a soldier, Marcellus, so you don't need me to tell you about my time in the legions. And beware of old soldiers' tales, for they're much exaggerated.' Lucius's brow furrowed. 'We have a more important matter to discuss.'

Marcellus dropped his head slightly in acknowledgement.

'Today we have to witness the crowning with oak leaves of a man who most certainly doesn't deserve it. I laid out the facts before you yesterday for your consideration and I noted a distinct lack of enthusiasm for what I said, acceptable when suddenly confronted with an unpleasant idea, but you have had time to reflect. Now I want you to explain to me why, in acting as I have, I have pursued the appropriate course.'

Marcellus sat silent, his head still bowed. He

knew the answer, or thought he did, but he was reluctant to oblige by stating it, when in his heart he knew it to be wrong. Rebellion in the Falerii household tended to be a painful experience, yet Marcellus felt the absolute necessity to do so well up in his breast.

'Well?' snapped Lucius.

Marcellus lifted his head sharply. 'I cannot fathom why you have acted as you have, Father. I believe that what you have done disgraces Rome, the Senate and this house.'

He stared hard at Lucius, whose face was frozen into an angry mask. His son had never dared address him so and evidence of the shock was apparent in his eyes. No shout would emerge; that was not his father's way. Lucius would fight to control his voice and the command to punish his son would be given in an icy, emotionless tone. The boy could not know that, much as his father disliked the idea of being checked, he also recognised that his son was growing to a point where automatic acceptance of the parental line was difficult. All sons disagreed with their parents, it was in the nature of things, and Marcellus's youthful sense of the value of principle was not surprising; had he not been like that himself at that age? So he sat back in his chair, making an arch of his long fingers.

'Explain.'

The words, pent up, came tumbling out, disordered and passionate. 'Vegetius is a corrupt slug. You told me in this very room that you sent Aulus Cornelius to Illyricum to put a stop to the man's blatant thieving. You know, acknowledge without reservation, that Vegetius left Aulus Cornelius in the lurch, left him to die like a dog so that he could come upon his triumph. Common gossip in the market-place has it that's something he doesn't deserve in any case, since a goodly number of the bones on his battlefield were innocent provincials, neither rebels nor invaders. How can you stand up and plead Vegetius's cause in the Forum when you should be demanding his impeachment?'

Marcellus fell silent. His hands, which he had been waving furiously, now lay at his side. Lucius looked at him without expression, the tips of each arched index finger stroking his lower lip. Slowly the hands parted and were laid flat on the desk.

'One wonders if the money expended on your education was worth it. That was the worst delivered submission I've ever heard. You have allowed sentiment to destroy your oratory as well as your argument. Yet I know that you have observed my dilemma. The only fault with your conclusion is this. You have come down on the wrong side.'

'It is the side of honour,' said Marcellus defiantly.

Lucius's voice was as sharp as a vine sapling and it cut as quick. 'Do not go too far, my son. You have exercised enough liberty for one day.' The head was shaking slowly, from side to side. 'Everything you say is perfectly true. What a fine thing it would be to always act honourably. Aulus Cornelius was like that, forever measuring each act against his personal *dignitas*. You admire him so much, yet it does not strike you as foolish that a man of his standing should allow himself to be killed commanding less than three hundred men.'

'Thermopyle,' said Marcellus softly.

'Rome!' snapped Lucius, his finger pointing toward the street on the other side of the wall. 'Do not presume to match any Hellenistic myths against the needs of Rome. I know you have read Ptolemy's histories. Alexander conquered the whole of Greece and Persia, he even subdued and overran Egypt, yet where is your Magna Graecia now, Marcellus? Dust, a mere memory, like Sparta and Thermopyle. Not so long ago we were a city like any other, prey to powerful neighbours. Now, we are masters of half the world. I have talked of this often enough and it did not happen by some accident. Upright citizens, acting in unison for the good of the state, and a system of governance that denied rule to one man, made it possible.'

Marcellus blinked. It was most unlike his father, a man careful in his words, to expound such a massive oversimplification. Added to that his normally calm demeanour was gone, his delivery every bit as passionate as Marcellus's own.

'It was not the rabble that beat Carthage, nor our allies or some tyrant, it was us. It was not generals and mercenary soldiers seeking supreme power who took control of the east so that we rub up against Parthia, it was elected consuls and an army of men who had something to fight for, the very land on which they tilled the soil. And who led them? Us, the families who provided the generals and the magistrates, gave them laws and justice in the courts. Out there are people who would destroy everything we've built and no doubt they prate on about honour as well. Such a concept is fitting in a boy your age, but as boys turn to men they should acquire wisdom. When you say that I have dishonoured this house, you fail to add that I have done my duty by both the family and my class. In securing Vegetius's triumph I have attached him, and those who support him, firmly to the aristocratic cause. Yes, he acted in a base and cowardly fashion, yet in the end he did his duty. Illyricum is at peace.'

Lucius, who in his passion had expended some saliva, stopped to wipe his mouth.

'What would have happened if he had been impeached? Some in the Forum would have been on their feet to take advantage of the confusion in our ranks, arguing for land reform and an increase in the franchise, so that every peasant in Italy would be a Roman citizen, that justice should become the plaything of the mob instead of the prerogative of the well-born. Do you think the demands would stop there? No, the rule of the empire would become a plaything of political faction. How long would we last then? We would crumble, like every empire before us. The Pharaohs, Persia, Magna Graecia, Carthage, the Seleucids. Thank the Gods I have enough sense to put my duty and the survival of Rome above my selfish desire for personal honour. Posterity will record that if I failed to put virtue above necessity, I certainly did right by the Republic.'

Lucius had lost control, and that was, to his son, a scary sight, for displays of passion were, to him, anathema. He stood up suddenly, knocking back his chair, his voice loud and rasping. 'Come with me, boy!' He marched out of his study, Marcellus trailing him unhappily as Lucius made his way across the courtyard to the small chapel. Once there he threw open the decorated cupboards, exposing the family death-masks. Then he turned and dragged Marcellus to the altar.

'Swear, boy, on the bones of your ancestors! Swear that you will never put your personal honour above the needs of Rome! Swear to defend the city against those who would give away our family

wealth, take away our family power, and turn
people like the Falerii into mongrels.' Lucius was
almost screaming now, shaking his son by the
shoulders, the thin fingertips digging painfully into
Marcellus's flesh. 'Damn you, swear. I'd rather see
you dead than let you destroy what I have fought to
preserve.'

Lucius Falerius Nerva was affable enough an hour
later, smiling and nodding to his friends, all clients
and all committed to his cause. The Falerii house
was overflowing with guests of all ages and both
sexes. The women had charge of the smaller
children and they had been relegated, with their
girls, to another part of the house. In the atrium it
was the togate men and older boys, with Lucius
occupying centre-stage. As soon as he decently
could, Marcellus wandered away from his father's
side, still troubled by the exchange they had had
that morning; the ceremonies that had attended the
triumph enjoyed by Vegetius Flaminus and his
legion had not served to wash away the feeling of
distaste.

A servant approached Lucius, whispering in his
ear, and he held up his hand before turning towards
the main door, causing everyone to fall silent. They
stood like statues as the door swung open and
Vegetius Flaminus made his entrance, followed by
several senators who were either relatives or close

clients. He was dressed as a soldier still, in his purple triumphal cloak, his face painted red and the crown of oak leaves on his brow. Yet Marcellus could see the rolls of fat under his armour, his fleshy jowls shaking in anticipation as Lucius advanced to greet him. They embraced like brothers, then his host turned, opening his arms to introduce his new guest, and the room erupted, men cheering and applauding. Lucius looked through the throng at his son, still unhappy about the vow he had sworn that morning, his eyes hard and glinting, while his hand still held that of the conquering hero. He seemed to be saying to Marcellus, 'Look. Here, on the day of his triumph, this man comes to visit me! Nothing is more honourable than that!'

'Your father seems euphoric?'

Marcellus turned to look up at a tall young man in a plain white toga. He had a quizzical look on his face, to match the remark that was a question, not a statement. Marcellus realised that, in frowning so hard at Vegetius's welcome, he had given this man cause to enquire at the reason.

'Vegetius honours him,' he said quickly.

The handsome face clouded, dark eyebrows drawing together in a black look, this as Marcellus tried to place him, knowing that he had seen him before. The face was tanned as though he spent much time in the open, the voice deep and the bearing soldierly.

'I've never been of the opinion that Vegetius could honour anyone, even himself.'

'I know you, don't I?'

The other man's eyes had not left the scene in the centre of the room. 'The final disgrace.'

Marcellus followed his gaze and saw Quintus Cornelius, now a frequent visitor to the Falerii house, step forward to embrace Vegetius. The bitterness in the voice of the man beside him provided the final clue and recognition followed swiftly, though he had not seen Titus Cornelius for many years.

Claudia Cornelia heard the cheers and, knowing what they implied, felt her heart contract, while at the same time wondering at the naivety of such a reaction. She had been raised in a senatorial household, with an indulgent father who treated her as an intelligent child, a man who explained the way the world really operated as opposed to the myth by which people were sustained; honesty was rare, corruption was the norm. Aulus had been the exception and that, along with his fame, was what first drew her to him. Perhaps Titus had inherited his father's ideas. He had certainly looked ready to kill his elder brother when he found out what was proposed, a sentiment she heartily endorsed, though they had kept silent. Quintus would suffer for his own crimes if the Gods were just.

The chatter of the other women interrupted her thoughts so Claudia turned her attention to their conversation, which seemed to consist entirely of the possibilities of being ravaged or robbed in the streets, the price and quality of household slaves, and questions as to the amounts being stolen from lenient masters by slaves entrusted with running their households, all tedious in the extreme. She would have been mortified to be told that those feelings were evident in her face; the cheering, plus the gossip she had heard, so utterly banal, from a group supposed to contain the cream of Roman society. Valeria Trebonia was watching her closely, something she had done since first coming to the room.

It was partly Claudia's beauty that excited curiosity; the wife of the late Macedonicus was famous throughout Rome for her regal bearing and exquisite looks, but Valeria was also taken with her detachment, the way that she seemed to fit into this scene, yet not belong. The simplicity of her dress had some bearing on the impression, since Claudia eschewed excessive decoration. For all the trumpeted virtue of the ladies in this room, many had succumbed to the latest Greek fashions, adorning their hair and edging their dresses with patterned borders.

Not so, Claudia Cornelia; the black hair was dressed very simply, a mass of curls at the top contained by a simple braided cap, with the remainder cascading freely down the back of her elegant neck. Her garment was just as simple, a plain white dress, hanging loose beneath her bosom, making her look as if she came from another, more austere age. For all the fullness of her figure there was nothing soft about her. She exuded hauteur, without any trace of cruelty, great beauty which carried no hint of vanity and a poise that marked her aristocratic lineage.

Valeria admired Claudia enormously. The noisy children, playing around her in their usual abandoned way, seemed unable to penetrate her stillness and yet the opinion she had of their mothers showed clearly on her face. The girl was at a precocious age, with the first signs of female maturity already evident. To be extremely impressionable during puberty was not unusual, but Valeria Trebonia carried it to a greater degree than her contemporaries. With pliable parents and a household full of brothers she was allowed a degree of liberty in her education denied to most girls her age. Few families bothered to educate a girl, beyond the preparation necessary for marriage and child-rearing, but her father had engaged learned slaves for his younger male children, which allowed his daughter access to the knowledge they imparted. Not that these things had been given to her; in a house, let alone a society, so dominated by men, Valeria had had to fight for every privilege she had won.

She railed mightily against the advantages vouchsafed to her brother Gaius, studying under the Greek pedagogue Timeon in this very house, but her parents had baulked not just at the cost, but at the very idea of asking someone as stiff on tradition as Lucius to include a girl in his class. He might have paid a fortune for Timeon, but had shrewdly recouped that outlay by selling his services to the sons of his neighbours, this having the added advantage of giving Marcellus playmates of the right sort.

Necessity, as well as the desire to manipulate, had made Valeria cunning, so that she was experienced in the art of playing with adult emotions to gain her ends. That ability was extended to those her own age, particularly her brother's friends, and recently she had discovered that there was more than one method of discomfiting these naïve boys. As her figure blossomed she put aside the taunts of the child, in favour of the disdain of a woman.

The object of her admiration looked at her suddenly, aware that Valeria had been staring for some time. Claudia knew the girl; in such a cloistered society, where the rich and powerful continually gathered at the same events, she had come across her many times. The girl did not blush to be discovered or try to look away and Claudia, in registering this, also saw that Valeria had grown, had flowered, and looked quite fetching in her simple, youthful dress.

The stare, very close to a challenge, was typical; she had always thought the girl a trifle temperamental, given to emotional tantrums, which her parents not only allowed but succumbed to, helpless in the face of their daughter's moods. Not, herself, a strict person, she nevertheless felt that a dose of good old-fashioned Roman discipline would do Valeria Trebonia the world of good. Yet the change made her curious; if the shrewish child had disappeared, to be replaced by a striking young woman, had the temperament gone with it? Claudia beckoned and Valeria stood up, her recently gained height, plus her carriage, reinforcing the impression of a burgeoning beauty.

'Sit with me, child.'

Valeria frowned, which amused Claudia, who had used the appellation 'child' quite deliberately. But the face cleared quickly; this young lady was not going to allow herself to be discomfited.

'Thank you, Lady Claudia,' she replied, and sat down after a perfunctory curtsy.

There is a ritual in these encounters, which no amount of self-possession can avoid. Claudia had to ask after her parents, even if her mother was plainly visible on the other side of the room, struggling to control Valeria's noisy young siblings. Equally they must identify the last time they had met and remark on the pleasant nature of that occasion. Mutual condolences had to be exchanged; Claudia had lost a husband, while Valeria's grandfather had been cruelly hacked to death by the same Illyrian rebels. But Claudia was determined to avoid one convention, that of saying to the girl that she had grown, partly to avoid the need to flatter her, but more, because in dealing with this young woman, such an observation was superfluous.

'At least you can comfort yourself that your grandfather died as a Roman should.'

Valeria looked a little excited as she replied. 'I wish I'd been there to see it.'

'What!' Claudia exclaimed, her composure quite deserting her.

'We found one of the soldiers who saw him die, a centurion called Didius Flaccus. My father brought him to the house, and paid him so that he could relate the story and swear, in the family chapel, that our name had been enhanced by grandfather's deeds.'

Claudia was still shocked, seeing in Valeria's flushed cheeks and in her eyes a gleam that was disconcerting. She knew that the Trebonii were lax in the way they raised their children, but she could not believe that they had allowed their daughter to attend on such an occasion.

'And you were there?'

That brought some of the shrew back to Valeria's face, and a level of bitterness to her voice. 'No. But Gaius was permitted to attend. I had to eavesdrop to hear anything.'

It seemed pointless to observe that what she had done was both impious and wrong; besides, it was no part of her duty to rebuke someone else's child. Not that she got the chance; the excitement had returned to Valeria's face and her voice had a breathless quality, as she recounted what she had heard. 'All the women were raped, of course, long before they hacked grandfather to death. They couldn't find any trace of him, you know, so we had to make a death-mask from memory. Then the rebels piled the bodies up in a heap. Flaccus said that they had laid them together, men and women, as if they were…'

Valeria faltered there, not sure which word to use, but Claudia had the distinct impression that, in her excited state, she had been about to blaspheme, and only collected herself just in time.

'I cannot imagine what makes you say you wish you'd been there!'

Valeria put a hand on Claudia's arm, pressing down to make her point. 'But don't you see, it would bring the stories alive.'

'What stories?'

'Those written by Posidonius, about the tribesmen in the Alpine mountains. He's a good historian and he tells you lots about the Celts and their customs, but he leaves out so much about what really takes place.'

'Like mass rape and men hacked to pieces.'

If Claudia hoped for a reasoned response from the girl, she was disappointed; Valeria nodded emphatically. 'Can you imagine what it must be like, to fight and spill blood, to kill a man standing before he kills you, to be wounded and bleed, or watch a man burn alive in a wicker cage?'

'No, thank the Gods,' replied Claudia, standing up, clearly upset. 'And if I were you, young lady, I'd turn my mind to gentler visions.'

Valeria grinned at Claudia's elegant back as she walked away. She still admired her and had not set out to upset the older woman, but it gave her a thrill of pleasure to have done so, even if it had been an unconscious act. The cries from outside, where the boys were playing, caught her ears. That broadened the grin as she went out to watch, promising, as it did, even more mischief.

The ball flew from one hand to another as the players skipped and leapt about. It never spent as much as a second in any palm, being caught and immediately thrown to someone else as the watching girls squealed with delight and called eagerly to their favourites. Marcellus caught the hard leather ball in his hand, spun on his heel and threw it underhand to Gaius Trebonius, wrong-footing him completely since he had moved to cover the obvious possibility of an overhead throw. He corkscrewed in mid-air as he sought to leap backwards, while still moving forwards, and his fingertips touched the ball, but he could not hold it and it flew past him to land in the dust. Gaius did likewise, landing heavily and painfully on his hip.

'He got you that time, Gaius,' shouted Publius Calvinus.

Marcellus had already moved to help him up, enquiring if he had hurt himself. The other boy's face was screwed up in pain, having come down on earth baked hard by the sun, but he shook his head nonetheless; he would never hear the end of it if he admitted to feeling pain. Marcellus dusted him off as he balanced on his good leg, then walked over to fetch the ball, which had landed at the feet of Gaius's sister, Valeria, though she had made no attempt to pick it up.

Marcellus's lower belly turned over as he looked at her, which made him feel ridiculous; he had known and disliked her all his life, yet something had happened to that gawky pest who had always contrived to ruin their boyish games. She had suddenly filled out and her face, with her hair dressed on this formal occasion, looked somehow different. As he bent to pick up the ball, his nose detected the scent of her body and he found himself staring at the outline of her long legs, easily visible through the material of her fine woollen dress, his eyes inexorably drawn up towards the vee at the top.

Marcellus stood up suddenly, mentally shaking himself; it was only Valeria dressed up. Indifference would re-surface the moment he saw her in normal clothing, with her hair around her shoulder, but that thought could not be held as he looked into her eyes. She was smiling slightly, and her nosed twitched a fraction, while even her lips seemed to have effected a change, being more full and inviting. Or was it just that she was smiling, given that she normally stuck her tongue out at him.

'I'm sorry if I hurt your brother,' he said, wondering why he had bothered to speak.

'Who cares about brothers?' She moved her hand across the front of her dress, a move which drew his eyes. Her smile broadened as she saw how his look lingered at the sight of her pubescent breasts, pushing against the fine material.

'Come on, Marcellus,' shouted Publius. 'If you don't hurry we'll award you a default.'

Marcellus turned quickly and threw the ball hard at Gnaeus, which was taken smoothly and aimed above the head of the still wounded Gaius, who ignored the pain in his hip and jumped to catch it. The ball was halfway back to Marcellus before he had got his good foot back on the ground. It was not hard; Gaius could not throw with much force from such a position, so it was all the more amazing that he, the best ball player of them all, missed it completely. He smiled weakly at such a silly mistake, then made a rude gesture in response to the farting sound that Publius sent in his direction.

Valeria raised her fingers to her nose, as if she was trying to contain the odour of fresh sweat, which had lingered after Marcellus had walked away.

'It is too soon, I grant you, but it is something that must happen.'

'Marriage,' replied Marcellus, aghast.

'Why does that sound so strange, boy?' asked Lucius. 'Have you never heard of such a thing?'

'It's just that I've never considered it.'

'It is not for you to consider,' Lucius insisted, 'it is for me to decide.'

Lucius had been drinking, more than was good for him, unusual in so abstemious a man and it was easy to understand why. The leader of the *Optimates* had, to his mind, pulled off a most telling coup. By attaching Vegetius and his clients to his cause, without at the same time losing Cornelii support, Lucius had guaranteed himself an unassailable majority in the Senate, something well worth celebrating. But it was the presence of all the wives and daughters at his house, adding to the atmosphere, that had led the conversation to this point.

'Still,' he said, with a slight bow, 'it would be interesting to hear if you have any suggestions.'

'I wouldn't know where to begin.'

'It's very simple, Marcellus. We have more power, especially after today, than anyone in Rome, so we do not require to form alliances to increase it.'

'Money?' asked his son.

Lucius nodded. 'Is always handy, provided the family is of the right stock. You understand, Marcellus, that though I inherited a decent estate, I have given my life over to the pursuit of political goals, staying here in Rome for that purpose. Therefore, lesser men have been able to line their pockets with military conquests, or provincial governorships, in a way denied to me.'

'Do we lack money?'

'Let us say that we have a fortune in need of repair. Therefore you must marry someone who has a great deal of wealth, but no power. They will be grateful for that which we confer on them, the Falerii name alone is something, and we can take a massive dowry, which will ensure that the family maintains its leading position in Roman society.'

Marcellus, who had had a few cups of wine himself, could smell Valeria's scent in his nostrils and as he conjured up a vision of her, standing before him, he felt his blood begin to race. 'Are the Trebonius family wealthy?'

Lucius actually hooted with laughter, his neck stretched out to make him look like a newly hatched fledgling demanding food. 'No, they're not, and it wouldn't matter anyway. The Trebonii have been noble for less than two hundred years. I might countenance a step down for a good dowry, but I won't go that far.'

CHAPTER SEVEN

———◆———

Cholon was tired, hot and dusty; drawn curtains could not keep either the heat or the filth out of his litter. He looked at the scroll on his knees for the hundredth time, praying that he would arrive in Aprilium soon. Many of the men who had died at Thralaxas had come from this region, so the box at his feet was full of silver denarii. The first part of his task would be simple; he had sent a message ahead to the local praetor, asking him to arrange for the relatives of those dead men who had lived close to the town to assemble and await his arrival. That would take care of most of the contents and please the bearers who had had to transport him and his treasure. After that he would deposit the remaining funds at the local temple of the Goddess *Roma*, then take a tour through the region, hoping to find the dependants of the others on his list. Each would be given a token that, along with proof of their identity, would qualify them for their share of the bequest.

Lying back, he tried to forget the heat, allowing the jogging of his chair to send him into a dream-like state. He had been on the road for weeks now, first to the north of Rome, now heading south. It was so good, no longer being a slave. Odd that the Republic put so much store by the aura of citizenship, yet they allowed any slave freed by a Roman to automatically assume the same rights as his late master. Aulus had left him with more than enough to live in comfort, though he would have given it all back if he could, just to have that man to serve. It was not to be and once this task was over he would have to find a new way of filling his time.

Relations with Claudia had not blossomed immediately, despite her plea that they should be friends, but they had improved, especially when they shared an equal rage at Quintus's behaviour. Claudia was as close to disowning her stepson as Cholon was to poisoning him, a fitting end to someone who was prepared to embrace his father's murderer. Titus, sickened by what he had witnessed, had gone back to Spain as soon as he decently could, leaving behind what he termed 'the stink of Roman politics'. Cholon half-wondered if, when this task was complete, he might not depart himself, perhaps to Biaie, which was by the sea and by all accounts a very idyllic place, more Greek than Roman. Eyes closed and curtains drawn, he knew they had arrived in Aprilium just by the babble of voices he heard through the curtain, so he put aside thoughts of a villa overlooking the sea, of the plays and poetry he would write, bringing his mind back to the present and the task in hand.

If the journey to Aprilium had been bad, this was worse. The first part of his route had been on a proper road, the Via Appia, now he was being ferried along badly maintained cart tracks; fine for a horse, passable for a cart, but worse than useless for a litter carried by four stumbling bearers. Finally, having been tossed about quite enough, he alighted from the chair and walked, looking over fields of crops and pasture to the mountains which dominated the eastern skyline, rising in ever-increasing ridges all the way to the centre of Italy.

The praetor in Aprilium had been most obliging; all the farmers on Cholon's list were Roman citizens, liable for land tax just as they were liable for service, so the directions he had been given were fairly comprehensive. The men had been exempt during their service, but now they were dead, their relatives would have to find the means to satisfy the needs of the Roman state. The praetor had avoided saying it, but he fully expected most of the money that Cholon was distributing to end up in his municipal coffers.

He and his now-empty litter had to leave the track to make way for a cart, laden with vegetables, the mule being pulled along by a bent old crone, with dirty white hair, spiked and unkempt, her face burnt near black by years spent in the sun. Cholon took the opportunity to check his directions, though he took care not to get downwind of her. The old woman stopped at his bidding, and in the way of country folk seemed to chew upon the question.

'My he's getting popular,' she wheezed, grinning and exposing her toothless gums. 'He had a whole lot of visitors the other day. Not that he had cause to welcome them.' She laughed then, though the sound was more of a cackle, her bony frame shaking with the effort. 'Happen he won't welcome you after what they did.'

'The fellow I'm looking for is dead,' said Cholon, ignoring the logicality of that remark. 'He has a son of the same name, I assume?' She did not reply, her eyes narrowing suspiciously, while her bony hand reached into a pouch on her side. Cholon felt that this old woman could close up, for country folk did not like authority and with his decorated litter and his fine clothes he might look very much like some authoritarian figure. 'I assure you that his family will welcome me. I bear a bequest coming to them from a very famous man, a reward for his service in the legions.'

If he thought she had been amused before, it was as nothing to the state she was reduced to following that remark. Her eyes opened wide, a great gush of fetid air escaped from her open mouth, and the sound she made, a single screech, seemed to echo off the surrounding hills. Another followed and the mule, frightened, shied away, but the halter was firmly held and the animal received a mighty slap. Then she bent double, her hands clutching her sides, gasping for breath through her gums, her spiky hair flopping about as she tried to get some air and she kept repeating the words he had used each time she stopped laughing enough to draw breath:

'Service…legions…bequest…'

Cholon looked round at his bearers to see if they could offer any enlightenment but they looked equally bemused, so there was nothing to do but wait for the crone to recover. Eventually her breathing grew more regular, her hand rubbing her aching ribs as she slowly returned to normality, until finally she looked Cholon in the eye.

'Turds float, friend, an' if you ever doubted it, you'll stand convinced when you meet your man. All used to laugh at him, sayin' that he would be a knight an' all. Happen they was wrong.'

Cholon was still confused. 'You've yet to furnish me with proper directions.'

The old woman pulled out a handful of bones

and threw them at the ground. What she saw there made her quiver and she fixed him with a beady eye, which suddenly seemed full of anger and hate. 'You can't miss it, man. Keep on this track till you see a new villa going up, three sided and a portico, like a proper gent's. That's Dabo's place.' He stood aside to let her pass and she started laughing again, though softly this time, repeating the same litany. 'Service…legions…bequest. I'll wait here for you, Greek. Be sure and come to me on your way back. Me and my bones have a message for you.'

Cholon pushed past angrily, barely giving the bones spread out on the track a second's glance. They were clearly an attempt to solicit a payment for some specious form of rustic fortune telling. He was near the farm, too late to turn back and ask, before it struck him: he was dressed as a Roman nobleman and had spoken in proper Latin. How had the old creature known he was Greek?

'What does that look like to you?' asked Mellio, from his vantage point on Dabo's roof, one hand pointing into the distance.

Balbus stood upright, a red tile still in his hand, shaded his eyes and followed Mellio's pointed finger, examining the litter as it approached, then he turned his attention to Cholon, walking alongside, holding, very obviously, a rolled scroll.

'Tax-gatherer,' he snapped, dropping the tile,

which slid noisily down the roof and flipped over the edge onto the dust below.

'That's what I thought,' said Mellio, looking anxiously at his mate.

Dabo shouted up angrily from the courtyard. He had been watching the two men, wondering how he could get them to speed up the work, which had slowed considerably since Aquila's departure. 'Careful of those tiles, you lout. They cost money.'

Balbus ignored him and spoke softly to Mellio. 'We don't want to meet any tax-gatherers do we?'

'No we don't!'

Balbus made for the ladder. 'Best quit for today, says I.'

'Where're you going?' Dabo yelled at them as he scurried across the yard. Again they ignored him, climbing down to ground level as he strode into the courtyard to confront them. 'I've been watching you two all morning, and I want to tell you I'm not satisfied.'

Balbus turned his back to him. 'Hide the tools, Mellio. We don't have time to get them away.'

'What do you mean hide the tools? You get back up on that roof, or you'll not see a denarius from me.'

'There's someone coming to see you, mate, someone you won't make welcome.'

Dabo's face paled under his broad-brimmed hat, the image of Flaccus coming to mind, but his meanness overlaid that. 'Get back to work. Now!'

They glared at each other for several seconds, the two workers weighing the cost of non-payment against the price that might fall on them if they were caught working as builders. They were officially classed as poor, entitled to free corn, and Balbus shrugged, bent down and picked up his hammer, before making his way back to the ladder. Mellio, following him, whispered urgently.

'What you doin'?'

Balbus turned and spoke sourly. 'Can you imagine what that tight-fisted bastard will do if he gets an excuse not to pay us?'

Mellio looked at their employer's retreating back and shrugged in agreement. Dabo had turned and hurried to the open side of the compound, casting his eyes down the track. It did not take him long to reach the same conclusion as the builders and his heart nearly stopped with fright.

'Nine years,' he moaned to himself. 'Nine years' land tax. They'll ruin me.'

He turned and made for the house, calling to his wife. His sons Annius and Rufurius were in the fields, so she would have to deal with this intrusion; after all, officially, he was dead. That made him stop moving and shouting; it was one thing being at home while someone else fought your war but he had never considered that Clodius would actually get himself killed. Silently, standing in the middle of the compound created by his new, half-built villa, he cursed the man; if he was officially dead, then everything around him belonged to Annius, his heir. Dabo fought to bring some order to his thoughts, regarding a son who disliked him nearly as much as he disliked Annius. If the boy ever found out about this he would probably boot him off the property. He could lose everything. Time to come clean. What he had done was illegal, but it was a regular if not a common occurrence, one to which the magistrates could turn a blind eye. As for the taxes, he could slip them a bribe that would be a lot less than he owed, with a grovelling apology for missing the census.

'There's no future in being dead,' he murmured to himself. 'Time for Dabo to return from Hades to the land of the living.'

Then he remembered he had been calling for his fat and lazy wife and she had yet to respond, so he stormed into the finished part of the house, glad to have someone on whom to take out his anger.

An odd feeling had come over Cholon as he approached the buildings; up till now the farms he had visited had been run-down, with untidy fields, places where he felt the money he offered would be insufficient compensation for the loss of the man needed to work the land. This was different; here was obvious prosperity, and a look around the place, fields well tilled and a full and thriving pigsty, revealed proper husbandry. The house itself was a mess, but that was because it was, as yet, unfinished. It required little imagination to see it as it would be, with a tiled courtyard, facing north, away from the heat of the sun. Did these people really qualify for a bequest from Aulus? The face that greeted him was full of the rural suspicion he had come to expect, a man of perhaps forty years dressed in a long smock, which reached below his knees, with a large straw hat on his head. He could not be the owner, since he looked nothing like the sort of person who would construct a place such as this. Indeed he smelt like a farm labourer who had just completed his most unpleasant task of the day.

Dabo, for his part, was wondering who he was about to greet, there being nothing official about his visitor's accoutrements – no rods of office – nor the livery of his plainly clad, dust-covered attendants. His nose crinkled as he caught a whiff of the scented water that the man wore, his eyes taking in the braided band that Cholon wore around his head, something in which no true-born Roman would be seen dead, and the voice, with his light pitch, to a ruffian like Dabo, sounded as though it belonged to a girl!

'I am in search of the relatives of Piscius Dabo.'

Dabo said nothing, trying to make sense of the words. Cholon mistook the look on his screwed-up face as a sign of bucolic stupidity, so he repeated the name slowly, and still lacking an answer, leant forward slightly and proceeded to spell it out letter by letter.

'I heard you the first time,' snapped Dabo, stung by the implication that he was an idiot.

His visitor was slightly taken aback, left with a wholly inappropriate and patronising look on his face. Dabo looked beyond Cholon to the four bearers, waiting for instructions to lower their chair.

'Who's asking?'

The Greek recovered his dignity, squared his shoulders and spoke sharply. 'You will first tell me, have I come to the right farm?'

Dabo nodded. 'You have, but I'll say no more until you tell me why you're here and who you are.'

'Please be so good as to fetch the owner. My business is with him.'

'I am the owner.'

Cholon blinked, then looked around the area, as though what had been said could not be true. The man was old enough to be a dead legionary's father, but the century scroll had said that the deceased was the head of the household. His eye caught the two builders, standing idle on the roof, listening to the conversation below, deep suspicion on their faces, so he tried to inject a friendly note into his voice.

'Then it is you I have come to see.'

Dabo declined to respond; if anything his frown deepened and his voice was now positively hostile. 'About what?'

Cholon was tempted to rebuke him, even tempted to turn on his heel and forget this prosperous fellow who dressed like a tramp. He did not need the money by the look of the surroundings and his manner was offensive, but it was not his place to interpret the general's instructions. So he took a deep breath and launched into the familiar litany, one repeated so many times in the last few weeks. But he refused to look this fellow in the eye, instead casting his gaze over his shoulder, to where Mellio and Balbus were eavesdropping.

'First I must express my regrets at the loss of the head of the household. Be assured that Piscius Dabo did his duty by the Republic and, at Thralaxas, died as honourable a death as any man can hope for. Already in Rome the tale is the stuff of legends. Before the final assault, the general in command, Aulus Cornelius Macedonicus, realising that few, if any, of the men he led would survive, bade me carry his wishes to his executors. These were that all the men who died with him should be remembered in his will and their relatives should not suffer by their death. I am here to fulfil that wish.'

'What does that mean spoken plain?'

'It means,' snapped Cholon, 'that Dabo's heirs are to benefit from the death in battle of Piscius

Dabo. Are you his next of kin?' Dabo threw back his head and laughed, a reaction which annoyed Cholon even more. After all, the dead deserved respect, so he shouted at the man. 'Are you related to the legionary, Piscius Dabo?'

Dabo grinned at him, tempted to tell him of his fears of the tax-gatherer. He was firstly relieved because those had evaporated and the second question had only served to increase his humour. 'I'm related to Piscius Dabo, all right. None closer, friend. You could say we was twins.'

'I'm wondering if we can stand by and let this pass,' said Mellio who, like his workmate, had heard every word of the exchange. Both men knew of the bargain struck between Dabo and Clodius, which was common enough knowledge locally.

'By rights any money should go to Aquila,' replied Balbus.

He was still musing, wondering if he should intervene, while the well-dressed visitor fetched a scroll from the litter, scanning it, talking all the while, explaining the procedure for the collection of the money. 'A twin you say? I cannot find any evidence of a twin on the census. Only a son, Annius.'

Dabo spoke quickly and there was a new note of respect, triggered by greed, in his voice. 'The twin was a joke, sir. Annius is Piscius Dabo's eldest. He's out in the fields, working.'

'Then it is to him that I must speak.'

Dabo was stumped; if he asked Annius for help the boy would do the opposite just to spite him, but he could hardly admit to being *hastari* legionary Dabo, alive and well. Not only would that pose some danger, but he could kiss goodbye to any coin that was going. At least the task of fetching Annius would give him time to think, so he touched the brim of his straw hat and headed off towards the ribbons of fields that made up his farm.

'Is it any of our business?' asked Mellio.

Balbus nodded, his eyes fixed on Dabo's retreating back. 'It is that. So if we're planning to say anything, we best be quick.'

Cholon was not shocked; being Greek he was more inclined to praise Dabo for his good sense rather than take a stiff-necked Roman attitude and berate him. Neither would he report him, it being none of his affair. The only question to be answered was how to get Aulus's bequest to this boy called Aquila, for he certainly could not countenance going all the way to Sicily to deliver it. The builders were back on the roof, working away, when Dabo came scurrying back into the courtyard with a young boy of about ten, surely too young to be the Annius Dabo listed in the census two years previously, a census that the parent had managed to avoid.

'Here you are, sir,' cried the father. 'This is the younger Dabo.'

'Is it indeed?'

Dabo, fooled by his visitor's smile, grinned and came close, wafting the odour of the pigsty in Cholon's direction. 'Small for his age, ain't he, but he's a good lad.'

'I'm sure he is.' Cholon looked at the boy, who immediately avoided his eyes. 'What's your name, lad?'

Dabo reacted with exaggerated surprise. 'Why, Annius!'

'Let him answer.' Cholon turned to the boy, pointing at Dabo. 'Who is this?'

Rufurius, clearly nervous, replied without thinking. 'My father, sir.'

'Your father?'

'What he means is…'

'It's perfectly plain what he means. Now boy, what is your father's name?'

Rufurius was utterly confused, his head turning between Dabo and Cholon, as the Greek favoured him with a look that encouraged him to speak. It was too much for the boy to make up a name on the spur of the moment, even though his father, with a screwed up look on his face, was willing him to do so.

'Piscius Dabo.'

The paternal hand took him hard round the ear

and Rufurius spun away with a painful cry. 'Idiot!'

Dabo made to go after the boy, but Cholon placed himself between them and put his hand on Dabo's stinking smock. It was not physical strength that stopped the farmer, more that he had no idea who this man was and it would never do to go belting someone important. Besides, the four litter bearers had started to move towards him, though their master waved his other hand to tell them to remain still.

'The boy has saved you a flogging, if not something worse. You would do well to remember that.'

Dabo just growled, glaring past Cholon at the cowering Rufurius. 'I wish I'd exposed you, you little turd, and I curse the day that Clodius found Aquila.'

'Found?' asked Cholon. He removed the restraining hand and rubbed his fingertips together, in a vain attempt to rid them of Dabo's smell.

'Not that he would've found the little bastard, if I hadn't have filled him full of drink. If anybody deserves a reward, it's me.'

'It is not a reward.'

'It's money ain't it?' Cholon nodded, moving backwards to avoid the spittle that Dabo, in his ire, was spraying around. 'Same difference. I looked after the boy and his mother for years, an' took him into my own home when she died. I'm not one to spit on a friend, even if the boy wasn't his own flesh and blood. Not many can claim to be a foundling twice.'

Cholon did not want to hear any of this; what he wanted was information about this Aquila, then he could leave this farmyard, as well as this stinking peasant. 'You are not making sense. What is all this about exposure and foundling children?'

'The boy, Aquila. He was found by Clodius after a night's drinking, lying a couple of leagues off the road in them woods you can just see from my roof. Only the Gods know where he came from, lazy little sod with grand ideas. Like his father: never done a day's work in his life.'

Cholon had a moment's thought, of that night many years before, the Feast of Lupercalia, when he and Aulus had placed a small bundle in some woods far from a main highway, but he dismissed it. Exposure was commonplace and such coincidences were the stuff of plays and comedies, not of real life.

'My sole concern is that the boy should receive the money due to him. Do you think he will return here?'

'Never!' said Rufurius. His father glared at him, but he did not disagree and Cholon turned round to face the boy as he continued. 'He has relations in Rome, a baker called Demetrius.'

'Not relations, the boy was never adopted

proper,' growled Dabo. Then his face took on a crafty look. 'There are Clodius Terentius's blood children, surely any money should go to them. There's a sister on the other side of Aprilium.'

'Did they live with their father?' Dabo shook his head. 'Then they do not qualify. The bequest was for dependants. Has this Aquila reached manhood?'

'No.'

'Which is?'

Dabo looked at his younger son, as if to confirm, by the difference in their ages, the truth of his reply. 'Thirteen summers, I suppose.'

'Then he is the sole dependant and the money is his. I shall leave instructions at the Temple of the Goddess *Roma* in Aprilium. Should he return here, you must direct him to that place.'

'And if he don't come back?' asked Dabo.

'I may seek to find this Demetrius Terentius in Rome. More than that I cannot do.'

She was waiting for them in the same place, crouched by the side of the track, staring at the bones laid out before her and since her cart blocked the way, Cholon's bearers were forced to stop. He walked towards her to see that her finger was stuck in the red earth, where she had drawn the outline of a beaked eagle, wings outstretched as if in flight. The old woman did not look up when Cholon coughed politely and he finally touched her shoulder when she failed to respond. The skinny frame fell to the side, the head falling backwards, and Cholon could see clearly that the black eyes held no life. He looked at the bones, lying in the dust where they had been cast, and the drawn eagle, wondering what message, if any, they contained.

CHAPTER EIGHT

———◆———

South went Flaccus and his party, past Neopolis, towards Rhegium and an ever hotter sun, with Aquila bringing up the rear of the column, his mouth full of the other people's dust. Minca was at liberty to run alongside the road, drinking freely from the thin watercourses which traversed the fields that lay on either side of the route. The paved roadway was busy, full of carts and wagons pulled by dull-eyed oxen, and messengers on post-horses galloped by, demanding right of way, as did the occasional official or wealthy traveller in a litter. Flaccus and his men moved in the morning and the late afternoon, resting up from the heat of the noonday sun, both horses and men sleeping in the shade. They stopped in a town for the night if they could, or at the post-houses along the way if the distance demanded it, flea-ridden establishments, with poor food and worse wine. Flaccus was careful now to pay for their needs in advance, so that any further expenses would fall on those doing the ordering. He laid out nothing on the boy, who was obliged to feed off the left-overs of other travellers and bed down in the stable with his dog and the horses.

All Aquila's attempts to engage Flaccus in conversation failed; the ex-centurion had no desire to talk of his times in the legions, nor of the exploits of Clodius Terentius, who had been at best an innocent, at worst an amiable buffoon who was always short of what he needed to get leave. And he moaned about everything: having to serve in place of Dabo, the seeming indifference of the wife he had left behind, always claiming that she had in her possession something valuable that would more than pay for any leave he took. Flaccus was not a fool, and he had heard every promise and excuse in the book from the men he had led. Clodius would promise the moon to get home, and that Flaccus knew would be the last he saw of him, never mind the money Clodius had lost to him gambling.

Indeed, every time the boy mentioned the name Flaccus thought of the treasure wagon in that poorly lit clearing and the wealth which, as far as he was concerned, Clodius had lost, of the prophecy he heard that he would die covered in gold and how near that had come to being fulfilled. Why had he tried to steal something so valuable with only someone like

Clodius Terentius to help him? The man was born to lose. If Clodius had a spirit that watched over him, it was *Egestes*, the Goddess of poverty.

Yet even heartless Flaccus occasionally turned his thinking to those he and Clodius had watched die and the manner in which they had been killed; they were, after all, fellow-Romans. The male civilians had been strung up on trees, to be used as targets for arrows and spears, the women and girls had suffered the fate of females in any lost fight, but he had seen the soldiers killed too, one by one, forced to make their way down a line of men who wanted to beat them into pulped submission before the final blow to despatch them. Those thoughts made him even more taciturn, and that was before he even gave any consideration to the men he had left behind at Thralaxas. These were things he wished to forget; they were not memories of which he wanted to be reminded.

Aquila reasoned, when Flaccus growled to be left alone, that the older man was regretting his one moment of weakness. He could not know that every grain of dust in Flaccus's teeth served as an excuse to curse the luck that had him on this road, with years of toil before him, in the company of a band of cut-throats whose loyalty could never be truly bought, when he had held a fortune in his hands, could not know that the boy's questions brought that all back. And there were other worries. It was soon obvious that Toger and his mates had access to money, though it was a mystery how they acquired it, for they had had precious little when he had taken them on. Every time the band stopped in a town, and after the men had eaten, Toger would disappear for an hour with a couple of the others, returning with the means to purchase the things he seemed incapable of living without: wine and a woman. His presence on every expedition clearly established that he was an alternative leader for these men, a source for certain of future trouble. Assuming they were indulging in a bit of thieving, Flaccus decided he would need to follow them one night. Not that he would interfere; he wanted these men for the very qualities he suspected they were employing, albeit there was a limit. If they were doing more than thieving, that could put him at risk.

His years in the legions had given him a nose for trouble. Tonight, being in a post-house several leagues from the nearest town, he should have been able to relax, but the men were restless. That might just be because, for once, they were out of coin. They had ordered no extra wine as far as he could tell, nor questioned the landlord about the other services on offer. Toger, particularly, was like a caged lion, striding about, his beetle-brow creased in anger and frustration, his beady eyes occasionally favouring Flaccus with a menacing glare. The centurion ate slowly and watched the whispered conversations, accompanied by much gesturing, with a lot of sideways glances in his direction.

They waited until he was in the stable, checking the horse's hooves, before slipping away under a strong moon, Toger and two others, Dedon and Charro, with Flaccus watching from the edge of the stable door. He waited till they were just out of sight and started to head after them, but the other men appeared from nowhere and, though it could not be proved, he was sure they would block his pursuit if he tried to continue. Flaccus was too experienced to risk an open breach, so he smiled at them, made a gesture to indicate he had forgotten something, and went back into the stable.

'Where are you boy?' he said softly.

'Here!' The reply came from above his head and he looked up to see Aquila laying on a bale of straw, the dog beside him.

'How would you like a proper bed to sleep in and food off your own plate?' Aquila did not reply, nor did he blink; the bright blue eyes held the older man in a disconcertingly steady gaze. 'Toger has gone for a little walk with a couple of his mates.'

'I know. They go out most nights. They'll be back in an hour or so.'

Flaccus spoke eagerly, his normally cautious nature overborne by his surprise at the boy's observation. 'Any idea what they get up to?'

'No.'

'Well, that's what I want to know.'

'And you can't go yourself because the others blocked your way.'

'How do you know that?'

For the first time the boy smiled. 'You can see a lot from up here. You can see that they turned north once they were over the crest of the hill and out of sight of the stable door.'

'Come down here,' snapped Flaccus, angry at the way, with his calm response, this boy was besting him. Aquila dropped from the hayloft, landing softly and bending his knees to break his fall. The dog chose a different route, jumping down into a pile a straw, and once there, it lay down to watch.

'Do you think you could follow them?'

'Easily. We're in the country, not some town. I've never heard or seen an elephant, but Toger must sound just like one in the undergrowth.' He jerked a thumb towards the dog. 'And Minca will pick him up a mile off.'

Flaccus took him by the ear, tugging it gently, ignoring the dog, which had stood up and was watching them carefully. 'You're a cocky little bastard, ain't you. I want to know where they've gone and what they do. Find out and I'll pay for your board, fail and you and that hound can start walking back to Dabo's farm, 'cause that mare of his will be forfeit.'

Aquila did not flinch or cry out as Flaccus tugged his ear harder, he just stared at the centurion, refusing to be cowed. 'I can only do that if you let go of my ear.'

Flaccus smiled, releasing him. 'You're nothing like Clodius are you?'

Aquila turned and was halfway out of the window, the dog eagerly following, but his reply was clear enough. 'Why should I be?'

The road was built on a causeway, with culverts running underneath at intervals to aid irrigation. Aquila headed in the opposite direction to that taken by Toger, crossed the paved highway, slid down the other side and ran north out of sight of the other men outside the post-house. With Minca at his heels, he slipped through the first arched channel and made his way to the small defile that he had seen the trio take. Turning north again, he ran swiftly and silently, dodging round the gorse bushes and skipping over any loose twigs. The dog was ahead, stopping occasionally to sniff the north-west wind, whimpering softly if he detected some strong odour. Aquila heard them well before he saw them, since his description of Toger was not over-stated, and soon he had all three in view, with Toger well in the lead, blundering along, parallel with the road, making no attempt at silence, as they strode on in the fading light.

Aquila slowed down, called Minca to heel and

dropped to a crouched position, using the bushes for cover as he trailed them. They were still heading north, clearly with a destination in mind. Toger stopped, threw out his arm, indicating something off to his right, and they turned that way. Aquila let them go, waiting till they were a fair way off, before shinning up one of the few wild olive trees in this sparse and barren landscape. The lamps from the main room of the villa shone out clearly in the twilight and the purposeful way that the three men were walking towards the place identified it as their destination, so Aquila dropped back down and ran after them, still keeping out of sight. He stopped dead at the sound of the barking dogs, grabbing Minca and forcing him to sit, his blood freezing as he heard Toger speak, not more than ten paces away. The wind had carried his scent away from Minca's nose and they had nearly blundered into them.

'Dogs bark at anythin', you know that.'

One of the other men spoke, his voice angry. 'We came at the place from the wrong side. They've picked up our scent on the wind. Besides it sounds like a pack of them. They'll tear us to pieces if we try and sneak in.'

The third one interjected. 'You're forever rushin' at these things, Toger.'

There was a slight scuffling sound, then a gasp as though one of the men was in pain and Toger's voice, never gentle, was truly threatening now.

'You mind what you say, you bastard.'

The voice that replied had a strangled quality. 'I was only trying to tell you.'

'You don't tell me anything, Charro. I tell you. Understand!'

The third voice had a note of fear. 'No more killing, Toger.'

'You going soft, Dedon?'

'Sense. We've already done murder on this road, if we do another a magistrate would need to be as thick as pea soup not to make the connection. We can't leave bodies all the way from Rome to Sicily.'

Toger's voice was angry. 'What are you suggestin', that we go dry of wine and women for the whole journey?'

'No, but if we can't steal without bloodshed, it's best left. An' I can't see how we can rob a farmhouse without hurting someone. It was a daft idea.'

'What if I was to say this farmer had a pair of prime daughters.'

'You can keep that as your wishful thinkin', Toger. I say we wait until we're stopped in another town.'

'I'm as dry as a Vestal's tit, an' I need a woman.'

'I've never known you not to, mate. Why don't we ask Flaccus for an advance on our wages?'

Toger's voice became angry again. 'I'll not crawl to that sod.'

'Like it or not, Toger, he's the boss now.'

Another strangled gasp accompanied Toger's reply. 'Maybe we'll see about that, one day. Maybe he'll order me about once too often.'

'Then don't turn your back, mate,' growled the third man. 'Without him there'll be no food or drink, let alone women.'

Toger snorted. 'What? One of you lot try to kill me? That'll be the day.'

'Well, I say this is never going to work. We've either got to go in there and kill everyone, including the dogs, or give up and go back to the post-house.'

'I vote we leave it.'

'An' I say we go in,' growled Toger.

For the first time Dedon's voice matched that of Toger in determination. 'Then you'll be doin' it on your own.'

Aquila heard the sound of a sword being dragged across a rock, a sound that had the dogs barking furiously again, and this time it was loud enough for a faraway door to open.

'What d'you do that for?' snarled Toger.

'Just to help you make up your mind, mate.'

A stream of curses followed, accompanied by the scrabbling sound as they stood up to leave. Aquila was up and away before the three men had turned round, running fast in the moonlight to put as much distance between them as he could. He took the same route home, arriving at the back of the post-house, unobserved by the men searching the road for some sign of their returning companions. He shoved Minca in the stable and went to find Flaccus, breathlessly explaining everything he had heard. The centurion looked thoughtful and questioned him about the talk of bloodshed, but Aquila could tell him no more than he already knew.

'Well you earned your bed and board, lad.' He pointed to the table. 'Help yourself to some food.' Having not eaten properly for days, Aquila was ravenous. He stuffed bread and cheese into his mouth and helped himself to a mixture of wine and water. 'You can bed down with the others in the bunkhouse.'

'Minca?' asked Aquila, through a mouthful of food.

'Can stay in the stable,' snapped Flaccus. 'And make sure you tie him up!'

The dormitory was full of sleeping travellers. The mercenaries, including Toger, sat outside, talking quietly, falling silent whenever anyone approached. The centurion had paid for Aquila's cot, plus the right to use the pump, and he took advantage of this privilege to launder his smock and his small clothes, all caked with dust from his days on the road. He stripped off everything, including his amulet, gently stroking the eagle as he pumped water into the stone trough, thinking of the dead Fulmina and Clodius, recalling happier times with the latter, when, as a toddler, they had swum together, engaged in mock fights, and the sadness of his departure.

Washing quickly, sluicing water everywhere, he threw his clothes into the now murky water, rubbing them vigorously. He was wringing the excess water out of his smock when, sensing that he was being watched, he turned round. Toger was standing in the doorway, with what passed for a smile on his brutal, ugly face. His piggy eyes dropped to Aquila's groin and the smile widened.

'Why you're a man already,' he wheezed. A finger flicked to indicate the hairs that sprouted between the boy's legs. 'Though I think you've got a way to go yet.'

He rubbed his hand over his groin. 'Like to see what a real man's got?'

Aquila put his smock on quickly, even though it was soaking, determined to cover his nakedness. He shivered as the damp cold cloth touched his skin, then reached out for his amulet.

'Let's have a look at that,' snapped the squat mercenary.

The boy looked at him defiantly, lacing the amulet onto his upper arm as he did so. Toger's face took on its habitual angry look and he lumbered over to the trough. Aquila tried to walk past him, but the older man put a hand on his chest and pushed him till his back was against the hard stone, his face close, his stinking breath making the boy turn away.

'When I tell you to do something, boy, you do it, 'cause if you don't I can be real nasty.' Aquila saw the lips part in an attempt at a smile and he felt the hand reach up to fondle his groin. 'Mind, I can be nice too. Strikes me you might need some looking after, you being as young as you are. Might be that a few of the lads'll take a fancy to you. They don't much care where they stick it, as long as it's warm.'

Toger's belly was now pressed against Aquila. The mercenary's free hand flicked his golden hair, then he reached down and fingered the raised eagle of the amulet. 'Nice that. Look good on me. I might decide to help myself one day. That is, unless you happen to be my friend. What do you say, boy?'

Aquila didn't answer, nor could he look the older man in the eye, and only the sound of voices heading towards the pump room saved him from the need to reply. Toger pushed him violently out of the way, dipped his hands into the water and fetched out Aquila's small clothes, still in the water, then he threw them at the boy's head just as the other mercenaries entered.

'Don't want to leave them lying around, do we boy? Might get someone excited.'

Everyone saw the object thrown and caught and,

once identified, it caused them some merriment. They might have wondered why the boy did not join in their ribald by-play, but Aquila suspected they probably knew.

The hand was over his mouth before he was fully awake and he felt the cot sag as the weight landed beside him. Toger's voice whispered in his ear as he forced his head down till his mouth was pressed against the straw of the mattress. 'Make a sound and I'll break your neck.'

Aquila struggled silently, his head turning from side to side. He could feel Toger stabbing his prick at him, trying to enter as he pulled the muscles of his buttocks tighter and heard the older man curse. Then the mercenary pushed his face into the cot, trying to force Aquila to lie face down. He fought hard but the man was all muscle. He crossed his legs and forced his knees together as Toger rolled on top of him. The mercenary had given up trying to coerce him, instead he placed himself so that his penis was trapped between Aquila's buttocks and his own belly. The boy felt him start to move, felt the hardness of his erection pushing into the small of his back. Toger was moving faster and faster, his breathing increasing as well till the spurt of hot fluid shot up Aquila's spine.

The mercenary stopped moving and pushed his mouth close to the boy's ear. 'I'll have you, mark it,' he whispered. 'And in time you'll be willing. I'd take you now excepting you'd wake the whole place, but I'll get you alone.' Aquila thought he heard him snigger. 'And the more you fight, lad, the better I'll like it.'

The hand was off his mouth now. Aquila spoke softly himself, not sure why. 'No you won't. I'll sleep with my dog from now on.'

Toger just laughed, using one hand to push the boy's head back into the straw of his pallaise while the other hand fumbled with the leather thong that held the amulet, untying it. It wasn't easy, but finally he managed to loosen it, then he bent forward to whisper in Aquila's ear again.

'If you want this back, boy, there's one sure way to get it. Just put those pretty lips of yours to work and as for the dog, don't put too much store by that, 'cause old Toger, he don't take no chances. I've dealt with dogs all my life. If you take a look in the barn, you'll see what I mean.'

The cot creaked as he stood up. Aquila spun round and saw him walk boldly back to his own cot at the end of the room. None of the other men had woken, or if they did, had not considered it their concern. He shoved his hand in his mouth to hold back the tears and stood up quickly, rushing to the trough to wash off Toger's filth. Clean, he made his way to the barn, wanting Minca's company, the warmth of something he could trust.

Toger had used the rope with which Aquila had tied up Gadoric's dog, and by sheer strength he had strangled it, leaving the great black body hanging from a rafter in the barn. Aquila sank to his knees, feeling utterly alone, more alone than the day Fulmina died.

They had gathered by the tethered horses, all saddled for the day's journey. Toger had his back to the stable when Aquila came out, his spear in his hand, balanced easily on his shoulder. His eyes, like the point of the spear, bored into Toger's back. Dedon looked over the squat man's shoulder and nodded his head to indicate the boy and Toger turned, his eyebrows rising at the sight of the spear.

'Get your weapons,' said Aquila evenly.

The eyebrows went up even further, completely removing any trace of a forehead. 'What, boy?'

'I said get your weapons. If you don't, I'll kill you anyway.'

'You kill me?' Toger pushed a stubby finger into his chest and turned so that the others could share in the joke. Flaccus, standing behind his horse, eased his sword from its scabbard. If the boy was serious, when Toger killed him, he would have to finish off the mercenary.

'Want this back, do you lad,' said Toger, rubbing his hand over the leather amulet which now adorned his upper arm.

The head of the spear moved slightly. 'That, and the fact that you killed my dog.'

Toger indicated the absurdity of the situation to the other men. 'Look at him. Skinny runt, he can barely lift the thing.'

Aquila's voice, so even, so cold, made them turn to look at him. 'Last chance, Toger. I shan't ask again.'

The mercenary should not have laughed and it was even more stupid of him to throw his head back in that exaggerated fashion. The point of the spear took him in the centre of the neck, thrown with enough force to come out through the back of the skull. Aquila followed up, yelling madly, but by the time his fists hit Toger on his leather breastplate the man was incapable of further suffering. The blood pumped out of his mouth and neck, frothing as it mixed with his breath and he fell, straight legged, landing in the dust with an almighty thud. Toger croaked once or twice, then his body went limp. Aquila, standing over him, his body shaking, dragged his spear out of the man's skull. The flow increased to a torrent as the heart pumped the life-blood out of the broken neck, forming a pool by Aquila's feet. With the spear on his shoulder he looked at the others, standing open-mouthed, dumbfounded by what had happened. They could not believe that a mere boy could kill a man they had all feared.

His voice brought them back to the present. 'If

any one of you ever attempts to do what he tried last night, I will kill you as well.'

Flaccus slipped his sword back into his scabbard and spoke loudly. 'I'd say the boy's done us all a favour.' The heads turned and looked at him, trying to make sense of what he said. Flaccus knew this was the moment; if they did not agree, he might as well leave them all behind. 'I was set to kill him anyway, so Aquila here has just saved me the trouble. Now dig a hole, bury the bastard, and let's get on our way.'

Aquila had put the spear down and stood, still quivering from head to foot, with tears now coursing down his cheeks. Flaccus walked over and looked down at the now inert body, then knelt quickly and removed the amulet, fingering the raised eagle before he tied it back on the sobbing boy's arm. When he finished, he patted him on the back, then he put a reassuring hand on Aquila's shoulder.

'We might have to nickname you Hercules, lad.' Aquila looked up at him, wet-eyed, for he had expected to die, if not by Toger's hand, then certainly at the hands of his friends. 'I think I'd best put you on wages and I'll even give you a special job. You stay with me at all times and if you think I'm in any danger, you use that spear the way you used it on that pig. Better still, you can have his weapons. Learn to use them too and even I might walk round you.'

Using the point of Toger's knife, Aquila sat unpicking the stitches as they dug his grave, in his mind going over the words Fulmina had used. 'Wear it when you fear no man', she had said. He was not sure if that was true now, only that the idea of wearing the amulet was impossible to contemplate, for every time he touched it he would think of Toger and what had happened in the blockhouse; blood had not washed away his feelings of revulsion. The gold flashed in the sunlight as he looked at his inheritance for the first time, marvelling at the way the bird, held up to the blue sky, actually seemed to fly. He unpicked the chain as well, threading it through the gap at the top of the charm, and he held it up in his hands, preparing to put it on, but the shadow that fell across him made the boy look up. Dedon stood there, his eyes fixed on the eagle.

'It's a good job Toger didn't know that was in the amulet, otherwise it would have been you hanging in the barn, instead of the mutt.'

Aquila put the charm on, pushing the cold metal against his warm skin. He closed his eyes and the faces appeared before him. Clodius, Fulmina, Gadoric and Minca. Utterly alone now, he could not help the tears that edged out of the corners of his eyes so he stood up abruptly and walked towards the two pits that the mercenaries had dug well away from the road. All eyes were fixed on the object which swung from his neck, flashing in the morning sun. He threw the leather amulet into the largest grave, and watched as it was covered over. Minca was buried with more ceremony than Toger, the animal's grave marked and prayer said, which was as fitting as it was heartbreaking.

He did not see Flaccus looking at that gold charm, cursing himself and wondering if he had, after all, been wise. Maybe he had misjudged Clodius Terentius.

CHAPTER NINE

———◆———

Marcellus knew, just by the atmosphere in the house, that something was brewing. If anything, his father's workload, plus the number of visitors to the house, increased. The *Equites* had instituted a move to increase their power by seeking control of certain juries, at present a prerogative of the Senate. The knights complained that these senatorial panels of adjudicators made it impossible to bring a member of the upper house to justice. Few senators were so blameless, so free of corruption as magistrates or provincial governors, as to open the floodgates by convicting one of their own. There had been rumblings of discontent for decades, all part of the eternal struggle between the Senate and the next senior class of citizen seeking to enhance their status, but matters, judging by the riots in the poorer quarters of the city, were coming to a head.

For once he was being spared inclusion in

whatever was about to happen. Quintus Cornelius had moved into the position of Lucius's confidant and constant companion, thus Marcellus was left to his studies and more importantly to his games and military training. He and his companions were free to go to the Campus Martius as soon as Timeon finished their lessons. The pedagogue, once so keen to chastise, had forsaken his vine sapling and long since eased up on his punishments; perhaps he had seen his pupils practising with staves and javelins and realised that these boys, growing to manhood, should they turn on him, would inflict too much damage. He might also have recalled a warning once given to him by Aulus Cornelius: that it was a bad idea to overly discipline a boy who might one day, should his father expire, be his master.

Lucius had engaged the services of an old soldier, Macrobius, to tutor his son in the great tradition of Roman arms. It was a duty he was well qualified to perform: having served all his life in the legions, his body was scarred from a hundred battles, and, despite his advanced age, the muscles still bulged from the constant exercise that was his daily routine. His purple nose and broken-veined face testified to the other part of his daily routine, he being a nightly visitor in the more rowdy wine shops. Marcellus, his body oiled and dusty, furiously attacked wooden posts with his sword; he wrestled, jumped, boxed, threw the discus and javelin, lifted weights and for light relief trundled the hoop and cast darts, all this before plunging gratefully into the swift-flowing Tiber. There he bathed alongside all the other wealthy young men of Rome, as well as the veterans who still came daily to the Campus Martius to practise their weapons drill.

This was the life of a young Roman aristocrat; Macrobius taught him how to ride as well as fight, took him out to the hills around the city and initiated him into the skills of the hunt. There, despite Marcellus's obvious prowess in all the arts of games, war and the chase, he berated him in a manner of which the boy's father approved. Mere competence was unacceptable, not even excellence was worthy of praise from the battle-scarred legionary, and Marcellus was excellent, good enough to have an audience of much older men, as well as his contemporaries. He ran fast and jumped long and high, wrestled with guile as well as strength, often beating boys much older than himself. He was dangerous with sword and shield, threw a javelin with both distance and accuracy, and none of this was achieved at the expense of his education.

Even Timeon, who disliked Marcellus more than any of his other pupils, had to concede that the boy did well at his lessons. His Greek was perfect, he was numerate and wrote and spoke well in Latin and as he approached the age at which a boy puts on his manly gown, Lucius Falerius could look at his son, now taller than himself, and feel that the predictions he had made upon the boy's birth, that he would achieve greatness in areas that had been denied to his father, were well on course to becoming reality. The summons to attend upon Lucius came late in the day, when Marcellus was tired from his exertions on the field, as well as the long swim he had enjoyed in the river. Macrobius had been summoned first, to report progress, while Marcellus ate a hasty meal and ordered a quick change of clothes, for it would never do to attend upon his father in a garment reeking of sweat. Macrobius emerged from the study, beckoning that he should enter, and he did so to find Quintus Cornelius in attendance.

'You may feel I've been ignoring you, Marcellus,' said Lucius, managing to make it sound like his son's fault. How the boy wished he could explain how much he relished his recent freedom. 'It is not through choice, I assure you, since what is happening now stands at the very centre of the difficulties assailing the Republic.'

Marcellus offered a silent prayer that he was not going to be subjected to a speech, but he realised that Quintus's presence would spare him a repetition of the standard report on the current state of Roman politics.

'It was ever thus,' said Quintus. 'Whatever we in the Senate consider we might surrender, unruly elements always demand more.'

'Surely your quarrel is with the knights?' said Marcellus, an intervention which produced an unwelcome reaction in his father.

'Who do you think whips up the passions of the mob?' he snapped, leaning forward. 'They do, promising them free food and a better life, then they stand aside while their creature attacks the most august body of men the world has ever seen. The life they live now is that which we gained for them. The world trembles to hear our name, fears to cause us offence. Kings and ambassadors come to Rome, and bend the knee to us…'

Lucius's voice tailed off and he sat back and closed his eyes, looking thin and tired. Marcellus glanced quickly at Quintus to see if he had formed the same impression, that such a careless outburst was unusual from a man who had always been famous for his self-control. Now his temper seemed, increasingly, to get the better of him. But Quintus sat stony-faced, as though what had been said was oratory rather than the start of an impassioned rant.

'You have often explained to me that any system will be one of continual strife, as each group, pursuing its interest, tries to enhance its power. It's like a natural law.'

That made Quintus take notice, smacking, as it did, of philosophy, something he considered to be exceedingly dangerous, since it was inclined to make men question the established order. He glared at Marcellus as though he had denounced *Jove* himself, while Lucius opened his eyes and looked at his son, a ghost of a smile on his face; he was clearly pleased with what he saw, but he did not respond to the question.

'There is a great difference in our ages Marcellus and I have long suspected that I may not be alive to see you take your rightful position as a senior magistrate.'

The boy replied quickly, thinking that this was a new departure; his father never spoke of his own mortality. 'I wish you a long life and good health, Father.'

Lucius acknowledged the sentiment with a nod, and Marcellus, who loved his father, meant it; he might be stern and demanding, but to a boy his age that was a parent's right and if Lucius had not often seen it as his duty to soften the rigour of his life, then at least he had shown his son a degree of respect rare in such a relationship. Whenever the father had asked for an opinion, he had had the good manners to listen to the reply, often patiently explaining a better solution when he thought he was wrong.

'Had you been born earlier, Marcellus, I would

naturally have passed my burdens on to you.' Lucius half turned, casually waving his arm to indicate the rolls of papyrus that filled every shelf in his study. 'That cannot be.' He then leant forward, calling Marcellus's attention to the silent Quintus. 'You must get to know Quintus Cornelius better. I have taken the liberty of discussing your future with him.'

The visitor smiled at him and there was a silky tone to his voice as he spoke; the words were designed to please the parent rather than the child. 'I am bound to say that I like what I hear, Marcellus. Both Timeon and Macrobius have commended your progress. Would that my own sons had the same degree of skill.'

'I have taken Quintus Cornelius fully into my confidence, Marcellus, and I intend to bend all my efforts to ensuring his rise to the consulship.' The man was beaming now; with Lucius Falerius Nerva behind him he was certain to succeed. 'He and I see things the same way, which is gratifying.'

'I would be a fool not to follow your advice in all things, Lucius Falerius.'

Both men bowed their heads slightly, as if to emphasise the truth of what Quintus had said. 'I think we have concluded our business, Quintus. Could I beg you for a little time alone with my son?'

It was polite, but it was, nevertheless, a command from a man who knew that it would be obeyed, yet Quintus hesitated slightly before standing, forcing Lucius to get to his feet first, making the point that he was more than a mere supplicant client. Marcellus watched, fascinated, as the two men said their farewells, noting every nuance of the way they dealt with each other; watched as Quintus edged Lucius into a position where he had to show his guest the door himself. All proper respect was shown, as befitted the difference in their ages and standing, but Quintus made it clear they were now the only things that separated them. Lucius was not offended by this; he was smiling, and seemingly reinvigorated, when he returned.

'That young man has his father's brain, Marcellus, and he puts it to better use. Even as a child, I noticed that he was destined to be more than a mere soldier.'

His son was wondering what Titus would have made of such a remark; the second son of Aulus Cornelius Macedonicus was content to be just that. In Marcellus's eyes he was, for that reason, the better of the two. When his father mentioned that very name, his son jumped as though he had been caught with an impious thought.

'Titus is always harping on about Spain, complaining that we don't prosecute the war with enough vigour, especially about the hill-forts. He seems fixated by this Brennos, just as his father was before him. We have, as you know, discussed it.'

Marcellus would not look at him, caught as he was between his admiration for a brave soldier and his fear of being seen to have doubts regarding his father's policy. 'I taxed Quintus on that score, wondering whether his brother's pessimism would colour his judgement, but, on that at least, he was as clear as he was clever. Let the tribes do their worst. He sees, as we do, Marcellus, that Rome has more pressing concerns than such banditti.'

'What did he actually say, father?' asked Marcellus, curious in spite of himself, half-suspecting that Quintus's opinion carried with it a good deal of malice.

'That Titus has placed himself too close to the problem and cannot see that we have time. Let Brennos and his allies raid the frontier. Nothing, Marcellus, will force Rome to attack him, until Rome sees it as necessary.'

Lucius sat down, still clearly pleased, and Marcellus wondered if his seeming exhaustion of a few moments ago had been an act. His face showed no sign of fatigue now; it was as lively as it had ever been.

'Quintus had some trouble with his father's debts, which have held him back for a while. Most fortunate, since it gave me time to wean him off some of his wilder notions. He might be sound on the problem of Spain, but he was less so on the path we *Optimates* must follow. I've often worried that everything I've worked for could fall apart but with Quintus committed to the cause and eager to carry the torch, I think I can rest easier at night, and so can you.'

Lucius fixed his son with that enquiring look, which demanded that Marcellus guess the conclusion to be drawn from that remark. 'You do not see what I'm driving at?'

'No, Father.'

'What would happen if I dropped dead?'

Marcellus protested quickly. 'Surely you cannot expect me to take such an event into consideration. It would be impious to contemplate your death.'

Even though he continued to smile, there was just a hint of asperity in Lucius's voice. 'You've inherited some of your mother's sentimentality. I am mortal like other men. I will die and, given my age, I shall very likely do so long before you can think of occupying the higher offices of state.'

'I hope that is not true, Father.'

Lucius looked at the low ceiling, his gaze dream-like. 'So do I, Marcellus. I have often seen you in my dreams as you sacrificed your bull, then taking your place as senior consul in the Senate.' He looked at his son again, and the eyes held something like love; at any rate it was an expression Marcellus had never seen before. 'I don't praise you, nor do I encourage others to do so, but both Timeon and

Macrobius have furnished me with glowing reports of your progress. You've a long way to go yet and the path you will follow is strewn with pitfalls, but I want you to know that, at this moment, I am proud of you.'

Marcellus dropped his head, aware that he was blushing.

'Quintus was here while they spoke and I think he was frankly amazed at their words, which is just as well, since if anything should happen to me, it is to Quintus you must look for assistance.' Marcellus looked up again as his father continued. 'As you heard I have promised to aid him to the consulship. He could well do it without my help, of course, given that he has talent and money, but you, of all people, will know what my blessing means.'

'He cannot fail!'

'I have offered him more than that. The Senate is full of aspiring and ex-consuls who lack either power or true dignity. I intend that Quintus will be different. He'll inherit the task I have laboured at all these years. Not only will he become consul, but he'll assume the leadership I hold. Men who are my clients now will become his, should I, either through death or illness, be unable to continue.'

'Are you ill, Father?' asked Marcellus anxiously.

'I ache from increasing age, but no more than that.' The boy's enquiry had touched him and he turned away slightly, just for a second. 'Back to the

subject of Quintus. As a quid pro quo for my
assistance, Quintus has taken an oath to assist you
in turn. He will not seek to advance his own sons in
place of you. Everything I have built, he will hold in
trust, until you are old enough to assume
responsibility.'

'Will he keep his word?' asked Marcellus. He
didn't trust Quintus, and the expression on his face
made that plain.

He had rarely seen his father laugh, but Lucius
did now, the thin body shaking with mirth. He bent
down to the floor and when he returned to an
upright position he held a small leather bag in his
hand. Lucius untied the thong that held it closed,
tipped it up and emptied a ball into his palm,
holding it up, between finger and thumb, for
Marcellus to see. The light from the oil lamps
flashed in the object, multiplying and moving as
Lucius twiddled with it.

'I had this made for you, Marcellus.'

Unused to presents from his father, his expression
was a mixture of surprise and pleasure. He had
never seen anything like this glittering object. 'What
is it?'

'I should have thought that was plain.'

'It looks like glass.'

'It is. And it is a perfectly shaped sphere.'

'How did the glassmaker do it?'

'Only the Gods know. Greek, of course.'

'What is it for, Father?'

'Is it not the same size as the leather ball with which you play?' Marcellus nodded. 'Then that is what it's for. Macrobius tells me you are a winner at the sport, the best he's ever witnessed, tells me that he's never seen you drop the ball all the time he's been tutoring you.'

'Everyone drops the ball at some time, Father.'

Lucius frowned. 'You'd best not drop this one, boy. If you do it could break into a thousand pieces.'

'Then I can't play with it?'

Lucius suddenly smiled again and sat back in his chair, his finger arched before his mouth in that familiar way, with the glass ball touching his lips. 'Why not?'

'I could be the best player in the world, but I cannot have a game without involving other people.'

Lucius nodded, still with that slight smile on his lips. 'True!'

'What I am saying is that I don't need to drop the ball myself. Any one of my friends could be the one to break it.'

Lucius leant forward, holding the glass sphere up to the light again. 'Imagine that this ball is you, your mind, your body, your future and your hopes.' Marcellus looked confused. 'You asked if Quintus could be trusted, said you cannot have a game if you don't throw the ball to another player. If I was to say that I agree with you, there is no one to whom you can safely throw this object without fear of it being damaged, then I believe I would have answered your question about Quintus Cornelius!'

Cholon sat gazing at the blank sheet of papyrus before him. Outside his window, to distract him, the sounds of the teeming streets of Rome, along with the smells, wafted up; that, at least, was his excuse for not writing. But deep down he knew it was untrue, knew that his imagination would not furnish the words of the play he saw so clearly in his head. A child, born to a noble family, exposed at birth but rescued, who grows up to manhood and ends up a slave in the house of those very parents who disposed of him. The themes were clear in his mind too. The Romans were forever prattling on about nobility, as though it was something in the blood. He wanted his foundling to be an uncouth lout, so that when the family found him to be their own, they sought to disown him all over again. He had toyed with the idea of introducing a touch of Sophocles, having the boy sleep with his own mother, but that smacked of tragedy and Cholon very much wanted to write a comedy; a piece that would expose, through satire, the hypocrisy surrounding the high opinion in which the Romans held themselves.

He heard a slave shout the hour in the street, and laid aside his stylus, pushing from his mind the picture in which all Rome hailed him as a comic master. He was due to dine with Claudia tonight, to report on his trip to the south and the payment of Aulus's bequests, and his mind turned to that villainous peasant Dabo.

'What was the name of the baker? Decius. Donatus.'

There he was, again, talking to himself. He really must engage the services of a couple of slaves. Nothing like the presence of inferiors to keep you on your toes. Later that evening, as he sat opposite Claudia, listening to her tales of Titus, her grandchildren and the appalling way that Quintus treated his wife, he could not help thinking how attractive she was. Not that he harboured any desire for her himself, but it seemed odd to him that, given her independent means, there was no queue of suitors outside her door.

Thoas the Numidian was outside her door, listening hard to see if he could discover any more information. He had taken a fancy to one of the women who ran a wine shop near the market-place but unfortunately she had expensive tastes. Since his only source of coin was from Lucius's steward, he needed a constant supply of information to maintain his suit. Callista, Claudia's maid, sat alone in her mistress's suite. She knew where her husband was, and what he was doing. Should she tell? If she did Claudia might send Thoas away, which was the last thing she wanted. Callista needed her husband back in her bed, demonstrating the same ardour he had shown when they first married.

'But surely the Claudians are a very illustrious family,' said Cholon, not in the least amused by Claudia's dismissive wave.

'There you are. That remark shows that you cannot acquire the mysteries of Roman bloodlines merely by being granted citizenship.'

'Oh, I know how exclusive you all are. What I cannot comprehend is why the thought of a Claudian marrying a Falerii causes such mirth.'

'It's because we are Sabine,' said Claudia.

'Forgive me, but how can you be? Your family line is full of consuls and the like.'

'Originally the Claudians were Sabine nobles. The last King of Rome, Tarquinus Superbus, invited us to enter his service, giving us comparable status in the city. To the full-blooded Romans, the diehards, we're still outsiders.'

'How long ago was all this?' asked Cholon.

Claudia waved a dismissive arm again. 'Three or four hundred years ago, but it's like yesterday to the Falerii.'

'Then why is Lucius betrothing his son, Marcellus, to a member of your family?'

'Money, Cholon. Old Uncle Appius Claudius is

close to being the richest man in Rome. Even Aulus, with all the wealth he brought back from Macedonia, barely surpassed him. The dowry will be enormous.'

Cholon was tempted to ask why Aulus had married her in that case, since the Cornelii claimed to be a much older family than even the Falerii, but he knew that it would have been tactless, as well as unwelcome, and would serve only to ruin the relaxed atmosphere of the evening. Claudia, for her part, was wondering how long she would have to wait to ask Cholon that all-important question. Her son, if he had survived, would be exactly the same age as Marcellus Falerius. There would be a ceremony soon, when the boy put on his manly gown, and since he was going to be betrothed to a Claudian, albeit from another branch of the family, then she was going to be invited to witness the event. It was not something to which she was looking forward.

'Let me tell you about the most startlingly odious cretin I met on my travels. This fellow had sent someone else to serve in his place in the legions, while he stayed at home and worked his farm.' Cholon leant forward, a look of amazed amusement on his face. 'Do you know, he had the gall to try and fool me into paying Aulus's bequest to him, even though he was hale and hearty…'

Thoas had already left the door. There might be

something to gain from exaggerating what the two of them had said about the forthcoming betrothal, but he doubted, once that Greek bastard had started telling tales of his travels, he would hear anything else of interest.

CHAPTER TEN

———·———

Lucius Falerius Nerva's grandfather, like so many other senators, had done well in the distribution of *Latifunda* on the island of Sicily after the Second Punic War. These 'farms' were not like those in Italy, being vast arable areas worked entirely by slave labour. The main property, on the northern coastal plain, was fertile, and, with the hills nearby, generally well watered. The other, in a valley towards the centre of the island, was less favoured, requiring a greater commitment to irrigation than Lucius had been prepared to either plan or fund. Both holdings had been allowed to stumble along without much improvement, under the control of a lackadaisical overseer; worse than that, he had allowed male and female slaves to mix freely, with predictable results. They built themselves comfortable huts; some had been on the land so long that their young children toiled alongside them, both generations working at an unhurried pace and eating a fair proportion of what they grew. Flaccus, having paid a quick visit to the other Barbinus properties, changed that in his first week by rebuilding the slave compounds – he would destroy any exterior lodgings – followed immediately by a severe cut in the food supply.

A surveyor had laid out the practical way to increase the area under cultivation and thus the yield, an improvement that would require an increase in the number of slaves. Such an investment might eat into Flaccus's profits, so he first determined to see what he could achieve with the resources to hand. No other farm on the island, as far as he could tell, had operated such a lenient regime and all produced higher profits, so an initial improvement should be simple. His next step was the separation of the families, a policy he explained to his band of mercenaries.

'They shouldn't have womenfolk and a litter anyway. Makes 'em soft. We're going to shift all the women and children inland. They're useless in the fields anyhow, especially at ploughing and planting time, and they spill most of the water they carry in the wrong place. We'll send them to the other farm. They can start work on the irrigation ditches.'

'They can't break rocks, Flaccus,' said Dedon, an interruption that was practical rather than sympathetic.

'No, but they can carry them. Breaking stones will be a punishment for those that give us trouble.' He looked around the assembled mercenaries, aware of their indifference. 'Don't make the mistake of thinking this is all going to go smooth. We'll have plenty of aid from the other farms to start with, but once we've sorted the place out we'll be on our own. I don't expect that all of you will be here in a year's time. One or two of you might be dead.'

That made them pay attention. 'There are only a few of us, an' hundreds of slaves. Some of them will work with us, the ones who'd rather flay their mates than toil themselves, but we'll always be outnumbered and Rome is a long way off. Other farms, barring the odd runaway, have got their slaves nice and pliant, but only because they've been hard. They work or they die and if they cause trouble they're worked even harder and die quicker. Our lot have had it easy and they're not about to take kindly to what I plan to do. There's only one way to keep the lid on any trouble. You've got to be ruthless. First sign of dissent, you crack down. Kill if you must, but remember slaves cost money.'

'What about the women?' asked Charro.

'Threaten 'em, but don't touch, that is unless you get any trouble. Then you can do with them what you like.'

Aquila, armed with a sword and shield to add to

his spear, acted as a sort of personal bodyguard to Flaccus, so he saw very little of the anguish these orders caused; having given his instructions, the new overseer was content to let his men carry them out. The mercenaries would be brutal, they were being paid for that, but he had no desire to witness what they did. Even Flaccus might have baulked at some of their wilder activities. The ex-centurion rode all over the properties, sketching his plans for the better use of the land and available water. Aquila did not see the women and children torn from their huts, know of the hardships of their march to the inland farm stockade with no food or water on the way, of protesting men hung by the thumbs from trees and flayed till they were nearly dead, or of the fate of the women who fought to remain themselves, victims of the slack observance of Flaccus's instructions. Some, having serviced the whole band, still had enough life in them to be fetched back to the men's barracks, with the stark choice of meeting their needs, or the offer of a painful death.

But Aquila saw the smoke of the burning huts on the horizon, looked into the glazed eyes of the men who had now been herded into the wooded compounds, watched as they worked, chained together, saw the vultures in the sky, before they swooped to feed on the bodies of those women and children who had died on the march. He had stood beside Flaccus on the day that those unfortunate men, who dared to protest at their treatment, with precious few tools to dent the solid rock, started on the first of the new irrigation schemes. He knew the inducements they had been offered were a lie; there would be no easy life after the punishment was served. Aquila had been with Flaccus as he drew the plans for the next natural aqueduct. And if they were not broken on that, they would be returned to the land, to ploughing and planting, just as soon as this channel through the hills was complete.

He ate with the mercenaries and listened to their stories, happy to be treated as an equal while they related the more salacious incidents. He was part of the band, accepted since the death of Toger as one of them, and he was growing up, turning from a boy into a man. Aquila was, at last, part of a family again.

'Time you dipped your wick, boy,' said Dedon, a remark which the others greeted with a small amount of ribald comment, accompanied by whistling and cheering. Aquila turned back quickly to look at the table, Dedon having observed his eyes locked on to the swaying hips of Phoebe, the youngest of the slave girls. The hut had a dozen such women, who acted as cooks, maids and concubines. Some, like the object of his attentions, were resigned to their fate, accepting the attention of the mercenaries rather than face the alternative; others had taken to it as if born to the life. All ate better than the other female slaves and if the work was unpleasant, it was less arduous than shifting dust and rocks.

They were sitting in the hut, at a long wooden table strewn with the remains of their supper. Aquila, determined to keep up with his new-found friends in the article of wine, was slightly drunk. They had the hard heads of grown men accustomed to drink; he was still a youth, not yet old enough to don his manly gown, so he treated everyone at the table to a knowing look, meant to convince them that the suggestion was way too late.

'You've got a full bush of hair on your balls now,' added Charro with an exaggerated wink. Then he looked at his mates and smiled. 'Wouldn't surprise me if you've been slipping it to one of the girls when we're not about.'

Aquila leered at him to confirm the truth of the statement, touching the side of his nose with a slow finger at the chorus of enquiries that followed. Dedon responded, his voice jocular. 'You say he got hair, Charro. How'd you know that? You been having a peek while he washes?'

'He don't just wash himself, brother. That eagle round his neck ain't the only thing he plays with.'

Dedon pretended to be shocked. 'Is that right! Found a use for his right hand has he?'

Aquila blushed furiously as they all laughed, making gestures with their own hands to illustrate their meaning. 'I say we should have a look and see what he's got.'

The others roared their approval. Aquila was on his feet quickly, but the hands of the two men on either side had already taken hold. Vainly, he struggled to get free as more hands grabbed at him as the rest of the band gathered round. A couple of the men took his legs and he felt himself lifted in the air. They laid him, still squirming as hard as he could, on the table, scattering the plates and goblets. He felt the hands at his small clothes and sought to turn as they were torn off, heard the whoops of joy and the ribald remarks, keeping his eyes tightly closed while he was minutely examined. Rough hands flicked at his private parts, with many a reference to size and function.

'Let's set him to a woman,' whooped Dedon.

Roars greeted this. They had his smock off before he was lifted into the air again. The men carried him bodily to one of the rooms at the end, calling out to all the girls to witness what was happening, and they crowded round for a view of this novel event. Only Phoebe stood back, unwilling to participate.

'Who's it to be?' Dedon leered, his finger pointing at those most eager to see. 'Come girls, off with your shifts and let our hero have a look.'

Two of the girls threw off their clothes and stood naked, ready for inspection. His captors dropped him to the ground, still holding his arms tightly, and made him face the pair, the roars that greeted the beginning of his erection louder than any that had gone before. He tried, but he could not help himself, having spent a good deal of time fantasising about the very act he was being encouraged to perform.

Dedon pointed at his groin. 'You're in for some pleasure girls by the look of that, but we still have to decide who's going to be lucky.'

They pushed him forward until he was standing by the first of the girls, a rather plump creature with huge breasts. Dedon had appointed himself judge, and he crouched down to see the effect this was having on the boy. 'By the Gods, lads, it's twitching. Aquila's prick has a life of its own.'

He was presented to the next girl, older than the rest, who waggled her hips a little to entice him. Aquila had that sensation in his groin, that mixture of pleasure and pain, and it was becoming unbearable. He shut his eyes and tried to think of something else, an act which Dedon misinterpreted.

'No. This one's no good.' The mercenary raised his head to pick out a third candidate and almost immediately his eyes lit on Phoebe, standing well away from the crowd. 'We've been going about this the wrong way, lads. I started all this 'cause our young cock-sparrow has his eyes on a certain swaying arse.'

Phoebe must have known what was coming, for she shrank back against the wall. That only encouraged Dedon, who jumped across the room to grab her. He hauled the girl close and growled in her ear. 'You're lucky you're still here, the way you carry on. Don't think I haven't seen you, making yourself scarce at night. Time you earned your fuckin' keep.'

He started to laugh, the pun being unintentional, then spun round and dragged her forward, repeating his remark to universal acclaim. 'This is the one for Aquila. He'll gain an inch, once he catches sight of Phoebe without her shift.'

The women, who knew which side to take for their own well-being, helped Dedon to pull off Phoebe's clothing. Aquila was shuffled towards her and he knew, even with his eyes still shut, that he was before the slimmest as well as the youngest of the slave girls, a Macedonian about his own height. Dedon was right. It was her hips he had been watching, moving enticingly under her woollen dress, and, to him, part of the attraction was her reluctance to indulge the others. He had had his eye on her for weeks, trying to pluck up the courage to get her alone, his confidence alternately boosted and crushed by the enquiring looks she gave him.

'Oooh!' He felt himself jerk spasmodically as her

cool hand brushed against him. He opened his eyes. She was standing very close, deliberately not looking at him, her eyes full of tears. Aquila looked down, to see that Dedon had hold of her wrist, and was pushing her hand, so that it rubbed gently against him. He opened his mouth to protest, to ask the crowd to stop, but Dedon spoke first.

'We best get them to it, lads,' cried Dedon, mistaking the sad look in the boy's eyes. 'I don't think our novice can hang on much longer.'

Aquila felt himself lifted bodily once more. Phoebe allowed herself to be led, unresisting, to the straw pallet on the floor. The women laid her down, forcing open her arms and legs to welcome him, as his bearers lowered Aquila into position. Dedon took hold of his gold charm, pushing it out of the way, as he whispered in Phoebe's ear.

'You've got two choices, girl. Either you see to the boy, an' show willing, or I'll wrap a rope around your neck and string you up from the nearest tree.'

'No, Dedon,' Aquila gasped. 'I don't want this.'

The mercenary spun his head, to look Aquila in the eye. 'Nonsense, boy. Don't be soft.'

'He ain't soft, an' that's for certain,' said Charro, with a whoop of glee.

Dedon grinned at him. 'Only goes to prove, friend, that a standing prick ain't got no conscience.'

He felt their arms on his back, pushing him. They'd taken hold of her legs, which were now encircling his thighs. Female hands put him inside her. Phoebe, encouraged by Dedon's threats, started to move against him. That feeling, which he fought to suppress, rose quickly; too quickly. His naked buttocks, accompanied by loud cheers, jerked furiously as he came in a woman for the first time, his head buried in the crook of her neck, and he heard the sob in her throat as he stopped moving.

Dedon's voice seemed very distant. 'I say we should leave them alone, lads. Then perhaps young Aquila can give Phoebe a real seeing to.'

There was much giggling as they all filed out of the room. Aquila lifted his head and turned hers so that he could look the girl in the eye. She gave him a sad smile then turned away again.

'I'm sorry,' he said softly.

That made her turn back, searching his eyes to see if he was sincere. Her hand reached out to feel the golden eagle that hung between them. The two youngsters stared at each other for what seemed an age. Then Phoebe's other hand came up to the back of his neck and she pulled him down, kissing him full on the lips. The way he subsequently took the Macedonian girl as his own personal concubine caused no resentment, nor did she complain again. Aquila was far from sure if she genuinely liked him, or was merely happy to serve the needs of a young and persistent lover, rather than go back to what she had put up with before, but over the days and weeks he came to realise it was more than just acceptance. Phoebe lost the hunted look she had worn before, not that she got much peace. He spent every free moment in her arms, trying to talk to her between bouts of lovemaking, difficult since he had no Greek and she only had enough Latin to serve as a slave. She learnt words from him, but he garnered more from her, starting with her name, which meant 'bright lights'. In time they could hold stilted conversations enough to explain how they came to be here in Sicily.

The mercenaries, having supervised his initiation, now seemed to adopt him fully. When not riding the farm with Flaccus, or locked in Phoebe's arms, they took upon themselves the job of teaching him the arts of fighting; how to ride bareback and fight off a horse, saddled or not. Dedon was a trident and net man, Charro a master with the short sword. Spear throwing he knew, but the others taught him to wrestle, to fight with staves, how to kill with the boss of a shield, the way to use a knife or a rope at close quarters and how to fire off an arrow from a proper bow, and they were not gentle, which led to many a bruise and more than one cut. Aquila never complained, never let them see if he was hurt. Phoebe dressed his wounds, and rubbed oil into the tired and burgeoning muscles, never failing to finger his pendant, whispering words in Greek as she praised her eagle.

Over the months Aquila grew in strength and speed so that the contests were no longer wholly one-sided. He fought well and never whined when he was painfully bested and was thus popular amongst the men. Because his manner was less rough than his fellows, and given his single-minded attachment to Phoebe, he was popular with the women as well. Hard-hearted Flaccus, obsessed with his need to increase the yield, even consented to the holding of a ceremony, with special food and some of his own wine, to celebrate the March day following the Feast of Lupercalia, when Aquila donned his manly gown. All the concubines helped in the preparation, weaving as well as cooking. Some of them cried as he stepped forward, in a new smock, his red-gold hair carefully combed and dressed, the eagle flashing on his tanned chest, no longer a boy, but a Roman citizen and a man.

There was never a month without trouble and much as Flaccus hated the waste he was forced to sanction the occasional hanging. Flogging was a daily occurrence as the men were driven at dawn into the fields to work, overseen by other slaves whom the mercenaries had recruited. They themselves acted as a sort of mobile reserve, available to impose an even harsher regime if the trouble became serious. Flaccus spent his time between his two farms, threatening and cajoling, with many a lying promise, all to increase the land under cultivation. It was hardly surprising that any slaves who caught their guards unawares, and who had the strength, did their very best to escape from such a regime but that was happening all over the island. More worrying was the fact that these escapees had only one way to feed themselves, and that was to steal from the likes of Didius Flaccus.

The first harvest had shown a drop in yield. Even though Flaccus had anticipated this, since it was caused by his restructuring, he manufactured a towering rage, tongue-lashing his men as layabouts and threatening to cut their pay. The slaves paid for this, of course; they were driven to work even harder by an increase in flogging, plus a couple of exemplary crucifixions. This was not confined to men either; women and children suffered just as much and the young bodyguard was no longer shielded from it. As he rode from place to place, just behind his leader, Aquila could contrast the atmosphere now with that which had existed when they had arrived. Not even a ghost of a smile anywhere, just hardship and pain. Those with some spirit, who had avoided death or serious injury and had not run away to the hills, were worst off, breaking rocks in the unyielding hills. The women dug trenches in the softer ground while their children removed the earth to build embankments on the lower slopes. As he rode by, the children, some of them approaching his own age, would look up, their eyes full of envy for the golden youth with his horse, his weapons, his healthy glowing skin and his full belly.

The spring ploughing was over, the fields planted. For the slaves it was normally a period of comparative rest. Not now. Some were kept to water the fields, the rest put to work increasing the irrigation, working up on the hillsides which had, until then, remained uncultivated. They cursed the earth, which was nearly as hard as their grim and ruthless master. Flaccus rarely slept and never relaxed, refused the services of slave girls and worried constantly, watching the stalks of wheat as they grew. He ranted and raved throughout the harvest, cursing the slightest waste. Only when he began to see some of his labours bearing fruit did he consent to spend some time away from his duties. It was no holiday; Flaccus was called to discuss joint measures against banditry with the other men overseeing the Sicilian farms. There had been an upsurge in attacks as increasing numbers of slaves went missing and coordinated action was needed to root these villains out of their mountain retreats.

If he had been unable to look his fellow-bailiffs in the eye, Flaccus would not have gone even then; now the centurion knew he could, for the summer harvest was up. Not by much, but it pointed in the right direction and he had increased the land under the plough. Next year, always assuming the Gods blessed them with the right amount of rain, he would see, in the number of bushels his farm produced, something to crow about. Determined on a final check in progress, Flaccus insisted on going via the inland farms, increasing the journey time by two-thirds.

Aquila was saddled up before first light, holding the second horse, waiting while his leader repeated his instructions for the tenth time. Dedon's voice sounded like a nagged husband, as he agreed to each point. Eventually Flaccus mounted up, but not without delivering a last command. 'Leave half your men here, Dedon, and take the rest back to the main farm. If there's any trouble, send for me, right away.'

'Yes, yes,' replied Dedon wearily, wishing the man gone so that he could go back to bed.

'That's it then!' But Flaccus didn't move, as though the act of tugging the horse's head round was too much to bear. Aquila leant down and pulled the reins for him.

'Don't look back, Flaccus,' he said, as they cantered out of the compound.

Once he had shaken off the dust of his own properties, the old centurion relaxed. They climbed the saddle of a steep hill, with Mount Etna to the south, rumbling and belching smoke. He was in a talkative mood, no doubt buoyed by success, and for the first time he allowed himself to indulge in a little reminiscence, speaking of Clodius and how close the pair of them had come to being rich, even admitting their plan to steal the gubernatorial gold.

'It was me that spotted the wagon, and I only chose Clodius 'cause he was lying next to me watching what was going on.' Flaccus was brief regarding what he and Clodius had seen before that, Roman soldiers running the gauntlet and mass rape taking place all around, the women eventually killed and mutilated. In his mind's eye he could see that wagon parked away from all that, occasionally lit as the fires of the other burning wagons flared. 'We had it in our hands, near all of it, and we buried it under a thick bush, but in the darkness we left a trail in the grass that stood out like a sore thumb at first light, so when we came back next day the rebels had pinched it. It should have been mine, because it's prophesied, boy.'

Aquila, riding alongside him at a slow canter, adopted a non-committal look. Fulmina had believed in her Gods, yet they had led her a hard life and given her a painful death.

'Don't think I'm a fool,' Flaccus continued, sensing the doubt. 'Any number of fortune-tellers have seen it. The first time a soothsayer told me I'd be burdened with wealth, I laughed at him, but a second told me the same, and then a third. The last one was the most detailed and after what happened with Clodius I went back to see him.'

'What did he say?'

'The same thing.'

'And you believed him?' asked Aquila, incredulous.

The older man's eyes narrowed, because after losing his gold he had gone back to see that soothsayer with his sword in his hand. Losing his temper, he had used it. 'They were his dying words, which is a telling thing when he confirmed what he'd said before.' Flaccus's voice took on a priestly tone, as if to lend authority to the words. 'I see a golden aura. There are men around, numerous and cheering. You will be covered in gold.'

'That's a lot of gold,' said Aquila, who clearly didn't believe a word of it.

Flaccus shook his head and looked back towards the flat, well-cultivated landscape. 'Maybe he meant I'd make my fortune here. I thought we'd done it then, your Papa and I. My prophecy come true, but it was not to be.'

'What do you think happened to it?'

That made Flaccus angry; in his mind it was still rightfully his and if anyone had got in the way of him possessing the gold it was that buffoon Clodius, not something he could say to Aquila.

'That bastard Vegetius Flaminus probably

nabbed it, an' if he did, he wouldn't hand it in.'

They fell silent. Aquila guessed that greed had caused the problem and for the first time in an age, he thought of Clodius, feeling a tinge of sympathy for his fate. But his mind soon returned to Flaccus and what he said about Vegetius Flaminus, thinking it was a bit thick to accuse someone else of a crime you had fully intended to commit yourself. The road had been rising for some time and as it wound round the spur of a mountain, they came to the spot at which it started to drop, a vast cultivated plain and the long seashore clear in the morning sun.

'I shall go there one day,' the boy said finally.

'Go where?'

'Thralaxas. I'd like to see the spot where Clodius died.'

Flaccus just grunted and he spurred his horse to make it go faster down the hill. The spear that flashed past Aquila's eye, aimed at his leader, took his horse just behind the ex-centurion's leg. The animal reared up, throwing Flaccus onto its wounded haunch. Aquila shot forward, his head behind his horse's neck, as Flaccus fought to stay mounted. Looking back, he saw the arrows, which had been aimed at him, thud into the ground. It did not register consciously, but he had counted six of them; nor that he had added that to the spearman and tallied up that they faced at least seven armed assailants. The boy had his sword out and he hit the centurion's horse with the flat of the blade, a blow that made it fall forward onto all four legs, and as Aquila rode by he grabbed the reins and yanked the animal into lumbering motion. Flaccus regained his saddle and adopted the same pose as Aquila, his profile as low as possible. Both horses were screaming, though only one had the pain to justify it, as they shot down the slope, hooves flying on the scree. As soon as he had Flaccus's horse moving, Aquila reached behind his back for the spear, pulling it from the harness and pushing out in front like a lance. There would be more; it did not make sense to attack from the side and not to block their path.

'The rocks,' he yelled, even before the three men rose up to stop them. He went straight on, catching the first in the chest before his sword was up. The blow, into a heavy man running forward, nearly dislocated his shoulder but at least it arrested the forward movement of his horse. He pulled on the reins to make it rear, his grip on the spear so tight that it hurt. That extracted the weapon from the dying man, freeing it for subsequent use. He pulled even harder to hold the animal up in the air, the hooves keeping another assailant at bay. That gave him time, as the horse fell back onto the ground, to alter his grip and cast the spear.

It was a bad throw, made off balance, but it glanced along his quarry's thigh, which forced him onto one knee. Flaccus had gone for the third man with his sword and they were now engaged hand to hand, with sparks shooting from their blades, the sound echoing off the hillsides as the metal clashed. Flaccus parried the blows with just enough skill to get past his man because he was not trying to kill or wound him, he was trying to get clear. Both could hear the cries of their original attackers, now running down the track to join the fray.

'Ride boy!' Flaccus shouted, as he spun his horse so it was facing uphill. He made a sweep with his sword, enough to make his opponent leap backwards, before hauling the animal's head round to chase after Aquila. They put a lot of distance between themselves and their attackers before pulling up, with both them and their mounts breathing heavily. Aquila looked at the centurion and grinned.

'That was close,' he gasped.

'You weren't worried were you?' asked Flaccus, his chest heaving as he spoke. Aquila raised his eyebrows. 'They can't kill me yet, boy, I haven't got my gold.'

CHAPTER ELEVEN

Titus had been ordered back to Rome and he was unsure why. Perhaps his constant carping about the need to mount a proper campaign had bored his superiors; during his years in Spain he had acted as *Legatus* to more than one arriving general, so had attended many a conference to hear their aims and ideas. He half suspected, when he heard their instructions, that the Senate did not want an end to the war. It provided a method of rewarding, or enticing, the members. Nothing tickled their vanity like the prospect of a triumph and since they were not short of that vice, ambitious men queued up for the chance to gain one in the only province that remotely provided an opportunity. Lucius always had a hand in such appointments, something that flowed from, and helped secure, his majority. If his nominees did go off to war, he hedged them about with so many restrictions that their dreams of a ride in the triumphal chariot were doomed to remain unfulfilled.

Right now he had to converse over dinner with the two people in the world for whom the mention of anything to do with Spain, and especially Brennos, was taboo. Unaware of the whole story surrounding those events, he knew nevertheless that Cholon and Claudia avoided any reference to his father's campaign. Hardly surprising; his stepmother could not welcome any reminder of what must have been a painful captivity, while the Greek would bridle at anything that in any way threatened to diminish his late master. The subject of what he had been engaged in could not be avoided altogether, but it tended to centre on how his service might enhance his political prospects, with Claudia insisting his career so far had been a success.

'A moderate one perhaps. All appointments are in the personal gift of the commander and I have had longer employment than most, which I can only put down to luck.'

'Nonsense. It was deserved,' said Claudia.

'What I really need is a proper campaign, with the chance to really make my mark. Nothing I've achieved up till now qualifies me for office.'

Titus smiled, his modesty completely natural, and at that moment his stepmother felt a pang as she saw his father, to the life, before her. The Greek too saw the image and longed to be near Titus, the fact of his being unattainable only making the longing greater. His nightly tours of the streets of Rome occasionally produced sexual gratification, but he got nothing else from the men he slept with, except, because they tended towards the rougher sort, the odd bruise. Yet here, before him, was the very thing he sought on those excursions, the image of his late master.

'Nonsense,' he croaked, trying, and failing, to disguise the catch in his throat.

'It's all very well being a military *Legatus*, Cholon, but I'd need to be a quaestor at least, and a very successful one at that, to find the money I need for a real career in politics.'

'I'm sure you'll achieve what you need in time,' added Claudia.

Titus shook his head, but he did not continue. His stepmother knew as well as he that the two careers complemented each other; few men would vote to give high military command to someone who had never held any kind of Republican magistracy.

'I don't have the kind of money I need for an aedilship. The campaign would ruin me, let alone the games I'd have to provide. I rather think my dear brother is suffering from that right now. You must remember they're nothing like they were in father's day. Now, with wild beasts and gladiatorial death fights, they cost a fortune.'

'Then Quintus should help you,' said Claudia.

Titus smiled. 'I won't ask and he has yet to offer.'

Cholon cut in. 'Then he ignores his responsibilities, and, I may say, your father's wishes.'

Titus just shrugged; as head of the house, Quintus had inherited a great deal of money and a lot more in assets. Given time to repair the depredations caused by Aulus's bequests, he was again among the wealthiest men in the city. What Titus had been left, while ample to live on, was nowhere near enough to provide him with the means to embark on a public career. If he could not find an alternative source of income, the *cursus honorum* was barred to him. Intent upon his own progress, Quintus saw it as no part of his duties to use some of the huge estate to advance his younger brother's political career.

'I have the funds you need,' said Claudia.

'It's not just money,' Titus replied. 'Quintus has inherited all of father's clients as well. They are committed to him, to his bid for the office of praetor. Then there's his attendance on Lucius Falerius, who practically controls the house. Unless he requests their aid, on my behalf, no amount of money will secure me office. My only avenue would seem to be a resounding success in the field, and right now Rome has no enemy so threatening that we must fight them.'

A slave stood in the doorway, silently waiting for a break in the conversation. It was Cholon who noticed him and he indicated his presence to Titus, who beckoned him forward.

'A messenger at the gate, your honour, who begs to speak with you.'

'At this hour?' said Claudia.

'He is from the house of the most noble Lucius Falerius Nerva.'

Titus frowned. 'Is he indeed?'

'He did not say so, master, but I recognised him.'

Titus had no need of Claudia's permission, this being his house as much as hers, but he requested it nonetheless. 'May I fetch him in, Lady Claudia?'

'The messenger has asked to speak with you alone, master.'

'See him at the gate, Titus,' said Claudia. 'I have a morbid fear of anything Falerii entering the house.'

She meant it as a joke, but it was one of those sallies that contained a measure of uncomfortable truth. Titus stood up and donned his slippers, making his way out of the dining room, across the atrium, to the postern gate. The Falerii slave stood just inside the door, with two of Quintus's slaves keeping an eye on him.

'Please leave us alone,' said Titus, softly.

'A request from the most noble Lucius Falerius Nerva.' The messenger hesitated, to see what effect the name would have, plainly disappointed that it had none; the man before him did not even flicker one of those heavy, dark eyebrows.

'What is the request?' asked Titus evenly.

'He asks that you call upon him tonight.'

'I am occupied tonight, dining with my stepmother.'

The slave frowned. The idea that anyone could put dinner with their stepmother above a summons from the leading man in Rome was absurd. 'I am empowered to say, by my master, that the request is of an urgent nature.'

'It must be, but that doesn't alter anything.'

'My master also asked that I invoke the name of your father, the most noble Aulus Cornelius Macedonicus. It is in his memory that he asks you to call on him.' Titus fought back his anger and the temptation to throw this messenger into the street; no good would come of taking his ire out on the slave. Besides, he was intrigued; Lucius could hardly be unaware of Titus's feelings towards him. The slave continued, his voice somehow taking on the silky tones of his owner. 'My master feels that he has failed his old friend, something he would wish to remedy.'

'He'd be in for a long night, fellow,' snapped Titus.

'Can I carry back a positive reply, sir?'

The silence lasted for several seconds, before Titus nodded abruptly. The messenger turned and departed immediately, leaving him to shut the gate.

Lucius came out personally and led him into the study, begging him to sit before returning to his own chair behind the desk. They looked at each other without speaking for a few moments before his host opened the conversation.

'Something tells me, Titus Cornelius, that you do not hold me in very high regard.'

'If anyone is aware of the reasons for that, it would be you,' replied Titus without rancour. He had decided, on the way here, that nothing Lucius did would make him lose his temper.

'I will not seek to justify myself.'

'You cannot.'

The older man smiled coldly. 'You misunderstand. I mean that I don't see the need. I sleep easily at night.'

Again they sat in silence, each weighing up the words that had been uttered, until Titus spoke, betraying a hint of impatience. 'The hour is late, I have been forced to leave my stepmother in the middle of dinner. Pray be so good as to tell me why you asked me to call?'

'I am grateful, Titus. Not everyone would abandon their stepmother to attend on me.'

The sarcasm was too much and Titus snapped out his reply. 'I may well abandon you, to attend upon someone whom I do respect.'

The insult did not dent Lucius's self-assurance one bit, his voice remained even. 'I'm glad to see you're not made of stone.' He picked up a roll from the desk and opened it. 'You remind me of your father, Titus, and according to your various commanders, you are his equal as a soldier. They are full of praise for your military abilities.'

'Have you been spying on me?'

Lucius sat back, his face a picture of mock amazement. 'Spying? What an odd word to use. If I was going to spy, it would be on someone with the power to harm me. You don't come into that category.'

'Yet you seek information on me?'

'Your father and I were good friends. Once, when we were young, we swore an oath in blood, to remain true to each other. Is it not fitting, given that oath, that I should seek news of his son?'

'No!'

Lucius was still looking at the scroll. 'You're right, of course. I have far more important matters to attend to, the doings of obscure military legates, however brave, are of little consequence.' Titus stood up abruptly, but Lucius looked up at him, still smiling. 'Sit down, Titus. I am no more prepared to be insulted by your assumed probity than you are by my apparent duplicity. I called you here so that I can aid you. If you wish to leave, do so. If you want a political career to match your military one, sit down.'

Titus paused, then sat down.

'Do I detect interest?' said Lucius, eyebrows raised.

'Curiosity,' replied Titus. 'You have said I remind you of my father. If I do, then like him, I cannot be bought.'

Lucius sighed. 'We could sit here all night discussing the relative merits of political systems and the need for expediency, but I fear what fascinates me would doubtless bore you.'

'Please come to the point.'

'Very well. I think your brother is behaving badly. I think he has let you down, you and the memory of your father.' Titus fought to keep his face a mask; they had been discussing that very point when Lucius's messenger called. It was uncanny; it almost seemed like sorcery. 'Do you agree?'

'I make it a point never to discuss private family matters outside the home.'

'Then you're alone, it's common gossip in the market-place.' He held his hand up to stop Titus interrupting. 'Are you aware that I have put my support behind Quintus in his bid for the praetorship?'

Titus raised his heavy eyebrows. 'I know he's exceedingly confident.'

Lucius bowed his head to acknowledge the compliment. 'I also intend to aid him to the consulship and, if he wishes the office, in time, the censorship.'

'Why?'

'That is not something I'm prepared to discuss. Let us see it as falling into the same category as your family matters. But I will say this. Rome needs good soldiers as much as good magistrates. Nothing would be worse for our city than inexperienced men being given command of armies during a serious war.'

There was a terrible temptation to bring up the subject of Spain, and some of the fools who had been sent there, but Titus kept quiet. Lucius knew more about that than he did himself, even if the old stringbag never left Rome. Perhaps different enemies threatened the Republic.

It was difficult to keep a tremor of excitement out of his voice as he asked, 'You anticipate a serious war?'

'We have a great deal, we Romans, so others are bound to try and take it away. I'm assuming that you, like your brother, wish to mix a career in the army with one in politics. No doubt you too would like to be consul one day?'

'I doubt I have the ability,' said Titus.

'Your father said the same thing,' Lucius snapped, 'and it was just as foolish on his lips as it is on yours.'

It was time, Titus decided, to make the older man aware that he knew where this conversation was leading. 'Are you offering me your support?'

Lucius waited a moment before speaking, weighing up his words. 'You sound as if you're prepared to reject it.'

Titus sat forward, the black look on his face emphasising his words. 'I'm not prepared to do anything to get it, if that's what you mean!'

Lucius sat back, but the movement had nothing to do with Titus's aggressive statement.

'I shall request that I be allowed to speak, for a while, without interruption.' His guest nodded and assumed a more relaxed pose. 'I have two concerns. One is Rome, and the other is the Falerii name and reputation. There are occasions when the two can be at odds. I have always put the *imperium* of the Roman state first and for that reason I engaged the interest of your brother. I have made certain commitments to him and in return he has promised me that, should I be unable to do so, through death or age, he will carry on my work.'

'You don't trust him?'

'I ask you not to interrupt,' replied Lucius sharply. 'Your brother has the makings of a great public servant. I have no doubt at all, having spoken with him, that we are as one on the really important matters concerning the future direction of Rome, but his failure to advance you troubles me. It is wrong and he should be made aware of it.'

Titus interrupted again. 'Why?'

'There is no conflict. You deserve advancement. Rome needs magistrates like you. It can only be personal dislike, or envy, or some other such useless emotion, that prevents him from doing his duty as head of the family.'

'You could just tell him.'

Lucius's self-control slipped at that point. 'Fool!'

'Have a care, Lucius,' shouted Titus, coming halfway out of his seat.

The older man put up both his hands in an act of submission. 'You are right, I should not address you so, Titus, but you are too direct, again too like your father. What if I say these words to your brother, in private, and he tells me, with all due respect, to mind my own business?'

'You clearly have reasons for not doing so, but I cannot fathom them.'

'Nor shall I bother to explain, but I wish to tell your brother, in no uncertain terms, that he is wrong and in a way that makes use of the message. My son Marcellus dons his manly gown tomorrow. I formally request that you attend the ceremony.'

'And?'

'You will discover that tomorrow, if you choose to attend. All I ask is this: that in public, you treat me as a friend. I would also like you to be generous to Marcellus. I doubt it will be an onerous task. After all, my son quite admires you.'

'Your son barely knows me.'

Lucius picked up several scrolls. 'Not so. He has read these a dozen times. Why, he will probably bore you with details of your own heroic exploits.'

Coming of age, in a patrician family, was as much a public as a private ceremony. It was certainly enough to induce a high degree of nervousness in Marcellus. The slightest mishap that could be laid at his door would shame his father and all the Falerii ancestors. Lucius had drummed into Marcellus that nothing counted so much as the family genius, the blood-line and fame by which they achieved and maintained prominence, so he shivered slightly in the early morning light as, for the last time, he donned the smock of a boy, purple-bordered and short. Slaves placed garlands about his shoulders as the noise grew, this coming from the crowd gathered outside the house to witness the event. His father's friends and clients, each one greeted by the host, were arriving at the house, filling the atrium with the noise of their conversation, as they prepared for the procession to the temple.

Titus killed the conversation with his late entrance, for it was no secret that he held himself at a distance from this house and all it stood for. Lucius made his way across to the gate to greet him, taking him by the hand in a powerful grasp. Titus, not certain why, responded in kind and Lucius turned and looked at Quintus, who had been one of the first guests to arrive. His face was set like a mask, but he recovered quickly, moving over to the gate, to remove the burden of his brother from Lucius.

'Guard him well, Quintus,' said Lucius, in a voice just a shade too loud. 'Titus may well be our conscience.'

Quintus was angry but he dare not let it show; only the tightness of the lips indicated his mood. 'I confess I've shamefully neglected my brother, Lucius. Like you, I have too many responsibilities and he is somewhat tardy himself. He's been home for a week and we've yet to discuss his future.'

'A glittering one, I'm sure,' Lucius added smoothly. Another guest, a grey-haired senator, arrived, flustered at being late. Lucius detached himself and went to greet him, waving aside his protestations of regret.

'Was this your idea, brother, or did Lucius Falerius think it up?'

Titus looked at Quintus, assuming a puzzled expression. 'Whatever are you talking about?'

Lucius came to fetch his son personally, looking him up and down to ensure he was correctly attired. 'Time to go, Marcellus. Remember you are a Falerii.'

'Yes, father.'

'I have invited someone special, just for you.' Marcellus looked confused. 'You must promise not to bore Titus Cornelius by asking him too many questions after the ceremony.'

'Titus Cornelius, here?'

'It must be a fine thing to be a hero, even in the eyes of a silly child. Still, he's destined to be a great Roman general, so I suppose it's fitting.'

The procession made its way out into the street, Marcellus at the head. The crowd greeted him with a roar, as if their reward depended on it. They were not yet sated with these ceremonies, which would go on throughout the month of March. People in the market-place flocked to see, since the Romans dearly loved display. They made their way to the Capitol where, flawlessly, Marcellus sacrificed the bull, immediately donning his white manly gown. Back at the house the guests were invited to give their congratulations to the boy personally. Titus, when his turn came, was struck by the youngster's height and build, so different from that of his father. His black hair was lightly curled, contrasting sharply with his chalk white gown, the eyes were dark brown and steady, the smile warm and without guile. He was forced to wonder how such a slippery customer as Lucius, thin as a sapling, could have produced such a handsome, outgoing fellow.

The impression was strengthened when the boy collared him to ask about the wars in Spain. He had read the despatches avidly, as well as the private letters to his father from Titus's commanders, so he knew most of the details already, but he showed a lively interest and a keen intelligence. The name Brennos engaged him, and he asked avidly about Celtic warriors in general, and the hill-forts in particular, with many enquiries as to how they could be subdued. Titus answered evenly and honestly, enumerating the problems, though careful not to lay any blame for the lack of any real success at any one person's door.

Having asked more questions than were strictly polite, the boy suddenly halted, biting his lip as if gearing himself up for something. 'Titus Cornelius. I wish to ask you a favour.'

'Then do so. If it's in my power to grant it, I shall.'

'Three years from now, I will be of age to undertake my military service. Nothing would please me more than that I should do so under your command.'

Titus smiled. 'You might do better to attach yourself to someone who's going to be a successful general.'

'But you are destined to be just that,' said Marcellus, genuinely surprised.

'And pray, young man, how do you know that?'

Marcellus pulled himself up to his full height, which was still a head shorter than his hero. 'My father told me it would be so.'

It was the older man's turn to be surprised. 'When did he tell you this?'

'This morning, but I knew that it was true years ago.'

'Why?'

Titus was almost the last to leave and Lucius looked at him closely before answering. 'You do not feel that you deserve my good offices?'

'Only you would know that, Lucius Falerius, but you strike me as a man who never does anything without a purpose. Even the ceremony today was put to good use.'

'Can I plead sentiment?'

Lucius was playing with him, but Titus refused to be drawn into an angry response. 'Please don't mention childhood oaths.'

'Perhaps if you knew the circumstances that brought about that oath between your father and me, you'd be less of a cynic.'

Titus smiled, not sure why. 'There's a degree of effrontery in that, coming from you.' The older man bowed slightly to acknowledge the truth of his words, while the younger man dropped the smile. 'I have a worry, Lucius Falerius.'

'Which is?'

'You have done me a service today. You will want something in return. I worry that I will not perform it, either through a disinclination to do so or perhaps because I've no idea what is required of me.'

The old man put a thin hand on Titus's shoulder, adding an encouraging squeeze. 'I trust that you are your father's son. When the time comes, you will know precisely what to do.'

'No explanation now?'

Lucius shook his head. 'Never fear, Titus Cornelius. When you are called upon to respond, it will be a duty you are happy to perform. It won't feel like doing me a service at all.'

CHAPTER TWELVE

They were now riding along a good road, a proper, paved Roman affair, straight as an arrow. Mount Etna was well behind them, rumbling and smoking in the distance, yet they could not see much ahead, with most of the town of Messana blocked out; in the warm southerly wind, occasionally gusting to the east, it was easier to see the mainland across the narrow straits. Smoke rose, thick and black, with the orange strip of flame just visible at the base, sometimes blocking out the sun and rolling out slowly over the bright blue strip of sea. The entire coastline had been sown with wheat; now they were burning the stubble after the harvest and behind the raging fires the fields lay blackened and barren, as though some great plague had struck the land.

'Look at that boy,' said Flaccus, pointing eagerly through the smoke to the grain ships loading in the harbour at Messana. 'There's a fortune before your eyes and a good part of it belongs to our lord and master.' Aquila waited while another black cloud drifted out to sea, finally clearing enough to make the harbour visible. He could see the ships, their single square sails furled against the masts, with the long rows of ports for the oars. 'Those are our proprietor's own ships, too.'

Flaccus's eyes gleamed; they always did when he contemplated the prospect of wealth, his or someone else's. The horses shied away from the heat as they rode past yet another band of flame, slowly eating its way across the stalks. Once through that, they were in the clear with the town now visible. White-walled, the Greek city still looked like the fortress it had been before the Romans took over the island. Inside the battlements, low buildings alternated with the numerous temples, each red tiled roof a slightly different shade, and at diverse angles. Stark against the blue sky, the row of crucifixes by the roadside stood out clearly. Flaccus reined in his horse as they came abreast and looked up at the men roped to the wooden crosses, examining them to see if they were dead.

'Fresh today,' he remarked, without emotion.

'Who are they?' asked Aquila, his eyes still firmly fixed on the ground. He had not enjoyed the thought of crucifixions on the farms and he did not want to acknowledge them now.

'Runaways, most likely. They've had more trouble with slaves here than elsewhere on the island. Stands to reason, they can see what they're missing more easily in a town.' He pulled the horse's head round and made for the low gate in the town wall. Halfway between the crucifixes and the entrance a series of stakes had been driven into the ground, each one with a man lashed to it. 'There's tomorrow's batch, that is, if those already strung up are properly dead.'

'What do they do with them when they're dead?'

'Easy, boy.' Flaccus laughed, then coughed as a last puff of smoke filled his lungs. 'They just lay them in one of the fields they're going to burn.'

It was the laugh, followed by the cough, that made one of the trussed-up men lift his head. The hair was shorn, slave fashion, so that it formed only a grey stubble on the grime-streaked head and his gaunt face was a mass of bruising from the beatings he had already suffered, his smock torn open to reveal the bloody weals that were caused by repeated whipping. Aquila opened his mouth to say something, then shut it quickly, kicking his horse in such a way that it moved Flaccus on as well.

The single eye of Gadoric followed him, his parched lips open in surprise, the great scar across his face, a stark white against the burnt skin of the face. The boy's thoughts were in turmoil as they rode under the arch of the gate, the horse's hooves

echoing noisily in the confined space. He fought the
temptation to look back, though he could almost
feel that basilisk eye fixed on him, and his voice was
slightly unsteady as called to Flaccus.

'Those men at the stake will be crucified?'

The old centurion caught the tone, and as he
replied, his voice echoed off the buildings that lined
the narrow street. 'You're not squeamish, boy, are
you? Don't fret for a dead slave, lad. It makes the
others work harder.'

The town was busier than any place Aquila had
ever seen. As they approached the centre, an open
space dominated by a large wattle and daub temple,
the crowd increased so that forward movement
became a struggle and Flaccus, to little effect, lashed
out at those who blocked his path; they could not
move out of his way because of the overall crush.
Aquila could see the packed steps of the temple, full
of people trading. In one shaded corner a teacher
addressed a group of young men, his arms waving
as he declaimed; in another moneylenders
transacted their business, with a great deal of
shouting and slapping of foreheads. Stalls lined the
spaces between the tall columns, each with its own
yelling vendor. Exceedingly colourful, little of what
he saw really registered; he could not put aside the
look of hate that had filled that single eye, the look
of a man who feels betrayed.

Flaccus turned away from the temple and headed

down the incline towards the harbour, still struggling to make any headway. Once out of the square the crush eased, though it was still difficult for a mounted man to move with any speed until they emerged onto the wharves, full of carts laden with grain, each one with a trail of exhausted-looking men filling their baskets at the tail. Flaccus asked one of the sutlers for directions; the man took in the freshly tended gash on the horse's flank, before pointing to a large warehouse.

The front was clear of carts, the slaves, instead, trudging in and out of the open warehouse doors. Armed men lined their route, with the occasional crack of a bullwhip or a vine sapling striking on a bare back, accompanying the loud exhortations that they should move faster. Down by the edge of the wharf a group of carpenters were working with great lengths of timber, which they had erected to form a triangle, now being threaded with ropes. Both dismounted and hitched their animals to the rail, and Flaccus stood for a moment watching the steady procession of labour: all men, all dull-eyed and every one looking undernourished. He nodded slowly, as if in approval, before walking into the shaded interior of the warehouse.

One rotund fellow, with a leather apron over his white smock, and a wax tablet in his hand, stood by a large set of scales. As each basket was filled from the grain store it was put on the scales. He then noted its weight before indicating that it should be removed. Nodding to Flaccus, and without interrupting his work, he pointed to the rear of the building with his wooden stylus. The air was full of fine golden dust, which covered everyone and everything, giving the slaves, with their bare ribcages sticking out, the appearance of skeletons rather than human beings.

Aquila followed Flaccus up a narrow staircase, through dampened screens, carefully placed to contain the dust. The top floor of the warehouse held the cargo that the ships had fetched in from Ostia: bales of cloth, large ampoules of wine, weapons and a whole stack of hardwood tree trunks, grown specially so that one branch at each end formed the point of a plough. At the front, overlooking the wharf, a table had been set up, laden with food and wine, with bales arranged to provide seating, so that the overseers of the various properties could take their ease and feed themselves, all the while able to watch the fruits of their farms being loaded onto the ships. One of them, a fat fellow with a bald white head, was talking loudly and Aquila had a vague feeling of recognition, without being able to place why. Better dressed than his companions, he had the proprietary bearing of a man who owned the place and he was busy explaining to the others his plans for the future.

'Every time you shift grain you lose a bit. Some ends up on the ground when you're loading your carts, more when they're bucketing along some of the interior roads. Now, that's our money dribbling out. Remember we get paid on the weight that arrives in Ostia, not the weight of what we grow.'

He turned to greet Flaccus and the boy could see that for all his well-fed, carefully barbered look, the round face was hard, the eyes calculating rather than friendly. He greeted them effusively, ran his eyes up and down Aquila, before he bade Flaccus to eat and take his ease. The ex-centurion returned the greeting, acknowledged the others present, then filled a platter for the boy, gave him a cup full of wine and sent him to sit on a bale well away from the table, before looking to his own needs. Aquila accepted with glum ill-grace, his mind still on the sight outside the gates, which earned him an enquiring stare from Flaccus. The look the large fat fellow gave him was different; more to do with his lithe young body than his mood. Aquila ignored him and he turned back to the table, eager to expound his theories. Flaccus, caught between two thoughts, had no time to enquire of the boy what was amiss.

'And every one of you complains to me about the weight I record, since it never tallies with your own.' Heads nodded at that, and despite the

friendly tone of the meeting, many a black look was
aimed in his direction. 'I lose too, friends. Just cast
your eyes over that trail of grain between the
warehouse door and the ship. That's mine, every bit
of it. There's a trail just like it at the unloading, with
half the folk of Ostia fetching their chickens down
to the wharves to feed for free, and it all adds up to
a pretty denarius at the end of the day.'

He stopped to top up the goblets of those nearest
him, turning as he did so to look at Aquila again.
The boy, slouched across a bale, did not notice; he
was looking at the sun, coming in through the open
doors, turning the stream of poured wine bright
red, which made him think of Clodius. He had seen
that very effect as his adopted father had held the
wine gourd above his head on a hot day, expertly
aiming the contents into his open throat, and the
sight further served to take him back to a world he
thought lost forever.

'You have something in mind to solve this,
Cassius Barbinus?'

That wiped any thoughts of Clodius and his past
from his mind as a flash of hate coursed through his
body, because suddenly he knew where he had seen
the fat man before. It had been the day the
supposedly tame leopards had attacked Gadoric's
sheep. The animals had been intended as a gift for
some important visitor, one of them, a scented prick
of a boy his own age, who had been just as

responsible as Cassius Barbinus for the fact that the leopards had been let loose within sniffing distance of the set of prey animals he was shepherding. The results were all too predictable, though Gadoric had pointed out, when Aquila told him of what had happened, the sheep belonged to Barbinus. If he wanted to feed them to a pair of big cats that was his right.

The man who had trained those leopards from cubs was furious; so was Aquila and there were many reasons why. He sat bolt upright and looked hard at Barbinus, but the object of his attention had turned to face his questioner. Was this really the rich senator whose woods he had raided for game, the man who owned the farm where he had last seen Gadoric, before encountering him tied to the stake today? He had, according to his overseer, Nicos, brutally raped the slave girl, Sosia, forcing from her throat a scream so plaintive that Aquila had mistaken it for the cry of a distressed fox, then sent her away, adding to the woes of that unforgettable day. The thought that anything he might have done these last months could have profited Cassius Barbinus nearly made him throw the platter in his hand at the man's head. Barbinus, unaware of the effect his name was having on the boy, looked around his assembled bailiffs and provided his answer. 'Indeed I do have a solution, my friends. If you look outside you will see I'm building a hoist.

Once it's complete, each one of you will be given a plan to make one of your own.'

'Using what?' asked Flaccus; as the newest member of this select group he was the most concerned about cost.

Barbinus smiled. 'Don't worry, Flaccus, I'll provide the timber. I will also provide sailcloth, specially cut, with eyeholes all round so that they can be lashed at the neck.'

He looked around to see if any of them had made the connection, only to be greeted by blank stares. Finally his gaze fell on Aquila, the senator mistaking the glare in the boy's eye for interest. Barbinus walked over, the wine flagon still in his hand, as Aquila dropped his eyes to the floor, in a stew of still-troubled thoughts and uncertainty. The youngster was dirty from his riding, but his tall frame, tanned skin and that red-gold hair were enough to attract a man like Barbinus. Then the senator's eye caught the golden eagle at his neck, which made his eyebrows arch in surprise.

Cassius Barbinus considered himself a connoisseur of Greek and Celtic art. What was a boy like this doing, wearing such a valuable object? Aquila, unaware of the interest, took the charm in his hand, then lifted his head, his eyes like two sapphires, boring into Barbinus. The senator did not know that the boy wanted to kill him but he did notice that Aquila was not cowed by his status, a fact which only served to increase his attraction. He poured some wine into Aquila's cup, his eyes never straying from the boy's face.

'Can you guess, boy?'

The answer seemed so obvious that Aquila obliged immediately, but his voice had a distant quality, as though he was talking to himself. 'You load the grain into the bales and the bales onto the carts. Then the bales are loaded straight onto, and off, the ships.'

Barbinus turned and beamed at the others, waving an expansive arm. 'Without spilling a drop. No more waste, and more important, no more arguments about being cheated.' A general murmur of agreement followed this, with much nodding of heads. Barbinus turned back, giving Aquila another head-to-toe look. Used to people wilting before his gaze, the stillness clearly disconcerted him. 'Who is this boy, Flaccus?'

The centurion, who knew Barbinus of old, was frowning. The man was a satyr, not to be trusted with two pieces of warm liver, let alone a girl or a young boy. 'Aquila Terentius. He's from a colony near Aprilium. His father was one of my men killed at Thralaxas. I picked him up on the way south. Sort of adopted him, you might say. Like a son to me now!'

'He's a bright lad.' Barbinus had not mistaken Flaccus's tone or the strength of the last statement;

the old centurion was telling him to keep his hands to himself. 'I have some land around Aprilium.'

The senator's eye dropped again and lingered for a moment on the charm round Aquila's neck as if he was about to ask its significance, but he stopped himself and looked up again. 'You stick with Flaccus, boy, he won't want to be here in Sicily all his life. Someone young and ambitious, who knows the farms, would be an advantage.' He did not turn round as he addressed Flaccus, but kept his eyes firmly locked to those of Aquila. 'Have you educated him?'

There was a distinct note of anger in Flaccus's reply; the way Barbinus asked the question sounded like a rebuke. 'Didn't see the need.'

'I would advise you to be less short-sighted. If this boy has a brain, take advantage of it. Teach him his numbers and if he can write, Greek as well as Latin, then he could have a future.'

'Right now he's learning to fight,' snapped Flaccus.

Barbinus still had not turned round. 'Admirable, but limited. Our world is full of those who can fight. Not many of them can think, as well.'

'Maybe you're right.'

Barbinus was now looking at Aquila's mail shirt and at the sword worn loose by his side. 'Do it, Flaccus!' He spun round on his heel to face the now blushing bailiff and Aquila was subjected to an angry look from Flaccus, as though what had happened was his fault. Barbinus went back to the head of the table, patted his newest overseer on the shoulder, and changed the subject. 'But, old friend, we have more important things to discuss.'

He looked at them all in turn, lounging about the place, forcing them to sit up and pay attention; for all his jovial manner Barbinus demanded respect. 'I've had a meeting with the other owners and they've agreed we must coordinate action against the growing threat of banditry.'

'We were attacked on the way here,' said Flaccus.

'Where?'

Flaccus explained what had happened like the soldier he was, making no attempt to sound heroic, concluding with the opinion that whoever had sought to ambush them did not appear to be either capable, or numerous.

'Not numerous now, Flaccus, but they could be if enough slaves escaped to join them.'

'None of mine will escape,' Flaccus replied, with a sneer. 'They don't have the energy.'

Polite coughing greeted what sounded like a bit of boasting, especially in the company of men who knew their trade better than he, men whose help he had sought on first arriving in Sicily. Flaccus realised what he had done and mumbled words to the effect that he still had a lot to learn and would be happy to take advice, but Barbinus cut right across him, producing another angry glare.

'That's what's caused the trouble we have now. People being complacent, thinking that it'll always be someone else's slaves that will cause trouble. Well it isn't, and if you doubt me just go out of the southern gate and you'll see.'

'Are those men yours?' asked Flaccus. He made a sudden, dismissive gesture with his head to Aquila, who had begun to edge closer.

Barbinus frowned. 'Sad to say, they are, and they weren't just trying to escape either, they were much more ambitious. Wanted to rise up and take the town, which is just as well for us, since the plans frightened enough of the other slaves into betraying them. Those bandits in the hills might not amount to much but they act as a beacon for all the other malcontents. That's why we have to root them out. Slaves are less likely to run if they've got nowhere to go.'

'Do we have a plan of action?' asked one of the others.

Barbinus nodded. 'We do. I've already persuaded the governor to call his auxiliaries out. The main base of these villains, at least the ones that worry us, seems to be here in the north. They don't go south of Etna much, so we'll use that as a pivot to work on. They have women and children with them, so they can't move fast. Most of our forces will gather to the west, sweep down through the mountains, skirting the volcano. The rest will form a barrier between Etna and the route south along the coast. If we can drive them out onto the plain we can deal with them easily.'

Barbinus laid both his palms on the table and leant forward to emphasise his point. 'I want to see every one of them either dead, or stretched out on a crucifix by the side of the road.'

'When?' asked Flaccus.

'It has to be soon. We've got cooler weather coming and the slaves have less to do so they don't need as much supervision.'

'That might be true for some,' Flaccus responded. 'I'm still working on the irrigation ditches.'

Barbinus fixed him with a look. 'One of the things these bandits are very good at is smashing up irrigation schemes. Seems a good idea to put a stop to that, and I haven't forgotten that you were very recently a soldier, Flaccus. Since the governor can't field the troops necessary to mount a proper campaign, then we must assist him.'

Aquila had withdrawn into the shadows, only half listening to Barbinus. In his mind he could easily imagine Gadoric, trying to persuade others that revolt was worthwhile and being betrayed for his pains. He thought about the men he shared a hut with; they would be involved in this and revel at the prospect. Given a clear command to kill they would do so with pleasure, not bothering much if those they murdered were guilty men or innocent women and children. It worried him that, having achieved manhood and a fair degree of martial prowess, he would have to go along, required to participate, indeed expected to enjoy the rape and murder that would be inevitable, all on behalf of a man called Barbinus.

'Could we not request troops from Rome?'

Barbinus threw his head back and laughed. 'What? To put down slaves? I think you've had too much sun, Didius Flaccus. When did Rome ever need soldiers to subdue slaves?' He patted the top of his head, stark white in contrast to his olive-skinned face. 'Do as I do, friend. Always wear a hat, especially in Sicily.'

He had said the same thing to Silvanus, the governor, at the meeting that morning, unaware that he, a more astute politician than Barbinus, had already sent off a despatch to Rome. Not that he disagreed with the landowner about the requirement for troops to put down a few slaves, but the governor knew that in the febrile world of Republican politics it was a good idea to cover all eventualities. Sicily was an exceedingly lucrative office, one of the best in the Senate's gift. It was therefore axiomatic that others, even those he could call friends, continually sought to have him replaced.

CHAPTER THIRTEEN

———◆———

Quintus Cornelius tried hard to concentrate on the reports that Lucius had asked him to read, but his mind kept returning to the games that it was his task to organise. They were going to be expensive, more than in a normal year, since it was necessary to head off the rising discontent of the poorer sections within the city. People continued to pour in from the countryside, quite a number being ex-soldiers, either citizens of Rome or former auxiliaries. Already volatile, their previous skill at the profession of arms made them dangerous. The corn dole had become an ever-increasing burden on the state and that, at least, meant that the reports from Sicily had his undivided attention.

One bad harvest in that island and the effect in Rome could be incalculable. Lucius Falerius, with Quintus as his willing helper, now controlled the Senate in a way that no faction had achieved for a hundred years but that had a negative side. Some of those who opposed them, aware that any attempt to change matters in the legislature was doomed, tended to seek exterior means of advancing their cause and what better method to choose than allying themselves with the bare-arsed mob whose slum dwellings disfigured the outskirts of Rome? Denied bread, that lot could well burn the city.

Chariot races were a useful way of allowing the populace to let off steam, but nothing worked as well as a proper set of well-organised games. As one of the urban aediles it was not something he could avoid, since it fell within his responsibilities as a city magistrate and he was cursed by the behaviour of some of his more profligate predecessors, who had sought to bribe those who voted in the Comitia by pandering to their whims. Gone were the days when a few wild boar, bear baiting by dogs and the odd raging bull trying to gore a criminal, satisfied the Roman multitude. Now it was wild beasts from Africa and Asia; elephants versus lions or tigers and mass gladiator contests that had to be fought to the death, something that increased the price ten-fold. How was it that a ceremony, once a graveside contest between specially chosen warriors to honour a dead chieftain, had grown so that it now dominated the way of entertaining the masses?

He shook his head, partly in disgust, but more to aid his concentration. Spain, Illyricum, Numidia,

Macedonia: all required his attention. He had never dreamt that there would be so much work involved in trying to maintain political superiority. His mentor passed over as much work as he could, claiming as he did so that Quintus could not advance in stature and maintain his position in the future unless he understood all the ramifications, the levers that constituted their means of holding power. Lucius Falerius stood in the background, ready to intervene when matters reached an impasse, leaving the younger man staggered by the apparent simplicity with which he solved thorny problems. Often he could bring a recalcitrant senator to heel with a few whispered words, and this after weeks during which Quintus had tried all manner of cajolery and persuasion. Really, all the difficulties stemmed from supporters; their enemies they could ignore but those who purported to share their views were a source of constant irritation. Fellow senators, supposedly august and dignified individuals, were really like a set of squabbling children, intent on endlessly pressing petty complaints.

One would have a grudge about the distribution of public land, to satisfy which required some form of compensation. Another would complain that the proper order of precedence had been ignored in some insignificant debate, this an affront to his dignity. Mollifying them could only be achieved if both the reigning consuls, and all their living predecessors, could be persuaded to yield the right to take the floor first. Quintus knew that money, in the shape of monopolies, land grants and dispensations, oiled the process more than political principle. A realist, he was not shocked by this, but it did add to his own woes.

Personally, he had to be seen as above any suspicion of corruption; the slightest hint that he was feathering his own nest by giving himself concessions that others would claim as their due could cause a haemorrhage in their ranks. So Quintus Cornelius was forced to endure endless toil, spend money to please the mob, while denying himself income to appease his peers. He complained about it loudly, though never once to the point where he even hinted at a willingness to lay down the burden.

A slave entered to remind him of the hour; he was due at the Forum to partake in a civic welcome to be extended to an embassy from Parthia, so Quintus threw aside the despatch from Silvanus, the governor of Sicily, warning of an increase in the problems caused by runaway slaves. His request for regular troops to help weed them out was absurd and surely the consuls would share his view; let the planters, who made the profits, pay to keep the peace. As he dressed, taking great care with his toga, his mind wandered from one problem besetting the Republic to the next. The frontiers were bad enough, but here in the city he had to decide what advice to offer regarding the activities of certain knights. Wealthy enough to advance to the Senate, they were being denied admittance on the flimsiest of excuses, mostly concerned with their personal morality. Would they, once elevated, behave as they should and drop any demands for reform of the courts? Or would they come to the chamber and try to tip the balance towards the class they had just left?

Could he do something to stop the other Italian states from bribing senators to advance the idea of universal citizenship, or find a means to shift some of the slum dwellers, non-Romans, back to their own lands? Each fold in the heavy white garment seemed to represent a different conundrum, which would require as much care in the tackling as the fuss he was making about his appearance. Quintus was not yet bored by such ceremony, still excited to be required to represent his city when external potentates sought either alliance or peaceful coexistence. He desired to be elegant without being overt. Against the gorgeously clad ambassadors from the east he wished to stress that Rome was controlled by men who required no glitter to enhance their *dignitas*. Today there would be, at the request of Lucius Falerius, no gold rings in the Senate. Plain iron, as of old, was sufficient for him, therefore it was enough for all. Finally satisfied, Quintus left his private rooms and made for the gate. He was halfway across the atrium when the door was opened to admit Cholon and the senator fixed the Greek with a jaundiced look.

'I don't know why you don't move in here.'

'I value my freedom, Quintus.'

Cholon took great pleasure from the way the double meaning of that upset the owner of the house and he was rewarded with a scowl. 'The number of times you dine with my stepmother! If it was anyone else I'd be worried, but then I don't suppose her virtue is in any danger from you.'

Cholon could not care less what most people said of him and that particularly applied to his sexual inclinations, but this man annoyed him enough to elicit a sarcastic response, no matter what he said. 'I do so agree, Quintus. She is in much greater danger when I'm not around. How gratifying it is that you take the precaution of observing her every move.'

The look of confusion on Quintus's face was genuine. 'I don't know what you mean.'

'Of course you don't. It's mere coincidence that Thoas always has his ear to her door.'

'Thoas. The Numidian?'

'Who else?' replied Cholon, pursing his lips at what he considered blatant obfuscation.

'You're imagining things, Cholon. My stepmother bought him and his wife off me on the very day the will was read. He's her slave now, not mine.'

That threw the Greek, who stood aside to let Quintus pass. He made his way to Claudia's suite of rooms in curious mode. There was no doubt that the Numidian listened at doors and Quintus did not actually have to own him to get information. He could be paying the man for it. His opinion of the head of the Cornelii household was so low he never even stopped to consider any other possibility.

'Why do I feel that you are always on the verge of asking me something?' Claudia smiled at him, giving a good impression of curiosity, but she was obviously flustered. 'May I speak plainly?'

'I was never aware that you did anything else,' she replied.

'I get the impression that often, when we talk, you have a question on your lips. When you speak, your expression does not always match the words you use.'

'Perhaps I have a singular expression.'

'Or an awkward question, Lady!' He had spoken more sharply than intended and the look of alarm on her face proved it. 'Please, forgive me. I did not intend to distress you.'

'Do you like me, Cholon?' she asked.

'I never dine regularly with people I hate,' he replied, flippantly.

But Claudia was serious, her handsome brow knitted with the lines of worry. 'That's not what I asked.'

'Yes, I do.'

'If I were to ask you for the one secret which you have, and I crave, would you tell me?' He shook his head, but that was because of doubt, not a refusal. Her voice was under very tight control, which gave it a hard quality, when she was really striving for a supplicant one. 'You must be able to guess what that is, Cholon. I want to know where Aulus exposed my son.'

He sat still for some time, his head shaking very slowly from side to side. 'I am given to wondering, having at last been asked, if that is the only reason I'm invited to dine so often.'

The voice broke and she was on the verge of tears. 'I'm so desperate for an answer, Cholon, that I would not be able to tell you if that is right or wrong.'

Cholon stood up suddenly. 'I must go.'

Her hand was out in panic. 'No. Stay!'

'I cannot. You asked me if I liked you. Would it serve as an answer to say that if I stayed here I would be tempted to betray a sacred trust?'

'Please?'

The tears came and he could not help crying too. 'The boy is dead, Lady Claudia. I betray no secret when I say that your husband made sure of that.'

'He wouldn't kill him. He couldn't!'

'Not by his own hand, but he was so far from a place where he might be found that he could not have survived.'

'Then it would do no harm to tell me where it is.'

Thoas, on the other side of the door, was willing Cholon to speak as much as Claudia. When the door flew open he was caught half-crouched and the tearful Greek, leaving in haste, nearly knocked him over.

Marcellus was privileged to be allowed to observe the unfolding scene from a good vantage point. Careful to remain hidden behind the pillar, he watched as the file of senators, each in a white toga bordered with a thick purple stripe, made their way out onto the steps overlooking the open space of the Forum Boracum. The ambassadors from Parthia, who had been accommodated outside the city for a week, made their entrance through the city gates a spectacle to remember. Ahead of them sweepers, with constant prayers to the Goddess *Deverra*, cleared the Sacred Way, while a line of slaves bearing water pots spread their load to kill the clouds of dust, the sunlight playing on the gold threads that spun through every garment. The Roman crowd did not roar, as they would for a conquering hero coming to the heart of Rome garlanded by success in war, but they did gasp at the sheer quantity of precious jewellery that adorned these gorgeous, dark-skinned creatures.

Every hat, each neck and all their fingers bore some evidence of the wealth of the Parthian Empire. Behind the ambassadors, their escort carried with them gifts for the people, each valuable object borne on a velvet cushion, these greeted with applause by a population who knew they would never see them again. Then came the animals, caught from the hinterlands of the east, from lands that even Alexander had failed to subdue. Tigers from across the Indus, lions from Arabia Felix, huge brown bears from the endless northern forests. The novelty was one black and white bear, in a cage of its own, contentedly sucking on some kind of shoot. Some reacted to it like they would to a pet, others wondered how such a creature would fare in the arena.

The horns blew as the party left the Via Sacra, crossing the open space until they stood finally at the steps leading up to the Forum. Marcellus knew that the esteem in which these ambassadors were held would be demonstrated by one fact: how many steps the august senators would descend to receive them. Conquered nations did not even warrant a move from the interior, while client states were graded by their importance to Rome, either by the tribute they paid or the troops they furnished. Few nations could bring the senators down to their level, an acknowledgement of equality, but the Parthians did.

Numerous inheritors of the lands of Darius, they could, if they wished, cause endless trouble in Rome's eastern dependencies. Thus, at a signal from the reigning consuls, the entire line of senators, to the accompaniment of trumpets, slowly descended to the bottom of the steps, timing their arrival by the rostrum to coincide with that of their visitors. The noise of the crowd, cheering mightily now, meant that the words they exchanged remained unheard. These, Marcellus knew, would be mere pleasantries. The hard bargaining, covering the renewal of a treaty, compensation for border incidents and the level of punishments to be meted out to those who had fractured the peace, would take place elsewhere and in private. This was the public spectacle of diplomacy: smiles, bows and the acceptance of the visitor's gifts. Lucius was well to the fore now, having stood back to allow the consuls to welcome the embassy. Here, in this setting, he had a rare opportunity to represent his status to the people.

Marcellus felt his lungs fill, just one manifestation of his pride, as his father accepted a jewel-encrusted diadem. Lucius beckoned to one of the twelve attendant priests to come forward, members of the College of Pontiffs charged with the duty to oversee the religious needs of the Republic.

He then made a great show of passing the gift over to them, a clear indication that in accepting such a valuable offering, he was merely doing so on behalf of the people of Rome. After such an example, no one could do otherwise. The cheering of the crowd became regular, as both consuls and each honoured senator passed his gift to the priests. They, in turn, would dedicate them to the temple of *Jovus Optimus Maximus*, which stood above them on Capitoline Hill.

Everyone from poorest peasant to richest citizen was thus included in the ceremony, made to feel that they, and their city-state, were but one hydra-headed entity, of which these white-robed men were mere representatives. Lucius called Quintus forward and he then engaged in a deep conversation with the leading Parthian emissary. Marcellus was given cause to wonder at what passed between them, since Quintus broke off at the end with his face wreathed in smiles, following that with a warm handshake bestowed on Lucius Falerius. But that thought faded as the consul took station with the Parthian leader, and led him up the steps towards the temple.

Later that day Marcellus was summoned by Lucius to talk over what had taken place during the more private meeting. His father was tired, his thin face lined with weariness, highlighted in the shadows cast by the flickering candles, but the voice was strong, if a little hoarse, and his conclusions as trenchant as ever.

'All that smiling and bowing was nonsense. They were so bellicose in private that I was given to regret advising the Senate that we should greet them at the rostrum. We should have made them climb the steps to meet us.'

'Does it mean trouble?' asked Marcellus.

'Not immediately, but it's only a matter of time before some incident on the border sparks a full scale war.' Lucius tapped both his hands on his desk in a gesture of frustration. 'It's not the Roman dependencies that cause the friction, those we can control, but we can never agree about client kings or rulers where we have mutual interests. They, quite naturally, favour candidates that incline towards Parthia.'

'While we have our own nominees.'

'Exactly!' Marcellus listened as his father ranged over the whole eastern frontier, naming each king and state that stood between Parthia and Rome: Commegne, Birythnia, Pontus, Cappadocia. Each was fragile, with no ruler able to guarantee that the succession would remain within their own family, and if it could they tended to play off their heirs against each other to secure their own well-being. Hardly surprising that the two great powers took an interest, even less surprising that they failed to agree a mutually satisfactory solution.

Lucius rubbed his eyes. 'It will come one day, Marcellus. The same conditions apply to Parthia as Carthage. We cannot live in peace and harmony, forever, with a state that threatens us or seeks to equal us in power. One must perish, the other prosper. When that day comes, I hope the Senate has the good sense to ensure that we're not occupied elsewhere.'

Marcellus stood up at the first hint that his father was about to do likewise. Once on his feet, Lucius passed his son a tightly bound scroll. 'Time for sleep I think. You will attend upon me in the morning, but before you do, examine the contents of the scroll. It lists all the complaints with which we were bombarded today. I want you to look at them, and have ready some solutions to the problems they present.'

Marcellus suppressed the inward groan. 'Thank you, father.'

As they left the study, Marcellus remembered Quintus, and his face wreathed with smiles. 'Why was he so pleased with himself?'

'You know he's responsible for the games to be held a week hence?' Marcellus nodded. 'Well, I asked the Parthians if, as a gift to the people of Rome, they would pay for them.'

'And they agreed?'

'More than that, my son. They offered their escorts as a gift as well, to fight any gladiators, or even soldiers, that we care to put against them. Quintus has every right to be pleased. He's going to have a really fine set of games, please the mob and enhance his prestige, and they're not going to cost him a penny.'

'I hope he thanked *you*,' said Marcellus, with a slightly sour note.

CHAPTER FOURTEEN

———•———

Aquila, picking up his weapons, slipped out unnoticed, leaving Flaccus, Barbinus and the other overseers engaged in a tedious discussion about crop yields and the rising price of slaves. The horses had been taken to a nearby stable and checking on them was his first priority. Both were feeding happily, each tail flicking the flies off the face of the other. Flaccus's mount, with the spear gash, seemed unaffected by the wound, which the ostler had re-dressed, covering it in an evil smelling compound. He placed his weapons alongside those belonging to Flaccus, which had been laid in the corner of the stall.

'When will you be wanting them?' asked the ostler, nodding towards the mounts.

'Who knows,' replied Aquila truthfully. 'Perhaps today, perhaps tomorrow.'

'Well, you can come when you like. Cassius

Barbinus owns the stable, so there won't be anything to pay.'

Outside, the men were still shuffling across the quayside, loading the ships with grain, and Aquila watched them while he tried to bring some order to his thoughts. Unaccustomed to choices, he was unsure which course to adopt; all the events in his life had been as a result of other people's actions, now he was on his own, with a muddy set of alternatives. His fingers sought the charm as an aid to thought, and he seemed to draw strength from that; at least it seemed to clarify his options. He pushed gently through the line of slaves, then turned off the quay, making his way back towards the concourse before the Temple of *Pallas Athene*. It was crowded still and much harder going on foot than it had been mounted on a horse, all elbows and cursing to maintain any forward motion. Finally he managed to push his way through the crush and reach the stone steps, worn away by the feet of countless worshippers.

The colonnaded portico was full of tradesmen selling all manner of produce, few, if any, having much to do with the cult of *Pallas Athene*. Luckily, he had some money, given to him by Flaccus, and this allowed him to buy things, which in turn permitted him to ask questions. General enquiries told him that the city gates would be closed at night, not against any real threat but through long habit. The crucifixion of slaves aroused little interest, the locals being much more taken with bloodier forms of retribution.

'Can't abide crucifixions,' said the squint-eyed man selling fresh figs. 'By they time they get them upright, they're half gone, especially when they've had a good beating beforehand.' He looked at Aquila closely with his good eye; the other was aimed in the general direction of Italy, only a few leagues distant across the straits. 'Then what happens?'

The boy sucked on the fig and shook his head.

'Nothing, that's what. Now I say they should be nailed on, not roped, with a chance for a citizen of the town to do the hammering. And they should be fresh, well fed and cared for before the event.' He winked at the mainland. 'Then they'd really feel it when we break their legs, eh?'

There was much more in that vein, a general discussion of the relative merits of stoning, public beheadings, breaking on the wheel and ripping apart with horses. Further questions revealed that Gadoric and the other men tied to the stakes would be left outside the gates, under guard. 'Not that they'll be goin' anywhere, lad. If the guards have a mind to sleep, they'll probably break their legs tonight. Makes no odds to a dyin' man and few are likely to be on hand tomorrow to complain about the difference.'

Aquila sat on the steps at one corner, listening to the pedagogue lecturing his pupils. The little Greek he had learnt from Phoebe was inadequate for a full understanding of what was being imparted, but he picked up the names of Hector and Patrocles, so he knew the man was talking about the siege of Troy, using gestures, as well as speech, to tell his class tales of heroes and their deeds of valour. Suddenly Aquila was back in the shepherd's hut, Minca at his feet, hearing Gadoric's long sagas of the men from the north, and the feeling he had had then came flooding back. The shepherd had always maintained that the Celtic way was superior to that of Rome, with everything in the Latin world put down in writing. Aquila, for the first time, wondered if Gadoric was right or wrong and it mattered, since it had a bearing on what he would do next. Barbinus's words he recalled too, given what he had said to Flaccus was tantamount to an order: he had the chance of an education, the opportunity to learn to write, a valuable asset in the world in which he lived. Barbinus had hinted at a comfortable future, overseers being well rewarded.

The alternative was stark: to put it all behind him, heading off for an unknown fate and quite possibly a painful death. The two did not compare, yet the memory of Gadoric, almost like a father to him, and the time he spent with him, haunted Aquila. He thought back to the raft of advice he had had from the shepherd, hoping to find in the man's wisdom and knowledge the words that would release him from this dilemma. Gadoric, if he had the chance, would tell him to stick with Flaccus and Barbinus; no one in their right mind would seek to help a half-dead prisoner to escape, regardless of how much he loved him. The boy looked up at the blazing sun, beginning to set in the hard blue sky. For all his speculation, he knew the decision had already been made, had been as he had watched that line of slaves and held his personal eagle talisman in his hand. There was really no choice. Aquila got to his feet abruptly and made for the stall of the man selling local wine, buying a complete rush-covered ampoule.

They were the dregs! Scruffy, lazy and foul-mouthed. Aquila remembered the day that Clodius left home to join his legion, with the metal and leather of his uniform polished and gleaming, his spear and shield slung in regulation fashion on his back. A proper soldier! It was a travesty to apply the name to these two layabouts. They were not Romans, of course, but locals; mercenaries, hired by the governor of the province. Aquila smiled and poured more wine into their wooden gourds, keeping them brim full.

'It's no fun for us, mark it,' said the taller of the two, flicking his thumb towards the three men tied to the stakes. 'That is, once they're outdoors.'

'No, lad, we get our laughs indoors,' said the other one, small, fat and just as untidy, giving a wheezing laugh. 'They start off with their heads high, spitting in our eyes, but we soon see to that. They'd lick our arse for a kindly look when we're finished.'

Aquila glanced towards the men slumped forward on the stakes. Even in the twilight he could still see the evidence, on their heads and shoulders, where they had been savagely beaten. The three men on the crucifixes were motionless, the last spasmodic jerk from the one in the middle had happened an hour ago. If they were not actually dead, they were so close it made little difference.

'The fig seller favoured stoning,' said Aquila. 'Said that was a real joy, second only to a beheading.'

The tall guard leant forward, his bony, unshaven face pained and his eyes full of hurt and doubt. 'Not for the likes of us, we have to just stand and watch and when they do a beheading, we're not the ones who get to wield the axe.'

'Who'd be a soldier?' said the other, holding out his empty gourd.

Gadoric had only raised his head once since Aquila had arrived, giving a look, with his single eye, that conveyed nothing. As they sat, talking and drinking, the carts had rumbled out of the town as the traders, farmers in the main, went home for the night. Those who had been out in the fields, and sought either comfort or distraction inside the city walls, had trooped through the gate as the sun dipped towards the horizon.

'Do you feed these men?' asked Aquila.

'We're supposed to,' the small guard replied, his hand rubbing the black stubble on his chin. The tall one was shaking his head to stop him talking, but drink had loosened his companion's tongue. 'Don't seem much point in wasting food, giving it to a dead man.'

'So who eats it?'

'Don't know. We sold it at the temple. They sell it on.'

The tall fellow spoke again, his face and voice reeking of suspicion, proof that, in his opinion, Aquila was asking too many questions. He seemed unconvinced now that this youth, liberal with his wine, had the deep interest he had implied, a desire to watch men die on the cross.

'You best be getting along, lad, before they close the gates. Otherwise you'll be stuck out here for the night, just like us.'

The small one opened his mouth to speak, but the other man kicked him on the leg. 'Best get the fire goin', don't you think?'

Aquila shook the ampoule. 'There's a drop left in here. Might as well see it off.'

They exchanged glances and an imperceptible nod, holding out their gourds. Aquila filled them, hearing in the background the sounds of their fellows shouting that the gates were about to be shut. He suspected that they would not be shut to this pair; they would light a fire, stack it high, wait until the town had settled down, then rap on the gate to be let in. The question was, would they maim their charges beforehand?

He stood up, wished them goodnight, and made off into the gathering gloom. The sun had just gone, the sky was black above and azure blue to the west, with only the odd star showing and the moon still below the horizon. As soon as his body was lost against the darkness of the town wall he turned towards the sea, heading for the patch of scrub by the shore where he had tethered the animals an hour before. Flaccus would probably be more upset about the loss of his horse and his weapons than the disappearance of Aquila, cursing at the money it would cost to replace, but it would be morning before he discovered that both were missing. He was at the governor's villa, eating good food and consuming too much wine. He would be overcome with the pleasure of dining with so eminent a figure, almost like the man's equal, and he would not give Aquila, who had hinted at a visit to the brothel, a second thought until he failed to appear in the morning.

He stood still listening to the sounds of Messana closing up for the night. Few would waste the oil needed to light a lamp, going to bed and rising with the sun. There would be activity around the temple but that was in the very centre of the city. Here at the edge, he had only sleepy and ill-equipped guards to worry about. He watched while the moon rose in the sky, felt the air chill as the heat of the day was sucked up into the clear night sky. The pinprick of light from the guard's fire threw the three crucifixes into stark relief as the light from the flames flicked across the inert bodies. He felt a chill in his own heart to equal that of the night; if he failed, his fate would be the same as theirs.

With his weapons, plus a small sack of food, Aquila moved silently across the flat, hard-packed earth, keeping close to the walls. He crossed the road, ducking into the well of the city gate so he could not be observed from above. Once clear of that he scurried swiftly to a point past the small exterior camp, moving in a wide arc so that he came back towards the fire from a point behind the three staked men. He moved up, half-crouched, until he was right behind Gadoric and laid down his spear. First he had to make sure the man was alive; no point in going on if Gadoric was dead. He said a few words in the Celtic tongue, his heart leaping as he saw the head jerk upright.

'You're alive,' he whispered.

'You!' croaked Gadoric. It took so much effort, just to say that one word, Aquila wondered if his friend had the energy to say anything else. He put his hand on his shoulder, squeezing it to reassure him. 'Don't talk, just listen. Soon, those two guards are going to go back into the city.' He squeezed harder to cut off the question. 'You saw me drinking with them. Before they leave, they're bound to come and check on you. They may even want to break your legs so you can't escape.'

Gadoric dropped his head, clearly exhausted as Aquila finished. 'If they just come to look, they will live. If they fetch the hammer, I shall kill them both.'

He reached inside his sack and produced a fig, holding it up so that the parched and starving Celt could eat it. Gadoric sucked greedily, the juice running out of his mouth and down his chin.

'Quietly.' Aquila pressed his mouth close to the other man's ear as the lips moved, the voice so soft that he had to repeat the words Gadoric said to be sure he had heard right. 'The others?' His hand squeezed the shoulder again. 'When the guards have gone, friend, not before. I don't want to kill unless I must.'

The fire had died down, though it still glowed enough to cast a circle of light. The two guards got to their feet and the tall one lifted his tunic and pissed against the feet of one of the crucified men, the stream of water playing up and down the broken legs. He was laughing all the time, making jokes that Aquila could not hear. The small fellow was tidying up their little camp and once he had finished they both picked up torches and started towards Gadoric and his companions.

'That nosy young bastard had good wine,' said the tall guard, loudly. Aquila froze, then slipped out his knife and jammed it in the ground in front of him as he saw the man swing the long-handled hammer onto his shoulder.

'He wasn't nosy, just curious. Never seen a crucifixion before, had he?'

'Beats me how you can tell the difference. Did you notice that trinket he had around his neck?'

'Much do you think it was worth?'

'Enough to retire, mate.'

Aquila lifted Flaccus's spear and waited, wondering if his suspicions were correct. Which one of the three prisoners would they try to immobilise first? He slipped further round behind the shepherd as they approached the one on Gadoric's left. The tall guard lifted his head and let it go. It dropped lifelessly.

'This one's a goner already.'

The small guard pushed his torch forward and peered closely. 'Makes no odds. Better safe than sorry.'

'Right then,' the tall one replied, lifting the

hammer till the head was halfway down his back.

Aquila threw the spear and followed on behind, grabbing his knife as it left his hand. It took the tall guard in the chest and his hands let go of the hammer as he stared first at the spear, then at the figure hurtling towards him. He tried to lift a hand to warn his companion, also transfixed by the protruding spear. The little one began to turn, but Aquila was on him, spinning him back again. His hand went under the man's chin and the knife slid easily through the soft tissue of the neck. The tall guard was still standing, swaying back and forth. He opened his mouth to yell or scream, but Aquila took his heels, causing him to fall heavily onto his back. The knife swung again, this time in a vicious arc.

Whatever sound he had intended to make died in his ruptured gullet and he expired a few moments later, as his blood pumped out through the gaping wound in his neck, draining into the hard earth by his glassy eyes. Aquila did not spare them a glance; he cut Gadoric's bonds first, easing the man to the ground, then he opened the sack of food and spread it out before him. The shepherd sat, head still bowed, unable to move as Aquila ran to cut free the others. The slave whose legs the guards had been about to break was, indeed, dead; too much sun and no water had probably killed him. The other one yelled in pain as Aquila cut his bonds and the boy clapped his hand hard over his mouth, begging him in three languages to be silent. The Greek made sense and Aquila helped him over to the point where Gadoric sat, then went to the campfire to fetch the jar of water he had seen earlier. When he returned both men were rubbing their wrists, biting back the excruciating pain caused by the blood flowing back into their limbs. Gently he fed them, cupping water in his hands so that they could drink.

'Do you think you can mount a horse?' he asked Gadoric.

The question took the Celt by surprise. 'You have a horse?'

Aquila smiled, his white teeth flashing in the pale light from the moon and the stars. 'I have two. You eat and drink. I'll go and get them.'

His voice took on a note of urgency, his finger pointing to the two dead guards. 'We must go soon. Those two will be expected, so the guards at the city gate will wonder, when they don't show, where they are. They might come out to investigate. Another thing, I can move myself without being seen or heard, but that won't apply to horses. There's no point in my trying to lead them over, so I will ride them. As soon as you hear the hooves, gather up the food, get to your feet and be ready to mount.'

Gadoric pushed himself onto his knee, then using the stake as support he got painfully and slowly to his feet. 'Best to be sure we can stand up.'

Aquila helped the other slave up and half-carried him to the other stake, addressing him urgently in Greek, ordering him to remain upright. He gathered up the food himself, pushing the bread and fruit into the sack, then went to make a last check on Gadoric.

'If anyone comes while I'm getting the horses, head off down the right hand side of the road.'

The shepherd just nodded slowly, then he lifted his head and smiled, hard to see in the darkness, but it was there and it cheered the boy. He ran back the way he came, stopping by the dark city gate to listen. The odd faint voice, but no sign of any discussion about the two men he had killed. Back at the copse he took the hobbling off the animals' legs and, mounting his own, leading Flaccus's horse, he set off at a trot. The sound of the hooves, on the hard earth, rang like huge drums in his ears. The voice he heard could have shouted for any number of reasons, but Aquila didn't wait to find out; he kicked his horse into a canter, then a gallop.

More shouts erupted as he approached the line of stakes and crucifixes. The two injured slaves were still hanging onto their stakes so Aquila dismounted and led the horses to them. He grabbed the stranger and threw him up onto the animal's back. The man, clearly no rider, could not mount properly so Aquila took the hobble rope and lashed it round his hands, ducked under the horse and tied the other end round the feet. Quickly he gathered the remaining food and lashed the sack to the saddle horn. The sound of shouting increased as the gates to the city opened. He made a grab for the reins, tied them to the saddle horn of his own horse, then led both animals over to Gadoric's stake.

The voice was cracked again, full of despair. 'I don't think I can do it.'

The boy pushed him towards the horse, bent down and lifted his foot. The voices were loud now, getting close and sounding excited. The lack of reaction from the two guards must have alerted them to what had happened. Aquila heaved on Gadoric's legs, throwing him up so the Celt fell forward across the withers. Aquila hauled his spear out of the dead guard and jumped up behind him, then kicked hard. The overloaded horse moved slowly. Too slowly! The soldiers from the city were running at them full tilt and the boy could see their uniforms now, as they caught the glim from the pale moonlight, and he also saw the tips of their spears, raised and ready to throw. He kicked the animal again and it started to trot. No time for sentiment, he spun the spear in his hand and jabbed it into the horse's flank. The animal tried to rear but the weight of two riders held it down.

Aquila jabbed again, and with a terrified scream the horse took off. Their pursuers kept pace to start with, but once the horses got going, the gap opened up. The thud of spears as they hit the ground behind him was loud, but not as shrill as the cries of frustration until they faded away. It was only a breathing space; they would go back to the city and rouse out some cavalry, and Aquila knew they would be an easy target on the open plain. He hauled hard on his reins, aiming the horse over the fields of still-smouldering stubble, heading for the black line of hills that stood stark against the moonlit sky.

CHAPTER FIFTEEN

❖

'No wonder father preferred life in the army,' said Titus.

Cholon had just finished his list of the latest scandals to rock Rome, most of which concerned her illustrious senators. There were the usual cases of attempted seduction, blatant pederasty and financial chicanery, yet most alarming was the way that some, including the most senior, had tried to recover the presents given to them by the Parthians. Informed by the priests, this had led to a thundering denunciation in the Forum from Lucius Falerius Nerva. Once on his feet, he had not spared them, alluding openly to the bribes that some members had taken to further the interests of Rome's eastern rivals, for once setting aside his normal reserve in addressing his peers and delivering some very unpalatable truths in words that had all of Rome talking.

'Your father always maintained that their reputation didn't bear too close a scrutiny.'

Titus threw back his head and laughed. 'Close. You can smell the corruption from the Pillars of Hercules to the Pontus. They ask men to die on the frontiers when every law that they have enacted to control their own behaviour is openly flouted. Senators make fortunes yet baulk at the provision of proper supplies for soldiers in the field. Don't they know that these men on short commons hear of how they feed dozens at their table with expensive imported delicacies, how they line each other's pockets with lucrative offices, which is an even greater scandal. It's about time someone told them so, though I never expected that it would be Lucius Falerius.'

Cholon looked out of his window though the height afforded a very limited view, confined to his nearest neighbour ten feet away across the narrow street. 'How goes the knights campaign?'

Titus pulled a face. 'Not well enough. People like Lucius are too shrewd to be caught out by tribal votes in the Comitia. He knows just who to bribe and he also knows those knights whose only dream is to be senators. As long as he holds the censor's office, or fills it with one of his nominees, the Senate is safe from everyone but himself. No one gets in of whom he does not approve.'

'Are you not, yourself, one of his nominees?' asked Cholon.

Titus looked at him closely, thinking he was still the same carefully barbered fellow he remembered from years past, though the odd line had appeared to spoil that smooth countenance. The question bordered on the impertinent, even if Cholon was a free man, but the Greek had always talked to his father in the same manner and in some ways it was flattering to be treated like that, rather than be subjected to the barely disguised contempt with which Cholon addressed his brother Quintus.

'Strictly speaking I am being supported by my brother, but since he is close to Lucius Falerius, the exalted one ensured that the Falerii votes were at my disposal.'

'Odd. I never imagined that you'd be beholden to the Falerii, after what happened.'

'Don't bait me, Cholon,' replied Titus with a wry smile, refusing to be drawn.

The Greek's eyebrows shot up in mock alarm. 'Was I baiting you, Titus?'

'You know you were, you slippery Attic toad.' This was delivered with a wider smile and caused no offence. 'For you, and for you alone, I will explain. Lucius merely asked me to attend his son's coming of age. That I did. Quintus, seeing me in the house of his own patron, took the hint, just as Lucius intended he should. I even went as far as to ask the exalted one what he wanted in return.'

'And?'

'He said that I would know what to do when the time comes.'

Cholon frowned. 'An unspecified favour at an unspecified time? Sounds as though he may be asking a great deal.'

'I'm content to leave that to the Gods, Cholon, and provided it's consistent with my principles, I will happily oblige.' He saw the Greek's frown deepen, and he knew the cause. His continuing dissatisfaction with what had happened at Thralaxas was well known. 'Quintus will not do what must be done, even if he is a senator, just in case it harms his long-term interests, so it falls to me to gain redress. That means, in turn, that I must also enter the Senate. I can only get the money to do that by successful soldiering. I'll never get hold of a million sesterces in Rome.'

'Are you not now, as Quaestor Urbani, in charge of the public purse?'

Titus ignored the interruption. 'Lucius Falerius has pressured Quintus by acknowledging me, so my brother will do everything he can to get me a profitable posting once my term of office is ended. Not because he loves me, but because Lucius has made him see sense. That it's consistent with his own dignity that I should prosper, but I don't think that will extend to a seat in the Senate.'

'You said, when you arrived, that you needed a favour from me?'

'I do. You're a clever fellow, Cholon.' He noticed the Greek puff out his chest slightly. 'Though my father did say, several times, that you're not as clever as you think you are.'

The eyes narrowed at the same time as Cholon's shoulders. 'That's an insult, Titus. It's not normally the way to elicit a favour.'

'True, but you won't do what I am going to ask for love of me. Once I'm in the Senate, if he's still alive, I intend to impeach Vegetius Flaminus for what happened in Illyricum.'

'You're wasting your time, Titus. No senator will convict him.'

'What if they aren't sitting on the case? Say the court that tries Vegetius is manned by knights?'

'You plan to become a senator, yet you want to ally yourself to the knights?'

Titus nodded vigorously. 'That's right and I want you to help me. Instead of sitting here composing plays that no one will ever perform, I want you to take up your duties as a Roman citizen. Father left you enough and if you put yourself forward you'll be in the knight's class as soon as they undertake the next census.'

Cholon was angry, though more because of the accuracy of his visitor's words than their impertinent delivery. 'Firstly, you inform me that I'm not as clever as I think, now you tell me that I cannot write either. Truly, Titus, you have a strange way of seeking support. Do you have any more insults left to deliver before I ask you to leave?'

'I didn't know my father as well as I should, but I think if he had his life over again, he might spend more time on the affairs of Rome than he did on the battlefield. Something has gone wrong, Cholon. Perhaps it is because we have grown too big in the world. The city reeks of licensed villainy. As Rome has conquered, the spirit that animated our forefathers has become corrupted by naked greed. If we are to hold what we have, we must change things at the centre. If we cannot rely on trust, we must make those with power accountable to their fellow citizens. If that means knights, sitting in judgement on senators, so be it.'

'I still don't know what you require of me?'

'Participate, Cholon, and when you feel you have something useful to say, or advice to give, then tell me.'

Cholon looked sideways at the sheet of papyrus, empty except for a few drawings scratched on the edges. 'Do you really think that we can challenge the likes of Lucius and Quintus?'

'Lucius Falerius wasn't born powerful, Cholon, he made himself so, and as far as I can tell, his personal probity is beyond question. But he believes that the Senate should have untrammelled authority over the state. The knights should be content with what they have and our Italian allies should merely provide troops to die on our behalf. Events in Spain are allowed to drift and the chief of the Duncani taunts our provincial governors.'

Titus saw the Greek's eyes narrow at the mention of Brennos and continued without pause.

'He either shuts his eyes, or his mind, to what goes on. Or perhaps he thinks that is the price that must be paid to retain senatorial power. I believe he is wrong, and I think that a successful impeachment of someone like Vegetius Flaminus could open up the whole tub of worms to proper inspection.'

'Vegetius could be dead before you get to the Senate.'

Titus favoured the Greek with a grim look. 'That is true, but believe me Cholon, there's no shortage of candidates for condemnation.'

The dust rose behind the wheels as Titus manoeuvred his chariot through the Campus Martius. He would have to wait a while, until the space cleared, to put his horses through their proper paces, charging from one end of the field to the other, but this human obstacle course presented a good opportunity for a more precise training of his animals. He handled the traces deftly as he swung right and left through the wrestlers, boxers and those practising with weapons. Soon he was by the bank of the river and as he turned upstream a crowd, all intent on watching a fight, barred his route. Titus could see, from his vantage point, young Marcellus, wearing a head guard. Sweat dripped off him, as the boy sought to nail his nimble opponent with a decent punch. The crowd around the dancing pair cheered him on, booing his opponent, who seemed disinclined to engage in a proper bout, merely concentrating on avoiding the blows aimed in his direction.

Titus hauled on the traces, bringing his chariot to a halt outside of the ring of spectators, his mobile platform affording him a perfect view. The boy was fighting a grown man, fully bearded, though the fellow was shorter than Marcellus by a head. He also had the air of a professional about him; the way he weaved and ducked proved that he knew his business and if he was being driven backwards it was not because of fear or pain. Titus realised that the opponent, back-pedalling furiously, was trying to tire Marcellus out, it being a hot afternoon, with the sun blazing down out of a cloudless sky. He could also see the old centurion, Macrobius, standing silently, watching his pupil; the look on his face was hard to place, seeming to be a mixture of disapproval and satisfaction.

The professional stopped dead and caught Marcellus with a blow on the pads that covered his ears. That was the prelude to a punch aimed at the boy's stomach, which Marcellus only avoided by an ungainly backwards leap, leaving him off balance for the next assault, as his opponent followed up quickly. He parried as best he could, but a fair number of punches got through and they were hard knocks; the man was not sparing the youngster, treating him as an equal. Marcellus kept his hands up, covering his face as he rode the sustained assault. Blows rained on his forearms and shoulders as he weaved untidily, till the man halted for a split second, setting himself up for a straight jab that would pierce the boy's defences, as soon as he looked through his fists to see why his opponent had stopped.

Marcellus did not oblige him by waiting. One of his upraised arms shot out and his guard being too low, it caught the boxer unawares. The left-handed blow took him on the cheek, raising and turning his head to the side, exposing his bearded chin for the punch that followed, but he was too wise to wait. He did not fight the force of the blow; instead he rode it, letting the punch carry his head back out of danger so that Marcellus's right hook missed the chin by a fraction. The man had got his feet right and he spun slightly, his own right hand swinging easily through Marcellus's guard, to land a blow that knocked the boy clean off his feet.

The watching crowd rushed forward to help Marcellus up as Titus hauled on the traces and took his chariot round the outside, bringing it to a halt alongside Macrobius. The boy's tutor had not moved but his head did, for he was nodding and the purple-veined face was set in a look that boded ill for his pupil.

'Who was he fighting, Macrobius?' asked Titus.

The old man looked up. 'Nicandros, a Greek professional.'

'Isn't he a little young to be taking on professional boxers?'

The purple, cratered nose twitched angrily. 'He wants to be a soldier. If you can assure me that all those he fights will be amateurs, I'll stop training him now.'

'What I meant, Macrobius, is that he'd be better off fighting boys his own age.'

The old warrior sniffed again, and the anger was tinged with just a trace of pride. 'No point, Titus Cornelius. He just beats 'em.'

Nicandros, the professional, had helped get Marcellus to his feet and he was talking to the boy encouragingly, patting his hunched shoulders and assuring him that he had put up a good fight. Titus passed his traces to Macrobius and climbed down and as Marcellus saw him approach he pulled himself upright, fighting to stay steady. Nicandros looked up too and though he did not know the charioteer, he could see by his dress, and the way others deferred to him, that he was important.

'I'll take care to avoid this lad in five years, sir. If he was to come to Greece for the Olympiad, fully grown, I'd back him to walk off with a branch of Zeus's own olive tree.'

Titus put his hand under the boy's chin and lifted the head. The eyes were still a bit glassy as Marcellus shook his head in an attempt to clear his vision, his face bearing the pain that accompanies defeat.

'Tell me, Marcellus, has Macrobius taught you to handle a chariot yet?' The boy shook his head very slowly. 'Then I shall take it as my duty to do so.'

Marcellus gave Titus a weak smile. 'I doubt I'd be much of a pupil today.'

'Nonsense. You've had a hard blow, but it's nothing that cold water won't cure.'

Titus looked around the assembled faces questioningly. 'Who are his friends?' Several claimed the honour, putting up their hands, and Titus smiled, looking into Marcellus's eyes as he gave them an order. 'Then it falls to you, as his friends, to revive him. Chuck him in the Tiber.'

Eager hands grabbed at the young boxer and he was lifted bodily and borne towards the nearby river, where, with due ceremony, he was swung through the air three times, before being released to land with a great splash in the water.

'Turn round, girl.'

The naked body, slim, olive-skinned and shining, spun slowly and Lucius Falerius noticed the uplift of the breasts and the erect nipples as she complied.

Her dark brown hair, freshly washed and still slightly damp, covered the whole of her back, all the way down to the rise of her firm buttocks. They were like two perfect orbs, with a straight dark line where they joined the legs. Gratifyingly, there was no excess flesh at the top of her thighs to spoil the rounded lines that extended from her narrow waist.

'Turn again,' the old man said dispassionately, and the girl obeyed, her eyes cast down in a maidenly fashion, her hands set likewise to cover the sparse hair on her mons pubis. Lucius's voice took on a note of anger. 'Take your hands out of the way and look at me.'

The girl obeyed quickly, fixing Lucius with her almond eyes, her full red lips parted to show even white teeth.

'Is she a virgin?'

Lucius noticed the overseer from his Campanian farm hesitate; the fellow knew better than to lie to Lucius, but it was obvious he had been tempted to do so, assuming that, even if it had not been specified, it was what his employer required.

'Well?'

'Unfortunately, no!'

The man's shoulders seemed to shrink into his body as a way of emphasising his regret but for all his apparent grovelling, he was damned if he was going to tell the senator the truth. According to the guards that had delivered her, Cassius Barbinus, before he sent her away, had used her as he used everyone: without feeling. Lucius Falerius Nerva would not touch anything that Barbinus had taken, even a gifted slave, but his overseer thought her wasted where she was, on a farm that her master rarely visited. Besides, she was becoming a problem – not herself, for she was a meek creature – but the male slaves he oversaw, a rough lot, were openly lusting after the girl and his own wife, who had seen his eye wander to her swaying hips, had scolded him for his own interest. Much better for her to be here, in Rome, where she could, if Lucius permitted it, form an attachment to a more refined household slave, with the added benefit that it would make his own domestic life a little easier.

'Do you not recall her, Eminence?'

'Should I?'

'She was a gift from Cassius Barbinus, sent to me two years ago. While she was his property she became attached to a boy her own age. It is thought matters might have gone too far.'

'That would be typical of Barbinus. The man can't even control his slaves.' Lucius stepped forward and ran a hand over the smooth olive skin, and she shivered slightly at the touch. 'The parents, both Greeks?'

'Yes. I was told the father's from Thrace, the mother Macedonian.'

Lucius nearly asked about the Thracian; famous

for their strength and fortitude, especially in the sun, they were usually employed in Sicily growing wheat. Then he remembered, just in time, that he had sold his property on the island. The need to do so made him frown angrily, so unlike him was it to lose touch. The barracking he had given his fellow-senators over the Parthian gifts, was, he realised now, unwise. His overseer mistook the look generated by such thoughts and spoke hastily.

'There are other girls on the farm who are virgins, Excellency, though none as pretty as this.'

'I don't want a virgin!' Lucius took the girl's chin in his hand, thumb one side, index finger the other. The grip was firm without being painful. 'I own you, girl, body and soul, do you realise that?' The girl nodded with difficulty. 'Please me and you will be well rewarded, thwart my wishes and you'll lose your looks down a lead mine. You will come here, to my house, as a normal household slave. The tasks I set you will not be too arduous and for that your duties will be light. Do you understand?'

Again the girl nodded. The overseer had told her all about the betrothal, so she knew that the daughter of Appius Claudius was not yet ten years old. The wedding, between her and Marcellus Falerius, would not take place for several years.

'My son is a handsome fellow and I think he will treat you kindly. If you do likewise then he will not see the need to expend his energies in the brothel. In time, he will have a wife, then I will send you back to the farm, with permission to take a man and bear children.' The girl, who had once dreamt of marriage and children on the farm where she was raised, tried hard to hide a smile; perhaps this old man would send her back there. 'What's your name?'

She whispered in reply. 'Sosia, master.'

'Well, you're a pretty specimen, Sosia, pretty enough to make an old man wish he was twenty years younger.'

'Where is my son? I sent for him half an hour ago.'

The household steward bowed slightly. 'He's not yet returned from the Campus Martius, master.'

Lucius looked up at the evening sky. 'Don't be a fool, it's nearly dark.'

'He has taken to stopping off at the Trebonius house on the way home.' The steward noticed the brow of his master furrow and spoke hastily, lest blame be attached to him. 'Or so his body slave informs me.'

'He sees the Trebonius boy all day, man. They attend school together, never mind their games.'

'It is not the boy he goes to see, master. I believe he has become attached to Gaius Trebonius's sister, Valeria.'

'How long has this been going on?'

'Several weeks, master,' the steward lied; it was

many months, instead of mere weeks.

The voice was like the lash of a whip, making the fellow cringe. 'And you did not see fit to inform me of this?'

'I'll send for him right away, master.'

'Go yourself!'

'But, master…'

Lucius stepped forward and grabbed the man by the hair, shaking him violently. 'Yes, idiot. They'll think that you've been reduced to a mere household dogsbody, a paltry messenger boy, and every slave on the Palatine will laugh at you for weeks. Be warned, messenger, that is what will come to pass if you keep information about anything from me, let alone the whereabouts of my son.'

Valeria rubbed her hand over Marcellus's forearm, still bruised from the blows he had fended off in his boxing bout, as he finished relating to her the latest news from the frontier of Hispania Ulterior. Being privy to the reports passed on to his father, he was probably the best informed youth in Rome, eagerly listened to by his contemporaries, avid for news of war wherever it occurred, but none had the passion of Valeria and no one demanded that he outline each detail with such diligent insistence. Another insurrection had broken out, this time caused by a tribe called the Averici. Mounted on small ponies, they were very mobile, the worst kind of enemy the disciplined Romans could face. As usual, such an uprising was backed, indeed fostered, by the Duncani, who lay in wait for any Roman legate stupid enough to pursue the lightly armed cavalry into the hills.

The Averici seemed particularly callous, not content just to kill but instead inclined to torture and rape on a scale not seen in Spain for decades. Originally, when setting out to relate such tales, Marcellus had tried to shock Valeria with his graphic descriptions. Not now; he still provided her with the gory details, but it was to see the way she reacted, the way she tensed and released her breath, that drove him, sometimes, to colour stories that were quite horrific enough without embellishment.

'I prefer it when you come like this.' Her hand slipped across his filthy red smock. 'Somehow it makes everything more real.'

'Smelling of manure and sweat?' Marcellus shivered, himself, at the lightness of her touch. Valeria was dressed in everyday clothes, a plain white woollen garment, tied at the waist with a decorated belt. Her hair was dressed in that same way, high and curled above her forehead. The dark eyes, seemingly amused, looked at the tall boy who stood before her. Part of him could not resist the temptation to administer a rebuke. 'That's a very odd notion, Valeria.'

He attempted to touch her arm in turn, hoping

that by doing so he could pull her closer, but she slid away from him, replying, with her back half-turned, in a little girl voice. 'Is it, Marcellus? To me it's like a soldier fresh from the very battles you describe, the blood of his enemies still on his sword. A hero who, having slain the barbarian, comes to claim his prize.'

'May the Gods preserve us from such poetic rubbish,' said her brother, Gaius, entirely spoiling the mood of intimacy.

Marcellus, who had been quite taken with the sentiment, was annoyed. 'Can't you go somewhere else, Gaius?'

'Nothing would give me greater pleasure, friend, but if I go, you'll have Valeria's maid to watch over you and she'll keep you ten feet apart. The only thing Valeria will smell is her rancid armpits and there will be none of these little caresses that I allow.'

Valeria turned and stuck her tongue out at him, in the way she had, until recently, reserved for people like Marcellus. 'Pig.'

'Better a pig than a snake, sister,' replied her brother, unruffled.

'Please don't talk to Valeria like that,' Marcellus insisted.

Gaius adopted a haughty expression, though it was impossible to say whether it was aimed at Marcellus, or the slave who had just sidled up to stand beside him. 'Sorry friend. Not even you can deny me a brother's privileges.' He turned to the slave. 'What do you want?'

The slave grinned, much to the annoyance of Gaius, which was not eased by the way the fellow addressed the other boy direct, ignoring his question. 'Marcellus Falerius, your father's steward is at the gate, requesting that you be fetched immediately.'

'His steward?'

The boy's response only widened the grin on the fellow's face, for the Falerii steward was a haughty bugger, yet there he was at the door like a common household skivvy. Many would take pleasure from his humiliation.

'Damn you!' snapped Gaius. 'I asked you a question.'

The smile disappeared off the slave's face and he pulled away fearfully from Gaius, though he was twenty years the boy's senior. 'Did I not answer it, sir?'

'No, you did not! In this house you report to me, not to my guests, however favoured they may be.'

'Why, Gaius,' said Valeria teasingly, throwing up her arms in mock alarm. 'You look quite grown up.'

Marcellus had his eyes on her, and the breasts that swelled up through her dress. There was no doubt that she was grown up and he had to drag his mind from the image of her body. He placed himself between the angry Gaius and the cowed servant, addressing his friend.

'I must go. If my father has sent his steward, it must be something of importance.'

He turned back and bowed slightly to Valeria. She smiled at him sweetly, though her nostrils flared slightly and her voice dropped to a compelling whisper. 'Remember what I said, Marcellus. Come to me each day, on your way home, and tell me all the latest news.' She was close again, her fingertips reaching out to a particularly heavy blue-black mark on his upper arm. 'Should you be wounded on the Campus Martius, properly wounded, I will dress the cut myself.'

Marcellus frowned, but he had no time to ponder why a high-born Roman girl should undertake the task of a slave. He left, thanking the man who had brought the message, who took the opportunity to slip away from potential trouble by following in his wake.

'I do not wish to forbid it,' said Lucius, 'but I will not have you turning up at another senator's house smelling like an overworked street sweeper.'

'Neither Gaius nor his sister seemed to mind,' Marcellus protested, 'and it is on the way.'

'I mind, and that is sufficient. You will come home first, bathe and dress in proper clothes. Is that clear?'

'Yes, father.'

'And remember that you are betrothed to the Claudian girl. That does not debar you from other pursuits, but it does call for a proper degree of discretion.'

There was no point in Marcellus stating that he preferred Valeria Trebonius, no point at all, and not just because of his father's views. Sitting here, it was easy to tell himself that he would avoid her, stay away from the house and her endless teasing, but his resolve always weakened. There was no way to avoid her front door on his way home from the Campus Martius and her attitude, on such occasions, was so markedly different from that she employed at other times. He was strong with other people, including girls, never allowing anyone the least liberty, but all that seemed to evaporate in her presence. She produced an ache in him that no amount of self-abasement could control. It was almost as if Valeria knew she was the sole object of his nocturnal fantasies and so took every opportunity she could to come just close enough to make his obvious arousal unbearable. He could see the light in her eyes, bordering on mockery. What did she see in his eyes? He dragged his mind away from Valeria, back to his father, who was still talking.

'I trust that you are as ardent as any boy your age.' He was smiling, despite the hard tone of his voice. 'Go to your room, Marcellus. You will find that your needs will be fully catered for, by me!'

Marcellus ran his nose from her armpit to her
nipple, taking in the musky smell of her body.
When the slave girl had first been shown into his
room, whatever reserve he had felt had now
completely evaporated. Sosia was Falerii
property, his to do with as he wished. That she
had shown little passion actually pleased him,
since that absolved him from the need to feel or
respond. He did not want to get to know this girl,
just to use her. She could be an image, in the
darkness, on which he would project whatever
thoughts he desired. His lips circled the erect
nipple, his tongue darting in and out as Sosia
tried to hold her reactions in check, fighting off
the sounds that would indicate intimacy. Yet it
was hard, for in the dark one man could very well
be another, and her body was so sensitive to the
touch, just as her mind could not reject the image
of Aquila. That was how she had survived the
callousness of Barbinus, and the same vision
would aid her now, blocking out the attentions
being paid to her by her new owner.

Sosia had no knowledge of Roman ways,
especially those of the nobility, so when his hands
took her shoulders and spun her so that she was
face down, she was confused. The tongue now
ran up and down the vee of her spine, just
touching the fine hairs that lined her back.
Staying as stiff as she could, she heard Marcellus

murmur a name and then his knee was between her legs, pushing them open. He grunted slightly as he pushed hard into her. The name he had groaned, Valeria, was blocked out of her mind by the pain.

CHAPTER SIXTEEN

———•———

The trail Aquila was leaving would be easy to follow, but he had no choice. They had left the coastal plain behind and started to climb into the hills long before daylight. Now, with the sun full up, he could look back at the foothills beneath him, with the burnt wheat fields, laid out in the regular Roman pattern, criss-crossed at strict intervals by roads and paths stretching all the way to the sea. Gadoric and his fellow rebel, called Hypolitas, were with the horses in a deep ravine and if there was no immediate pursuit, that was where they would spend the day. There was pasture for the horses on a nearby ridge, quite possibly water too, since the grass was green, and the same ridge would also provide a convenient place to look out for anyone hunting them. He slid down the scree slope into the gorse at the mouth of the ravine and pushed his way through to find Hypolitas flat on his back, sound asleep, while Gadoric had fought to stay awake so that the boy should not have the entire burden of the rescue placed on his young shoulders.

Aquila knelt down beside him, speaking quietly. 'No sign of anyone chasing us.'

The Celt's red-rimmed eyes lingered on the gold charm, swinging slightly before his eyes, then he shut them tight, as though the effort of staring was too much. 'They will. They wouldn't go blundering about the countryside, at night, once they'd lost our trail.' Great coughs racked his body, but he kept talking. 'But they'll be out in strength at first light.'

'Are we that important?'

Gadoric rubbed a hand across his forehead. 'To them, yes. If they have people that can follow our trail, we shouldn't wait here.'

Aquila smiled; a problem he should have thought about before had just occurred to him. 'Where will we go, Gadoric?'

'We must join the other runaway slaves in the hills. There are hundreds of them out here somewhere.'

The boy decided to say nothing of what had happened the day before; Gadoric was too exhausted, so he put his hand on the shepherd's shoulder to push him back into the grass. He felt the man resist, though in truth it was feeble. 'Rest, my friend. They cannot surprise us. I can see the whole coastal road from here.'

'We must find the other runaway slaves.'

'No, Gadoric. You need rest, food and time to recover. If these runaway slaves are any good, they will find us before the overseers.'

They were like insects, mere specks in the distance as they made their way slowly down the tracks between the fields, stopping occasionally so that the man following their trail could check on their spoor. He counted thirty men, and though he could not be sure at this distance, he thought that Flaccus was leading them. Behind him the horses munched at the juicy grass, below the two slaves slept. Aquila had already drunk his fill of the fresh water that gurgled out of a fissure in the rocks before disappearing underground. The supply of food he had brought would not last long, so he had set snares to catch game. Using some saplings he constructed a canopy with his cloak to keep the hot sun off his back and from that shaded position, with water to hand, he could watch the progress of the pursuit without discomfort.

Their trail was, as he had suspected, easy to follow. A heavily laden horse, bearing two people, leaves a much deeper hoof print than normal. The task would become more difficult as they made their way into the hills, but they would come on, regardless of the problems, he knew that now. It was not just Gadoric's words; they would not have set out, in such a large party, if they did not intend to see the three crucifixes fully employed. Besides, Flaccus must have added his own disappearance to that of the condemned men. Given the presence of Cassius Barbinus in Sicily, the ex-centurion would be mightily embarrassed by the loss of his attendant, his horses and his weapons. Aquila thought back to the men who had ambushed them the day before, ten, maybe twelve people, not very well armed. Was that just one roving band, or were there more?

They only had two possibilities. Either they must disappear, or join a group that would frighten off the men coming after them. First he had to slow the latter down; Gadoric and Hypolitas needed time to recover their strength but if they were allowed to come on at their present pace he would be forced to move right away. The important people were the trackers; kill them and the whole enterprise would falter. But how? Against thirty men he had a spear, his bow and a quiver of arrows, two swords and one knife. He slipped out of his makeshift tent, rolling up his dark brown cloak, checked that the horses were properly hobbled, before climbing down to look at his companions. They slept, the remaining food and water between them, and he lifted the food and placed it under a bush, tucking the empty sack into his belt. A quick arrangement of twigs, something they had played at so long ago, left a message for Gadoric that he would be back. He took his spear and headed off downhill, looking for a place to attack, preferably as close to the coastal plain as possible.

Moving swiftly and silently, he was able to enjoy the sensation of being back in wooded countryside. At every opportunity, Aquila would make for an outcrop that afforded him a view of the progress of their pursuers. The party had left the plain and started up the hills, but even though they were out of sight he knew their location. Such a large group of men made a great deal of noise and you could place them by the flurries of birds scared out of the trees. He was following the trail down and they were following it up. They were bound to meet!

He found his spot, a narrow ravine where the sides rose some fifteen feet above the trail. Ideally he would have liked a place further down but there was no guarantee he would find anything as good as his present location. Aquila surveyed both sides, careful not to step on the trail, for if his pursuers had any sense they would not just blunder through a dangerous gully like this; at the very least they would be prepared for an attack. Odds of thirty to one were somewhat lessened by the narrow defile which would confine them to a maximum of three abreast, but those three and the men behind them would be ready, quite possibly with bow and arrows. Anyone standing up to cast a spear would present an easy target so he had to unsettle them, to do something to spoil their aim. First he collected dry twigs, laying them across the gaps in the trees that led round the ravine to the spot he had chosen for his attack. If anyone came by those routes he would be warned and could get away.

The next bit was harder, and given the lack of available time he was blessed with good fortune. Catching snakes is never easy, even when you know where to look, especially during the middle of a hot day. Aquila searched carefully through the long grass with the end of a specially cut branch, food sack in hand, concentrating on the shaded areas, under rocks, where they would sleep. He found two adders, pinned them with the head of the stick, then picked them up and slipped them into the sack. Taking up position, he laid his bow and three arrows in front of him. Then he was still, so that the forest around him, disturbed by his presence, could settle back into normality.

Those ascending were making a tremendous racket, blundering through the undergrowth at the side of the trail and scaring animals large and small, some of which ran past Aquila. He froze at the sound of breaking twigs, then spun round as a massive wild boar shot past his outstretched feet, too intent on escape to afford him even a passing look, but being a huge beast Aquila stared after it eagerly. Thigh high to a standing man, the curled horns on its snout were long enough to disembowel him, backed up by enough weight to break both your legs if it ran into you full tilt. In better times, he and Gadoric would have had great pleasure hunting such an animal.

The noises stopped, his pursuers having reined in their horses, and he strained to hear the voices, but the only sound was a faint hum of murmured instructions, followed by hooves muffled by the loose sandy trail. He loosened the neck of the sack, easing it towards the edge of the ravine as two men appeared, one looking at the trail, the other scanning the sides of the gully, shortly followed by several more riding in pairs abreast, bows at the ready, with arrows slotted into the gut. The man in front was a tracker and he was Aquila's target. He turned and beckoned behind him and Aquila inhaled sharply as Flaccus appeared. The old centurion stopped his horse at the head of the column and raised his head, seeming to look straight at Aquila, sniffing the air, as though that would alert him to any hidden danger. Clearly in command, he turned and beckoned for the others to follow. If Aquila was going to stop them, this was the moment, but Flaccus, in the lead, was blocking him from his favoured target. Logic told him that killing the leader would do just as well but sentiment made that impossible. Flaccus might be cruel and avaricious yet he had been good to the youth who now held his life in his hands.

The snakes were hissing madly and trying to wriggle out of the sack, their heads waving from side to side. Aquila took hold of the material at the bottom, jerked his arm and propelled the reptiles down onto the sandy track. They landed with a thud, two feet in front of Flaccus, and immediately wriggled away from him in panic. Flaccus's horse, right in their path, was rearing within a second of their arrival, which caused the horses behind to buck and turn. Aquila stood up and there was a fraction of a second when the two pairs of eyes locked. Flaccus must have seen Aquila whip an arrow into his bow, must have been sure, with the boy's prowess, that he was going to die. Aquila was pulling on the string, the head of the arrow still aimed at the old centurion's heart. He twitched it to one side, no more than half an inch, but it was enough. The tracker, whose horse had turned right away from the snakes, took the bolt, which missed Flaccus's head by a fraction. The thud was quite audible as it struck the man's back, feathers quivering on the long shaft.

He fired off one more arrow, then ducked quickly to his right as the return fire whistled through the trees above his head, one or two passing the spot where he had been standing, but all, in the melee, were badly aimed, because the horses, still spooked by the snakes, had tried to bolt. The confusion was evident in the mass of shouted and conflicting instructions, until the roaring voice of Flaccus raised itself above all others, commanding everyone to be quiet. Aquila slung his bow over his shoulder and retrieved his last arrow, then he was off, running diagonally across the hillside, spear in hand, through thick undergrowth that men on horses would not attempt. Flaccus was no fool; he would have some dismount to chase him on foot and he could only hope that he could either outrun them, or through superior skill in these woods, evade capture.

He moved swiftly, ignoring the disturbance his passing caused, for the woods were now in turmoil, with every bird calling in a unified chorus of alarm; that, added to the sound of men pursuing him, calling to each other as they came crashing through the undergrowth, spurred him on. He burst through a clump of bushes to another trail, made by animals over the years, and started to run uphill. The huge boar was coming down, so close to him that he would die if he tried to throw his spear so Aquila dived to one side, throwing himself into a thicket of painful nettles. Unable to turn swiftly the boar shot by, but it pushed out its hooves and finally shuddered to a halt.

Aquila leapt up and threw the spear to one side. His bow was up and the arrow slung, waiting for the animal to attack, even though he wondered if such a weapon would be of any use against such a creature. But it did not turn; the sound of the men chasing Aquila, to an enraged and short-sighted animal, was a stronger lure than his proximity. It lumbered off down the trail, rapidly gaining momentum on the steep slope. The youngster was up and running by the time he heard the screams, the first being of a man in danger, swiftly followed by that same man in agony as the boar took him. Then his howls mingled with those of the boar, high pitched and squealing, as his companions tried to save their friend by killing the animal. The whole forest reverberated with the screeching of man and beast, both, judging by the sound, in their death throes. Aquila hoped that the boar had failed to kill, for a badly wounded man would slow the chase down even more.

Gadoric and Hypolitas were obviously still asleep, there being no sign or sound of movement as he made his way past the hidden ravine to check on the horses and his snares. He saw the grass, discoloured by the angle of the sun, at the spot where he had lain earlier that day. After six hours it could not be flattened, that is, unless someone else had lain in the same place. Aquila stood still, listening, his eyes darting around the area, seeking clues. Gadoric might have come up to the ridge but if he had, why was he not here now and if he had lain there recently, he could not have failed to observe Aquila as he covered the last patch of territory through the sparse trees. Perhaps what he hoped for earlier had happened. If so, he must move carefully, to avoid creating alarm.

Aware that there was even higher ground from which he could be seen, every move he made was carried out with slow deliberation. The horses, now rested, watered and grazed, kicked skittishly as he removed the hobble ropes and they followed readily as he led them down to the hidden ravine. Nothing would get them through the gorse bush, so he tied them off to the branches before pushing the gap open and making his way through. He knew by the way his two companions were standing that they were not alone; Gadoric had him fixed with his single eye and he rattled off the warning in his heathen tongue, not that it did any good. The two spears were pressing gently against his side before the man had finished and hands removed his own spear, his bow and quiver, his sword and his knife as he was pushed into the centre of the small clearing.

'Well, this is no slave,' said a voice, speaking Greek, behind him.

Another voice replied. 'Looks like a Roman to me, Tyrtaeus.'

'His name is Aquila. He works for that bastard Flaccus, who took over the Falerian farms two harvests ago.'

'Bit young, Pentheus,' said the first man.

The voice that had spoken his name was full of hate. 'He's old enough to kill women and children.'

Aquila turned slowly; three men, no metal or leather, not soldiers. The man in the middle, the tallest of the three, curly haired with a hooked nose, stood with his sword swinging easily by his side. The others had spears, which were aimed in his direction, not that he feared them; if they decided to kill him it would not be done with a spear.

'Flaccus himself is just down the mountain, with about thirty men.'

'Just down the mountain is too far away to save you, boy,' said the man called Tyrtaeus.

'If Flaccus catches me, I'll suffer a worse fate than he'd mete out to you. I've stolen his horse and weapons, killed at least one of his men, but worse than that, I've shamed him before Cassius Barbinus.'

Pentheus sucked in deeply at the mention of that name as Tyrtaeus looked past him to Gadoric and Hypolitas. 'These men say they've escaped and looking at them it's easy to believe, but you, well fed and well armed?'

'These men would not have escaped if I hadn't helped them. By now they'd be strung up on a cross of wood.'

'Why did you help them?' demanded Pentheus. He was a sallow-faced individual, with prematurely grey hair and a pair of large brown eyes with dark rings underneath. It was plain by his look that he found the idea preposterous.

'He helped me,' said Gadoric.

The explanation that followed was disjointed and, by the look on Tyrtaeus's face, totally unsatisfactory. Gadoric was still weak and he had poor Greek. Hypolitas, when asked, could at least reply clearly, but he did not know Aquila at all, so he could only confirm that the boy had, indeed, helped them both to escape.

'A neat way to trap us, perhaps,' said Tyrtaeus. 'Free a couple of slaves, make your way into the mountains and hope to find some more. You say that Flaccus is chasing you. Perhaps he's following you instead.'

'Then why would I kill his men?'

'We only have your word for that,' Pentheus hissed. The spear dropped slightly as he addressed his words to Tyrtaeus, who was obviously the leader. 'I tell you I know him. You would too, if you'd ever seen that hair on his head, let alone the thing on his neck. I remember when they first arrived. He was like a son to that Flaccus, rode everywhere with him while the mercenaries brought from the mainland did the dirty work, flaunting that gold eagle and a well-fed body while women and children starved.'

Tyrtaeus looked at Aquila enquiringly and the

boy held his gaze, forming the words in his mind that he would need to save himself. Phoebe had only taught him a small amount of Greek, which did not extend to explaining the impression he had: that part of Pentheus's anger was probably compounded of jealousy as much as hardship and the way he looked at the eagle talisman was clearly suffused with greed.

'He speaks the truth. I was close to Flaccus, for reasons that it would be of little use to explain.' He raised his hand towards Gadoric, still struggling to follow the conversation. 'But I was closer to this man, who helped to raise me after my father went off to war. When I saw him tied to a stake, and heard what his fate would be, I could not leave him to die.'

Pentheus jabbed his spear into Aquila's stomach. 'Don't trust him, Tyrtaeus. Let me kill him.'

'I don't trust him,' replied the taller man, 'but neither will I behave like our late masters and condemn him out of hand.'

'I'm in a poor position to offer advice, but Flaccus and his men are headed this way, following our trail. All I have done is make him cautious, which will slow him down, but he'll be here before nightfall. Either you have enough men to stand here and fight him, or you too have to flee.'

'How many men we have is our business. Tie him up, Pentheus.'

The ex-slave grinned, dropped his spear and

dashed to obey. Tyrtaeus walked over and addressed the other two, his hand indicating the marks of fresh wounds. 'You are welcome, whatever else. Your scars are like the insignia of our tribe.'

'I'll take care of you myself,' whispered Pentheus, pulling the rope that held Aquila's arms tight. Then he grabbed the eagle on the chain, and jerked Aquila's head forward until their noses were nearly touching. 'I lost a woman and two children to your lot. I've dreamt of killing Flaccus ever since, but you'll do in his place. One thing I promise you, and that is a slow death.'

Tyrtaeus walked back, his arms through those of Gadoric and Hypolitas. 'Pentheus, help these two fellows onto the horses.'

'And him?'

'He's well fed. The bastard can walk.'

Marcellus read the despatch while his father watched him. They had become more like equals now; not that Lucius had mellowed, it was just that his son was becoming too mature to be treated as a schoolboy.

'My first impression is that Silvanus is exaggerating.' Lucius nodded, as Marcellus continued. 'Obviously he has to pay for calling out his auxiliaries, but sending troops to Sicily would be a burden on the state. How venal is he?'

'I daresay he'll make a goodly sum out of his governorship, but I doubt that it will be excessive.'

'What would be excessive?'

'Two million sesterces per annum. Half of that is about what the governorship should be worth.'

'How can we tell what he is making?'

'By the cries of the islanders. If he was milking them we would have an endless stream of complaints.'

'So there is the possibility that this request is prompted by genuine fears, rather than any dent it might make in his purse?'

'Runaway slaves are not unknown,' said Lucius.

Marcellus lifted the scroll and waved it. 'Which is just what this is, a few hundred slaves got into the hills, and they must steal grain and livestock to survive. It's banditry. I think he'll find he has quite enough men for this sweep through the mountains he's planned.'

Lucius smiled and nodded his agreement. 'I would have had serious doubts about putting the idea up to the Senate anyway. They're never keen on spending public money, so the idea of sending soldiers to Sicily would not be well received.'

Marcellus put the scroll down on Lucius's desk. 'Am I free to go now?'

'Yes, but take the scroll to my steward. This is the second despatch Silvanus has sent us on the same topic. I want it taken round to the house of Quintus

Cornelius. Let us see what opinion he has.'

'Would it not be easier just to tell him what you think?'

Lucius gave his son a sharp shake of the head. 'This was sent to the consuls, so it will require a debate and he will be proposing the response to the house. Let him make up his own mind.'

Marcellus made his way through the house, for even after this session with his father, he was still smarting from the way Valeria had humiliated him. The look he had received on making his delayed entrance, washed and dressed, was full of hauteur. Gnaeus Calvinus, still in his dirt-streaked smock, had benefited, though there was some doubt as to his level of appreciation. From what Marcellus knew, he did not even like girls, yet she had treated him like a heroic suitor and all for the purpose of annoying him. It rankled even more that Gnaeus had entered into the spirit of things, playing up to Valeria and even surpassing her in his flights of poetic hyperbole. All his friend's gentility had evaporated as they challenged each other, in rhyming couplets, to ever increasing degrees of bloodthirstiness. He vowed that he was finished with her games; never again would he allow her actions to make him jealous.

The room was dark, which was the way he liked it; he did not want to see Sosia at all. She was there, of course, as usual and the cot creaked as he knelt over her. The cool skin he touched was, in his mind, Roman skin, the hair the same as he pulled her head off the bed. The lips, even the resistance was the repugnance of a high-born lady, but she succumbed as he thrust his hips forward, and, in his mind, the insistent teasing voice was still.

CHAPTER SEVENTEEN

The runaway slaves might know the mountains that provided their refuge, but seemed sadly lacking in the skills necessary to evade a pursuit. The trail they were leaving, given their number, was so obvious it bordered on the ridiculous and the few tentative suggestions their prisoner made were cut off by the sallow-complexioned Pentheus with the butt of his spear. Aquila, trying to find out as much about his captors as he could, probed guardedly, aware that any direct question addressed to the leader, Tyrtaeus, would not be answered. But as they stumbled along the rocky mountain trails, he had time for an oblique approach, so he quickly established that this trio had nothing to do with the recent attack on him and Flaccus. From that, and other hints, he deduced that the slaves were in fragmented groups; they were not the organised bandit force that Barbinus imagined.

The party stopped as the sun went down and, permitted to rest alongside Gadoric, he was able to explain all that had happened since they had last met. He also enlisted his support, knowing that he had to persuade his captors that, if they continued in a like manner, Flaccus would catch them the next day and they would all die, so Gadoric called Tyrtaeus over and Pentheus followed. The moon made the latter's hair look silver, like the head of some benign old man, an impression quickly erased by the harsh voice.

'He stays tied. I don't care what anyone says!' These words were accompanied by a glare aimed at Tyrtaeus.

It was Gadoric who replied. 'He doesn't need to be untied. All I ask is that you follow the advice he and I give you.'

Tyrtaeus scratched thoughtfully at his hooked nose. He must have guessed that Gadoric, in his weak state, would leave everything to Aquila. Pentheus certainly seemed to, being quick to shake his head in disapproval. The leader examined the boy closely, struck by the maturity and assurance so evident in one so young.

'May I be allowed a question?' said Aquila. Pentheus shook his head again, but Tyrtaeus nodded. 'I would guess that, normally, soldiers never bother to pursue you very far into the mountains.' Another sharp nod. 'I mean no disrespect when I say that they don't think you're worth it. What are a few slaves, scratching an existence in the hills, to men who have so many?'

'One day we'll show them,' snapped Pentheus, jabbing the spear.

'Some have already. They've started attacking the outlying farms and either stealing or destroying crops. The governor and the owners are preparing a sweep through the mountains, in strength, to catch them.'

'We have done none of these things!' said the Greek. Aquila indicated the sacks of grain they had been carrying and Tyrtaeus answered the implied question. 'A pittance and always taken far from our base.'

Aquila smiled. 'That won't save you. Not that it will make any difference. At this pace, Flaccus will catch us all tomorrow.'

'He'll give up,' said Pentheus.

'He's not chasing you, idiot. He's chasing me.'

It was Pentheus's turn to smile. 'Then why don't we just tie you to a tree so that he can find you?'

'No!'

Gadoric pulled himself upright with some difficulty, his single eye flashing in anger. Tyrtaeus looked long and hard at both Gadoric and Aquila. He could leave them all, given it was the progress of these sick men that slowed them down, but no runaway slave could do other than help a fellow-escapee and in a clear recognition of Aquila's altered status he addressed his question to him.

'What do you suggest?'

The boy did not hesitate; for all his lack of years he knew exactly what he thought they should do. 'First, we can't afford to stop for the night. We must carry on.'

'Your friends aren't up to it.'

Aquila shrugged. 'They'll just have to be. None of us will survive if we don't.'

Tyrtaeus did not reply for quite some time, while everyone stood still waiting on his decision. 'Untie him, Pentheus.' The younger man opened his mouth to protest but he did not get the chance to speak. 'Do it!'

The night seemed endless as they slid and slithered through the mountains, partly in clear moonlight, but more often in pitch darkness. Aquila used all the skills that Gadoric had taught him, laying false trails to frustrate Flaccus and his soldiers, while obscuring their real destination by the use of a leafy branch, tied to the rear horse, when they took to the paths. They kept moving throughout the whole of the next day, with Tyrtaeus giving Aquila general hints of the direction they needed to go. The boy was not fooled, knowing that his guide was taking them in a wide arc, avoiding their true destination until he was more sure of his companions.

To the south, now that they were high enough, the smoking volcano of Mount Etna acted as a fulcrum for their route, appearing every time they entered an area clear of trees. There were constant diversions into the forests as they cut through from one trail to the next and every stretch of water and every rock or scree-covered slope was put to use. After two days, Aquila and Tyrtaeus, dropping back to check the progress of the pursuit while the others rested, could report that Flaccus had given up and turned back towards Messana.

Tyrtaeus finally set them on a straight course and Aquila, using the most prominent peaks and the position of the sun to fix his location, knew that after a slight trek to the west, they had turned north into the range of hills that abutted Flaccus's inland farm. He also knew, since he was told so often, that Pentheus had escaped from there, the place where he had toiled with his family, before the arrival of Flaccus and his murderous new regime. Revenge for what had happened then consumed the man as he harped on about the fate of his loved ones. The words made Aquila think of Phoebe, so gentle and kind, and of the rest of Flaccus's mercenaries, who were anything but. He missed her more than he did them, yet he had lived with those men for nearly two years, eaten with them, drunk with them and been trained to fight by them. They were cruel but so was the world and for all Pentheus's litany of the abuses visited upon the slaves, Aquila could not bring himself to condemn them.

The last few days had been harder on Hypolitas than Gadoric, who was a much tougher physical specimen. Hypolitas had spent the last three days lashed to the saddle, his face becoming more and more grey. He was too exhausted to show any relief when they finally arrived at Tyrtaeus's little settlement, six badly constructed wicker huts alongside a stream in a barren upland valley which made Aquila look around in wonder. The soil was rocky and shallow, hard to plough and near impossible to grow food on, and the grass was sparse, providing indifferent pasture. No wonder they had to steal grain. How did people survive in such a place, especially in winter? When he saw the inhabitants, emaciated men, scrawny women and bow-legged children, he knew that they could not.

The three newcomers were put in the most dilapidated hut, which had apparently belonged to a runaway who had failed to survive in this harsh landscape. Aquila tended to the two men and, given back his weapons, with permission to seek food, he was able to increase the diet of the entire settlement. Gadoric mended quickly and was soon able to join him, and as they hunted, they talked. The Celt showed no surprise when the boy told him that Clodius and Fulmina were not his real parents, while the eagle round his neck fascinated him. He questioned Aquila closely, and seemed frustrated by the younger man's inability to shed any light on its provenance, frequently taking it in the palm of his hand to examine it minutely.

'There was a time when every charm had a special meaning, a story of its own. But this!'

'That had a meaning,' said Aquila, sadly.

He was thinking of the day he had first set eyes on it. The Celt nodded, his look grim, and he too remembered Minca as he turned the charm over. Gadoric was a superstitious soul, convinced that he could feel a strange power emanating from the object in his hands. Aquila had felt that too, ever since the first time he had worn it, but it was something he was reluctant to admit, even to someone so close. That would mean explaining Fulmina's dreams, as well as the old crone Drisia's prophecies. It was not that Gadoric would laugh at him for giving credence to such tales, quite the opposite; the Celt would believe every word he said, but his young friend did not want to speculate about the nature of dreams and fortune-telling. He had done too much of that already. If Gadoric could have given him some kind of answer, some clue, perhaps where it had come from, that would have helped. It was clearly of Celtic origin and obviously related to his true parentage, but Gadoric could not help, so Aquila took it back and placed it round his neck, deciding that a change of subject was to be welcomed.

'You've never really told me how you came to be lashed to that stake?'

Gadoric was good at telling stories, and this one was no exception. Working with Hypolitas, he had tried to engineer a mass escape, after two years of surviving, half-starved and regularly whipped, on the loading wharves of Messana. He and the other ringleaders had been betrayed. Hypolitas, the only other survivor, and by Gadoric's testimony the moving spirit behind the attempt, was an ex-household slave, adept at magic, who had so displeased his master that the man had sent him to the wharves instead of selling him.

'You've no idea how brave that fellow is,' said Gadoric. 'Or how he can inspire men. I've spent half my life as a fighting man. Hypolitas has never raised a sword in his life, yet there was never any doubt who the others would follow. He has the gift and he can find the words that touch a man's heart and move him to great deeds.'

'We're going to have to move soon.' Aquila had said this so often that he could not keep the note of petulance out of his voice.

'A few more days could make all the difference.'

Gadoric was speaking of the health of Hypolitas; Aquila was thinking of the governor and his militia, of a still enraged Flaccus and his men, sweeping through these very hills. The note of petulance turned to one of anger. 'Very true. They could see us all dead.'

'They won't have moved so quickly,' said Gadoric dismissively.

Aquila frowned, well aware of one thing: only Gadoric stood any chance of persuading Tyrtaeus to abandon his huts and move to the south. Anything he proposed would be derided by Pentheus.

'There are women and children here. If we're shepherding them they don't have to move too quickly to catch us.'

Gadoric hauled the horse's head round to face the boy. 'What if I say we should stay and fight?'

Aquila looked meaningfully back towards the settlement, even though it was well out of sight. 'I'd reply that your ordeal has turned your wits.'

'It's not just us, Aquila. There are other runaways in these mountains. If we could gather them all together...'

'Is this Hypolitas's idea too?'

Gadoric smiled as he nodded slowly. 'You always did have a brain, but think on this. If we run away, what do we gain? Tyrtaeus and his dependants swap one barren valley for another. They're not hunters or fighters and this soil won't support them. In time they'll either die or be forced to give themselves up. Us, do we settle down and try to farm this landscape? I'm no farmer, nor is Hypolitas and what about you?'

'If we could get back to the mainland…'

It was a thought Aquila had been nursing ever since they had arrived, one that he had kept to himself until now. Regardless of what little remained there, it represented home.

'Perhaps you could do that. I have no desire to set foot in Italy ever again.'

'There are other places, Gadoric.'

'What do I do? Present myself, a branded slave, to some ship's captain and request passage?' They both knew that for a runaway slave, that was no option. He would be lucky to be put back to work in the fields, a death at the oar of a galley being the more likely fate. The ex-shepherd continued earnestly. 'Aquila, you are a free-born Roman. I was free-born once and so was Hypolitas. We want to be free again.'

Aquila opened his mouth to speak, but there were no words to say, so he dropped his chin onto his chest in an embarrassed silence. Gadoric could never be free in Roman territory, unless Barbinus gave it to him, plainly an impossible prospect. He knew the older man was looking at him with that one bright blue eye, as if waiting for him to draw an obvious conclusion.

'There is a way, boy,' he said encouragingly.

'Against Rome?'

'Talk to Hypolitas. He has the power to see into the future. Last night, as we talked, he told me of his vision. Of a slave army to make Rome tremble...'

Aquila did not know what made him grab his charm as he answered, but he did, and somehow it gave him the confidence he needed to contest such a wild claim. 'You trust visions?'

'With my life,' replied Gadoric, unaware that the boy was also addressing the question to himself. His face registered a slight degree of shock that anyone should even suggest the opposite. 'How else would the Gods talk to us?'

'Do they talk to us?'

'The day you came upon us, Aquila, tied to those stakes, Hypolitas said that you would come.'

The grip on the charm tightened. 'Me?'

'Not you, but he spoke of rescue. I thought it to be the words of a man in despair, yet before the sun went down, I looked up to see you. After such a thing, how can I doubt him?'

'You may be right, Gadoric. Perhaps the Gods do speak to us, only I wonder if they always tell the truth.'

'They talk in riddles, Aquila, but men like Hypolitas can see the true meaning.'

'Always?'

Gadoric smiled. 'Not always, otherwise he would have known we were to be betrayed.'

'And if he's wrong again?'

'He will tell you what I would. That for us, it is better to die than be a slave.'

'If you fight Rome you will most certainly die.'

Gadoric laughed, just as he used to when they had hunted in the woods together at home. 'We might win.'

Aquila threw back his head and laughed too, but his was not the laughter of mirth, more a hoot of derision. 'I was right, your ordeal has turned your wits.'

There was something about Hypolitas that made disagreement near-impossible. It was easy, out of his presence, to say he was a dreamer and quite possibly, with his spells and potions, a charlatan, but once he started talking he reduced everything to such simple ideas that the difficulties inherent in the solution seemed diminished as well.

'There are ten times as many slaves on the island as Romans.'

'The locals,' said Tyrtaeus.

'Hate them as much as we do!'

Aquila cut in. 'They won't fight Rome. They can't!'

'We don't want them to fight. We want them to stand aside.'

The voice was low and compelling, the eyes large and unblinking. His head was bald through nature, not because, as Aquila first supposed, he had been shaved. The large nose and prominent chin dominated the elongated face and his hands, with long bony fingers, never still, seemed to weave a spell as he talked. Aquila had discovered that he hailed from Palmyra in Syria, without having the faintest notion of where the place was.

'These hills are full of men, all runaways and all in small groups, easily destroyed. I have looked into the future. I see them combined.'

'With or without arms?'

Hypolitas ignored Aquila's sceptical tone. 'They can be made, or even better, stolen and these men trained to use them. Likewise food to sustain them. The farms are full of it and instead of sitting still waiting to be attacked piecemeal, what if we take the offensive?' The fingers darted about as though the entire island was set out on the hard-packed earth of the hut. 'First here, then there, striking by day and night, never still, always on the move from one side of the mountains to the other, with every slave we free another soldier in the fight.'

'Rome won't sit still,' said Aquila, leaning forward to make his point. 'You'll face an army one day.'

The eyes gleamed, the fingers joined together in front of them. 'We will be an army one day.'

His hand shot out, catching hold of the golden eagle that swung loose. 'There is power here, I can feel it. Perhaps one day, Aquila, I will ask the spirits to tell me where this came from, for I can see the past as well as the future.'

'You believe he's mad?' Aquila nodded, as Gadoric put his hand on the boy's shoulder. 'Yet you will go along with him.'

'You say you have no future, Gadoric, only that of a slave. Neither have I. I'm not a free-born Roman any more. I was outside the law from the day I freed you.'

'So you will join Hypolitas and me?'

Aquila turned and faced his friend, his heart heavy. 'There is one thing I must say to you, something you must pass on to Hypolitas. You cannot win, but I will join you, even if I am a Roman.'

'The reason?'

He had thought long and hard, feeling for the first time like a fully grown man who had to make his own decisions. The process and the conclusion were equally uncomfortable and he knew the words he wanted to say, just as he knew he would never say them. How could he tell Gadoric he loved him; that he was the only family he had. For all he had discovered and witnessed he could not condemn Flaccus and his mercenaries, nor Rome. He looked at Gadoric closely. The Celt probably thought his sole interest was a hope that Hypolitas spoke the truth; that he could, with his spells and incantations, see into the past as well as the future; that one day, he would put Aquila on the path to finding his true parents.

Then there was Phoebe, still a slave and in the hands of a man who had become his enemy. He could not admit that he missed her company, feeling that his friend would laugh at him. Deep down, he knew it had something to do with his own destiny, without being absolutely sure what that destiny was. Those words he could not say, even if Gadoric, with his faith in the Gods, would swallow it whole, so he gave an answer that would satisfy the Celt without enlightening him.

'Ever since you first taught me to cast a spear, it seems everything I've done has been designed to train me for war.' He looked straight into the single, blue, unblinking eye. 'Would you believe me when I say that I cannot resist a fight?'

CHAPTER EIGHTEEN

———◆———

Flaccus, when he woke, was still very drunk; he had been since his return from Messana, able to recall every word of the bawling out he had received, a tongue-lashing his employer had chosen to deliver before the entire group of overseers, so adding humiliation to the brew. No one had addressed him like that since he was a common ranker and because Barbinus had it in his power to dismiss him from this farm, to throw him back to a life of relative privation, he had had to stand still and swallow it whole. His grovelling apology, plus his vow to kill Aquila, had stemmed the tide of abuse as well as removing the threat to his prosperity.

The retching sound outside his window made him even angrier, realising it had been that noise which had woken him. The old centurion pulled himself off his cot and staggered to the window, yelling abuse at the culprit. As his head came out into the cool morning air, Phoebe spun round to look at him, her hand automatically going to her lips to wipe off the last of her vomit. To Flaccus, her face was like a red rag to a bull.

'You,' he growled.

'I'm sorry, master,' replied Phoebe quickly. The girl had done everything in her power to stay out of the way since Flaccus had returned alone. She was unsure what had happened, but since he had sent all his mercenaries out, yelling orders at them to find and kill her man, there was little doubt that Aquila would not be coming back. She tried to walk away, but a sharp word from Flaccus halted her.

'Get in here, girl. I want a word with you.'

He was talking to himself when she entered his room, growling under his breath about betrayal, his hand rubbing furiously at his groin. Phoebe stood before him, meekly, hoping by her attitude to dent his temper. That failed; Flaccus suddenly shot out a hand and grabbed her hair and she squealed painfully as he pulled on it, forcing her to her knees, then bending her head back so that she was forced to look up at him.

'Do you know what that boy has done, girl, do you?' His breath stank of sour wine and his spit was cold by the time it landed on her face. 'He's betrayed me, that's what. Betrayed the man who saved him.'

'Please?'

The weak, plaintive word did nothing to calm Flaccus. If anything it inflamed him. 'Please, girl. That's what you did. You pleasured the ungrateful brat at my expense and he was soft on you, too.'

Flaccus pulled her head into his groin, forcing her face against his sweaty leather small clothes. 'There's a price to pay girl and since your hero ain't here to cough up, maybe you'll have to do so in his place. Happen I should get my lads to take it out on you, mount you till you bleed. Then maybe young Aquila will ride in to the rescue.'

Having pulled down his breeches, the overseer was pulling her head back and forth across his groin, but he had been drinking for days, and no amount of concentration, or vivid imaginings, could help him. Even if she had been willing, the effect of the wine robbed him of the ability to do what he wanted and take out his anger on this young girl's body. Suddenly he stopped, as he remembered that she had woken him by being sick outside his window and he pulled her head back again, so he could see her tear-stained face.

'You're expectin', ain't you?' Flaccus still had a tight grip on her hair, so she nodded with some difficulty. 'Must be Aquila's. You ain't been near anyone else for months now.'

The terror in the girl's eyes made him laugh, a horrible sound that made her start to shake with fear, but he stopped laughing. In Flaccus's drunken imagination, he was back in that mountain ravine with an arrow aimed right at his heart. Aquila could have, and should have, killed him. The old centurion was well aware how good he was, had seen him take Toger with a spear. He knew that had the boy fired right away he could not have missed, but Aquila had hesitated, then aimed for someone else, deliberately sparing Flaccus's life.

'It's hard to kill someone like that,' he muttered, gazing out of the window at the sky, releasing the girl's hair as he spoke, so she fell in a heap at his feet. Phoebe said nothing, not knowing what he was talking about. 'The Gods could blight a man for such an act.'

Flaccus looked down at her again. 'I must kill him, girl. He made me look a fool, but I can spare his brat, trade one life for another, which will appease the Gods.'

Phoebe did not give Flaccus a chance to change his mind; she left as soon as she had gathered her few possessions together, clutching the old centurion's instructions to the slave vendor in Messana to take her as a trade-in for a pair of field hands. Flaccus watched her go, then emptied the contents of his goblet, which had stood by his side throughout the night, onto the black earth.

'No more time for drinking,' he said to himself. 'There's money to be earned.'

Aquila and Gadoric spent the next two weeks in the saddle, as they searched the mountains for runaway slaves. They met many who heeded their warning to flee, but found very few willing to stand and fight, lacking the persuasive quality that allowed Hypolitas to excite such people's imagination. It was he, still quite a sick man, who proposed the solution. Instead of asking them to stand and fight, he requested that they make their way to a high valley near the northern slopes of the smoking volcano of Mount Etna, there to sit and listen. If he could persuade them they would stay; if not then they would have ample time to move out of the way of the advancing Roman reprisals.

Then, despite Gadoric's pleas to the contrary, he announced that he must leave the camp. Hypolitas insisted on mounting the horse himself with the same determination he had displayed when he told them he needed to go into the hills on his own, putting aside all suggestions that anyone should accompany him, promising to be away for no more than two days, and requesting from Tyrtaeus that he strike the camp and be ready to move as soon as he returned.

'I must be alone. Only then can I call upon the spirits of the dead to show me the way.' These words were accompanied by a glare that made even the most stalwart man present tremble with fear. 'There is too much doubt here to see clearly, but alone, under the stars, I know that I will hear from the Gods. They will say what must be done.'

All watched anxiously as his retreating frame swayed in the saddle and at least one pair of eyes stayed fixed on that spot for the next two days, until, with the sun going down, Hypolitas, even more emaciated but with a firmer gait than that with which he had left, rode back into the camp.

'The omens are good,' he said, as they all gathered round him. 'The Gods have given me a clear message. It will be hard and not without loss, but if we have faith, then we can prosper.'

Those who had accepted the invitation and congregated around Mount Etna must have wondered if the smell of sulphur, which filled the air, presaged a horrible death. Not everyone had come, indeed the number totalled less than a third of those Gadoric and Aquila had asked, yet the Greek, brought to the spot on a litter, was quite changed by the sight of this ragbag assembly. He rose to speak, pushing aside any attempts to support him, seeming to gather strength from the mere act of addressing a crowd. As he walked behind the fire, lit as a beacon, but now no more than smouldering embers, he raised his arms and all present immediately fell silent.

'Fellow-slaves,' he shouted. His voice, with an odd hollow quality, echoed off the surrounding hills. 'Look at us, dressed in rags and half starved. I wonder how much you would laugh at me, if I named you heroes to rival Heracles.'

They did laugh at this, an association with the most potent warrior name amongst the Greek gods, nervously at first, then louder, with much digging of ribs to stimulate their mirth, until the sound filled this makeshift arena. Hypolitas let them indulge their humour, which worked just as well to calm their nerves, before raising his arms again to command silence.

'Yet you have laboured, just as Heracles laboured. You have fought a monster greater than ever he faced. You have triumphed where great kings have failed.' The voice dropped, till in its deep timbre it seemed to rival the grumbling volcano. 'You have defied the might of Rome.'

This statement was followed by a bemused murmur. 'You doubt that, do you not friends? Yet you are sitting here, in these hills, nearly free from the yoke that Rome has placed about your neck.' He paused to let those words sink in, before raising one cautionary hand. 'You will observe that I say "nearly".'

His voice was husky, a compelling quality that made them attend his words as he talked of the lands they had left, of the battles many had fought, the defeats suffered and the low estate to which such conflicts had reduced them. The hands moved slowly, combining with the cracked and deep voice, to lure them into the web of hope he was weaving. Aquila had heard him speak before and had been impressed despite himself, but never had Hypolitas spoken like this. He turned to look at Gadoric; the Celt's chin was up, his head held proudly and the single eye gleaming with anticipation. The other men and women in the crowd were the same. Hypolitas moved them to tears as he outlined his own fate, the loss of his own family, a tale with which they could identify, it being so very like their own. Then the voice changed abruptly. It was full of anger as the slave from Palmyra catalogued the crimes of the Roman state, which had left them in the hands of men who cared nothing for their well-being, even less for their happiness.

'They have their profits, these senators in Rome, and that allows them to remain blind. They have eyes to see, but few come to look. Let every man and woman on this island die, rather than dent their increasing wealth, yet these are men who have conquered half the known world and carried off its treasure. A state that wants for nothing will kill us all in back-breaking toil to have even more.'

The voice changed again, rising even higher now, and as if to give credence to his words the volcano started to rumble. Hypolitas, now in a glassy-eyed trance, seemed able to time his words to the sounds of the mountain, each conclusion he elaborated accompanied by an underground response.

'And who has had the courage to defy them? Not the kings and their armies. Us! Ragged-arsed slaves who have dared to say enough!'

He pointed at the volcano in the background, his arms open to embrace his audience. 'Listen friends, for the Gods are speaking to us. We have made a stand by our escape, but that is not enough, that is what the mountain is saying. What farm numbers in guards the men we have assembled here?'

There was a loud crack and a huge cloud of sulphurous smoke shot out of the volcano as Etna belched. Hypolitas threw out his hand, his voice matching the roar. 'That is the sound of war, of the Gods telling us to take what is ours, the food we grow and the land we plough. The Gods command us to combine, to attack the farms one by one and free our fellow-sufferers.' The voice dropped to a whisper, which made his enraptured audience lean forward to hear his words. 'I went into the wilderness, alone, to talk to the spirits. I had a vision, friends, and I saw fire.'

Hypolitas seemed to suck in his cheeks. He raised his hands and clapped them before his mouth. A stream of flame shot from his mouth, forming an arc between him and the glowing embers. Those closest to him fell on their faces, frightened to look upon such magic. The orator clapped his hands before his mouth again and the flame died.

'I saw in my dream that we, not in rags, but well

fed and clothed, would treat with Rome as equals. We would live in villas with servants to attend our needs. Slaves, in numbers enough to make the legions tremble, mightily armed, would make the conqueror relent.' He paused, holding them. Etna cracked again and Hypolitas really shouted for the first time, surprising everyone with the carrying power of the voice. 'I will obey the Gods as I will obey my vision. I will defy the might of Rome and I will make them treat with us. Who will join me?'

A split second elapsed before the whole semi-circle of slaves erupted in a resounding cheer. Those few with spears waved them in the air, yelling war cries, and Etna rumbled mightily again as if to spur them on.

Through Gadoric's intervention, the mood of euphoria was short-lived and good sense prevailed. Invited by the Greek to lead the cheering slaves into battle, he immediately poured a douche of cold water on the prevailing excitement. They could not fight the Romans as they were, so Hypolitas was reluctantly persuaded to move south of Etna until the sweep through the mountains had passed.

'You are not accustomed to war, Hypolitas. If we stand here we will be massacred. The Romans will use trained men, which we are not.'

It was clear, by the look on the man's face, that the Celt had, by his reference to Hypolitas's lack of military skill, angered him. Others, impressed by his sorcery or because they saw where the true power lay, were willing to tell him otherwise, but publicly, Hypolitas had acknowledged Gadoric as his military commander. He would be content, as he said, to study the art until he too was proficient in war.

Flaccus knew, after they found the third abandoned settlement, that the quarry had flown but he said nothing to the commander, since to do so would only bring more trouble down upon his head. Aquila had been present when Barbinus had outlined the plan for the sweep through the mountains and clearly the slaves had heeded his warning, and got away before the governor, Silvanus, at the head of his militia, backed up by every bailiff in northern Sicily, had set out on what was now a fruitless campaign. Barbinus had left before the raid commenced, to go back to Rome, determined to vote in the forthcoming consular elections, attend the Aedile games and keen to assure the Senate that, despite the worries of that old woman Silvanus, everything in this Roman province was under control.

The games he attended on his return were the talk of Rome for years to come. Quintus Cornelius had contracted for some unusual animals before the Parthians offered him theirs, so he had an overabundance of events to place before his audience, so many that the day might end before the entertainment. His planning was meticulous for he knew that the excitement of the occasion must build to a crescendo, which would occur when all of his important guests were present. These included the Parthian ambassadors, the reigning consuls, and the two consuls-elect. Recently voted in, Servius Caepio and Livius Rutulius would take office at the beginning of the year.

Rutulius was already badgering Lucius Falerius for permission to take a consular legion to Spain, boasting loudly that he would bring the frontier war to an end and present the Senate with the head of the troublesome Brennos on a silver salver. Servius Caepio, less bellicose, would smile ruefully and remind Rutulius, his junior colleague, that nothing could happen without his agreement and that until they knew the thinking of the Senate, no decision could be made. Rutulius was not fooled by that; he knew who had power and who was weak and had been lobbying both Lucius and Quintus with great vigour.

The priests sacrificed before the noisy multitude, announcing the day auspicious, and Lucius, in his capacity as president, declared the games open. The programme commenced with some old favourites – dogs hunting stags and bears – before moving on to one that always pleased the crowd: a bull and a bear chained together, condemned to fight until one was dead. The bull had only sharpened horns as weapons, while the bear, which could not move more than a few feet from those dangerous points, needed brute strength enough to snap the muscular neck if it was to survive. Being animals that rarely fought each other there was always a hiatus while the pair adjusted to the unfamiliar dangers.

Their minders had to prod them, opening up painful wounds, and these, angering the beasts, left them no alternative but to take out their rage on each other. The bull gored the bear twice, producing a sound halfway between a scream and a roar, before the black-furred creature finally realised its plight. Raising itself onto its hind legs, the great paws took hold of the horns, holding them with such strength that the bull could not move its neck, then the ursine beast set about trying to tear out the bull's eyes with its teeth. The roar of the crowd drowned out the horrendous bellowing this produced, a sound which rose to a deafening level when one of the eyes was removed, along with half the animal's face.

Young, lean and strong, maddened by the pain, the bull spun with such power that it dislodged the bear's grip. There was little room to use its hooves but it managed a kick of enough force to break its attacker's lower leg. Unable to stay upright on one leg, the bear dropped down, but it kept its grip on those horns, dragging the bull after it. That act, set against the efforts of the bull to stay upright, twisted and broke its neck. Suddenly, far from straining against the mighty pull, the bull went limp. The bear, still hauling hard, fell backwards, and the dead creature followed it down, one of the sharpened horns slicing through the bear's chest as they hit the blood-stained sand. The animal went into a frenzy, as it tried to dislodge the weight now crushing its body, but such an action only served to end its life, as the horns of the bull did in death what they had so singularly failed to achieve while the animal was alive.

'What a result, Quintus,' shouted Lucius Falerius, struggling to make himself heard over the delighted crowd. 'The priests did not lie. Your games would be remembered for that alone, even if they ended now. I've never seen the like.'

The audience shared his opinion and all present stood to applaud the podium. Marcellus and Titus, favoured guests, stepped forward to congratulate him. Lucius, as president, acknowledged the cheers of the crowd, but he was careful to ensure that his hand pointed towards Quintus Cornelius, so that the true author of this remarkable occurrence could take the credit. Even the Parthian ambassadors stood to applaud and they, splendidly attired as always, excited the crowd even more. From then on it was as though he was blessed with the power of *Jove* himself.

The elephant, set to fight four lions, was as brave as a creature of that species could be, not content to stay on the defensive, but determined to attack its opponents. It charged around the arena, bellowing mightily, taking one beast that allowed itself to be caught against the fencing, and having gored it, expertly, with one metal-tipped tusk, it used its trunk to toss it into the crowd. The packed audience parted as if by magic and the fatally wounded creature landed in an open space, writhing and roaring, its back clearly snapped. Careful to stay away from the still potent jaws, the mob set about it with anything that came to hand, beating at its body till it lay still. Meanwhile, inside the arena, the other lions had attacked. The elephant now had one hanging on to its swinging trunk, while another clung precariously to its back, claws dug into the grey flesh, trying to bite through the thick skin of the neck to achieve a kill. The third lion, circling on the ground, was foolish enough to wander too close and died, crushed like a gnat, under the elephant's great feet.

The beast swung its trunk, desperately trying to dislodge the lion that, snarling and ripping, was intent on tearing it off, finally showing it had a brain. The elephant suddenly charged the barrier, swinging so that the animal was forced against the wooden palisade, and then it just leant sideways. The crushing of the bones was audible above the screaming din of crowd approval, and was accompanied by a great fount of blood as the lion was flattened. The elephant's final opponent was still on its back, great fangs tearing chunks out of the thick grey folds, exposing the flesh and bone underneath. Primitive instinct told the starving lion that survival lay at the point where the elephant's head was joined to its body; break the slender bone that held them conjoined, and the great beast would collapse to the ground, easy prey to further assault.

Suddenly the elephant went over, like a falling tree, and the whole structure of the arena shook as it hit the ground. The lion flew twenty feet before it hit the sand and rolled a further ten before it regained its feet. The elephant was seriously wounded, that was certain; the slow way it tried to stand was evidence of that. The lion did not wait; it went for its opponent as soon it could, racing forward to resume the assault on the lacerated neck. As it leapt the last ten feet, the elephant raised and turned its great head, an act done in slow motion, and in anticipation the crowd suddenly went silent. The lion, committed, could do nothing. It tried to twist away but the metal-tipped tusk could not be avoided. It speared itself, the body moving forward with such force that the end of the tusk came shooting out of its back. The elephant, clearly exhausted, did nothing more, merely laying its head on the ground, content to wait until the death throes of its last adversary ceased. Then it struggled to its feet, and with the body of the lion still impaled on its tusk, it stumbled out of the arena to tumultuous applause.

The *hastarii* were on next, to fight all manner of creatures. Lions again, panthers, bears and wolves. For all their expertise, some of these trained animal fighters died, but more of their quarry suffered that fate than they did. This was followed by some light relief as first gazelles, then zebras and finally giraffes were set, pitifully, against various big cats. By the time the Parthian ambassadors' escort entered the arena, raking the sand did little to remove the deep coating of blood with which it was caked. The line of a hundred men took their places at one end of the arena, lined up, shields and weapons at the ready, to await their opponents.

A hush fell over the crowd as they strained forward to observe the arrival of the Roman contingent. Then the horns blew, and the tribune of the *corpus urbanis*, the city's own cohorts, led his men into the arena. Fingers pointed eagerly at various members of the unit. Those who knew the faces could see clearly, even under their helmets, that neither Quintus Cornelius, nor Rome, was prepared to commit inexperienced troops against the Parthians. Men who had stood down from the colours, loaded with decorations, were part of the troop. Many of the city's centurions, wearing rankers' uniforms, had been brought in to fight. Not one of the men was anything less than a *principi*, the senior, most heavily armed and experienced group of legionaries. The tribune marched forward, and raising his short sword, saluted Lucius Falerius.

'I come to receive your instructions, Excellency.'

Lucius had already discussed this with Quintus, adding his own opinion that a fight to the death was unwelcome. He did not doubt that the Romans would win but feared the effect such a result would have on peaceful relations with the eastern empire. He also pointed out how undesirable it would be to have to provide an escort to get these gorgeously attired creatures safely home. Quintus had not demurred at this, saving his opinion until the games were in progress; if they had not gone so well, he would have insisted on a fight to the death to round off the event. After all, he had his reputation to consider.

'Groups of ten, tribune. Kill if you must, spare life if you can. As long as all fight nobly, then your fellow Romans will be satisfied.'

The tribune favoured him with another salute, before turning back to his men. At a shouted command, the first ten stepped forward, to be matched by a similar number of Parthians. Lucius raised his hand, and, allowing the silence that followed to raise the tension, held it there for what seemed an age. Then he dropped it abruptly, gratified to observe that the first Roman javelins were on their way to their targets before his hand was back in his lap. The Parthians returned fire, then rushed forward, but the legionaries stood their ground, locking shields to break the attack. Two men died on their protruding swords.

As soon as the Parthians had lost cohesion, the line broke and several attackers were pushed aside, allowing the Romans to double up on their opponents. They had received and understood their orders; the blades of the short swords stayed unblooded, but the pommels were used unsparingly and clubbed men fell into the dark sand. It was not all one way; a pair of over-confident Romans collapsed, speared by the more alert Parthians, but soon the remainder stood above their foes, eyes turned towards the podium, looking to Lucius for the final decision. He signalled with an upraised thumb and the dead and comatose were dragged out of the arena.

Each subsequent fight followed a similar pattern, with the Parthians only once managing to best the battle-hardened legionaries. Quintus could sense, by the time the last set faced up to each other, that the crowd were getting bored. The level of noise in the arena had diminished at these near-continual Roman victories so he leant forward to whisper in Lucius's ear. His request was clearly ill-received since the older man shook his head furiously.

'He's asking for a fight to the death,' said Titus softly.

'It would end his games on a high note,' replied Marcellus.

'Trouble is, your father has just, very publicly, said no.'

They could not see Quintus's face but the set of his hunched shoulders told them how much that refusal had angered him. The tribune had saved his best men till last and he stepped forward himself, at their head, to confront the last group of Parthian infantry. He too must have sensed that the crowd was less enthusiastic now than hitherto. At a sharp command his men, instead of standing still, rushed forward in a disciplined line, casting their javelins with deadly accuracy. This took their opponents completely by surprise, throwing them into confusion and utterly negating their attempts at defence. Four died on the points of spears, three more were wounded. The last trio fought bravely, but were easily forced to the ground by the superior numbers of their foes. The tribune, his face alight with pleasure, turned to the podium and Quintus again leant forward. This time Lucius's head stayed still as he considered the request. The crowd must have sensed what was afoot, and the noise of their cheering died away. Marcellus was holding his breath too, wondering what his father would do. To deny Quintus, at his own games, might shame him; to accede after his previous public refusal would diminish the older senator.

Lucius turned to the Parthian ambassadors, his hand, outstretched, clearly offering them the decision. This was flattery indeed and the fact that the ambassadors were conscious of this signal honour showed in their delighted expressions. Their leader stood up, bowed to Lucius and raised his hand towards the arena. His thumb stood out sideways from his hand, and being well aware of the drama of the occasion, he held it there for a full minute. Then, to the delight of the crowd, he turned it down. Nothing that had gone before compared with the noise now as the citizens of Rome, hoarse from a long day, raised a last rousing cheer at the sight of their heroes spearing and stabbing the recumbent men they had defeated.

CHAPTER NINETEEN

———◆———

The assassin tried to kill Lucius Falerius Nerva after the sacrifice of the bulls, as the line of senators made their way towards the Forum for the opening session. Servius Caepio, as senior consul, led the procession, with Livius Rutulius one pace behind. Lucius, acknowledged as *Princeps Senatus,* was so close to Rutulius that none could say who had precedence. Marcellus marched alongside, proud of the position his father, through both age and eminence, now held. He noticed the man detach himself from the crowd and he alone saw, given the angle of his approach, that he was not reaching into his toga for a petition but for a weapon. The glint of the long thin shaft of steel acted on the young man long before he knew the intended victim.

He shot forward as the blade swung and time assumed a different, almost stationary dimension, each movement taking an age to complete, each one destined to be clearly etched on the boy's memory. He was too slow by a fraction; his outstretched hand only managed to deflect the blade slightly, yet that saved his father's life. The knife seared across his chest, causing a deep gash and a fountain of red blood, rather than going straight to the heart as intended. Lucius fell backwards, shocked and silent, yet to feel the pain. Out of the corner of his eye, Marcellus saw the other senators back away, registered the bright red stain on his father's whitened toga, but his main focus was still on the assassin, who had turned to face him, swinging the blade round to gut his belly. The boy hit him right-handed, with all the force he could muster, his left hand pushing forward to parry the knife.

It sliced across the fleshy part of his outstretched arm just as Marcellus grasped the wrist that held it. His right hand swung again, a true boxer's punch, smashing the man's nose, which sprayed his blood in all directions. His knees buckled and Marcellus hit him again, this time on the ear as the sounds of panic began to impede upon his senses: the senators crying out for protection, the mob shouting and screaming. The assassin had fallen back towards the crowd, too dense to admit him and allow escape. Marcellus, still hanging on to his wrist, hit him again, but, surprisingly, he arched forward, his mouth opening to emit a high-pitched scream. The young Falerii raised his fist to strike again, feeling the wrist, which he had been struggling to hold, go limp; the knife dropped from his opponent's grasp and stuck upright in the earth. The man's knees gave way and he fell forward on the boy, eyes and mouth wide open, as if in shock, then, too heavy for Marcellus to hold, he crumpled to the ground. The whole crowd could see the short sword which had been rammed upwards into his back, with such force that only the hilt showed.

Lucius had been lifted onto the rostrum, a platform from which he had spoken many times, and he lay now with his eyes shut tight as the lictors rushed around like disturbed geese, counter-manding each other's orders. Quintus Cornelius, who had been a long way behind, pushed his way through the other senators and jumped up on the platform, shouting for order in a parade ground voice, sending one of the lictors off to fetch a surgeon. Then he organised a guard round Lucius, with his brother Titus, who had been standing on the Forum steps, taking command. They pushed the curious onlookers back so that the wounded man could breathe. Marcellus found himself pushed back too and the feet of many men trampled over the body of the dead assassin before Titus pushed his way through to mount guard over that too.

'Marcellus,' he shouted, indicating his

whereabouts to the soldiers who had obeyed his instructions. 'Fetch the senator's son.'

Swords came out of their sheaths, with that rasping sound familiar to anyone who had ever stood near a soldier, and the crowd seemed to melt away as they pushed through to where Marcellus stood, tears in his eyes.

'He's alive!' Titus called out, praying he was right, because the breath the old senator was drawing looked mighty laboured to him. He took Marcellus by the arm and led him towards the rostrum, helping him up and shouting for those surrounding Lucius to stand aside. Blood soaked the front of his father's toga, but the eyes were open, brittle, hard and angry.

'Get me out of here, Marcellus. Am I to be gazed at, in my distress, by the mob?'

Aquila lay on his back, staring at the stars, his fingertips toying with the wings of the eagle charm, as men moved restlessly around him. The fires were low now, merely embers glowing in the dark, but he was too troubled to sleep, going over in his mind the events of the last few weeks and relating them to the dream he had just had, so unusually clear in his mind. He thought back to that day when they had gathered at the base of Mount Etna. He had found Hypolitas's speech as uplifting as the runaway slaves, been equally stunned by the magic fire he produced from his mouth and that feeling had lasted while they remained south of the volcano, probably because he had been too preoccupied to truly examine that with which he had become engaged. Not that things had eased off after the governor's men had gone back to their normal lives; the slaves commenced training for action as soon as they returned north, to hills and mountains now clear of the Roman threat.

The young man, so well trained in the profession of arms, had entered into things in good heart, helping Gadoric to sift out those who had soldiered before, so they, in turn, could take small groups to teach, showing them the very basic skills necessary to be a disciplined fighter. He had stayed away from the leaders at night but he knew that as they sat round their fire, Gadoric, Tyrtaeus and Hypolitas had discussed various targets and that was as it should be; too many voices meant confusion. But he had also heard Pentheus's excited talk of retribution and not thought of the blood that would be spilt, or the mortified flesh that would go to settle these old scores.

Yet his nightmares had reminded him, possibly for the first time since he had agreed to take part in this venture, that he was a Roman. A younger Fulmina had appeared, her hair black instead of grey, and spoken to him of his glorious destiny and so had Clodius, in his legionary uniform, asking if he had died fighting Rome's enemies so that the boy he had found in the woods could betray him to Greek slaves and help them spill Roman blood. Worst of all, he dreamt of the old crone Drisia, who had told Fulmina his fortune so many years before. In the dream she had the gold eagle in her hand, telling him to beware of angering the Gods, and repeating, over and over again, what she had intoned years before. 'Go to Rome, go to Rome.' Was Drisia dead too?

Aquila had woken suddenly, with his hand round the charm, which provided immediate reassurance, and free of sleep he felt less alarm, as well as a resurgence of the healthy scepticism he had about the Gods and their interventions, having seen how often they misled their worshippers. All Clodius's singing and Fulmina's beseeching had not saved them from a painful, penurious end, but dreams were different; that was when the souls of the dead, who could see so much more than the living, spoke to those they had left behind in order to guide them. Aquila believed it, Gadoric the Celt swore it was the key to all life, and even Hypolitas had used the power of his dreams to sway the crowd of runaway slaves. Aquila lifted the eagle and rubbed it against his lips, then he got to his feet and went to find Gadoric. He would explain to him first, then together they could go and talk to Hypolitas.

'Remember, no killing the overseer or his family,' said Hypolitas quietly.

It was not the first time he had said this but that did nothing to lessen the angry looks on the faces of the men around him, some of whom had escaped from this very farm and could not grasp the point. Pentheus, naturally, had been the most vociferous in his objections, citing yet again the litany of crimes from which he had personally suffered, his sallow complexion turning white with passion. Yet Hypolitas would prevail; for all his thin frame he was able to dominate these burly fighting men. It was not Aquila's dreams that had persuaded the Greek to show caution but the source: as the young man recounted his reasons, he had taken hold of the charm, which swung from the boy's neck, glinting in the light from the fire. Hypolitas closed his eyes for a second, before opening them suddenly, to fix Aquila with a hypnotic stare.

'You woke holding this?' he asked.

Aquila nodded slowly but he could not move his eyes, which seemed held by some exterior force. Hypolitas was talking, his free hand weaving slowly just outside Aquila's line of vision, but the words made little sense, since the only thing which registered was the droning, soporific quality of his voice. He felt Hypolitas tug at the charm slightly, as if he was trying to pull it off his neck, and that snapped whatever spell he was weaving. Aquila shook his head, then reached out to remove the eagle from the Greek's grasp. It was impossible to say what he saw in the other man's eyes, but it looked remarkably like disappointment.

Those eyes were as hypnotic and the hands weaved just as much in the firelight as he explained his reasons to the assembled soldiers, looking like an evil spirit as the rising sun lit his eager face. There was no mention of dreams, nor of the mystical powers of a gold talisman; for once, Hypolitas relied on plain common sense, even if it seemed to emanate from a supernatural source.

'Nothing will do more to condemn us in the eyes of the Roman Senate than that any of their citizens should be harmed. They will see that as an act of war and respond in kind. Remember our aim, which is freedom.' He glanced sideways at Aquila, as if to ensure that the younger man would remain silent. 'I did not see this at first, but I do now. If we spare their people, we can appeal to justice.'

'Justice!' snapped Pentheus. 'From a Roman?'

It was Aquila who replied. 'If you seek justice it may be forthcoming, if you seek war, Rome will destroy you.'

'Destroy us,' he sneered, with a heavy emphasis on the second word. 'Has the turncoat, Aquila, turned his cloak yet again?'

Gadoric's hand restrained Aquila's response but he spoke to Pentheus in the same angry voice the boy would have used. 'Beware, Greek. If you insult this Roman again, he may kill you.'

'Are we to leave the Romans to live while we murder each other?' Hypolitas's angry words brought them back to the matter at hand: their first attack, which had to be a success. If they failed here, no amount of visions or dreams would keep the hopes of the multitude alive.

They left the mountains in darkness, progressing halfway across the coastal plain before dawn to crouch by the roadway, which led straight to their destination several leagues distant. In his capacity as military commander, Gadoric had chosen a small farm on the north coast near Tyndaris. For this he advanced several sound reasons: first, it was well away from their base and unguarded. It would be an easy way to blood their troops and it would also serve notice, once news of the attack spread, that no farm, even one relatively close to a large town and far from the mountains, with armed support readily available, was safe. Finally, after the attack, it would be clear to anyone who knew the country that the runaway slaves had marched past many more tempting opportunities. That, in turn, would induce a feeling of nervousness in the Roman overseers.

It was even easier than Gadoric anticipated. The whole of the province of Sicily, having had Roman rule for a hundred years, had become complacent. The local inhabitants had long since ceased to cause trouble, content to serve their Roman masters as they had served the Carthaginians before them. The few who noticed the party of armed men on the road, in broad daylight, could barely be bothered to afford them close scrutiny and they took over the farmhouse well after midday without a blow being struck, for the Roman overseer and his guards were out in the fields, supervising the slaves. His fat wife fainted clean away at the thought of her fate in the hands of these ruffians but she was roused and told, in the company of the other members of the household, to prepare a proper meal, first for their captors, and after that for the returning slaves.

The overseer's son, who had originally hidden behind his mother, showed more grit by trying to run away to warn his father. Aquila spotted him and shouted a warning, setting off in pursuit just as he heard Pentheus laugh. It was the first time he had noticed the sound the man made, an odd, high, cackling affair, of the sort that would be produced by a witless fool. He also saw him raise his spear, and, ignoring the cries of alarm that were aimed in his direction, set himself to cast it at the running boy. Aquila changed direction and cannoned into him. The spear had already left his hand when Pentheus was bowled over, Aquila following through with his fist. Pentheus's nose burst open as the spear thudded into the ground, just in front of the overseer's son. The boy stopped dead, shaking like a leaf, his nose up against the swaying shaft.

Pentheus was cursing through his hands, covered in the pumping blood from his nose, claiming that he had aimed to miss, but Aquila had seen his eyes as he cast the spear. He knew, if the others did not, that only inexperience had saved the boy. Hypolitas, called upon to adjudicate, was even-handed; he cursed them both while the men round the farmhouse, arguing amongst themselves, seemed to divide into separate groups. There were those who agreed with Aquila and were content to obey orders but there were others who clearly felt, like Pentheus, that sparing Roman lives was a mistake.

Gadoric, with an angry shout that silenced even Hypolitas, brought everyone's attention back to the present. The sun was starting to dip in the sky and it was time to get out of sight, because the overseer and his slaves would be coming in from the fields and everything must look normal. Hypolitas, annoyed by the challenge to his authority, seemed set to argue and for a moment the two leaders were locked in a mutual glare, but the Celt's single eye triumphed in the contest of wills. Hypolitas took station behind the grain store, acceding to Gadoric's request, the rest going to where he dictated.

They heard the crack of the whips from their

hiding places, a sound which held a deadly familiarity, and they could easily imagine the shuffling mass of tethered slaves staggering along, chained together between the lines of guards. Soon they were in sight, tired, covered in dust from the fields, it being impossible to tell the men from the women. Every time one stumbled, the guards fetched them a hearty blow with a vine sapling; a child, falling to his knees, was treated to a mighty kick that sent the poor mite flying. He would have been left to lie there if two others, who looked as if they barely had the strength to lift their own heads, had not bent to help him to his feet. The sound of his sobbing also carried across the flat ground, aided by the rapidly cooling air of the short twilight. They waited until the slaves had been shepherded into their stockade for the night, and as the gate shut, Gadoric's men appeared from nowhere, rushing in small groups to capture their quarry, outnumbering the guards ten to one. The Roman overseer was the only one who attempted resistance, drawing the sword he wore at his side, but Gadoric and Aquila overpowered him easily.

The guards were quickly disarmed and bundled against the wooden walls of the stockade. Hypolitas, called from behind the grain store, emerged with a hammer, which he waved under the terrified overseer's nose before he opened the gate and, entering the stockade, indicated that none should follow. He did not have the volcano in the background to help him on this occasion but he had no need of it. Those outside only heard him when he raised his voice, yet all knew the words he used, for the choice for these people, compared to that of the runaways, was even more stark. Should they decline to follow him, the Romans would probably put those who stayed behind to the sword as an example to other slaves tempted to revolt. The oratorical magic he had worked on the slopes of Etna was employed again, bringing forth growls and cries of acclamation, which rose until his final promise, audible to those outside the stockade, that the Gods were on their side, was drowned by a roar of approval.

The hammer was employed to strike against the metal of the chains, the Greek keen to be seen as the saviour of each one individually as they went from slavery to freedom, until finally the gates opened and Hypolitas emerged, followed by three gaunt looking men. First he showed them the overseer, tied to the wheel of a wagon. The potency of Rome as an enemy was apparent in the man's carriage; he fully expected to die, but he would not beg, nor plead with slaves. Instead, he stared at them defiantly and Aquila could not help but admire him. Hypolitas, denied the grovelling he had expected, quickly led his dusty companions over to inspect their guards, now cowering against the walls, unarmed.

'Some of these men are ex-slaves?' he asked.
Fingers pointed eagerly at three of the guards and
one of the slaves summoned up enough saliva to
spit at them. Hypolitas greeted this with a grim
smile. 'Nothing is worse than a slave who turns
against his own. Go back into your stockade. We
will give you these vermin one by one.'

The buzz of excited conversation rising from the
enclosure as they re-entered was evidence that, in
their eagerness for revenge, they were not alone.
Hypolitas called to Pentheus, whose swollen nose
was smeared with dried blood. 'You are eager for
vengeance, Pentheus. Strip these men and throw
them to their fate.'

Pentheus looked around, seeking those who
would gain the honour of helping him. There was
no shortage of willing hands and they gathered
round the guards, now on their knees, pleading, to
no avail, for mercy. Pentheus just laughed at them –
that same high-pitched cackle that made him sound
insane – then, eagerly assisted by those who shared
his bloodlust, he stripped them of their helmets,
breastplates and finally their tunics, till they stood,
naked and vulnerable, in a tight, terrified group.
They grabbed the first one, lifting him bodily to
contain his struggles, while others opened the gates
to the stockade. Inside the slaves, men, women and
children, stood silent, their eyes glassy but fixed on
the struggling guard as Pentheus and his helpers

threw the victim at their feet. At first they barely moved, shuffling round and cutting him off from the sight of those outside the circle, in which the guard was still pleading for mercy, his voice rising to an imploring scream.

Hypolitas ordered the gates closed as the screams turned from fear to pain and Aquila closed his eyes. He knew that, inside that gate, the fellow was literally being torn apart by bare hands. One of the other potential victims, taking advantage of those around him who were transfixed by the sounds emanating from the stockade, grabbed a sword and fell on it. He screamed as it thrust into his belly and Hypolitas, in a rare show of emotion, rushed over and kicked him repeatedly, then ordered that he be thrown over the wall so that those inside could get to him before he expired. The last victim did not struggle; he was like a limp, naked rag as he was taken to the gate. It opened and the circle of slaves parted to show the mangled corpses on the ground. Their dusty rags as well as their faces were streaked in blood, some of it dripping off their chins. Even Hypolitas blanched at the thought of that but the last victim had to die. Still in a trance he was pushed towards the slaves and the doors were shut again. No shouting or screaming this time, just the steady thud of a human body being reduced to bloody pulp.

'Gadoric, the yoke,' called Hypolitas, as he

walked towards the overseer. He gave Aquila, who was standing beside the cart, a quick glance, then spoke softly. 'You deserve the same fate, pig.' The Roman did not react, even though he too had been able to see through those gates. 'Perhaps we should throw your fat wife in there?'

Still nothing but a defiant glare. 'Or your son, perhaps?'

For the first time the face showed a trace of fear, then his shoulders drooped and the voice was hoarse as he spoke. 'Take me, spare the boy.'

'And your wife?' asked Hypolitas with a thin smile.

He squared his shoulders again. 'She is the boy's mother and a Roman. If you ask her, she will say the same.'

Hypolitas pushed his face close to that of the overseer. 'So if I really want to hurt you, to make you suffer as others have suffered, I need only torture your son before your eyes.'

Aquila moved to intervene, to tell Hypolitas to desist. The Greek held up his hand, but the words that followed were addressed to the prisoner. 'Never fear, pig. We do not make war on children. Nor will you, or your wife, suffer more than the loss of your dignity.'

He pointed to the yoke, now held aloft by two men. 'You will pass under that, all of you, acknowledging that your slaves have now become your masters, and you will bear a message, pig. Tell all your fellow overseers, and the greedy owners gorging themselves in Rome, that the slaves are no longer prepared to die in their fields.'

He turned slightly, raising his voice so that all could hear, including the blood-spattered slaves, who had finished their sport and emerged from the stockade. 'Rome can have her grain, as much as Sicily yields now, and more in the future. The people who grow it now will continue to do so, but not as slaves. We will grow it as free men.'

He ordered the overseer untied, his wife and son were fetched from the house. 'Remember the message, pig. Rome can have her grain.'

They and the remaining guards were paraded beneath the yoke, the eternal sign of servitude, the proof that a power lay vanquished. The food that the household slaves had prepared disappeared quickly down the throats of the starving field workers and everything that could be carried or moved, farming implements, oxen, tools, as well as food and weapons, was stripped out of the farm. Hypolitas, who had been watching this work, sent everyone away from the house and he stood alone, his head back and his arms outstretched, as if seeking power from the heavens for what he was about to do. Then the hands came together suddenly, clapping hard in front of his mouth, and a jet of flame shot up towards the edge of the thatch that covered the farmhouse roof. Dry as tinder, it took light immediately until Hypolitas clapped his hands again and the jet of flame ceased. Then he turned and looked at the frightened prisoners, his bald head and prominent features giving him a demonic appearance.

'It is not just the slaves you must fear, Romans. The power of the Gods is against you. Now go, and tell of what you have seen.'

All the buildings were burnt out long before the overseer and his family were out of sight. The freed slaves were herded along again, this time by friendly runaways, who cajoled them to hurry without the aid of whips, heading for the hills and freedom. Gadoric, Aquila and the best trained men formed a cordon at the rear, ready to turn and fight if the armed men from the town of Tyndaris should venture out to investigate the column of smoke that rose from the smouldering buildings.

From that day they were rarely still. They had to raid to feed the extra mouths and each raid produced more racked bodies in need of nourishment. Also they were short of weapons and the weather was deteriorating, so the provision of shelter became an acute problem. The original small band had grown substantially as freed slaves and runaways joined them until the worried military commander called a conference to discuss this, and further operations.

'We can no longer operate as one unit, nor should we,' said Gadoric.

Hypolitas did not enjoy being told what to do by anyone, but, lacking knowledge, he had always bowed to the Celt in such matters. Yet he was taking a closer interest himself, asking advice from a variety of sources, so that each act of persuasion seemed to take longer and longer. Aquila, though invited to attend this conference, stayed out of the discussion. Others, particularly Pentheus and those who thought like him, were present and any interventions from that source, however sound, would be unwelcome, even if most accepted that, despite his years, Aquila was Gadoric's second-in-command.

'Surely the larger our forces, the safer they are,' replied Hypolitas, looking around the assembled faces as if seeking support for his view.

Gadoric cut in quickly, aware that only those who disagreed with him would speak out. In doing so, he responded in a more dismissive way than normal. 'We rely on speed more than numbers. When we attack a farm, it makes no sense to use a hundred men where thirty would do.'

The Greek's black eyes flashed angrily. 'The governor has patrols out all the time now. What if thirty men run into a hundred of them?'

'I seem to recall our desire to avoid a war. Even if we outnumbered the governor's patrol, I would recommend that we avoid a fight.'

Hypolitas frowned and clearly, to him, that sounded very much like cowardice. Gadoric was obviously aware of the impression he had created, both by his manner of speech and the words he had used, so he added quickly, 'Better to attack three farms at once.'

There was a long silence while Hypolitas weighed up the options but he used the time to fix everyone with an intimidating stare, as if to ensure that they understood that whatever the advice, the final decision was his. 'Who would lead them?'

'I would command one, Aquila another and Tyrtaeus the third.'

'Who will obey a mere boy?' snapped Pentheus.

Gadoric's reply was icy. 'Would you care to fetch your weapons, Greek? I have no objection to you fighting Aquila for the post.'

Pentheus's sallow face went as grey as his hair and he shook his head quickly. Hypolitas put his fingers to his lips to demonstrate the depth of his thinking, and Aquila, bolstered by his friend's support, volunteered an opinion.

'I agree with Gadoric, and I believe in the end we'll be safer.' Their leader gave him an enquiring look, so he continued. 'Smaller groups move faster and I don't think the Romans are just sitting waiting to be attacked. Staying together offers them a single target, a chance to snuff out this rebellion in one engagement.'

'Only if they know where we're going to attack.' Pentheus, with his usual malice, now underpinned by humiliation, managed to imply, without saying it, that Aquila the Roman was not to be trusted.

'I've had occasion to call you a fool before this, Pentheus, so I won't bother again. You have made much of my association with Flaccus. What do you think he did before he came to Sicily?' Pentheus just glared at him; he knew the answer to that as well as anyone. 'He's spent half his life soldiering, mostly fighting rebellious provincials. Up till now, if we've faced any resistance it's been from half-trained militia. If they had any real soldiers we'd have been caught months ago but it's only a matter of time before Roman troops arrive. Then all the knowledge he and the others have acquired will be brought to bear against us. If we stick to the same methods long enough, Flaccus and men like him will catch us and when they do they'll make sure we are outnumbered. They will annihilate the fighters and crucify the rest. Right now the governor will be working on some plan to thwart us, based on our policy of single raids. If we start to attack in several places at once, that will throw their calculations out.'

'Well said, boy,' put in Gadoric.

Pentheus favoured him with the kind of look humans normally reserved for rats. 'Anything else?'

'Yes!' snapped Aquila. 'We need to set up

meeting places for incoming slaves. Right now our best equipped fighting men are going all the way to the plains, then returning every time into the mountains. If some of our less able people could be put to use, shepherding them up through the valleys, the fighters could get on with what they're best at, raiding farms.'

'We're going to have a lot of people to look after,' said Tyrtaeus. 'Winter is coming. How are we going to feed them?'

'Don't imagine the Romans haven't thought of that,' replied Gadoric.

Hypolitas, who had remained silent, finally spoke, voicing an opinion that many had thought of but few saw as realistic. 'We can't stay in the hills anyway. Sooner or later we must attack and take one of the fortified towns.'

CHAPTER TWENTY

———— ◆ ————

They shifted a dining couch into Lucius's study, which at least quelled the continual angry shouts that had emanated from his bedchamber, and he lay there, throughout the day, chafing at the bandages that circled his meagre frame. No amount of lectures by his doctor could persuade him to rest, so the man took the unprecedented step of talking to Marcellus behind his father's back.

'You must have noticed how drawn he looks,' said Epidaurianus. Fittingly, Lucius was attended by the most eminent medical practitioner in Rome, who not only worked as a doctor but served as a priest at the temple of *Aesculapius*, the God of Healing.

Marcellus nodded, not sure that he should say anything.

'He must rest. Hand the burden over to others. Really it would do him good to get out of Rome.'

The doctor waited for Marcellus to speak and it pleased him that the youngster took his time, giving due consideration to his words rather than gabbling a response, something which would have come from most young men his age. But, of course, he was his father's son, by all accounts a paragon of all the Roman virtues and destined for great things. He certainly looked the part. Epidaurianus studied him carefully, almost dissecting Marcellus with his acute observations. The dark hair was curled, but in a manly way, in the careless fashion redolent of an earlier age, not barbered as was the modern, Greek custom. The face, though young, showed all the *gravitas* associated with his family and its responsibilities, both present and future, the brow indicating brain as well as brawn. He seemed to combine a scholarly demeanour with patent physicality, being taller than his father by a good head; broad and muscular, his skin darkened from a life spent in the open, with hands callused through the use of weapons. Yet the fingers were long and elegant, used sparingly, which only added to their effect. The young man fixed his eyes on the doctor's own. They were dark, unblinking, but the long silken lashes took away any hint of arrogance.

'You must understand, sir, that my father is engaged in what he considers to be his life's work.'

'For which all Rome is grateful,' said

Epidaurianus smoothly. Lucius was a hefty benefactor to the various temples, and wisely included that of *Aesculapius*.

Marcellus smiled, lighting up his otherwise grave face. 'We could debate that remark for some time, doctor.'

'Surely there are others who could deputise for him?' Now Marcellus laughed, which made Epidaurianus drop his sepulchral tone, in fact he spoke quite sharply. 'As you said, all Rome may not be grateful. After all, someone, as yet unknown, tried to murder him. If you don't want that section who do admire him to be dressed in mourning, you must stop him working.'

'Would that I had the power,' Marcellus replied.

'Marcellus Falerius, no one knows how much power they have until they attempt to exercise it. You are born to power, now you must ask yourself this. At what point do you wish to come upon your inheritance?'

Marcellus had done his best to look like a fully grown man but there was no disguising his youth. Quintus Cornelius suppressed a smile, noting the way the lad kept his face set, like a Greek thinker in repose, which was quite amusing.

'We do not yet know who was responsible, which, apart from all the other cares he has, is driving my father to distraction.'

'We may never know, for certain,' said Quintus.

'Please don't tell him that,' Marcellus replied hurriedly, dropping his studied demeanour.

'Lucius Falerius must know that he has many enemies, fellow-senators and knights. Some of our Italian allies would readily commit murder if they thought that by doing so they would gain the citizenship, and we did not entirely satisfy the demands of the Parthian ambassadors, for which he will bear the blame.' Marcellus was studying Quintus, savouring and testing every word, seeking for any meaning that might be hidden amongst them, but the Cornelii face was like a mask, and his words lacked emphasis. 'The real question is, having failed, will the people who tried to kill him make a second attempt?'

'His doctor advised me that he should leave Rome to recuperate.'

That made Quintus sit upright, though he tried to control the movement. He was the acknowledged heir to Lucius's power, everyone knew that, and like most successors he was eager to grasp power. There was a slightly crafty edge to the voice now. 'I am troubled by that, Marcellus. Your father has been kind to me, taking me into his confidence. We think as one, and though I am prepared to assume whatever burden he places on me, I confess to a feeling of nervousness.'

'He won't go,' said Marcellus, gratified to see the slight jerk of protest that ran through Quintus's body. 'Even if Epidaurianus tells him he will die from overwork.'

'We must, at all costs, keep him alive.'

The attempt at sincerity left Marcellus wondering just how badly Quintus wanted power – after all, anyone could have hired that assassin. It was not something he, himself, craved, though his father had arranged that he would come upon it in time.

'I lack the wit to think of a way of moving him, Quintus Cornelius.' The young man bowed his head slightly. 'Which is why I've come to you.'

The senator sat fingering the edge of his toga, ruminating on those words. He was not fooled; this youngster had the brains to conjure up a solution, he just lacked the stature to enforce it. The question he was posing to Quintus was plain.

'If he could be persuaded to undertake an important task, one that got him out of Rome...'

'Yet one that was not too arduous,' added Quintus, solicitously.

'A deputy of sufficient stature could do most of the actual work.'

'I will call upon your father today, Marcellus, at the ninth hour,' said Quintus. 'It will be of some benefit if you are present.'

'You look like a stuffed magistrate,' said Valeria, under her breath, her hand flicking at his pure white toga.

They were sitting in the garden of her father's house, with her personal maid less than six feet away. Marcellus, sensing her anger, wanted her more than ever. He had tried to keep his own promise, to stay away, but somehow his resolve always failed. Not that abstinence in regard to Valeria was easy, Gaius being one of his closest friends. Besides that, because patrician Rome was really rather small, they tended to meet at every function or festival. It was always the same for Marcellus: the desire to dominate her, to make her perform as Sosia did, doing everything he commanded, was overwhelming. However, the opposite occurred, often to the point where Valeria delivered a very public humiliation. Only a fool would stand for it, yet, in pursuit of a kind word from this girl, Marcellus had even defied his father by calling at the house each day since the attempted assassination, without first changing. He tried to edge closer, inching along the stone bench, but she moved away.

'I have not been to the Campus Martius today, Valeria. I had to call on Quintus Cornelius. Are you annoyed that I still came to see you?'

Her head jerked away from him, the nose lifting in the air, which stretched her slim neck. Admiring it, he was wondering if he wanted to caress it with his lips, or squeeze it between his hands.

'That is something I've yet to decide upon, Marcellus Falerius.'

The formality forced him to suppress a curse. He had nearly gone home to change into his fighting clothes before coming here, knowing he was in no danger of a rebuke. While his father had been confined to his bed, Marcellus had done very much as he pleased, but he had decided against it. How could someone who had just called on one of the leading senators of Rome, and been received in his house with honour, humble himself before a mere girl, however much he desired her, by changing into battered old armour and a smelly smock? Some of that feeling still persisted, making him speak more directly than normal.

'What is wrong with being clean? You make that sound like a crime.'

'Did I not ask you, Marcellus?'

Valeria had never asked him in so many words, but by hints and the way she reacted he knew that the look of his battered accoutrements, as well as the feel and smell of his exertions, brought the more hair-raising parts of his stories alive. It was as though she was some kind of Amazon, denied her true vocation through being born at the wrong time, who was determined to live her true life, vicariously, through him.

'My father forbade it, yet I have defied him more than once.' Marcellus stopped. He had never told anyone about his father's instruction and the frown on Valeria's face was evidence that doing so now was winning him no plaudits. He searched his mind for an excuse, aware, as he spoke, of both the lame, illogical words and the equally pusillanimous way he delivered them. 'I cannot take advantage of his illness. Until he is well enough to conduct his own life again, I must obey him.'

Her eyebrows were now arched up, giving her an aura of heightened beauty. 'Why did he forbid it?'

'He said it was undignified, unbecoming of a Falerii.'

'I suppose it's all right for a Trebonii?' Valeria replied sourly, making it plain she had not missed the snobbery, even if Marcellus had not intended it. 'You choose to please him rather than me?'

Marcellus was genuinely non-plussed by that. 'He's my father. I have no choice.'

'What did you say when he arranged the marriage with the daughter of Appius Claudius?'

'Say?'

The tone of voice that followed, wheedling and anxious, struck a false note. 'Do you care anything for me, Marcellus?'

He looked around, partly to avoid an answer, more to make sure that the slave girl had not heard her mistress's words. The maid seemed to be concentrating very hard on her sewing, as though she had no desire to listen to their conversation.

'Answer me!' whispered Valeria, urgently.

'I don't know what to say.'

'It's very simple, Marcellus. The answer is yes or no!'

They had never talked of this, though he had often tried to move their conversations in this direction, but he had never insisted, partly because he was unsure if the emotions he felt consisted of love or sheer possessiveness. There was such a lot he disliked about Valeria: her vanity, the way she treated her parents as well as the rest of her family. She was cruel to slaves, in a way that he felt was unbecoming, making them grovel before her over trifling misdemeanours, but most of all he hated the way she behaved with people her own age. She was like a cat with other girls, either seeking to be stroked, or scratching painfully. With boys it was worse, since she could not bear to see them pay court to anyone else. Her coquetry infuriated him, especially when her sole intention seemed to be to make him jealous.

'Yes,' he whispered.

'So what did you say to your father about the betrothal?'

'I didn't say anything!'

'Why not?' she hissed. 'If you love me, you should have told him.'

That put Marcellus on the horns of a dilemma. First of all, the question had changed: she had moved effortlessly from the one word, care, to another, love, which was quite substantial. Even

Valeria, self-obsessed as she was, must know that no one told Lucius Falerius what to do, least of all his son. Quite apart from that he could hardly admit that he had put forward her name as a tentative suggestion, only to be informed that the Trebonii were not considered good enough to be connected with the Falerii. So he took a deep breath, which puffed out his chest, and replied with the only answer he could think of, unaware, as always, that by adopting such a pose he looked and sounded pompous.

'My father demands, and deserves, my complete obedience.'

'Then why, Marcellus, having been forbidden, do you come straight here from the Campus Martius?' His mouth opened and closed, like a fish breathing in water, but there was really nothing to say. 'You don't love me, Marcellus. You want me, that's all, and what would you do with me once you're finished?' The girl stood up suddenly, causing her maid to look up from the garment she was mending, noting that her charge was angry. Valeria was halfway to her bedroom before she called over her shoulder. 'Marcellus Falerius is leaving now. Please be so good as to show him to the gate!'

Marcellus stood on the other side of the postern, disconsolate and angry, cursing both himself and Valeria. She had made her way to an upstairs room, and was leaning out slightly so that she could watch him. Forced to dodge back to avoid being seen when he finally started walking away, she had caught sight of his furious countenance, which made her laugh so much, she had to lean against the inside wall for support, allowing the cool stone to quell the heat that came from her tingling body.

Quintus Cornelius paced the study, his mind racing as he tried to weigh the advantages to be gained by the absence, from Rome, of Lucius Falerius Nerva, agitated because his appointment was close, leaving him little time to think. The latest despatches were strewn across the table, evidence of his haste as he had sought to find, in them, a solution to the problem of where the older man should go. Not that he would depart willingly; persuasion would be required and that, in turn, meant that the matter had to be important enough to qualify for such elevated scrutiny. Lucius had the power to change whatever he chose, so his presence would not be welcome outside Italy, even by his own appointees.

Not all the scrolls on his desk came from official messengers, some were petitions from the provinces asking for help to contain the rapacity of the Roman proconsuls. There was corruption a'plenty seeking redress, yet that was known to Lucius and considering he had lived with the knowledge up till now, it seemed unlikely that he would relish the concept of heading any commission to bring his peers to a better execution of their responsibilities.

Spain was the logical place for him, since that benighted land caused the Republic more trouble than any other, and the idea of a buffoon like Livius Rutulius going there was risible. Given his nature, and his pea brain, he would court the kind of disaster that Rome had spent years seeking to avoid. Perhaps a man like Lucius could see, as others had not, a way to control this Brennos and nullify the danger presented by dominant hill-forts like Pallentia and Numantia. Was it possible, with his cunning brain, that the leading man in Rome could outwit the ex-Druid priest: either bring peace to the provinces, or establish, once and for all, that nothing could be done? To Quintus, Spain had decided advantages, for at the very rim of Roman power and still involving a sea journey, it would remove the old man from affairs for a very long time, allowing him to enhance his own prestige at Lucius's expense. Against that was the fact that his mentor would see that as clearly as he.

Then there was this slave revolt in Sicily, which, if Silvanus was to be believed, was rapidly spinning out of control. If it was true, it would be the governor's own fault. Silvanus, if he supported the *Optimates,* was a trifle lukewarm. Would the chance to either neutralise him, or bind him closer, tempt Lucius Falerius? The senator left his house for the short walk to the Falerii gate, mentally rehearsing the arguments he would use, well aware that the cunning old fox he was about to visit would sense any disloyalty almost before it was stated. He tried to put to the back of his mind the insistent voice which told him he was engaged on a fool's errand.

The mere mention of the word Spain produced a look that told Quintus, quite clearly, that further discussion on that score was fruitless, so he quickly substituted his second idea.

'Sicily?' said Lucius, still far from pleased. His face looked sour, as though he had just bitten into a lemon.

'It's no longer an isolated revolt by a few slaves, Lucius Falerius. Recent reports talk of a slave army.'

'I have read the reports, Quintus, and dismissed them as exaggerations, which is what you should have done.'

'I agree, Lucius,' replied Quintus smoothly, 'but they would provide a wonderful excuse for you to leave Rome, without really going out of Italy. You could head a commission to enquire into the disturbances. It may be that there is some truth in the rumours. Silvanus is still insisting that we send legions. Nonsense, of course, the day will never come when Rome has to field an army against slaves.'

Lucius glanced at his son, who was attempting to look innocent. 'I have no desire to leave Rome, Quintus. Just because a few of our fellow-senators ran away, does not mean that I should.'

Several dozen of his peers, all adherents to the *Optimates* faction, had suddenly found pressing reasons to visit their estates the day after the attempt on his life. They would remain out of the city as long as they thought there was a risk.

'Why did they try to kill you, father?' asked Marcellus. All three fell silent. The glare that Lucius aimed at his son spoke volumes, but Marcellus was now too old to be rebuked before an outsider, even one as eminent and close as Quintus. The youngster ignored the look and kept talking. 'If that assassin had succeeded, the whole of Rome would have been in turmoil. How many senators would have fled if you had actually died?'

'That I cannot tell,' Lucius replied, but Marcellus noticed that his father's look had changed: the glare had been replaced by a rather arch expression of enquiry. He knew his son too well to believe that what he was saying was spontaneous, but he held his tongue, his curiosity being that much greater than his potential wrath.

'It is my opinion that those opposed to you in the Senate were behind this act.'

'Senators do not stoop to murder,' said Quintus, dismissively, a remark which produced a polite cough, as well as a bland look, from Lucius. 'I'm more inclined to think that the Parthians were responsible. What happened, especially the immediate murder of your assailant, smacks of eastern intrigue. But I think I see what your boy is driving at. You have named me as the heir to your power, and you have informed all your clients that this is the case, yet in the immediate aftermath of a murder, I'm not sure that I could muster all the support we normally hold. What if others, prepared and waiting, chose that moment to cause mayhem?'

'How many times have you discussed this?' said Lucius sharply, looking from one to the other.

Quintus opened his mouth to say never, but the youngster got in first. 'Once, father, and I would not grace it with the title discussion, just as I will not be chastised for showing concern for your health.'

Lucius was fighting to keep the mask of anger. Failing, he turned to Quintus, lest Marcellus detect a hint of his gratitude. 'What you are implying, Quintus, is that you need to establish yourself well in advance, so that no one can be in any doubt of your position, should anything happen to me.'

'Yes!' replied Quintus, hoping that his attempt to grasp this lifeline wasn't too obvious.

'Sicily?' said Lucius, rolling the word around his mouth.

'There's no panic, Lucius. You can take all the time in the world to get there.'

'Nonsense, Quintus. No one would believe that I would trouble myself unless the matter was serious.'

'No one will believe that you've actually gone, father. They'll think you're sitting just outside Rome, waiting to pounce.'

Lucius gave Marcellus a rare smile, wondering if the boy had deliberately set out to warn Quintus, or merely done so by accident.

'You will need a military legate, Lucius. Might I suggest my brother Titus. His term of office is nearly up.'

'An excellent notion, Quintus.'

The other man spoke as though he could not believe what he was saying. 'You agree, then?'

'I do. You shall have access to all my papers, Quintus. Added to that, you shall be free to act as you see fit. This wound may prove a blessing.'

'How so?'

Lucius fixed Quintus with a gimlet-like stare. 'Perhaps I can retire earlier than I had supposed.'

He sent word to Servius Caepio as soon as Quintus had gone, despite Marcellus's protests that he would tire himself out. The senior consul needed no pleading to attend; after all, his year of office, which he had expected to be peaceful and profitable, had started badly. Had he not been consul, he too would have fled the city, if only to get away from the rantings of his junior, Rutulius, who was all for a decimation, killing one in ten of the city population; this so that those who attacked Lucius, and through him the faction of which they were members, would know that their foul deed would not go unpunished. Gently, without being too overt, he outlined Rutulius's ideas to Lucius, gratified to see that the *Princeps Senatus* held them in equal contempt.

'Is he still set on going to Spain?' asked Lucius.

'It's a constant refrain, as if he hopes, like water on a stone, he'll wear down my resistance.'

'I have agreed to undertake a task in Sicily.'

Caepio, small and sharp-featured, showed great control. If he was shocked by this news, nothing in his demeanour was allowed to show it. 'Indeed. Then the people of that province should consider themselves flattered.'

'It's on doctor's advice, added to the pleading of my son. They say that being out of Rome will help me to recover. Quintus Cornelius half-hinted that I go to Spain.' Lucius paused, sure that someone like Servius Caepio, given a few moments to think, would work out all the ramifications of that notion. 'I said no, naturally.'

'How very wise.'

'What worries me, Servius, is that while I'm in

Sicily, Rutulius might just get himself enough votes to put pressure on your good self, and have his way.'

'I think that Quintus Cornelius and I can contain him.'

'It is something I'd rather see settled before my departure, one way or the other.'

Servius was abreast of Lucius, if not one or two steps ahead. He knew that Rome would be unsettled by Lucius's departure. The final responsibility for events lay with the consuls, and if matters got out of hand they would bear the blame. 'The only way to ensure your peace of mind is to appoint someone else to go.'

'Which is why I asked you to call.'

Servius held up his hand, counting off the arguments on his fingers. 'Spain deserves attention, but it's too far for you to travel. Rutulius is not to be trusted in such a situation, yet whoever proceeds there must have the stature necessary to ensure that the wishes of the Senate prevail. That doesn't leave many people to choose from.'

'No!' replied Lucius. 'And what the Senate needs in Spain is someone well versed in politics, not war. I have advocated for years that this Brennos should be suborned, not attacked. I would rest easy, in my Sicilian bed, if I knew that the man who went to Spain not only shared my views, but had the brains to carry them out.'

'I have been short-sighted, Lucius Falerius, for which I beg your humble pardon. Perhaps the constant drip of Livius Rutulius's ideas has blinded me to what is required. If you will give me your support, I will move that I go to Spain myself.'

'And Rutulius?'

'With Rome unsettled, there will be plenty at home to occupy him.'

Servius stood to say farewell, a man well content. The *Princeps Senatus* had just done him a great favour. Right now, despite all the trouble on the frontier, Spain was probably a safer place than Rome. Any mistakes made at the centre of the Republic would haunt their perpetrator forever; errors at the periphery, especially in a posting that had fooled cleverer men than he, would not count. He would have been less pleased if he had heard what Lucius said to his son after he left.

'Ambitious, venal and an intriguer. Quintus will be much better off with Rutulius. Him he can control, but Servius Caepio, presented with an opportunity to enhance his position, could not resist the temptation to take it.'

CHAPTER TWENTY-ONE

Marcellus was sick of looking at scrolls, but his father had insisted; only he could help him to remove the ones he wanted, and he did not trust his steward. Once Quintus had access to this room, the man might tell him that papers had been removed, even if he had no idea what they contained. Once the extra strongbox was filled, Lucius locked it, affixed his seal, and instructed Marcellus to hide it in the cellar. He then had himself carried to the Senate on a litter, and moved the motion himself, with Quintus seconding, that a senior member of the house go to Sicily to investigate the disturbances. The vote was carried easily; true, there were those who owned land there who feared for their revenues, but most sought a respite from the eagle eye of Lucius Falerius, who was quick to enumerate their faults if they debated against him.

The only thing that marred Lucius's day was that

Cassius Barbinus, with the nose of a ferret, guessed that the proposer wanted the job for himself. He put the Falerii name forward before the man they had lined up to do it had a chance, speaking of his fellow-senators, especially Lucius and Quintus, in such fulsome terms that everyone in the chamber knew he was lying.

'What could be more appropriate than this: that our most august member should personally see to matters in the Republic's most important province? I had the good fortune to buy some land in Sicily recently, from none other than our august colleague. If I'd ever doubted that he cared more for Rome than his own well-being, those farms would have convinced me. Not for Lucius Falerius Nerva the husbandry of his estates. No, my friends, they had been allowed to go to rack and ruin while he saw to the affairs of this house. I feel almost criminal. After all, I paid a fair price, but now I find that the yield has increased so much that I'm in profit already.'

Barbinus turned to Quintus, his large round frame shaking as he tried to contain his mirth. 'I most humbly beg Quintus Cornelius, who shares with Lucius Falerius a love of the Republic, to combine good husbandry with politics. Let Lucius go to Sicily, to ensure that all is well, to see with his own eyes how the land prospers, and if he agrees to do this, I, in gratitude for his sacrifice, both now and in the past, will dedicate the entire annual revenue from his old farms to the Temple of *Aesculapius* as a token of my relief that he has been spared for such an onerous task.' He waved his arm, in a huge theatrical sweep which took in all the benches. 'Fellow-senators, I move the motion.'

Lucius had smiled at Barbinus on the way out, pushing himself up on his litter, determined that the man would not see he was upset, but once outside he allowed Marcellus to glimpse how bitter he was. He knew, as well as all the others who had attended the debate, that Barbinus would never have dared to treat him so if he had been fully fit.

'I must do something to reward that man's eloquence when I return. Cassius Barbinus could find he has a more prominent place in the Senate. Or no place at all!'

'I shall make slow progress, Titus Cornelius, stopping to rest frequently, I must since the doctors insist. Besides, I must keep abreast of what is happening in the city.'

Lucius arranged for a continual stream of messengers to meet him on the Via Appia; he did not want to be too far south if Quintus proved utterly incapable. It was not just his health that would slow him down.

'I will need authority to act,' said Titus.

'You will have all the authority of my position

and my person,' Lucius replied. He could see Marcellus out of the corner of his eye, hopping from foot to foot in a most uncommon, and to his father's mind, most unbecoming display of impatience. 'I fear that I must burden you with my son, Titus Cornelius. If I tie him to the pace of my litter he will drive me to an early grave.'

Marcellus stopped moving and stood erect. 'I would see it as an honour to stay by your side, father.'

'A duty, Marcellus.'

'No!'

Marcellus wanted to go with Titus more than anything in the world, yet he was worried about leaving his father, for what Lucius thought was impatience, was really indecision. The old man felt a tear prick the corner of his eye and it shocked him, since he was not the lachrymose type, but this son of his had pierced the armour that normally surrounded his heart. He rarely touched Marcellus, or showed any sign of affection, but he did now, bidding him come closer for a painful embrace.

'Go with Titus Cornelius, my son, and behave in a manner to make me even more proud.'

'I do hope that your departure from Rome is nothing to do with me, Cholon.'

'Please be assured that it is not, Lady Claudia.'

She gave him a grim smile. 'Yet I rarely see you

these days, even though I have promised not to pose embarrassing questions.'

Cholon could hardly tell her the truth: that on behalf of Titus he had taken an active political role, seeking out those knights who honestly sought reform, rather than the mass, who generally confused such things with the need to advance their personal interests. His efforts had just begun to bear fruit, had indeed advanced to a point that made some form of action imminent, when the attempt was made on the life of Lucius, an event that had brought everything to a halt. Some knights, like their senatorial superiors, had found pressing reasons to be out of the city; others, less cowardly, had counselled delay. To press matters immediately would look suspicious, in some way connected with the assassin's blow.

Cholon had argued the opposite – that an opportunity existed which might not be repeated for years – but he had been unable to muster enough support. Then, when Quintus had informed Titus of his new task, accompanying the *Princeps Senatus* to Sicily, the Greek's nimble mind had made the connection. Despite his best efforts his machinations were known; worse, Quintus and his colleagues were aware of the involvement of Titus. Common sense dictated that he too leave the city for a while. None of these thoughts showed on his face, which held the same look as before: concerned, if slightly amused.

'What could I possibly say that would convince

you? All I seek is a more Greek environment. I feel stifled in Rome and with Titus leaving too...' Cholon shrugged, but said no more.

'Where will you go?'

'I will go as far south as Biaie, Lady, though I admit the temples of Sicily do attract me. Especially Syracuse, which, as you know, was an Athenian colony.'

'So no plays, Cholon, no comedies lampooning our stiff Roman manners?'

The mocking tone of her voice made him quite brusque. 'Perhaps, once I'm away from the city, I will be able to see you Romans more clearly.'

'You may even see some virtue.' Claudia smiled, and gently touched the back of his hand. 'And me, who shall I have with both you and Titus gone?'

Cholon thought, if Claudia had any sense, she should have a stream of lovers, but he did not say that. 'You have your grandchildren.'

'So I do,' she said sourly, making him realise how tactless he had been.

To find himself staying in the same city as Lucius Falerius Nerva gave Cholon quite a shock. Only the sheer volume of traffic had allowed them to meet in the first place, for Neapolis was, if anything, busier than Rome. Their litters, caught in the jam, ended up side by side. Lucius, peering through the gap in his curtains, recognised him immediately.

'Cholon Pyliades!' he cried. The Greek acknowledged the greeting but declined to reply and the senator's face took on a mocking frown. 'Oh dear, Cholon, still harbouring a petty hatred for nasty old Lucius Falerius.'

Cholon did not know the old man all that well but he had been more privy to the thoughts of Aulus Macedonicus than anyone else. To Cholon, Lucius represented the other side of the Roman coin; where Aulus had been kind and generous, he was cruel and mean. He knew they had been childhood friends, that was not unusual, but they had remained committed to each other, which had mystified him, given they seemed to have nothing at all in common. While he could readily see what Lucius gained from such an upright friend as his late master, he had no idea what benefit accrued to Aulus by the connection, and if anyone stood in the way of the family getting justice for what had happened at Thralaxas, it was he.

He had observed Lucius often enough, going about his business in Rome, striding through the crowd, either accompanied by lictors or, when out of office, by a personal slave. The man had always struck him as sour of face and single of purpose. Now he was grinning from ear to ear, something which Cholon had never seen. It was as though the southern heat had thawed his normally icy exterior and Lucius, thin though he was, showed evidence of some strength and a fair degree of charm, in the way he insisted they dine together.

'Titus Cornelius told me you'd taken to writing plays,' said Lucius, with a face, and tone of voice, that made it sound like an occupation akin to torturing kittens. Then there was the suspicion that his host was being disingenuous, deliberately not mentioning his political activities.

'You know what we Greeks are like, Lucius Falerius, forever idling the hours away. As a race, we lack purpose.'

Cholon had intended a degree of irony, but it totally missed his host, who took his words at face value. 'Plays are bad enough, but at all costs you should avoid philosophy.'

'I cannot see what harm can come from a study of philosophy. Surely the whole point of the subject is the improvement of that flawed creature, man!'

'The whole subject does nothing but breed discontent. Stoics are so wedded to virtue that no man could escape their strictures, while Epicureans are devoted to pleasure, which must be funded by blatant corruption.'

'Lucius Falerius, that is the worst summation of philosophy I've ever heard. Mind, I agree with you about the insufferable priggishness of the Stoics...'

Lucius interrupted, a wicked look on his gaunt face. 'So you don't see the continual pursuit of pleasure as morally debilitating?'

Cholon realised that the old man only intended to be provocative, a humorous diversion to create conversation, having correctly tagged Cholon as a follower of Epicurus, but as they talked, despite his claims to despise the whole subject, Lucius showed his true colours. Some adherence to the tenets of the philosophers was essential to a man in public life and it was plain that Lucius Falerius was, if anything, a Cynic. They discussed virtue and the pursuit of knowledge, the common threads of Socratic discourse, with Lucius always playing the advocate against whichever view Cholon espoused. It was a great pleasure and extremely taxing, since the older man, with all his experience of pleading in the Roman courts, was a cunning adversary. Course after course came and was consumed; they had evacuated once already, but with the quantity of rich food, Cholon wondered whether he might need a second vomit.

He belched loudly in mid-sentence. 'At the risk of repeating myself.'

'A privilege you've exercised more than once,' said the senator with a grin.

'It would be good manners to let me finish.' Lucius, still smiling, nodded for the Greek to continue. 'All I'm saying is that if all the philosophic concepts could be brought together in one; if a man could love pleasure and virtue in equal proportions, have a healthy respect for the Gods, while still living in harmony with nature; accept that the Universe is greater than he and that what is pre-ordained cannot be changed, but must be suffered, indeed enjoyed...'

Lucius shook his head in mock wonder. 'That would be some man, with all those qualities. *Jove* himself would be envious of such a paragon.'

'He would, deservedly, stand head and shoulders above the herd,' replied Cholon, with a slightly arch tone.

'True, and I'll tell you the difference between Rome and Greece, Cholon. You Greeks would elevate him, even to the point of suffering tyranny. We, the Romans, would cast him out of the city, that is if we didn't throw him from the Tarpian Rock.'

'But then you are barbarians,' said Cholon, coldly.

'Rather successful ones, don't you think,' replied Lucius wickedly.

'Is that the secret of Roman hegemony? Barbarism?'

'No!' Lucius continued in a more serious vein. 'Our success is based on three things. Stubbornness, manpower and flexibility.' Cholon raised an eyebrow, inviting him to continue. 'In times past, even the best class of Roman citizens were not much given to purely intellectual pursuits. We are farmers who have had to plough a hard furrow. The attitudes that forced the land to yield were transferred to the battlefield. Remember we never let a man fight who has nothing to defend. Every soldier in the legion is fighting for his own hearth, thus they do not require ringing speeches, or generals who must pretend to be Gods. But the real difficulty for our enemy is this: that he can beat an army, but not the state, for without kings, Rome is flexible. The next consul will raise another army. If he is defeated, even killed, we will elect someone else to take the field. The Republic is relentless.'

'So you have ground the world down, like sand on a tooth?' asked Cholon.

Lucius nodded, smiling, accepting as a compliment what the Greek had intended as a mild insult. 'Might I suggest a walk in the night air, it has cooled somewhat now.'

They were walking now, warm without being hot, at a slow pace set by Lucius, with the crickets numerous enough to make hearing difficult and the heady scent of the flowers filling their nostrils. 'There is still a great deal to do, Cholon. Before that man tried to kill me I was preparing a motion to put before the house, which would have secured the rights of the patrician class for all time. It is a sad reflection on how diminished we are, that so many fled the city. I had to put aside all thoughts of introducing my *Lex Faleria*.'

Cholon had several thoughts to contend with: if

Lucius was being so open with him, perhaps his earlier fears were unjustified, but then this gaunt old man was a master of intrigue, so it could be just a ploy to trap him. One thought was paramount, however: he silently thanked the assassin, who had unwittingly done Rome a great service.

'I'm surprised, in such circumstances, you decided to leave.'

'At first I could not sleep,' said Lucius, taking Cholon's arm for support. 'Worrying about how matters proceeded in Rome, but the further away I got from the city, the more I realised that things were out of my hands. Quintus has the responsibility now and since there is nothing I can do till I return to Rome, then conjecture is fruitless. Besides, it gives me a chance to see how he performs. After all, it is possible I may not live to see matters settled. It may well be that my motion will end up as the *Lex Cornelia*.'

'A very stoical response,' said Cholon with deep irony.

'Let's not start that again. I don't think I have the energy for any more philosophy.'

The old senator was tired; he had always been thin, now he looked cadaverous, the light from the oil lamps strung around the garden threw his gaunt features into sharp and skeletal relief and even the eyes, at this late hour, had lost their sparkle.

'It still seems a strange step for you to take.

Sicily is somewhat beneath your dignity.'

'It may have appeared so at first, but according to the latest despatches, matters are getting steadily worse.' The old man sighed, rubbing his hands over his eyes. 'Perhaps Silvanus was right. If we'd sent troops in the first place, we would have snuffed this thing out a lot earlier.'

'You are weary, Lucius Falerius.'

'I am indeed, Cholon, the wound still troubles me, yet here I am, faced with a delicate problem. I have stood in the Senate and caused the assembly to vote down the proposal to send troops and so has Quintus. It will look mighty odd, a request for soldiers, coming from me.'

'If they are necessary...'

Lucius let that go, too tired to explain the complexities: that it would do Quintus little good if his first major proposal in the house was one, originally, he and Lucius had so vehemently argued against. 'There is one consolation. Perhaps at this late stage I will finally get to command an army.'

'Would you like any advice on the standard you should aspire to?'

'No,' replied Lucius sharply, aware that Cholon would only use it as an excuse to praise his late master. 'But I wonder if you would be so good as to call on me tomorrow. I might seek another sort of advice.'

'You are a Greek. They too are Greeks.'

'That is an over-simplification, Lucius Falerius,' replied Cholon. 'I'm an Athenian. The slaves on Sicily are either Macedonian or boneheads from Asia Minor.'

Lucius, looking refreshed from a good night's sleep, waved that objection aside. 'It is something I wish to try before calling on Rome to provide a legion. If I'm successful I can claim to have saved the Republic money and lives and if it makes any difference, the idea was brought on by something you said last night.'

Again, Cholon had the feeling Lucius was being disingenuous, not prepared to fully explain his motives, but really he was grateful for that. Knights were bad enough, but the tendrils of senatorial politics were too baffling for him, nor could he think of anything he had said the night before that could cause the senator to propose such an idea. The offer was tempting, regardless of the element of danger, for he would be acting in the name of Rome, with the kind of authority, to make peace or war, once enjoyed by Aulus Cornelius Macedonicus. And, as he had said to Claudia, he had half a mind to go to Sicily and visit the temples, anyway.

CHAPTER TWENTY-TWO

———◆———

Aquila could not have been more wrong about Didius Flaccus; while he paid lip service to the idea of another attack on the rebels, his main interest remained in the yield from his own farms and he was not alone, which made the task of the governor that much harder. He had little true strength at his disposal; apart from a handful of Roman cavalry, most of the men under his command were locals, poorly trained, ill-equipped and badly led. Fine for guard duties, useless for battle with a growing force of rebels, if they could not be stiffened by a levy of veterans from the farms. The scheme for another sweep through the mountains had suffered from endless postponement, the actions of those who had pledged support beyond coordination. He had sent to Rome for the tenth time, requesting assistance, a plea which had again fallen on deaf ears. The city had too many other troubles to contend with; a few slaves running from their masters barely registered, especially since the owners had yet to see their profits severely dented by this insurrection.

The news that he was to receive a senatorial representative, instead of soldiers, sent Silvanus into a towering rage, all the more potent for the fact that the person coming was Lucius Falerius Nerva. As a result of this missive, he sent off despatch after despatch, outlining the deteriorating situation while calling all his own militia back into barracks, so that the three separate bands were free to roam almost at will. They avoided places that had strong protection, which meant that Flaccus was left well alone, free to worry about the winter sowing. His irrigation ditches were finished, the land under cultivation increased by a quarter, so that he had nearly replaced his fallow sections, and since he had put women and children back to work in the fields, he had enough slaves to do the job for this year, aware that he would lose a percentage, those who could not do the work on the poor rations they were given to eat.

The rain teemed down, soaking everyone, carried on a wind seemingly strong enough to quieten even Mount Etna. Aquila, slithering and sliding as his horse sought a foothold on the muddy tracks, urged speed. The sooner he could get these freed slaves under some form of shelter the better; weak from work, hunger, the strain of their escape and now this foul weather, many were already being carried. Surprised to see Gadoric at his rendezvous, he rode ahead, leaving the rest of his men to bring in their charges. There was no welcome in the Celt's eyes and he beckoned Aquila away from the encampment so that they could speak privately. They dismounted and huddled in their cloaks under a tree, Gadoric eyeing the line of slaves shuffling into the camp.

'We must stop for the winter.'

Aquila cast an ironic look at the grey, cloud-filled sky. 'We might be too late.'

'I've tried to persuade Hypolitas but he won't listen. He's obsessed with freeing as many people as possible, even if we can barely feed them. He thinks the more we have the stronger we'll be.'

'Surely it's your decision, Gadoric. You're a free man now, you can stop this when you like.'

The Celt ignored the barbed remark. 'Tell that to Hypolitas. He's not so keen to take my advice these days.'

'I doubt he was ever keen.'

The two of them looked at each other, one a tall, fully grown man, scarred from numerous battles, the other a golden-haired youth, nearly as tall but unscratched. Neither wanted to be the one to say what was on their minds: that the Greek was falling victim to his own rhetoric. Hypolitas was beginning to think of himself as invincible and in that mood had no desire to take advice from anyone.

'If we can persuade Tyrtaeus to join with us, Hypolitas will have to give way. We must find him and persuade him.'

Aquila just nodded, unconvinced, and went off to see to his charges.

It was still raining steadily when they found Tyrtaeus's encampment. The rain ran off his arched back and down the flanks of the horse. Gadoric lifted his head to examine the throat, cut raggedly from ear to ear.

'That's what happens when you're soft,' snarled Pentheus, who, with grey hair plastered over his head, looked more like a corpse than his late leader. 'He was like you, afraid to spill blood.'

'What happened?' asked Aquila.

Pentheus shrugged, as though what he had to say mattered little. 'One of the guards had a knife. He wasn't searched properly.'

'Stay here,' snapped Gadoric. 'No more attacks till you hear from me.'

Pentheus opened his eyes in surprise and he looked at Aquila with that deep, ingrained suspicion which was now habitual. He also looked as though he was about to protest, for as second in command, the leadership of this group would naturally devolve on him and with Aquila holding a similar position, his lack of years could not be held against him. Gadoric, towering over him, spoke first.

'You'll get your fill of fighting, Pentheus, never fear. Maybe a bit more than you really want.'

Persuading Hypolitas was not easy. He saw himself as the sole cause of the banditti's success, forgetting that he, personally, could not wield a weapon. Aquila was right when he had hinted that the man had fallen prey to his own speechifying, but those who surrounded him contributed too, slavishly agreeing with everything their leader said, often flattering him outrageously. Gadoric soon realised that the Greek would not yield for all the right reasons, so the Celt wisely decided to play him at his own game, painting a golden vision of a great slave army making stupendous conquests. Towns would open their gates, cities would offer tribute, not to slaves but to their leader Hypolitas, and Rome itself would tremble at his name, but all this would be jeopardised if they continued with piecemeal raids.

To begin with Hypolitas made no attempt to hide his disdain for Gadoric's most recent military advice but that changed inexorably as this image of personal greatness was outlined for him. His eyes, slightly raised, looked above the other man's head at the sulphurous smoke rising from the distant, smoking volcano, just visible against the grey overcast sky, then they began to glaze over, as if he could see everything that was being offered quite plainly in his mind. His lips moved silently as Gadoric, in the tradition of his race, borrowed freely from one epic to create another. The Greek's lips had started to move first, soon followed by his head, nodding at each imagined triumph. Gadoric ended up almost singing his tale, but he brought his voice under control, returning it to normality.

'But to do all this we feed our men to make them strong. We must train them to fight properly, as a real army, or they will take the field as a rabble.'

Aquila interrupted; he thought that Gadoric had gone too far, since Hypolitas was clearly harbouring dangerous God-like tendencies. This feeling was evident in his voice when he spoke, carrying, as it did, a hint of irony. 'You wouldn't care to have your name associated with a rabble, would you, Hypolitas?'

The Greek came out of his near trance-like state to stare at the younger man and for the first time Aquila saw undisguised dislike. Then the eyes dropped to the gold charm at his throat, and the look changed to one of greed. Knowing that Hypolitas coveted it, Aquila took the eagle in his hand, wondering if he had spoilt Gadoric's whole idea by that one mundane, slightly ironic comment, and the look his friend gave him certainly indicated that he had.

'You are a wise man and such a man moves with care,' he continued, trying to repair the atmosphere. 'We must take a city, you have said so yourself. Which city? How will we attack it? How many men will we need? These things cannot be left to chance.'

This string of questions brought matters to a head, since Hypolitas, even in his most deistic mood, knew that he was unqualified to made such judgements. Slowly, now without difficulty, he was forced to concede each point. He would stop the raids, except where there was a need to acquire food, initiate more training and set others to the forging of weapons. Gadoric, with Aquila and a small band of mounted men, would reconnoitre the various Sicilian cities and decide which one was most susceptible to attack.

'Can we really take a city?'

The question was asked as they gazed at the distant walls of Agrigentum. To Aquila they looked just as formidable as all the others he had seen these past weeks and even though he was at home in the saddle he was tired out by their endless travels. Not all the time had been spent in riding, or gazing at walls, a great deal had been expended talking to the local inhabitants, all of whom seemed to hold similar, unflattering opinions on the benefits of Roman rule.

Here in the south, if they knew of the slave revolt around Messana, it barely registered. They had no suspicion that these well-fed, mounted men, who spoke near unintelligible Greek with such barbaric accents, were anything other than legitimate travellers, so they were free in their criticism of Rome, hankering for a golden age, long before the tutelage of Carthage, when the island had been ruled by the Greek oligarchy in Syracuse. And following on from that, Gadoric had gone off on his own to look at the landscape with the eye of the warrior he was. It was after one of those lonely excursions that they had come to this place. He acknowledged the question, smiled, and spoke quietly so that only the boy could hear.

'Not by assault, Aquila. We've none of your Roman siege engines and the like to batter the walls, nor do we possess the skill to make them. But perhaps by negotiation.'

The reply was larded with heavy sarcasm. 'We'd like your city, please surrender?'

Gadoric pointed past the walls they overlooked, his finger aimed towards the angry, grey-blue sea. 'Agrigentum is the closest Sicilian city to Africa. It lies, unsupported, between two wide rivers, something which, if the local farmers are to be believed, has always made it vulnerable.'

'Why?'

'Any city under siege looks at the means of relief.

Agrigentum is a port, so it should most easily come by sea. That was true when the city was Carthaginian, but where is the Roman fleet? Most likely scattered across the whole of the Middle Sea.'

'Soldiers?'

'Any army coming by land has to cross an easily defended river, whichever route they choose.'

Aquila cast his mind back to his childhood, to Clodius teaching him to swim, something every legionary was trained to do. 'That won't stop a Roman army.'

Gadoric grinned at him. 'What Roman army? Imagine you're inside those walls, which are not as formidable as they appear from this distance. I know, I have looked. Lacking any credible threat, they've been left to rot. You've heard rumours of trouble in the north, a few slaves raiding and looting, then one morning you wake up and find a whole army camped on your doorstep.'

'I don't think you can yet call us a whole army.'

'We will be by the time we get here. I intend to march south along the coastal plain, picking up every slave we can on the way.'

Aquila looked at Gadoric with a degree of apprehension; had he also become a victim of his own vision? He made it all sound so simple, as if his potential opponents were people of little account, instead of the formidable legions that had conquered where they marched. It was a tempting dream, which would ease all their difficulties. Unfortunately his pride in Roman military prowess, deeply ingrained, would not allow him to share it.

'And if the negotiations fail? What happens if you're stuck outside the walls when the Romans arrive?'

Gadoric fixed him with that solitary eye, his voice dropping again, and the words he used highlighted two facts: first, that the Celt had his feet firmly on the ground, and secondly, even as the closest of friends, they faced very different dilemmas.

'Then we might as well fight, Aquila. We must go on because we cannot go back. Only you have that choice.'

Pentheus had moved his men back to the main camp, his first act being to get Hypolitas to confirm him as Aquila's equal. From that position he set out to dominate the men left behind, and this was harder than his other task, which was to become the sole confidant of the leader. This he managed by raising the art of flattering Hypolitas to new heights. The Palmyran was increasingly seen in Pentheus's company, nodding sagely as his companion outlined some point regarding the future management of the slave army. At every gathering the others would hear Pentheus repeat, to welcome applause, the same message.

'Remember, Hypolitas, that you alone are our leader. We look to you, and no other, to guide us. You command and we obey.'

Insidiously and assiduously he undermined Gadoric, not by belittling him but by praising him. Hypolitas could not fault the Celt's military ability but the constant drip of Pentheus's praise, liberally sprinkled with allusions to his superior, if unclouded genius, rapidly eroded any feelings Hypolitas might have had for the man with whom he had escaped. Pentheus, seemingly ever eager to please, subtly exploited this, gradually feeding the leader's burgeoning ego.

'Look at me, Hypolitas. I was no soldier. I was a farmer before I became a slave, yet I took up a spear and went out to fight. I may, modestly, claim some success.'

'I hinted, to Gadoric, that I should do the same.'

'And he said no! Perhaps he fears to risk your person?'

The older man frowned at this and Pentheus did not add anything else; it was sufficient to let Hypolitas draw his own conclusions. Instead he seemed to change the subject.

'I wonder if it is wise to do nothing at all for the whole winter. Will the Romans not see this as a sign of weakness, a sign that the rebellion has burnt itself out?'

Word of their homecoming spread quickly and a sizable crowd gathered before they had dismounted. Hypolitas greeted the returning Gadoric like a long-lost brother, taking his arms with a smile, embracing him, then hauling him into his own hut. Aquila followed slowly, content to allow the two old comrades a moment alone. He looked around the camp, now a well-ordered affair, with scores of new huts replacing the makeshift wicker tents that had been there when they first arrived. A few of the men he had led pushed forward, eager to greet him, but the smile was wiped off his face when they told him what had happened, information that caused him to spin round and rush into the hut.

'Pentheus!' The single shouted word made both men turn to face him. Gadoric looked confused, Hypolitas angry. 'How long has he been gone?'

'You dare question me!' snapped Hypolitas.

'Aquila?' said Gadoric, shocked at the expression in his young friend's eyes.

'He's gone after Flaccus with eighty men.'

'Who?' the Celt enquired, still confused.

'Pentheus did so with my blessing,' said Hypolitas, with an airy wave of the hand. 'We agreed that...'

'You old fool!' It was a long time since anyone had even checked Hypolitas, let alone insulted him, and the shock on his face was total, almost like a man who had received a hard slap. 'He's wanted to get his revenge on Flaccus ever since we started this revolt. Gadoric kept him well away from the area for that very reason.'

The Celt still looked confused and Hypolitas's thundering response did nothing to help him. 'I lead here! Don't think that bauble round your neck gives you the right to question me.'

Not in the least cowed, he grabbed at his charm, pushing it out towards Hypolitas. 'I'm not sure of what you trusted, my dreams or this, but the message was clear. No Roman blood, remember? That was the policy and it was supposed to give us some hope.'

For the first time Hypolitas, his eyes fixed fearfully on the eagle, seemed to falter, his voice, for once, devoid of confidence. 'Pentheus knows that as well as anyone.'

'He didn't tell you where he was headed, did he?'

'We must remind the Romans that we are here.'

'Hypolitas,' said Gadoric, sadly.

'Get out! I will not be addressed like this,' screamed the Greek. 'I will be obeyed.'

Gadoric took him by the shoulders and shook him, speaking quietly. 'We didn't escape one tyranny, Hypolitas, to endure another.' They stared at each other for several seconds before Gadoric spoke again. 'Go after him, Aquila. Stop him if you can.'

His nose informed him that he was too late before his eyes; the smell of burning wafted into his nostrils on the northerly wind. The horse, which he had pushed to the limit of its endurance, was winded, so he could not urge it to greater speed. The black smoke rose into the sky and as he came closer he saw the flames at the base. Then he heard the screams, high pitched, mixed with loud and maniacal laughing. The fire rose above the barracks which had, at one time, been his home. When he saw what Pentheus and his men were doing he jumped off the horse and ran as fast as he could towards the blaze. The screams grew louder, so did the laughing and he barely noticed the row of flayed bodies hanging from the trees. Had he looked closely he would not have recognised any of those he had lived with, men like Dedon and Charro. The skin had literally been stripped from their bodies, leaving a bloody pulped mass dripping into the dark soil and onto the heap of broken staves under their feet.

He saw one of the women break out through the window, her hair on fire so she looked at this distance like a flaming torch, a small child cradled in her arms. One of Pentheus's men tripped her up, grabbed her as she fell, lifted her and the child bodily, then threw them back into the burning building. Aquila was amongst the raiding party now: some of the men, disgusted as he was, had stood back from this outrage. Pentheus was in the middle of the compound directing operations, his face and arms purple from the blood that had spattered all over him. In the flames, with his wild staring eyes and grey hair, he looked like a madman, laughing in that high-pitched cackle that came upon him in the presence of death. He screamed with crazed delight as his men poked their long spears through the windows to drive back the maddened women who were trying to escape from the all-consuming flames.

Aquila grabbed him and spun him round, slapping his face to try to bring him back to his senses. 'What are you doing?'

'Whores!' spat Pentheus, pointing to the bodies swaying on the trees. 'They pleasured that vermin. Some of them are with child by the bastards. This fire will cleanse that plague.'

Aquila hit him, knocking him to the ground, then ran towards the inferno screaming Phoebe's name, but no one was alive in there now, for the flames had started to suck in the surrounding air, and they rose to a flickering peak, carrying the souls of the dead women and children with them in a huge funeral pyre. Some of Pentheus's men, as bloody and wild-eyed as their leader, had seen him strike the blow, seen their leader knocked to the ground, and they turned on him angrily. Others, mainly men who had served with Gadoric, and who had stood off from this barbarity, rushed forward to protect him, swords and spears at the ready. For a moment the two groups stood facing each other, until one of his rescuers took Aquila's arm and led him away. Only when he got away from the heat of the fire did Aquila realise that he was crying.

They led him towards a steep-sided pit which had been dug in the ground, surrounded by bulging grain sacks, and Aquila leant on one and looked down. Flaccus was there, as bloody as the men on the trees, but still alive. His hands and feet had been hacked off and Pentheus had laid the hands where the feet should be and the feet in place of the hands.

'There he is.' Aquila turned to face Pentheus, who had lost none of the crazed look he had before. The man was giggling insanely as he talked. 'He's not so mighty now, is he, your Roman friend?'

Aquila wanted to kill him, but if he tried now, others would die. These two groups of men, still eyeing each other warily, would fight, and once joined who could say how many would be killed? Flaccus and Phoebe were beyond any help he could give. Pentheus came closer, the smell of his sweat mixed with the odour of dried blood.

'Have you heard his prophecy, Aquila? That he would not die till he was showered with gold? He told me all about it as I tore off his skin.'

He threw his head back and laughed out loud and those who supported him laughed too, a crazy cacophony mixed with the loud crackling of the flames. Aquila turned and jumped down into the pit to kneel beside Flaccus. The centurion's eyes, staring out of a bloody smashed face, flickered in recognition.

'I never did thank you for not turning your back on me, Flaccus.' With that he slipped a coin out of his pouch and started to place it under Flaccus's tongue. 'I cannot avenge you or Phoebe now, but I will, I swear. Think well of me when you've crossed the Styx.'

The eyes flickered again and the lips parted to expose the pulverised teeth. A slight hissing sound escaped from the centurion's throat as the coin slipped into the pool of blood in his mouth. He was trying to speak, but no words came. Aquila stood up and, pulling out his sword, he saluted him like the Roman soldier he had once been. Hands reached down to help him out of the pit and he stood watching silently as Pentheus's men cut open the sacks. Then, to the sound of loud cheering, they poured the golden grain into the pit, suffocating what was left of the life, as well as fulfilling the prophecy of the one-time centurion, Didius Flaccus.

CHAPTER TWENTY-THREE

He had no choice but to send a verbal message; Gadoric could not read or write, so Aquila sent his farewells with one of the men he knew the Celt trusted. Surrounded by the smouldering ruins of the farm he had watched as Pentheus led his men back into the hills. The bloody bodies of the mercenaries still swung on the makeshift gibbets, so he cut them down and transferred the corpses to the embers, then piled loose wood on to make a proper fire. A flaming ember was enough to torch the grave of Flaccus; grain burns easily, especially when dry. It was only then that he remembered Pentheus's words about the women bearing the mercenaries children. Had Phoebe borne him a child? It was possible. He fingered the eagle round his neck, seeking guidance, at the same time recalling the way she had stroked it, which made him feel guilty; he had never really made any attempt to free her from a life she must have hated after he had gone.

The flames behind him again shot into the sky, fired by the grease from the numerous bodies of the mercenaries, and he knew that it was time to leave, for the smoke would bring others from the nearby farms to find out what had happened. Retracing his route without really having any idea where he was going, Aquila abandoned his original intention, to shadow the party ahead of him until he could find Pentheus alone and kill him. That would bring him back into an orbit he was determined to avoid, having, as he had, lost all feeling for this revolt, which seemed designed more to satisfy Hypolitas than as a fight to free more slaves. Gadoric would at least know what troubled him and he hoped he would understand, and perhaps detach himself from that hopeless endeavour before it was too late.

He rode till he was too exhausted to go any further, then, dismounting, he made up a bed for the night and spent the dark hours, clutching the eagle, pursued by dreams of fire and death. The following weeks were spent alone, close enough to the slave camp to observe them, but far enough off to hunt and fish in peace. He slept under the stars, wrapped in his cloak, the nights growing warmer as spring came.

'Where are they now?' asked Titus.

Silvanus glanced at Marcellus before replying, wondering at a youngster, not yet old enough for military service, being included in these discussions. Come to that, he was twice the age of this legate, Titus Cornelius, and he had held many important magistracies in Rome before becoming governor of Sicily, yet he felt that he was being obliged to explain himself like a nobody. He jabbed a finger at the map on the table between them.

'They moved out of the mountains some three weeks ago, turned south, bypassed Catana and Leontini. We believe they are marching on Syracuse.'

'What is their strength?'

'Their numbers increase daily,' the governor replied, as though that was too obvious to require explanation.

'Numbers mean little,' said Titus. 'What I want to know is their fighting strength. Could we, by levying all the Romans on the island, make up a force strong enough to offer battle, or at least reinforce Syracuse?'

Silvanus bridled, unaware that Titus had not intended to be rude. He was just too wrapped up in the military problem to consider whether he was being polite.

'What do you think I've been doing, sitting here on my thumbs? I wrote to Rome last year, warning them, but no one took a blind bit of notice. If I'd had an ounce of real support then I could have gone into the hills and easily flushed them out.'

Titus, with the powers vested in him by Lucius Falerius, did not have to choose his words even if this noble senator considerably out-ranked him, and it seemed to him the man was intent on laying the blame for everything at any door other than his own. 'You could have done that anyway without the need of troops from Italy. You even called in the militia and left them lounging by their own hearths. Sitting on your thumbs seems to be exactly what you've done.'

Silvanus, who was a plain-speaking man, raised his eyebrows, his voice heavy with sarcasm. 'I know. All I had to do was get the largest group of avaricious cretins it's ever been my misfortune to meet, who are spread all over the island, and persuade them to let their crops rot in the fields while they chased all over Sicily trying to bring back a load of slaves, people who would disappear again at the drop of a straw hat.' He leant forward, his finger pointed insultingly at Titus. 'If you're so clever, Titus Cornelius, with your little scroll of instructions from the Senate, you do it.'

Silvanus then turned round and stormed out of the room.

Aquila had trailed them round the saddle of Mount Etna, which was, as usual, smoking and rumbling threateningly, then followed them through the foothills until the whole mass of runaways, with their women, livestock and children, debouched onto the littoral north of the city of Catana. Coming down onto the plain, in their wake, he found empty farms, with the houses ransacked and storerooms stripped bare, but no bodies. Word spread quickly of this slave army and every overseer for miles around, and his guards, deserted their property and fled south to Syracuse. Even from a distance Aquila noticed the increasing size of the host as every freed slave, exposed to the flowing ideas of Hypolitas, flocked to join them. By the time the walls of Syracuse showed on the horizon their numbers filled the landscape.

Marcellus stood on the walls. To the north he could see the dust cloud created by the insurgents as they marched towards the city, behind him, if he had cared to turn, he would have seen numerous ships pulling out of the harbour as the less stalwart Romans, with those Greeks who had helped them, sought to escape across the narrow straits to Italy. Titus's attempts to persuade them to stay had come to nought; indeed he had been asked, caustically, what he was doing on the island, supposedly a military legate, without a couple of legions to back him up.

'They'll be outside the walls tomorrow,' said Titus.

'Do we stay?' asked Marcellus.

'Yes. They have no ships, so they can't blockade

the harbour. They'll soon find out it's impossible to take Syracuse without a supporting fleet. We need to get a message to your father. If we can pin them down here, it will be easy to bring troops into the town by sea. If another legion came down the coast from Messana, we could trap them between two forces and destroy them.'

But they did not stop for the city; Gadoric was wise to the notion that he needed a fleet to subdue such a place, just as he knew, from the locals, that Syracuse had a history of withstanding lengthy sieges, even against enemies who possessed ships in abundance. It was too Roman and too well fortified to be easily taken. They invested it nevertheless, but only so that they could strip the countryside bare for miles around of food and slaves. The inhabitants of Syracuse who had stayed behind, under Titus's command, and who had set themselves to fight until help arrived from Italy, woke one morning to find the plain before their city devoid of their foes, who had decamped during the night and headed south. Aquila watched the party of twenty mounted Romans, their red cloaks billowing behind them, leave the town and set off in pursuit. Too few to fight, they were obviously intent on shadowing their enemy.

Gadoric, turning west along the southern coast, ignored the offers of surrender from the small conurbation of Camarina, moving on quickly to stay ahead of the spreading panic, by-passing the major city of Geta by fording the river well to the north. He forced-marched his trained bands to the next river, one of the two that hemmed in the city of Agrigentum, leaving the mass of untrained slaves to follow. Mounted detachments were sent to cut the bridges and hold the fords on the river to the west and he ordered the straggling mass of slaves into the foothills north of the city, then spent two days sorting them into manageable groups. Finally, with no moon to warn of their arrival, he ordered everyone down onto the plains that stretched away on either side of Agrigentum.

The inhabitants, who supposed this threat, if it existed at all, was still well to the east of Geta, woke one morning to find what looked like a huge army camped outside their crumbling walls, with a simple offer available to them. Open your gates and you will be spared; resist and the whole city will be put to the sword. The recently freed slaves, in truth useless in a fight, looked formidable enough in their newly rehearsed and static formations, so for someone looking out from the crumbling walls of Agrigentum, the position seemed hopeless. Hypolitas, with Gadoric and Pentheus at his side, rode forward to talk to the leading citizens who lined the walls. He spoke of the tyranny of Rome, told them that he had no desire to hurt fellow-Greeks, and promised that his army would not occupy the city in strength, but would instead disperse to the surrounding farms to assist, as free men, in the cultivation of the land. He promised to respect the temples and the women and to abide by the statutes of the city, as long as he was afforded the same civility he intended to give to them.

Even those who wanted to resist knew that it was impossible. Given time, the walls could have been repaired, making the city as formidable as it had been a hundred years before, but there was no time, the enemy was at the gates. Only Roman legions, backed by a strong fleet of ships, could oppose this slave army. The legions were nowhere to be seen and, besides, in such a Greek city, they would scarcely have been any more welcome than Hypolitas. He capitalised on this, talking of freedom for the whole island, of throwing off the Roman yoke, with slave and freedman combining to create a prosperous future. Such a dream, such words, in the mouth of another man, would have been risible, but Hypolitas had that compelling voice, which could hold the attention of the largest crowd, plus the finale with his magic fire. For him, the gates were open before the sun had reached its zenith.

Marcellus looked at Titus to see how he would react but the face was still, as if set in stone, gazing on the gates of Agrigentum, wide open, with the runaway slaves as free to enter as the citizens were to leave. Hypolitas and his ramshackle horde had a city and a fine harbour and they could see that some of that army was already busy repairing the walls.

'Well, Marcellus,' said Titus finally, gesturing towards the white walls. 'What do you suppose this means?'

'A long hard fight, a fleet to blockade the harbour, siege engines to batter the walls and several legions to carry out the assault.'

Titus swung his horse round. 'The first thing we must do is seal the approaches east and west. That army is big enough. When word gets out that they've taken a city, every slave in Sicily will be trying to join them.'

Marcellus pointed towards the solitary horseman watching them from the ridge. 'He's still there. Is he following us, or the slaves?'

'Time to find out,' shouted Titus, who had studiously ignored the man trailing him, though the constant presence, like an itch you could not scratch, had annoyed him greatly. He kicked his horse and headed straight for him, followed by Marcellus and the rest of his men.

Aquila watched them for a moment; they were aimed at him like an arrow, with the billowing clouds of dust raised by their hooves adding to the effect of their streaming red cloaks. He hauled his horse's head round, and calmly trotted off the ridge. Only when he was out of sight did he kick the mount into a gallop, heading for the deep ravines that furrowed the foothills of the mountains surrounding Agrigentum. Losing his pursuers was simple.

'A fleet is the first priority,' said Titus. 'We must commandeer ships from Rhegium and Neapolis. Anything will do, just as long as we can man them with proper soldiers.'

Lucius listened carefully, his face drawn; still feeling the effects of his chest wound, the journey had not been kind to his health. 'You fear they will seek allies?'

'It's what I'd do, Lucius Falerius. There are enough people on the coast of North Africa that still hanker after a strong Carthage. We may have razed the city, but I'm sure the dream persists and we can't be sure how far afield they'll go. The thought of conquering Sicily will appeal to more than one of our enemies.'

Lucius turned to his son. 'It is central to Roman policy, Marcellus, that no other power holds Sicily, remember that. The whole of Italy becomes vulnerable if we allow such a thing to happen.'

'Yes, father,' he replied.

'What I'm saying, Lucius Falerius, is that there is no time to consult Rome.'

'Consulting Rome would be a waste of time, anyway, even though it must be done, but any legions we can muster will get here too late.' Titus frowned, wondering what Lucius was talking about, but enlightenment followed swiftly. 'What chance is there of a decent harvest coming out of Sicily in the present circumstances?'

'None whatever.'

'Well, Marcellus, what do we deduce from that?'

Having been away from his father, Marcellus had lost the habit of being prepared for searching questions, yet the answer came easily enough, having already occurred to him. More and more he found himself assessing a situation as Lucius would, often surprising himself by the complexity of his conclusions.

'Disquiet in Rome as the price of grain rises. They may have to cut the corn dole in the spring and that will certainly cause riots. As soon as news reaches the city that the situation demands a consular army to subdue the slaves, those who have grain will start hoarding it, so we won't have to wait for the actual shortages. Riots could break out just as we're trying to raise the legions. It is absolutely certain that our allies will suffer from increased prices first, so they won't wish to denude their farms to provide us with auxiliary troops when they need every man to be busy at his plough.'

'Untidy, Marcellus, though accurate,' said Lucius. 'You really must work on the way you arrange the presentation of your conclusions.'

For all the acidity, it was plain he was pleased with his son; it was in his eyes as he turned back to talk to Titus. 'That infernal corn dole is the real problem; ever since it's been in place, more and more ragged-arsed scum have poured into the city to claim it. Anyone who tried to reduce it, or remove it, would be strung up. Worse than that, anyone who promises to sustain it, regardless of the cost to the treasury, can have any office they want. The mob will vote for bread today and damn tomorrow.'

'I am lost,' said Titus. 'I won't pretend I don't understand the politics of Rome, but I can really only see a military problem requiring a military solution.'

'Let us first see if we can find another way.' Titus looked even more bewildered. 'I met that Greek in Neapolis, the man who served your father.'

'Cholon?'

'He has undertaken a little errand for me. We shall wait till he returns, before we alert the Senate to the scale of the problem.'

Cholon had no difficulty in entering the city of Agrigentum, being clearly no threat, a wealthy traveller on a litter with eight attendants. Four carried him; the rest carried another open litter, which held his possessions. He was, of course, stopped at the gate and asked his business.

'Why have I come here? Are you mad, fellow? Right now this must be the most interesting place in the whole of the Middle Sea. Great events, man!'

'You've come to see the King of the Slaves?' said the guard, with obvious delight.

'I was not aware of any kingship. I am familiar with the name of a Palmyran Greek called Hypolitas.'

'One and the same person, sir.'

'So, fellow, he aspires to the diadem. I must gaze upon this King, considering he has made Rome shudder. I would dearly like to speak with him. Is he accessible?'

'None more so, your honour. No airs and graces attach to our King. He remembers that he was a slave, just like the rest of us.'

'He is acknowledged by all then?' asked Cholon.

The guard leant forward and Cholon tried not to flinch at the man's stink. 'Locals don't bend the knee, but they will. All it needs is an assembly so that he can be acclaimed. A few prods from our spears will do the trick.'

'It sounds as if this is already arranged.'

The guard half-turned, then winked, with all the subtlety of a poor stage comedian. Clearly the man was looking for a coin. 'When will this assembly take place?' asked Cholon, reaching for his leather purse.

'Tomorrow noon.'

'Could you secure me a good place from which to watch?'

'I can that, sir, though not till my duty is done. One of the men who guards our King is a friend.'

Cholon slipped the man two silver denarii, which he palmed expertly. 'Take this, fellow. One for you and another for your friend. If he asks who wishes a good view, say that a wealthy traveller from Athens, by the name of Cholon Pyliades, seeks a sight of this paragon. I will rest at the Temple of *Diana*.'

That presented even less of a problem than entry into the city; the normal source of donations to the temple had dried up since the slaves arrived. Wealthy men, fearing the future, hoarded their money and dressed in rags. Cholon was more than merely welcomed, he was feted and the priests, like priests everywhere, seemed happy to grovel for a few coins, dropped noisily into their finely wrought Corinthian salver. He was happy; bribable Greeks were so much easier to deal with than sententious Romans. Mind, Lucius Falerius had practically given him proconsular power, so sour remarks regarding Roman faults had been avoided of late. He wondered what Titus and the Lady Claudia would say if they could see him now.

Claudia had never thought of her life as restricted until the problems associated with searching for her lost child surfaced. Aulus had left her independent, but that did not release her from the natural constraints attendant upon any woman, let alone one of a noble family, and she could not just travel around the country like a man, asking questions. While her husband had lived such an extended search as she was now planning was impossible. The short excursion she had taken, and her talk with the midwife who had delivered her baby, had been fruitless. After Thralaxas Claudia had pinned her hopes on Cholon and she refused to accept that her son was dead, as Cholon insisted he must be, so she combed his words, which were etched on her memory, for clues. The Greek had mentioned a road; the child had been placed in woods far from some highway. Such roads were not numerous and there had been even fewer when the boy was born.

'A map, Lady? asked Thoas, who had never seen or heard of such a thing.

'Yes.' Claudia explained, first what they were and how she thought the slave could get one. 'If you cannot find someone who sells such things, there must be maps in the Temple of *Juno Moneta*.'

The slave repeated the name slowly. He knew the place, a wooden structure at the summit of the Capitoline Hill, next to the building where they minted coins. He had often looked at it, wondering if it was possible to dig a tunnel from one to the other.

'I am a slave, lady, and no worshipper of your

Gods. Can I go into such a place with this request?'

'This is Rome, Thoas. Even a slave is allowed to worship in our temples. I will give you something to pay the priests, plus a written request that any map be entrusted to you.'

Quintus Cornelius now found himself working as hard, if not harder, than Lucius had done in the past but he was happy, for he wanted nothing more in life than to be the leading man in Rome. He would need a military victory to ensure that, but given sufficient prestige, he could pick and choose his Consular year and thus his campaign. He was in a happy mood as he made his way from his bedroom to his study, for once leaving his mouse-wife with a delighted smile on her face.

It never occurred to Thoas that his mistress's stepson would want to work so late and he had checked, listening as Quintus and his wife noisily made love. Odd that such a meek creature should be such a screamer in bed! She had exhausted her husband by the sound of it, so he was out of the way for the night. Apart from them, the entire house was fast asleep. The lamplight in the study first alerted Quintus, so he approached the door cautiously, then the rustling of the papers alarmed him. After what had happened to Lucius Falerius, he never travelled anywhere without a long-bladed knife. Since he did not share a room with his wife, he was dressed in the same clothes he had been wearing all day, including the weapon, so he pulled it out now, eased himself through the open door, and saw his mother's Numidian slave rifling through the scrolls in his tall map cupboard.

The thought that the man was a fool was the first thing that entered his mind: there was nothing of value amongst those maps. It was unlikely he could read, so he had tried the wrong cupboard but that did not alter the fact that Thoas was trying to steal something from his papers and there was only one way to deal with such a thing. The Numidian was tall, muscular and could prove a difficult opponent. This was no time to take a chance.

Thoas started to turn as Quintus stabbed him, which meant the blade took him in the side of his leg rather than the back, and in turning he added effect to the sideways motion that Quintus used, tearing his thigh muscles even more than the senator had intended. Quintus was a soldier, as adept in the martial arts as any of his contemporaries. The left-handed punch hit the slave on his open mouth, removed several teeth, and killed the sound that Thoas had started to make. Quintus kicked his other leg from under him and dropped, with his knees thudding onto the slave's chest as he hit the floor. Then the knife was at the Numidian's throat.

'Make a sound and I'll take out your gizzard.'

Terror made Thoas's eyes look white against his dark skin, fear made him gurgle, the knife pressed into his throat made him stop. The slave's mind was racing, since there seemed no way out of the trouble he was in. Then he had an idea. It would be pointless to plead mercy on the grounds that he was acting on Claudia's behalf, but what about Lucius Falerius Nerva? Everyone in Rome was afraid of Lucius and gossip in the wine shops had it that this included Quintus Cornelius, so when the question came, he gave the answer that he thought would save him.

They found his body in a street leading to the market-place, the throat sliced open. Rome at night was a lawless enough place for murder to be commonplace and Thoas, who was much given to staying out drinking in places he could not afford, spending money he should not have, on women he could never hope to get, had met a deserved end, probably at the hands of someone jealous of his attentions to his paramour. Claudia, as a favour to help her heartbroken maid, paid for a funeral for the Numidian, even though she did wonder what he was doing out at that hour. Even more mysterious was the way that Quintus, without a word of explanation, handed her the note she had written out for the priests at the Temple of *Juno*

Moneta. As he did so, her stepson cursed himself again for that moment of blind fury, when he heard the name Lucius Falerius. That had made him slice the man's throat without asking him what he was looking for.

CHAPTER TWENTY-FOUR

It was immediately obvious that the slave army, despite the promises of their leader, had taken over the city. The guard at the gate had been an ex-slave and the entrance to the palace, normally the meeting place of the local oligarchy, was also guarded by runaways, simple questioning establishing that it was now the sole residence of the 'King of the Slaves'. Cholon waited, in a very privileged spot, as the crowds gathered and watched this paragon emerge into the square before the palace. He was surrounded by his advisers, one of whom, a tall blond fellow with a single eye, towered head and shoulders above his leader. The crowd, now a dense mass of bodies, who had gathered for a mere glimpse of this man, erupted into wild and unrestrained cheering.

Hypolitas was still thin, just as bald with the same wild eyes, but he had shed his simple smock for more elaborate garments, made of finer materials. He wore jewellery on his wrists and neck and the way he carried himself, the gestures he used to acknowledge the cheering, made it easy to imagine him wearing a diadem. The speech, to Cholon's ears, was less impressive, but he was prepared to admit to himself that bias could play a part in his judgement. The ritual with the fire, shooting out of Hypolitas's mouth, to form a great ball above his head, certainly stunned the crowd, even those runaways who had seen their leader perform this magic before. Then came another speech full of messages of peace and brotherhood, which ended with six white doves flying out from Hypolitas's sleeve.

As soon as the assembly was over Cholon composed his request. The leading priests from the Temple of *Diana*, who would add their voices to his plea for a private audience, would deliver this. Discretion had to be exercised if he was to keep his head on his shoulders, but the relish he took in his new role was undiminished by the danger. His impression of the man he had seen, that morning, contrasted greatly with the little information available to Lucius and the Romans.

That hinted at some person, near God-like in his simplicity, a man beyond avarice, yet he sensed that he was, in his fine clothes and flashing jewels, not like that. The apparent magic with the flames might

impress an ignorant crowd, but it did not have the
same effect on him, since he was sure he knew how
it was done. If anything convinced Cholon that he
could talk, profitably, with Hypolitas, it was the
way he had accepted the accolade 'King', shouted
from numerous throats. There was no attempt to
curtail this, no modesty, more an apparent welcome
in the eyes and an acknowledgement in the gestures
that such a title was nothing less than his rightful
due.

The message he sent had to be couched in
language that hinted, discreetly, at the nature of his
mission. If, indeed, this Hypolitas was an upright
man his request would meet with a blank refusal.
The venal priests, accepting the largesse that he
bestowed with ill-concealed greed, listened carefully
as, verbally, he outlined his instructions. Nothing
that could compromise him, or the recipient, could
be committed to paper.

'Say that Cholon Pyliades, a native of Athens, an
ex-slave yet also a citizen of Rome, seeks private
audience. I would speak with the King of the Slaves
personally and alone. Take care to acknowledge his
majesty, since he relishes the title. You may say that
I bear an offer from the chosen representative of the
Roman Republic, one that will guarantee him and
those he leads, peace, life and prosperity. I exert no
pressure for this meeting and I am willing to depart
without it, sure that the fates have already laid out

the future course of events. Perhaps his enterprise will prosper, perhaps every road in Sicily will be lined with crucifixes. As a Greek and an ex-slave, I can sympathise. As a Roman citizen, I am only too aware of the power available to that state.'

He looked around the assembled priests. Well-fed men of few real scruples, they would accede to only two things: power and money. He tossed the purse, full of gold, in his hand.

'They have a saying about the Romans. When they sack a city, they are very thorough, they even slaughter the animals.' He raised his head and looked around the rafters of the wooden temple. The way the priests shuddered convinced him it was enough. 'They will come and they will burn and be assured, the Romans will kill every man, woman and child in Agrigentum if this revolt is allowed to continue. Hypolitas is bound to ask you, as augurs and priests, for a prediction. You will tell him that you see this temple a smoking ruin, the city razed to the ground, the plain before the walls a mass of dead. Do that, and I promise you that this wooden structure will be replaced by a larger one, made of the finest stone.'

'How much did you pay the priests for that doom-laden prophecy?' asked Hypolitas.

Cholon raised his eyebrows in mock surprise. 'Pay? I've given them something for my lodging.'

'I think you lie.' Hypolitas, lounging, like Cholon, on a gilded divan, put no emphasis in the words, but he sought to hold Cholon's gaze with those compelling eyes.

Cholon replied smoothly. It was no business of envoys to show temperament, even at personal insults. 'If you're convinced of that, I fear no words of mine will sway your opinion.'

'So Rome is afraid of me?'

'That could be a fatal assumption. It would be more accurate to say that Rome is cautious. You have succeeded, Hypolitas, but only up to a point.'

The Palmyrian Greek was prepared to play the same game. If he was angry, he kept it in check. 'Which is?'

'Rome cannot grow enough food in Italy. Too much of the land has been given over to rearing cattle, so it depends on Sicily for grain. If that crop is less than normal...' Cholon tailed off with a shrug, sure that his host knew the rest as well as he did.

'I have offered to supply grain, quite possibly more than Rome receives now. All the grain you need, as long as we are left alone. Get the Romans out of Sicily, and leave the slaves. It's very simple.'

'What a tempting prospect,' said Cholon, wearily. 'Yet you know it cannot be. You are, after all, no fool, Hypolitas.'

'By the time your legions arrive the walls will be

impregnable. Not that I'll wait here in the city. I'll meet you, with a properly trained army, at the river crossings. Your fleet will have to fight my ships if they want to blockade the city.'

'I saw few ships in the harbour, certainly not a fleet.'

'There will be one, never fear. Is it worth it to Rome, to sacrifice men and money for something they can have without a fight?'

It was a good time to alter the course of the conversation, which, judging by the rising tone of Hypolitas's voice, was threatening to become a confrontation. 'It seems that these people want to acclaim you as their king.'

Hypolitas sat up suddenly, his voice earnest. 'A mere title, less than what I am to them now.'

'What are you to them now?'

'All powerful, close to the Gods, a seer who reads their dreams and speaks with fire through my mouth.'

Cholon had been looking forward to this claim of divinity. His voice was like silk. 'Take care the walnut shell does not pop out one day.' The Palmyran tried not to react and he very nearly succeeded, but he could not keep the surprise out of his eyes. 'It is a walnut, is it not, with holes in it and you will be wearing flints on your wrists. I have never come across the fluid you secrete in the walnut. I daresay that is where the mystery lies.'

Then he smiled; by his previous actions Hypolitas had betrayed just how much he coveted the trappings of kingship. 'So, you would like to be King Hypolitas?'

'I told you, a mere title.'

'Yet pleasant, nevertheless, though I fear such a move would only serve to anger the Romans even more.'

'I enjoy angering Romans!'

'I wish to speak freely, Hypolitas, putting aside the finer points of diplomacy, because your illusions will cost you your head.' He continued, despite the angry look on his host's face. 'The first thing you must understand is that no other force will be allowed to hold Sicily. It is simply too important to the Republic. If necessary, they will sacrifice Spain to keep this island. The second illusion is that the men who hold power in Rome act as a rational body.' It was now Cholon's turn to sit forward. 'Whose land do you think you've despoiled, whose slaves do you think you've freed? Some of the senators make millions of sesterces a year from their holdings in Sicily. Do you really think they'll give that up?'

'The price!' snapped Hypolitas.

'Why should they worry when others will have to pay it? They will vote to crush you to protect their wealth, then sit in Rome carping if it takes more than one campaigning season, and care nothing for the farmers you kill. The third illusion is the worst.

Do you really believe that a people who have conquered half the world will permit slaves to defy them? They'll crucify every one of your men and throw you personally into the pit of the Tullianum to be eaten by rats, as you die of starvation, just to prove they're invincible.'

'Did you come all this way to tell me that, you Athenian donkey?'

Cholon sat back suddenly, leaving the angry Hypolitas looking slightly foolish. 'No, I did not. I came here to offer you all your lives.'

Hypolitas reclined then, struggling to compose his features. 'Go on.'

'The person sent here by the Senate was given the task of enquiring into the disturbances. This could easily be stretched to include the causes.'

'Those are plain enough,' said Hypolitas coldly.

'This man is that rare creature, someone entirely free of personal avarice. He is also a man with the power to change things. On top of that he has the power to protect you.' Cholon began to speak quickly, since he had reached the nub of his proposal. 'Steps will be taken, in the Senate, to limit the excesses of the landowners, so the slaves, when they return, will come under the protection of the Roman state. You and the other leaders will be freed, given pensions, and allowed to live out your days in comfort.'

'You're asking me to betray my army?'

'Getting them killed or crucified would be the ultimate betrayal. I mean no threat, Hypolitas, but there will be no more emissaries after me, only legions.'

The silence that followed lasted for a full minute. Hypolitas held his visitor's gaze, as if by doing so he would somehow establish the truth of what he said. Finally he spoke. 'I could have you torn apart.'

Cholon stood up, then gave a small bow. 'So you can, King Hypolitas.'

In the hothouse atmosphere of this revolt, suspicion was natural; the first time Gadoric rode out alone his departure caused little comment, but as it became a regular occurrence, Pentheus, particularly, was afire to know where the Celt went on these solitary trips, leaving at dawn and returning before the gates closed at night. The answer, when he followed him, afforded the man no pleasure at all. As soon as the Celt returned he was called to face Hypolitas, who without confiding that he already knew, asked him gently where he had been. Gadoric made no attempt at concealment, openly admitting that he had ridden into the hills for a rendezvous with Aquila.

'The boy represents no threat to us.'

'Then why is he there?' demanded Hypolitas, who disagreed, even if he was not prepared to say why.

Gadoric shrugged, reluctant to explain his conclusions: that he was the only living person to whom Aquila now had an attachment. He had been as surprised as Pentheus and Hypolitas were now when the message from his young friend first arrived. They had met and embraced, talked and reminisced. Advised to get away the boy had refused, unless they did so together. Explaining why such a thing was impossible, Gadoric had the impression that Aquila harboured some fanciful notion of rescuing him when the legions finally arrived. None of this would make any sense to these two, so it was better left unsaid.

'You haven't answered Hypolitas's question,' said Pentheus coldly.

'I don't think he knows where to go.'

Hypolitas had the blank look of the truly innocent on his face as he spoke again. 'He can re-join us if he wishes.'

Gadoric was not fooled: Pentheus hated Aquila, as well as fearing retribution for the death of Flaccus, and Hypolitas did not trust him. The young Roman's life would not be worth a bent denarius if he came within these walls, not that any invitation would attract him. Aquila was scathing about the revolt and its leader, just as the high office Pentheus now held enraged him. Anyway, Gadoric enjoyed the clandestine meetings as much as his friend. They gave him a chance to talk freely, to air his doubts about the direction in which the whole enterprise was headed.

'He feels that, as a Roman, he cannot kill his own kind.'

'We should never have trusted him in the first place,' growled Pentheus.

Hypolitas threw up his hands in a gesture of futility. 'Well, there's nothing more to be done. Thank you for being so open, Gadoric. I must say, when Pentheus first mentioned your little trips, I was worried.'

'You have no need to worry.'

The hands went up again, this time in exasperation. 'What if anything happened to you? What would I do?'

'You didn't forbid him another meeting,' Pentheus complained, as Gadoric disappeared.

'No, Pentheus, I didn't.'

'Why not?'

'What would you think his reaction would be, if I told him that there is a chance of a settlement with the Romans?'

Pentheus had become practised at being this man's courtier. He also knew of Cholon's visit, without having the least idea of its purpose. But he was clever enough to make an immediate connection so he did not bat an eyelid and his voice showed no trace of emotion. 'What kind of settlement?'

'One that I could accept. Let us say that our position, as leaders, would be recognised. That we, at least, would be spared a return to servitude.'

'Gadoric would tell you to jump off the walls.'

Hypolitas smiled grimly. 'I wonder if that is good advice. I think you hate him.'

'Do I?' asked Pentheus guardedly.

'You are a man who hates easily, Pentheus.' The Palmyran laughed suddenly. 'But then so am I. You asked why I didn't forbid him to go and see his Roman.'

'Yes.'

'When I asked him where he went, he told me, right away. Gadoric does not yet know that he was followed. Let us, for the sake of our future, keep it that way.'

'Nothing would please me more than the sight of Aquila's body hanging by his feet,' said Pentheus.

'Then perhaps we can arrange for you to have it.' Hypolitas looked at his fingernails, as if the words that followed were of no account. 'Should that be possible, you would please me greatly by fetching back that gold eagle that hangs round his neck.'

Pentheus emitted that cackle, which made anyone who heard it wonder if he was mad. 'I shall bring you his head and his neck, with that charm still on it.'

The senior priests from the Temple of *Diana* entered and Hypolitas acknowledged them, before turning back to Pentheus. 'Forgive me. I have been invited to worship with these men. It would be impious to decline.'

The other man said nothing, but in light of the meeting with Cholon he could guess what was taking place.

'There is one of the leaders who Hypolitas says will never agree. The others will do as he tells them.'

'He is?' asked Lucius.

'The man who commands the army, a Celt by the name of Gadoric. Apparently, he's as venal as the rest but he hates Rome too much to ever agree to a truce.'

'Then Hypolitas must be rid of him.'

'He would rather we did that,' replied Cholon. 'He cannot be seen killing his own when he is promising them all a better life.'

Lucius nodded. 'That is fitting. Roman blood has been shed. It will quieten some of those who wish to protest if we take some revenge. The other terms?'

'A show of force, especially ships.'

'Titus and my son are arranging that.'

'He intends to be acclaimed and wishes to be treated with all the honours due to a client king.'

'The other leaders?'

'The future King Hypolitas seemed to care little for them. He spent most of his time telling me what kind of villa he required, how many servants and the size of his annual stipend, which is substantial.'

Lucius smiled, his thin face lighting up. 'The landowners can pay it and they can afford to, especially people like Cassius Barbinus. Perhaps it will still his tongue and make him treat his slaves properly.'

'They'll squeal, Lucius Falerius. Their income will be dented already by the reforms you propose to introduce.'

The other man's face was wreathed in smiles, which made more prominent his already well-defined bones. 'Let them squeal, Cholon. That is a spectacle I will certainly enjoy.'

Marcellus's only experience of the sea had been the short crossing from Italy to Sicily on a cargo ship, but this was different. He and Titus, at the head of a makeshift fleet, having received a bare set of instructions from his father, were now sailing south round the island. Most of the ships were merchant galleys commandeered against the wishes of their owners; they were aboard a proper trireme, its three banks of oars manned by fighting men, which had been fetched round from Brindisium, taken from its normal duty of subduing piracy on the eastern trade route.

He loved it; the rise and fall of the waves felled Titus from the first day, but not Marcellus. The smell of the salt water, the feeling of unlimited space, the way that the ship steered when he was given a turn at the great sweep that stuck out from the stern, lifted his heart. He had a turn on an oar, eliciting some admiration from the other rowers for his stamina and for his determination to keep up, though the effort left him an exhausted heap on the deck. Marcellus was back as soon as he recovered, keen to master the art and progress to the peak of efficiency achieved by those who manned the ship.

With the wind dead astern, and the great square sail drawing taut, they sighted Agrigentum just after dawn on the third day. The master, at the request of a slightly green Titus, cleared the ship for battle, taking in the sail and sending all the rowers to their stations. The man at the drum started to beat time causing the sleek trireme to edge forward and as the tempo increased the rowers strained harder, increasing the strokes without ever losing their rhythm. The catwalks above the rowers' heads were lined with soldiers, the first shock wave in an attack, who would be joined by those below once the need to manoeuvre had passed. The trireme head-reached the accompanying merchant ships with the water flying in a great spray over the prow.

They could see the few vessels in the harbour, grain ships, which the defenders had spread across the mouth, the sides lined with heavily armed men, which would be precious little use against the weightier Roman ships, Quadremes and Quinqueremes, built for close combat rather than ramming. But Titus and Marcellus were in a trireme and the master felt it was his duty to point out some of the limitations inherent in such a vessel. They were aboard a ship built for speed, whose prime method of attack was to ram the enemy, then board, but they were alone, so any conflict would be costly. He pointed instead to another galley, busy laying a wooden boom. The insurgents were using a wide beamed merchant ship to lower great tree trunks into the water, attached to each other by stout chains. Titus, eager for a fight, and dying to assault the enemy's main strength, nevertheless deferred to the captain, who brought his trireme round a touch, so that the bows were aimed directly at the ship laying the boom.

The men aboard her were not soldiers and the galley, of a type used to transport stone, was slow to manoeuvre. As they realised that they were the intended victim, they abandoned their task and tried to turn for the inner harbour, well aware that they were ill-equipped to withstand an attack. The other rebel galleys, which had already pulled in their anchors, took some of the men off the deck to man their sweeps. Marcellus saw the rows of oars swing back and down, biting into the water, sensing the strain that was being exerted to get these ships into motion. They rose and fell, and the water began to cream down the sides as the ships got under way.

'We should haul off, sir,' said the master, who had not foreseen this development. 'We cannot take on such heavy odds.'

That did not please Titus, who, at the prospect of action, seemed much improved. 'If we can prevent them laying the boom it will make any future attempts on the port much easier.'

The master, a grizzled sailor with a tanned, weather-beaten countenance, shook his head fiercely. 'If we ram that ship we'll be stuck in her when the others come up. We won't last two minutes against all those soldiers. I decline to risk my ship.'

Marcellus was looking at the galleys, on course to intercept. He did not see Titus's eyes on his back, did not know that the legate, who had the power to command this grey-haired sailor, decided against an attack because he had no wish to risk the only son of Lucius Falerius Nerva.

'Very well, Master, you may decline the action.'

The sailor was aware that he had displeased Titus, who was certainly powerful enough to break him, and not knowing the legate, he was unaware of his innate fairness. It could be the beach for him if he did not do something to salvage his reputation.

'Be a pity to without giving them something to chew on, sir.'

He called out a series of orders, bringing the trireme round on a converging course with the nearest of the grain ships. Marcellus, in the bows, watched closely as the distance between the galleys shortened. He ran back along the catwalk and begged for a spear, grabbing it eagerly and heading back, past the waiting soldiers, into the bows. Titus opened his mouth to order him below, but he said nothing, suspecting that the boy, close to his first taste of real battle, would probably ignore him. They were nearly on them now and the leading grain ship edged round to avoid being rammed, the side crowded with armed men, spears at the ready. That was when the master gave his order, reasonably sure that no one aboard the vessel he was attacking had ever seen a trireme in action.

The drum beat faster and the speed of the Roman ship increased slightly so that they were closing on their enemy rapidly. The first javelins started to fly, falling into the water between the ships as the master, leaning on the sweep, aided by men hauling on ropes, yelled another command that had the drum beating an almost continuous tattoo. Marcellus saw the oars beneath him disappear inboard and the trireme swung round. With perfect timing, the other oarsmen first raised their oars out of the water, held them for a second, them dipped then again. Their action brought the trireme in close to the grain ship, running alongside, and the prow took the first enemy oar almost immediately.

Marcellus felt the ship shudder and he held his arm up, spear ready, choosing as his target the biggest man on the grain ship, a huge fellow with a thick black beard. Oars were snapping like twigs beneath his feet as the trireme glided along the side of the grain ship, whose rowers, less disciplined than the Romans, had not pulled in their sweeps, despite the desperate orders being yelled at them to do so. As he came level, the black-bearded man, distracted like his fellows by the mayhem below decks, looked up just in time to see the danger. He raised his shield and his spear, his arm hauling back for a powerful throw.

Marcellus beat the shield by a fraction, his spear skipping over the very rim as the man raised it, and embedding itself in his chest. A well-aimed foot took Marcellus's legs away and he fell heavily onto the trireme's deck, just as the men on either side of his victim cast their spears in return. They flew harmlessly overhead, to land in the sea on the other side. Marcellus lifted his head and looked into the smiling face of Titus Cornelius, who was crouched protectively over him with his shield shutting out any danger.

'I think more men die in their first fight than at any other time. I can't quite decide whether that is because of excitement, or stupidity.'

Marcellus, hauled onto his knees, found himself

staring at the stern of the grain ship as it spun round, totally disabled, with a mass of wounded men on the deck. Every fighter aboard the Roman ship had cast at least one javelin as the trireme cleared the oars from the side of the enemy ship and now, as if by magic, their own oars reappeared from the ports and as they bit into the water, the master hauled on the sweep and the trireme spun round, in its own length, to outrun the other enemy galleys coming up to engage. Titus and Marcellus made their way back to the stern as the master handed over the sweep to one of his subordinates and pointed to the pursuing ships.

'If I can get them to chase me far enough, we might get that boat laying the boom after all.'

As if they had heard his words, the oars on the rebel ships shot up in the air, completely clearing the water. Below decks the men who had rowed those ships would be hunched over their sweeps, gasping for breath. There was no way that galleys like these could pursue a trireme, even one rowing easy in an attempt to draw them on.

CHAPTER TWENTY-FIVE

———————◆———————

Titus threw his few troops ashore as soon as he could, setting up a proper Roman camp in a bay about five miles from the city, well inside the river barriers to the east. They would never hold the place if the slave army chose to attack but it served to remind both the runaways and the inhabitants of Agrigentum that Roman power still existed. The trireme was given the task of patrolling the approaches to provide early warning of any intended incursions from the sea and Marcellus spent most of his time aboard the ship perfecting his rowing, never straying far from the master between shifts, pestering the man with an endless stream of technical questions.

The days dragged on into weeks as Cholon travelled between the camp and the city, finalising the arrangements that would return the slaves to their farms, albeit under the less brutal conditions

that Lucius intended to force through the Senate.
Titus had instigated a regular service from the
mainland and legionaries, taken from the various
city garrisons in the south, were quietly shipped to
his camp. Lucius was most adamant that nothing be
done to alert the Senate, but Roman strength grew
daily, boosted most importantly by a detachment of
cavalry.

Lucius arrived to find his son ashore for once, in
the kind of regular encampment he had served in as
a soldier all those years ago. Paternal greetings were
brief; the senator took over Titus's tent and, with
his health finally and steadily improving, went into
deep consultation with Cholon.

They met at the agreed rendezvous again, happy to
see each other in good health. The tall Celt, riding
a magnificent if slightly skittish horse, now wore
elaborate, expensive attire: light wool clothing and
a fine decorated leather breastplate and greaves. A
plumed Greek helmet was looped over his saddle-
bow and his shield was embossed with carefully
worked gold and silver images. Even his weapons
gleamed. Aquila wore the battered armour that had
served him for the last two years, carried the same
sword with the sweat-stained pommel, so beside
Gadoric he looked like a peasant. Ritual greetings
exchanged, it was not long before they were
discussing the situation of the slave revolt.

'Are you still planning to fight?' asked Aquila.

The Celt scowled. 'Right now we talk. You'll have seen that Roman camp by the shore to the east.'

Aquila nodded, but did not add how tempted he had been to enter it; the sight of those soldiers dressed in the same manner as his 'Papa' Clodius had acted as a powerful draw upon his primary allegiance.

'We could drive them into the sea in an hour,' said Gadoric, looking over his shoulder, 'and leave their bones to bleach in the sun.'

'They wouldn't stand and fight, Gadoric. They've kept enough ships to get away if they have to.'

'True, but it would be nice to try, instead of just sitting doing nothing.'

'How is Hypolitas?'

That produced a wry smile. 'King Hypolitas, if you please.'

'A strange title for an ex-slave.'

'He says that it makes negotiations with the Romans easier, but in truth he loves the name, as well as the trappings of kingship. He's become quite regal these last few weeks.'

Aquila spoke with genuine concern; he knew, regardless of the risks, that his friend would be better off away from the likes of Hypolitas. 'The Romans grow stronger every day?'

Gadoric nodded. 'We are supposed to finally decide on our actions tomorrow, whether to fight or accept the Roman terms.'

'What are the Roman terms?'

'Ask me tomorrow. So far only Hypolitas knows them all. He does all the negotiating privately.' Aquila's eyebrows showed clearly what he thought of that. 'He has a point. I shudder to think what might happen if our people even got a hint we were talking. Anyway, he knows where I stand. I've told him nothing less than complete freedom is acceptable.'

'Still determined to fight and die?'

The older man smiled. 'After all I've taught you, Aquila, you're still too Roman in your thinking.'

Aquila pulled a face. 'I know. I'll be happier on the other side. Do you really welcome death, you Celts?'

'It's not something I'd lie about,' said Gadoric sadly.

That sadness indicated the truth: no man likes the idea of leaving life, even if all his days he has been told that death is something to look forward to. Gadoric had as much trouble with his faith as any man, never sure whether those who were supposed to know, the Druid priests of the Celtic faith, could really see the promised Asgard, that paradise for the souls of warriors, or whether their pronouncements were just a ploy to excite bravery in men who might be afraid of death in battle.

'It makes no difference,' he continued. 'Death, when it comes, answers those questions, but the manner of a man's going is everything.'

He reached out and took Aquila's Celtic eagle in his hand, grasping it firmly. The youngster bowed his head, grabbed the chain and took it off. 'Take it, Gadoric.'

That brought a smile to the older man's face and he examined the charm for a moment, twisting it so that it gleamed in the sun, then looked up at its owner. 'This was meant to keep you alive, Aquila, not me.'

'How can you be so sure?'

'Just by holding it.'

Aquila opened his mouth to respond, but Gadoric stopped him. He slung the charm back over Aquila's neck, shook his shoulders in a fatherly way, then turned and walked over to his horse to fetch the sack of food and wine he had brought out from Agrigentum. Aquila's eyes, following him, caught the flash of the sun on metal somewhere far off.

'Did you bring a bodyguard this time, Gadoric?'

'No, I came alone.' He turned, sack in hand, and seeing the look on the youngster's face, mistook the cause. 'Come on, enough of this talk of death. Let's eat.'

Lucius Falerius looked at the scroll Cholon had given him, nodding contentedly as he read it.

'Hypolitas has sounded out all the other leaders. They will accept our offer of freedom and pension. That is, bar one.'

'The one-eyed Celt you told me of?'

Cholon nodded. 'He stands head and shoulders above them all, both figuratively and in life. Hypolitas is a compulsive talker, who's reached his pre-eminence through overuse of a silver tongue and the odd piece of primitive magic. The others are nobodies, hanging on to his coat-tails, more afraid of losing their skin than anything else. If this Gadoric was the leader, they would never have agreed to talks in the first place.'

'Yet he hasn't prevented Hypolitas from talking?'

'No.'

'Then he's a fool for all his nobility.'

The tent flap flew open and Titus stood framed by the daylight behind him. 'A messenger for you, Cholon Pyliades, from the Temple of *Diana*.'

Cholon looked quickly at Lucius, who was angry at this interruption. 'I must see him. It has been arranged.'

'Very well,' said the older man sourly. 'Show him in.'

Despite the heat of the day the man who entered was wrapped in a heavy hooded cloak, which he declined to remove even for the eminent senator. Cholon stood while the man whispered his message in his ear. Once it was delivered he turned and swept out of the tent. In a matter of seconds they heard the sound of his horse's hooves as he rode swiftly out of the Roman camp.

'Good news?' asked Lucius.

'I think so,' he replied.

Yet Cholon did not look as though he had received good tidings, he looked like a man whose favourite dog has just died. Later, as he watched the Decurion lead his cavalry out of the camp, with Marcellus in full uniform by his side, his expression was even more bereft of joy.

Aquila rode steadily along just under the rim of the ridge, with an occasional turn to the top to check on Gadoric's progress, grateful that the Celt had not allowed his horse its head, given that Aquila's stunted upland pony was no match for that magnificent animal; he was having trouble keeping up at the moment and the other man was barely even trying. The heat had gone out of the sun now and it was warm at this altitude, without being stifling like the lowland plain. The hills on his left nearly joined the track, leaving him a narrow ledge to ride along, so Aquila cursed when he saw the rock fall that had blocked his way and looked vainly at the steep slope below him and the sheer face of the newly exposed rock to his right.

There would be no tailing Gadoric now, but that flash he had seen earlier, which could only have come from something metal, worried him. He pulled his horse's head round, retraced his steps and dismounting, started to haul the pony up the slope to the next ridge. The creature slithered and slid, but it was made for this sort of terrain and eventually they emerged onto a scrub-covered plateau. Having made his way to the end he saw a clear path by a dried-out riverbed winding all the way down into the valley. Gadoric was there, a good league ahead now, a tiny figure with a trail of dust billowing behind him. Aquila looked towards the city, its white walls seeming to move in the haze of heat rising from the coastal plain.

From that height he saw the trap long before his friend: horsemen blocked the route ahead of him where it narrowed into a gorge, the sun glinting on their spears, while the other half of the party, some twenty men, were hidden behind a thick clump of gorse and trees, ready to come round behind the Celt when he passed. Even at this distance he could tell by the uniform colour of their cloaks that they were Roman cavalry. He yelled a futile warning but there was no chance that Gadoric would hear him so he pushed his pony onto the path, forcing it to descend at a frightening speed, not caring whether he or the animal was killed in the process.

Gadoric hauled on the traces as soon as he saw the Romans stretched across the valley floor, over twenty horsemen, completely blocking his way, and the sound of hooves made him spin in the saddle to see that the same number now stood behind him.

The steep slopes of the valley might have been possible on a really agile mountain pony, but this horse, sleek, fine-boned and bred to speed, would never make it up the hillside. Two men detached themselves from the party before him and rode forward and it was only when they got close up he realised one of them, regardless of his imposing height and build, was a youth.

'You are the slave commander named Gadoric?' said the older Roman, who wore the insignia of a Decurion.

The Celt fixed him with his one good eye, taking in the insignia on his armour, plus the torque on his arm, which was a mark of a man who had proved himself brave in battle.

'I am Porcius Catus,' the Decurion continued. 'I command the cavalry of Titus Cornelius, military legate to the *Princeps Senatus*, Lucius Falerius Nerva.' Gadoric glanced at the youth, observing that his armour was finely wrought like his own, but it bore no mark of distinction and the Decurion, noticing Gadoric's interest, added, 'This is the senator's son, Marcellus Falerius. As you can see, Gadoric, your position is hopeless. If you will surrender your arms we will escort you back to our camp.'

'Then?' asked Gadoric.

'That is not for me to decide,' replied Porcius.

'I will be a slave again.'

'Perhaps you will.'

Gadoric shook his head slowly and his hand reached out to take his plumed Greek helmet from the pommel of his saddle. His voice, when he spoke, was without emotion and without fear. In fact his mind was on the words he had so recently said to Aquila. 'You're too Roman in your thinking, friend. I'd rather die in battle.'

'That is stupid,' said Marcellus, impressed with the man despite the fact that they were enemies.

'To a Roman it is stupid, boy. To a Celt death is but a beginning.' He looked at Porcius. 'I offer single combat. I challenge Titus Cornelius.'

Porcius grinned. 'Which I must decline on his behalf. Perhaps if you had an army at your back our legate might oblige.'

Gadoric raised his helmet, smiling just before he put it on his head. 'That is one thing I always wished, to meet you Romans with an army at my back.'

'Your last chance,' said Porcius.

'I am on my way to Agrigentum, Roman. Stand aside.'

Abruptly the helmet was thrown aside. Gadoric loosed his blond hair so that it hung down to his shoulders, and detached his spear and shield from the rear of his saddle, putting the round buckler on his left arm. Porcius hauled his horse around and, followed by Marcellus, made his way back to the line of soldiers that still blocked the valley floor.

They turned to face Gadoric, now armed and ready for combat.

'May I make a suggestion to the men, Porcius Catus?'

The officer looked at him; this was the son of Lucius and he was not stupid. 'You may issue them with orders if you wish, young man.'

Marcellus raised his voice to address the others. 'Don't attack him. Stay still and try and bring his horse down.'

There was a dissatisfied murmur from the cavalrymen who were obviously looking forward to a kill. Porcius's voice cracked through the air, stilling the dissent. 'Do as you're told, damn you. We want him alive, if possible.'

Behind the line that blocked the Celt's retreat a single horseman in a heavy cloak rode slowly into the middle of the valley, emerging from the same clump of gorse and trees which had hidden the soldiers who had formed the second part of the trap. He had thrown back the hood and his face was now clearly visible in the evening light. Gadoric, looking behind him to assess the odds, saw him too. Marcellus knew instinctively that the sight enraged him by the way the Celt hauled mighty hard to bring his horse round.

He was charging the line at the other end of the valley before the turn was finished, aiming himself straight at the man in the cloak whose horse, no doubt unnerved by his rider, started to back up, its rear legs bending as it sought to retreat. The soldiers in the other line had received no instructions, so they lowered their spears and charged Gadoric, though they would have no time to get up speed before the Celt was upon them. Porcius kicked his horse hard, riding to intervene, but he must have known it was hopeless; the distance was too great. Marcellus trotted forward, watching the action as it unfolded.

Gadoric ignored the Roman cavalry. He raised himself in the saddle, one hand on the horse's neck and the rest of his body weight held by his knees. It was stunning horsemanship and he seemed to tower over the men coming at him. Just as they converged he threw his spear, aiming it over their heads at the solitary horseman behind them, but the man was too far away, so it was defiant rather than effective. The Roman spears, cast at close range, took him in the exposed chest, piercing his decorated leather armour, but the weight of his charge carried him on and he burst, still upright, through the line of attackers like a maddened boar. The horse, which had also taken a spear, faltered, but Gadoric hauled on the reins to keep its head up, using his other hand to pull out his sword. Marcellus heard the shout as it filled the valley, not a shout of pain, but a high-pitched war cry, emitted from the throat of a fatally wounded Celtic warrior.

The man he was trying to reach spun his horse awkwardly, attempting to flee as the Celt broke the Roman line. Sheer speed carried Gadoric on and he closed on his quarry, but Marcellus saw the shoulders slip as they came abreast, saw the upraised sword slip from the warrior's hand. The huge body slid sideways at the same time that his animal's forelegs gave way and both horse and rider crashed to the ground, the sound of breaking wood quite audible in the evening air as the weight of the falling horseman snapped the spear shafts still embedded in his chest. A great cloud of dust billowed up in the air as both horse and rider slithered along the hard earth, grinding to a halt, the animal twitching wildly, the warrior totally still.

Marcellus kicked his own horse and rode up, like everyone else, eager to examine the body. Porcius was looking down at the corpse unhappily, but the stranger, who had approached cautiously, was smiling, his sallow-complexioned face lined with pleasure. The prematurely grey hair took the dying sun, seeming to shine. He pulled his head back, filled his mouth and with an over-elaborate gesture spat on the corpse of the dead Gadoric.

'We'll take the body back to the camp,' said Porcius.

'No,' snapped the stranger. 'Leave him here. Let the vultures feed on his bones.'

'He deserves better,' Porcius replied.

'Does he, Roman? I say you leave him here.'

Porcius's voice took on a hard edge. 'Why should I listen to you?'

The cloak was thrown back, to reveal armour every bit as gorgeous as that of the man who had just died. 'I can't see it will help in the negotiations or please your legate, Titus Cornelius, if you choose to insult the new leader of the slave army.'

The man laughed, a high-pitched cackle which echoed off the surrounding hills, then with a mocking air, he bowed low in the saddle.

Aquila's pony had tried, but eventually he had had to dismount and run, leaving it, legs splayed and chest heaving half a league from the spot where Gadoric had ridden into the trap. He heard the war cry loud and clear, knowing as he did that he was too late to intervene, but he ran on nevertheless. The silence made him stop in the trees, and breathing heavily he walked carefully to the edge. The ring of horsemen was still, looking inwards, so Gadoric was in there, dead: there was no way his friend would have allowed himself to be taken alive. He heard the orders for the cavalry to form up, watched as the ring broke and horsemen fell into formation. Three people still sat over the inert body, easily identifiable by the finely wrought armour. One was a Roman officer, the other a youth who looked about his own age, but it was the third man that took his attention.

The silver grey hair on that sallow-complexioned face was unmistakable. So was the voice.

'Well, Porcius Catus, will you and this young man consent to accompany me back to Agrigentum? After all, it is fitting that a general should have an escort.'

The head went back and the man let out that slightly mad laugh, the same one Aquila had heard when Pentheus had buried Flaccus in six feet of golden grain.

Hypolitas and Pentheus, with four of the other leaders, left by one of the smaller city gates and made their way through the Roman lines with just the occasional creak of harness as evidence of their passing. The legionaries slipped into the city through the same gate, spreading out quickly, house to house, to take and disarm the slave army in manageable groups. Titus, with a small escort, made his way to the square before the palace, there to coordinate the actions of his men, while Marcellus, fretting and impatient, waited with Cholon and his father outside the city till the outcome of the operation was certain. No amount of pleading had gained him a place on such a dangerous enterprise.

Men died, Roman and slave, despite Titus's attempts at a peaceful takeover, but he was successful. The slaves greeted the dawn in a city controlled by Roman soldiers, while the bulk of their forces, camped on the plain or holding the river lines to the east and west, found that their refuge, the city of Agrigentum, had been taken from them. Worse for their morale was the news that Gadoric was dead: that their leaders, in return for personal safety, had sold them back into bondage. Even against the smaller numbers of Romans, whatever hope they had seemed to crumble, for they lacked the heart to put up a proper fight.

Cholon stood by the main landward gate of Agrigentum as the recaptured slaves were marched out. He recognised one face, that of the man who had greeted him at the very spot the day he arrived; then he had been happy, a mite cocky, his eyes full of hope and laughter, now those same eyes took in the figure of the Greek in a different way. They had lost all expression, as though the man behind them had ceased to exist, was in fact a mere shell, not human. Two young boys stumbled along beside him, his sons by the likeness. One carried the same lacklustre expression as his father but the other son looked at Cholon with such spirited loathing that the Greek had to steady himself to avoid taking a step back.

'You will have the thanks of the Senate for this, Lucius Falerius,' said the governor. 'A magnificent result, without blood or financial loss.'

'Just as long as we have a harvest I'll be happy. As for the thanks of the Senate, I fear that will be muted when I introduce a statute to protect the working conditions of the slaves.'

The governor, Silvanus, did not want to talk about that, lest by words he became associated with such a dangerous decree. 'You sail today?'

'I sail tomorrow. That pompous windbag, Hypolitas, sails today.'

'I thought you would depart together.'

'I cannot abide another day with that man,' snapped Lucius. 'How he ever came to lead this revolt escapes me. Anyone with half a brain would run a mile from such a creature. As for the others, the so-called leaders, they're no more than a bunch of peasants, for all their stolen Greek finery. Mutton dressed as lamb.'

Marcellus felt the same as his father; having been exposed to the Palmyran Greek for the entire journey across Sicily, he found his wheedling tone and constant self-regard offensive. He could not know that the fire that had made his words so effective was gone. Only one Roman had ever heard him address a crowd, or listened to him expound the cause of liberty in hushed tones, his hands weaving a spell.

Aquila would be immune now; the arrangements Hypolitas had made with Lucius Falerius Nerva, which were the talk of the island, meant that no one cared about him any more. He did not wait to see the slave army brought back to their farms in chains; he built a pyre for Gadoric, burnt his friend's body with proper honour, then rode across the island, ahead of Lucius's party, to Messana. There he took working passage on a small trading ship to Italy and he was waiting in Rhegnum when they landed. A crowd had gathered to see this spectacle, since every boat that put into the port had foretold the event.

His anger, so close to being madness, nearly boiled over when he saw the fine clothes they wore, worse still was the litter waiting to take them to their new home and the escort of cavalry provided by the praetor. They attracted crowds wherever they went, so trailing the party presented no difficulty; it was like a royal progress on the busy road through Brutium, Lucania and on, to the upland Samnite city of Beneventum, which stood at the centre of Italy, surrounded by high mountains.

Their villa overlooked a fast-flowing river, standing on a rocky promontory, affording fine views over the city on the opposite bank. The escort departed to be replaced by a smaller number of locally recruited guards. Hypolitas was ecstatic, standing on his terrace, knowing life would be good, knowing he would no longer have to obey the dictates of other men, and if he had to suffer the company of Pentheus and his like, who seemed incapable of thought, could not read or write, whose sole intent, as they had travelled towards this place, seemed to be the best way to fill the villa with wine and women, that was a small price to pay for a man who, at best, had never occupied any accommodation better than a small square room shared with other household slaves.

He turned from the terrace, looking at the spacious bedchamber that was now his. There were other rooms, a private bath-house for his use alone, a study, and a grand atrium in which he could receive guests. The local magistrates would come, as would the leading citizens of the Samnite state, after all, the King of the Slaves was famous. He would hold banquets that would be the talk of the city, build a library that local scholars would come to consult, engage in learned discussion with philosophers and perhaps write a treatise that would, when he was dead, keep the name Hypolitas alive for future generations.

The local Samnite guards were dumbfounded, for they had heard nothing in the night. Every bedchamber had the same names on the walls, written in blood, but they meant nothing to these men. Who were Gadoric and Flaccus and Phoebe? And what did it mean, that drawing of an eagle in flight? The only thing in Hypolitas's bedchamber, apart from that and the bloody signatures, was a crushed walnut shell on the floor of the terrace.

They found the bodies over the next few days as they were washed up on the rock-strewn banks of the rushing mountain river, well downstream. Four of them had died through having their throats cut, including Hypolitas, who had also lost his tongue.

The grey-haired one who had been known as Pentheus was different. The skin had been flayed from his back, his face was a hollow pulp and they had neither the time nor the inclination to search for his missing hands and feet.

EPILOGUE

━━━◆━━━

The news of the murder of Hypolitas and the others reached Lucius Falerius fifty leagues north of Neapolis, where he had stopped his journey to rest. Titus had gone ahead, to take his news to the Senate, something that would raise his name in the public mind and aid his bid in the forthcoming elections for the praetorship, which would, in turn, provide a route to the command of armies. Marcellus, naturally, had stayed with his father, using the time to visit the nearby shrine of the Sybil at Cumae, one-time home to another, who had made Tarquinus Superbus squirm to get hold of only part of her predictions.

Lucius was on the mend; the conclusion of events in Sicily and weeks in a static camp had raised his spirits and allowed his body to recover. Not that such a thing allowed for any softening in his rigid interpretation of right and wrong. His response to the news from Beneventum was entirely lacking in sympathy. 'Whoever did this had the best interests of the Roman treasury at heart, don't you think, and I cannot believe the world will mourn for the likes of Hypolitas.'

'I thought you'd be pleased,' said Marcellus, with a look that Lucius understood.

His father ignored the implications of the look, that perhaps he had sent the assassins; his mind was on other things. Given this bloodless success in Sicily, Lucius was probably more potent now than he had ever been, so he would probably find it easy to push his reforms through the centuries, which would secure the power of the *Optimates* and consign the *Populares* and their madcap ideas to the scrap heap. After that he might retire; one more speech to the Senate would suffice, to say his farewells and watch as the tears of hypocrisy flowed. His son was pushing a scroll towards him that he could not really be bothered to read.

'You saw the Sybil?' he asked quickly.

'Heard more than saw,' Marcellus replied, dropping the scroll on the desk. He tried to keep the unhappiness out of his voice, talking quickly to cover it up. 'She hangs in a wicker cage, in a huge cavern, high above the heads of those who visit. I think they have it there so that her voice echoes off the walls to increase the effect of her prophecies.'

'And did she prophesy for you, Marcellus?'

'She did not, father. All I got, for my over-generous donation to the Temple of *Apollo*, was a single sentence telling me that I would inherit everything I needed to secure my future from my father, who had secured the past for me.'

'By name?' asked his father.

Marcellus nodded. 'The priests must have some method of telling the Sybil whom she's addressing.'

Lucius treated his son to a thin smile. 'You will inherit from your father. Did she say how soon?'

'No!'

'No prophecy, ever given, is plain and clear.'

'Nor are they always the truth, father. It is a trade full of charlatans.'

Lucius agreed with his son, but he still hated to be interrupted and it showed on his face. He had a paternal duty to perform, which was to give his son a faith that he himself had never possessed. He knew Marcellus to be different from him, despite all his years of training; the boy would always need something to believe in, other than the mere concept of Rome. Prophecies could fill a void and cause Marcellus to act wisely instead of emotionally. Despite the reforms he was about to introduce, the Republic would always be in danger, always need men to defend it against the threat of tyranny. As he opened his mouth to speak, his mind went back to that prophecy he had heard as a child, with Aulus Cornelius. Lucius had seen that prediction off, had even survived an attempt to kill him. He was about to cap his life's work with a triumph sweeter than any celebrated by a mere general.

'You must look behind the words for the meaning. If they are not plain to you, they are to me. Perhaps approaching death gives one a clearer sight of things.'

He saw the look of consternation on his son's face and pushed out a hand to touch his arm. 'I have no fear of death, Marcellus. I had one fear, that all I'd striven for would disappear when I died; that the Republic would fall into the wrong hands, then disintegrate. As you know I have seen the Sibylline books in Rome. There are many portents in those, but they are written as verse riddles and difficult to comprehend. Only one thing seems clear. Rome will always be in danger, both from external foes and ambitious men, but the Republic will last and prosper, if the right men lead the state. I must have you accept that.'

'I do, father.'

'This Sibylline prophecy, being spoken, has a clarity the books lack. One day you may get to see them and I'm sure you'll be just as confused as I was.' Lucius rubbed his ribs where the knife had struck, making his son wonder if he was still in pain. 'This prophecy of yours has eased my mind.'

Marcellus frowned. 'It is little enough.'

'It is everything.' His hand gripped Marcellus's arm, and for the first time the boy noticed the translucent skin, over prominent bones, and the brown patches of age. 'Despite what I'm about to do, there will still be work. My reforms will need to be protected. That is your task. The Sybil has said so.'

'What about Quintus?'

'You'll be ten times the man he is, Marcellus. Trust Titus, but do not consult with him, for he will help you out of nobility. Quintus will help you too, but he will demand a price. You must pay that price, but slowly. In the cellar lies that chest of scrolls and in there is everything you will need…' The voice trailed off for a few moments. Lucius lay back, again rubbing his chest. 'I know you. I have raised you like the Romans of old, to be upright and honest. I was like you, Marcellus, until I realised that the Gods had given me a higher aim. What you find in that chest will not please you but I made you swear once to do as I did, and put Rome before everything. The Sybil has confirmed your oath. Do not think badly of me.'

His hand took an even firmer grip on Marcellus's arm and he looked his son in the eye. 'Rome first and always, Marcellus. Not pride, nor expediency and never a faint heart.'

Marcellus picked up the scroll, more as a way of

changing the subject than from any real interest. 'They sent you this from Beneventum, father.'

'What is it?' Lucius asked, as his son unrolled the papyrus.

'Whoever killed Hypolitas and the others was obviously acting out of vengeance. He wrote several names on the walls in blood.'

'You've already told me that. Apart from Gadoric the names meant nothing to me.'

'Apparently there was a drawing in each room, of an eagle in flight. They wondered if that might give us a clue as to who committed the murders.'

Marcellus held the open scroll before his father. He was looking at the drawing himself, so did not see the look of horror in Lucius's eyes, but he heard him mouth the words and turned to look. What he saw shocked him, for what blood Lucius had had drained out of his father's face.

> *Look aloft if you dare*
> *Though what you fear cannot fly*
> *Both will face it before you die.*

At once Lucius was back in that cave in the Alban Hills, a mere boy alongside his friend Aulus Cornelius, both pretending to be men, and the words of the prophecy they had heard filled his mind, and the moment a piece of papyrus like the one he was looking at now had burst into spontaneous flames in his hands. With a vision only granted to a man on the verge of death he knew that

Aulus had seen this very thing at Thralaxas, that same blood-red eagle that was before him now, telling him that everything he had striven for all of his life might not now come to pass.

'Call my litter,' he gasped, clutching at his chest now. 'I must get to Rome.'

Marcellus looked set to protest. His father, whose eyes never left the drawing of the eagle, shouted, 'I am your father, boy, you must obey me!'

Lucius Falerius Nerva's heart gave out before they had gone ten leagues. Marcellus had the body drained and embalmed, before loading it onto a chariot. By forcing his pace, and constant changes of horses, he was in the capital within three days. His father's pyre would rise from Rome and his genius would disperse with the clouds of smoke, into the air above the city which had consumed his life.

THE JOHN PEARCE SERIES

London 1793: Young firebrand John Pearce is illegally press-ganged from the refuge of the Pelican tavern to a brutal life aboard HMS *Brilliant*, a frigate on its way to war. Follow his adventures on the high seas...

'A salty blend of seafaring adventure and whodunit... Cunningly spliced battle scenes which reek of blood and brine'
Literary Review

'A clever blend of fact and fiction... A rollicking yarn of boldness and redemption'
Good Book Guide

'A must for armchair mariners... It's superb stuff'
Manchester Evening News

In the John Pearce series
By the Mast Divided
A Shot Rolling Ship
An Awkward Commission
A Flag of Truce
The Admirals' Game
An Ill Wind
Blown Off Course

a&b

WWW.ALLISONANDBUSBY.COM

For more information and to place an order, visit
our website where you'll also find free tasters,
exclusive discounts, competitions and giveaways.
Be sure to sign up to our monthly newsletter to
keep up-to-date on our latest releases,
news and upcoming events.

Alternatively, call us on
020 7580 1080
to place your order.